I0584482

Ford's Terror
By Richard A Wiggins

2nd Edition

Copyright© 2025. Richard A. Wiggins. All Rights Reserved.

No part of this work covered by the copyright herein may be reproduced or used in any form or by any means – graphic, electronic, or mechanical without the prior written permission of the publisher, RAWiggins Books. Any request for photocopying, recording, taping, or information storage and retrieval systems of any part of this book shall be directed in writing to the author.

This publication contains the opinions and ideas of its author and is designed to provide useful advice in regard to the subject matter covered.

Dedication

To Bob:
College roommate, Best Man, and fellow explorer. May memories of the time we canoed the Antler River forever haunt your dreams.

Acknowledgments

I want to thank my wife, Dena, for inspiring me to write the story, for her patience while it was being written, and for her generosity in getting it to market.

I want to thank my mom, Ruth, for reading it at the age of 96.

I want to thank son Isaac and his wife Tonya for their input while trying to do all the things they do to raise those two boys.

I want to thank my son Aaron and his wife Megan for their love to family.

I want to thank Khyla for the girly insight she insists she doesn't have.

Table of Contents

Chapter One - Au Revoir

Under a clear blue sky, the immature bald eagle we'll call E. Pluribus gripped the salmon in his formidable talons, fighting against the strength of the twenty-two-pound fish thrashing its tail in a desperate attempt to free itself. Driving his yellow beak into the flesh, he tore through scales, pecking as fast as he could to kill his prey. Keeping his grip was a challenge; he weighed only ten pounds. To make matters worse, he was stationary on a river sandbar, unable to lift his heavy catch into the air. If he had been in flight, momentum would have made the task easier.

Above him, other white-headed eagles circled, watching the battle unfold, ready to pounce should the fish escape.

Suddenly, a mature female, her wings as wide as a man's tall, slammed in, claiming the Coho as her own. She used her larger body and sharp beak to attack, asserting her dominance. Unable to fly, hold the fish, and fight at the same time, there was no choice but to let go. Beating his wings furiously, the young male bird lifted into the air, fleeing the attack. He stayed just above the water, turning his head to witness his hard-won prize being torn apart by his adversary. His piercing screech echoed across the river, a cry of frustration and loss.

Gaining altitude, E. Pluribus ceased flapping and soared on a warm current rising from the summer-heated earth. He circled effortlessly, scanning the ocean below for the faintest shadow signaling food. Spotting one, he plunged a hundred feet toward the water, pulling up just in time to extend his talons and snatch a fish mid-flight. His momentum carried him skyward; the fish secure in his grasp.

A sudden screech startled him. E. Pluribus hadn't seen the attacker diving from above. The impact sent them tumbling through the air, both refusing to release their hold on the fish. Clawing and pecking in midair, their struggle ended with a heavy thud as they crashed onto a sandbar. His left wing struck the ground hard, and the pain forced him to release his catch.

1

Bested once again, the young bird struggled to lift off, finally finding a draft to carry him back to the skies.

Ignoring the pain, he continued hunting, scanning the water for fish and the land for small mammals. To rest his injured wing, E. Pluribus soared higher than usual, riding hot updrafts effortlessly. Higher and higher, he climbed until he was above the nearby mountain peaks, gliding for miles. Below, the first snow had dusted the mountains in white. Waterfalls, fed by fresh meltwater, tumbled like silver braids down the slopes. Immense hemlock, cedar, and spruce forests line the coastline. He circled islands, scanning the land and water below.

E. Pluribus then flew over vast ice fields as the temperature around him dropped to freezing. He glided over the broken snowy surface as it sloped downward toward the sea, looking into the deep crevasses at the dark blue ice deep inside. The cold wind at this back buffeted him around, pushing him towards the end of the glacier. But hunger and injury were taking their toll. His strength waned, his wing stiff and unresponsive. He flapped awkwardly, his movements growing clumsy.

As he faltered over the end of the glacier, the clear waters of the glacial melt were flowing out from under the ice into a small lake. The water was erupting into great waves that tossed spray high into the air and created a mist above the chaotic surface. The lake water was being thrown around as if continuous earthquakes were occurring underneath it, waves washing high up on the bedrock.

An enormous tree, long ago, fell into the water and was battered by the wave until the roots and limbs were not attached, and it bounced as if it were nothing more than cork.

Unable to stay aloft any longer, E. Pluribus spiraled downward, losing control, aiming as he could for the bobbing tree as a refuge. Struggling with all his might but to no avail, the world blurred, and he crashed through the mist into the churning water and blacked out.

"Harry! Wake up! Harry!" Clara's voice pierced the darkness.

"You were jerking! You woke me up. What were you dreaming about? Were you having a nightmare?" She shook him gently.

Harry stirred, slowly coming to his senses. Lying beside him, Clara propped herself up on her elbow and brushed the damp hair from his forehead.

Still caught between dream and reality, he murmured, "Aah, hmm… that was some dream."

"What was it? You looked terrified."

"I was flying… like a bird. Like an eagle. It's hard to explain now, but I'm sure I was in Alaska. The mountains, the ocean—it all felt so real. I could see everything from ten thousand feet in the air. It was beautiful. I was trying to eat a salmon, but other birds kept attacking me. I was hurt… and then I fell. Right when I hit the water, you woke me up. That's so weird. How did the timing work out like that?"

Clara stopped running her fingers through his hair and let out a quiet sigh.

All Harry thought about—and now even dreamed about—was Alaska. Clara had never been there and couldn't understand what made it so intoxicating for him. Why was he so drawn to this distant wilderness? What was it about that place that held more allure than the life they had here in San Francisco? Most of all, why wasn't he dreaming about her?

"How wonderful," she said flatly. "I need to get some sleep. I have work in the morning."

"I'm sorry."

"It's alright. Goodnight."

"Goodnight."

They lay back-to-back, eyes open. Neither spoke as they imagined how they wanted their lives to unfold. He envisioned his journey to Southeast Alaska while she contemplated his absence.

The next day, drab, curtain-like clouds settled over San Francisco Bay as the marine layer rolled in. Shades of gray—some pale, others nearly black—drifted low in the sky. A light mist fell from the darkest ones. People strolling through the city kept their heads down, avoiding the fog and gloom.

Harry and Clara had lived together as an engaged couple for the past year in a small, sparsely furnished second-floor, two-bedroom apartment on Market Street, not far from his parents. He was a twenty-five-year-old hydrographer who, when home, spent his days studying papers and drafting charts, unaware of basic needs such as eating, bathing, or changing clothes. He loved taking measurements in the field and turning them into navigation charts. He felt responsible for showing every mile of shoreline, every reef, and all the rocks and other features that might pose a hazard. It was as much an art as it was a science—transforming numbers into contour lines.

On any given day, he was likely wearing his tattered, scarlet-colored flannel nightshirt and wool socks, which served as his day-to-day clothing, and had it not been for Clara cooking and making him eat; he undoubtedly would weigh far less than his underweight one-hundred sixty-five pounds. His sloppy appearance at home was in stark contrast to how he maintained himself while on duty on the ship as a naval officer and draftsman.

Harry L. Ford was a Master at Arms in the United States Navy, responsible for the security and safety of all on board the survey vessel *U.S.S. Carlise P. Patterson*. He accepted his Navy role, but Master at Arms was more of a means to an end: hydrography. The officer role suited him; he liked the privileges that came with the position, one of the most important being a shared room with a bunk rather than sleeping in a hammock with twenty-five other men in the crew quarters.

Clara Miller was twenty-six and devoted most of her time to caring for her ailing parents. The burden weighed heavily on her, and her prematurely aging face had the faraway look of a nurse after many days on the battlefield. Harry's indifference didn't help, and she usually went about her day with a negative attitude.

They had met one November day on the beach at Point Reyes, a popular spot for San Francisco locals. He was there to fish; she was there to escape from the constant burden of caregiving. They continued to see each other, and after a year of courtship, Harry proposed before he left for the 1888 summer survey season in southeast Alaska. They decided to wait until his return to get married. In the meantime, Clara moved in, primarily to get away from the relentless demands of her family. Now, it was late March, four months after he returned from the ship, but they weren't married. It didn't seem to matter to either one, so they continued with the living arrangements, never discussing actual marriage.

4

Living with Harry provided her with respite, but the work of caregiving followed her home. Constantly exhausted and often irritable, she withdrew, and their intimacy suffered. Whenever Harry's parents visited, she would retreat to the bedroom for the entirety of their stay, avoiding everyone.

One dreary day bled into the next. Harry's departure for the six-month summer survey season loomed, and his focus remained on his work. Clara had not been home for the past two nights, as she often stayed at her parent's house when they required full-time care. He realized he had barely seen her in the last two weeks and that he was leaving in just three days. Setting down his pencil, he wondered if they would see each other before he left.

She returned late that night after he had already gone to bed, but he was still awake when she entered the room.

"Hi," he said in the dark as she readied for bed.

"Oh. Hi. I didn't think you'd still be awake."

"Couldn't sleep. I worked too late, and then I started thinking about you… about how I haven't seen much of you, and I'll be gone soon."

Clara crawled under the bedsheets.

"Have you been drinking?" he asked, surprised by the smell of wine on her breath.

"Uh-huh. I had wine tonight."

"I was thinking—there isn't much time left. We should go out and do something tomorrow."

"Oh, Harry, right now I just want to sleep. Can we talk about this later?"

She rolled over, and he was left wondering.

The next day dragged, the only movement in the apartment coming from the shifting shadows on the walls. Clara didn't go to her parents' house— her sister had agreed to take over for the day. Harry remained at his drafting table, working in silence. Their only close interaction came when she cut short his straight brown hair and trimmed his beard, as per regulations.

By evening, Clara kept glancing at the clock on the mantel. The glances became more frequent as the hours passed. Finally, she set her book down and said, "It's your last night at home. Wouldn't you like to go out and have a little fun? Maybe a beer or two? You can order fish and chips! You said we should go out and do something." She mustered her most convincing expression.

"Oh, you remember that from last night?" He sighed, then nodded. "Okay, let's go out. Where do you want to go?"

With a playful kiss on his cheek, she smiled and exclaimed, "The Elixir!" She grabbed her purse and jacket, eager to leave.

The lobby was chaotic in downtown San Francisco's Elixor Hotel, filled with people eager to see and enjoy the new electric lighting fixtures and the most luxurious washrooms in town. Fishermen, longshoremen, sailors, miners, businessmen, their wives, and flirtatious women filled the pub. A drunken pianist pounded away at the keys, forcing people to raise their voices. The dimly lit room was thick with the lingering scent of cigar smoke and stale beer. Small tables occupied the center of the floor, while booths lined the walls, seating eager drinkers. Wooden posts, worn smooth by years of contact, supported the high ceiling of ornamental tin sheeting.

Harry and Clara took a booth against the far wall. The club was bustling. The bar stretched along the left side of the room, curving at the far end, where a hallway led to the privy and washroom. They ordered two beers and watched the crowd as they waited.

Harry faced the room, absentmindedly scanning the scene. Clara reclined beside him; her green eyes fixed on the bar. The server arrived with their drinks and took their food order. They sipped in silence, each absorbed in their own thoughts. He wasn't focused on anything, just taking in the movement of people, the occasional burst of laughter, the lively shuffle of bodies. A particularly rowdy man was making a spectacle of himself, but the constant ebb and flow of patrons created the real energy in the room.

When their food arrived, he noticed Clara shift slightly. It was subtle, but something had caught her attention. She straightened her shoulders, brushed a lock of her auburn hair from her face to behind her ear, and wet her lips.

"Harry, the food's here, and you're hungry—go ahead and start eating. I need to visit the washroom. I'll be right back."

Without waiting for a response, she wove her way through the crowd. Harry watched her from the booth, following the progress of her pale blue dress with a pink sash tied in a bow in front and pink petticoat underneath. She sauntered past several tables, heading toward the bar. The far end, where the hallway began, was another thirty feet away, crowded with patrons. When she reached it, she turned left, disappearing from Harry's view. But just before she did, he saw it: her hand falling lightly onto a man's shoulder. The man caught it, fingers closing over hers.

They held hands.

"What did I just see?" Harry's mind reeled.

Clara walked out of view, heading toward the privy. The man followed her.

Heart pounding, Harry sprang from his seat, pushing through the crowded room, trying to get a better look. Customers jostled past him, blocking his view. When the man finally returned to the bar, Harry couldn't see his face—too many people, too much movement.

Frustrated, he took a step back, pressing himself against a wooden support beam. He waited. Watching.

"Bartender, another whiskey." The man he was watching held up his glass. The bartender nodded, finished his financial transaction, and came over to pour from a red-labeled bottle. At the sight of the bottle, he recognized the man at once.

"Reeves. John Reeves."

He flashed back to an afternoon when he was about sixteen. His father had invited an insurance client to a picnic at a local park and brought his wife and three children. One of the client's sons, John, was Harry's age, and they hung out together that day. A couple of years later, he and Clara ran into John at a restaurant, which sparked several years of adult

7

friendship between them. They would get together for drinks occasionally and at holidays and birthdays, often exchanging gifts.

When he arrived home from last year's voyage in October, she had been at her parents' house while he was cleaning up their home. As he removed the household trash, the bag's contents spilled onto the floor. While picking up the mess, he uncovered a Maker's Mark whiskey bottle cork lost in the corner. At the time, he hadn't thought much of it, assuming it had dropped during one of the several visits John made when bringing over his favorite whiskey.

Breathing deeply at the realization that Clara might be seeing Reeves, he pushed back against the flow of guests to his table and sat down. He refused to look, to see what she and Reeves might be doing. Clara found him with his eyes closed.

"Harry!" She shouted above the noise of the room to get his attention.

He opened his eyes and stared at her. At that moment, their past no longer had any meaning to him; the long beach walks and late-night moon-watching they did together were no longer relevant.

His change of expression startled her, and she asked if everything was all right.

"Ah, no. The beer upset my stomach. I'd like to go." He did not want to lose his emotions in public.

"But we haven't been here long." She tried to grasp his arm, but he pulled away.

"No, I don't feel well."

Hailing a cab to take them home, they left in silence, Harry vowing not to say anything out of anger. Arriving at their apartment, Harry went right to bed, but he didn't sleep as his imagination ran wild.

The next morning, the smell of dead sea creatures drifted in through the open window, courtesy of tidal pools, fishing boats, and processing plants. Harry woke before Clara and lay in bed, breathing in the rotten smells. The smells reminded him of the ocean, and he looked forward to leaving. He turned and looked at Clara, still asleep. The jealousy from the night before no longer burned in his heart, but an ache was there, nonetheless. He realized she had a life without him, and he needed to let her have it.

Harry had scheduled a Hansom cab for eight o'clock, leaving him two hours to prepare and spend with Clara. He dressed in his uniform and gathered his surveying supplies and charts. Their conversation was limited to pleasantries; Clara paced to release her anxiety, eventually resorting to folding Harry's clothing and extra uniform, strategically placing each item in his duffle bag.

The driver arrived, and they boarded his rig for the trip to the docks. They sat in the quiet of the cab as it bounced over the cobblestone streets. Harry reached over and held Clara's hand for the thirty-minute ride. The cabbie stopped when they reached their destination, jumping from his seat to unload Harry's bags. Harry stepped out and walked around to grab his gear. The driver crawled back to his bench while the anxious sailor looked up at Clara's expressionless face.

"I'll be back in six months."

"I hope you have a safe trip," said Clara.

"I will, thank you."

"Harry, what's wrong? You seem angry about something. You haven't been the same since last night."

"Like I said, my stomach was upset last night; My nerves got the best of me. I'm better now. No, I'm not angry."

"Then I need to say something to you." She paused, her hands trembling but resolved solid. "I've been thinking about us. You..." She collected her thoughts. Harry could tell a blow was coming. "I don't think I love you. I'm sure I don't want to get married. I think that during this time you are away, we should emotionally and physically separate."

With a deep sigh, Clara explained.

"When you get back, I'll have moved out of the apartment. You won't have to do anything. I'll move my own things out. Harry, you haven't done anything wrong other than you being you. You wouldn't understand how I'm feeling. I want to be married and have children, but you never want to talk about our future. I want a future with someone who puts me first, but you put your career first. I feel lonely. I feel like I want more than what you can give. It doesn't help that once you leave, I have no idea what you are doing if you're even alive."

Harry felt ashamed, for Clara was right; he neglected her, he avoided talking about what might be, and he had no right to be angry about her wanting to fulfill her needs when he wasn't helping.

"I'm sorry. I could have done more; I see that. My focus is on my work and not on you; it's not on us. But why didn't you say something sooner?"

"I was afraid. I didn't want to face the consequences of my actions. I wanted to tell you the truth earlier, but I wasn't ready for what would happen. Now that I've told you the truth, I'm more afraid than ever of what will happen."

Standing on the street alone as she left in the cab, Harry, too, felt more afraid than ever. What had he done? What else besides quitting his job could he do?"

Chapter Two - Gangway

That morning in March 1889, the *U.S.S. Carlisle P. Patterson* was one of dozens of sailing ships and schooners anchored near San Francisco's harbor. Their masts were pale in the morning mist, the rigging appearing like cobwebs attached to burned-out trees in a forest. Within the decade, as the era of sailing waned, many of these same vessels would be scuttled. Steam was replacing sailing; just as subsequent technologies would replace steam. The *Patterson* straddled history, boasting both sails and steam propulsion.

The harbor was full of wind-driven vessels, passenger steamers, warships and navy support vessels, merchant ships, and fishing boats. Smaller skiffs and rowboats maneuvered between them, shuttling crew and supplies from ship to shore and back. Flags from countries all around the world fluttered in the breeze. Textiles, raw materials, tea, and seafood filled the waterfront loading docks, waiting for dockworkers to move them to warehouses or load them onto departing cargo ships. Immigrants from China filled the streets, bustling between home and work. Trade, transportation, defense, and culture defined San Francisco's harbor that morning, as it had become a critical link to China, Japan, and the Philippines for their silk, porcelain, and spices and to Mexico and Chile for their silver, copper, and other ores.

The intense activity of the harbor was in sharp contrast to the immobile man standing forlorn in the fog, his belongings on the wet sidewalk. Pedestrians stepped around his cluster of items while passing cabs splashed him from the street. Harry sobbed, shielding his face from the passersby. His stomach hurt, and his eyes burned. His world had dreadfully turned on him, and now he was alone—a practically divorced man.

Grabbing his things, he lifted them and turned away from the ships, walking away from his ship. He reasoned he wouldn't go this season; it was time to quit, to leave the Survey and find another position. He would take time off and travel. He could not go on this trip—he was too ashamed. In his torment, he felt small and immature compared to the officers he was supposed to serve with. He had a failed engagement in an era when only three marriages per thousand failed.

"Mr. Ford!" yelled a tall man in uniform approaching from behind. "Mr. Ford!"

He froze, caught abandoning his crew and his duty. Pulling a handkerchief from his pocket, he wiped his eyes and blew his nose.

"Harry, where are you going? The ship is this way."

"Mac, is that you? Ah, you're right. Where am I going?"

"Are you all right? Your eyes are bloodshot."

He couldn't answer, unable to put his thoughts into words.

"Harry, what is going on?"

John McDonald was one of the older ensigns onboard but also an old friend of Harry's. He knew Clara well, living six blocks down Market Street. The two households often combined activities and helped each other as they could. Attending the same church, they were each strong in their faith, while McDonald functioned as the *Patterson's* de facto chaplain. His white hair and solemn demeanor enhanced his pastoral appearance.

Harry gave McDonald the news.

"Mac, Clara doesn't want to get married. She's leaving me."

"I'm so sorry. I don't know what to say. What happened? You two seemed fine the last time I was there."

"She doesn't want to be with me anymore. She says it's because I won't return. She doesn't like the not knowing part."

"She's right, you know. You might not survive this voyage."

Harry shuffled his feet, embarrassed by what was to follow.

"Do you remember last December when we met at the Polaris?"

"I do. Quite a few of us were there that evening. We had an enjoyable time."

"We were celebrating Foust's engagement," he said, referring to another ensign from the *Patterson*. "He celebrated too much that night. Anyway, do you remember a man named John Reeves? He sat with us for a while— dark hair thinks he's the best in any competition. Remember? He said he could beat anybody in tennis, golf, rowing, whatever."

"I do. He was a pompous ass. Didn't care for him. He seemed greedy too—everything was about money or how expensive his things were, like his boots. Oh, I hope I didn't offend you. He is a friend of yours."

"I think he and Clara are getting involved. Clara and I have drifted apart. I realize she wants, she needs, more than I give her. I think, in the end, it's probably more my fault than hers. I pay more attention to my work and Alaska than I do her."

"My friend, if there's anything I can do, let me know. I can't think of what that might be right now."

"No, thanks. There's nothing either of us can do at this point. She and I have never really agreed on things. I say something's white, and she insists it's black."

"Harry, just a minute ago, you weren't thinking of..."

"No, Mac, I'm not. I mean, I may have been distracted for a minute, but I'm fine now. Let's get on board."

He slung his duffle over his shoulder as McDonald helped with the loose baggage, carrying it to the gangway about a hundred yards away. A group of landsmen was loading provisions, placing them in netting to be hauled on board, and calling out the name and number of each item loaded. Assistant Paymaster Davenport recorded the items in one of his many ledgers, repeating what he just heard from the deckhand.

"One dozen pairs of galvanized pintles and gudgeons."

"One dozen pairs of galvanized pintles and gudgeons."

"Two boxes of wood screws, number six. Two boxes of wood screws, number ten."

"Two boxes of wood screws, number six. Two boxes of wood screws, number ten."

"One hundred feet of one-inch sugar pine. One hundred feet of half-inch sugar pine."

"One hundred feet of one-inch sugar pine. One hundred feet of half-inch sugar pine."

"Four barrels of salt."

"Four barrels of salt."

Harry watched as they rolled the barrels into the netting, noting the drag they played on the net as it lifted to the deck for loading onto the ship.

Speaking to McDonald, he said, "No matter how much we prepare, there's always something that goes wrong that we don't expect—some part we don't bring, some piece that doesn't hold. How many times this season do you think we'll need to take a launch somewhere for something we need? Last season, we went, oh, what, a dozen times?"

"Yeah, or for food, water, and fuel. We never have enough."

"Davenport! How much more?" asked McDonald.

"Sir, we still have several tons of supplies—weights and lines, more lumber. We also have the water to load," the paymaster replied.

Davenport went about his business as Harry and McDonald ascended the gangway, stopping at the top before stepping onto the main deck. Addressing the watch officer stationed there, Harry asked, "Permission to come aboard?"

Ensign A. C. Almy, the watch officer, replied,

"Permission granted, Mr. Ford. Nice to see you again. You too, Mr. McDonald." With the watch's approval, Harry and McDonald stepped onto the main deck.

"Good to see you too, Andrew." Harry knew A.C. from last season. He didn't like calling him A.C., the initials sounding more like the word 'ace,' and Harry didn't feel Andrew was any sort of ace, more like an arse. He couldn't name why Andrew rubbed him the wrong way, other than his eyebrows, which were continuous from one eye across the bridge of his nose to the other, so he did his best to team up with the other officers instead when paired for work.

"How was your leave? How is Clara?"

Harry scoffed at the irony and pain of what was happening and evaded the question.

"She's fine," he said, averting his eyes.

Since McDonald already knew about the breakup and Harry didn't want to tell Almy his personal secrets, he changed the subject to avoid further questions by asking,

"What's our status? Is everyone onboard?"

"No, we're still waiting on a few of the crew. We have a new commander—Lieutenant Mansfield. He relieved Commander Thomas just two days ago."

"Where did Thomas go?" He wasn't surprised, as commanders usually lasted only one or two seasons.

"Washington, D.C. He was promoted to Hydrographic Inspector for the Survey," Almy replied.

"Hydrographic Inspector. Impressive. That is quite an honor. What would it be like to work for headquarters in Washington, D.C.?" wondered Harry.

"Too much politics, if you ask me," interjected McDonald. "Like the change of administration from Cleveland to Harrison this past winter. All the letterhead has to be changed—what a waste of paper."

"They have the best of the best when it comes to equipment, though," countered Harry. "We use their hand-me-downs in the field. I could work there, in D.C."

"Maybe you'll get the chance, Harry," concluded Almy.

"Do you know anything about our new commander?" Harry asked.

"I sailed with him some years back. You can't ask for a better man—fair, keeps his word, and wouldn't let anyone do something he wouldn't be willing to do himself."

"Agreed," added McDonald.

"That describes every officer of the Navy," Harry said.

He was beginning to feel better. Being back on board the ship had raised his spirits. Preparing to set sail was the distraction he needed; his focus had to be on his work—the two jobs he performed while out at sea.

Harry and McDonald excused themselves from Almy and headed to Harry's quarters.

"Mac, you've met the new commander. What's your opinion?"

"Mansfield's going to be great. He respects and values input from his officers, makes decisions when needed, and usually has ideas for handling situations. He's also an excellent sailor—preferring sails over steam. He'll have us under sail more than Commander Thomas did last year."

They arrived at Harry's quarters, a small, two-bunk room lit with two gas lamps and shared with Ensign Foust and hosting nothing more than a table, two desk chairs, two small clothes closets, and a mirror on the wall by the window. Foust had already been there and put his items away. Dropping the bags he had been carrying, McDonald left Harry to settle in. Harry filled the closet and drawers with uniforms and clothes, made his bed, and placed his wash items by the sink. Adjusting his uniform, he headed to the pilot's house to meet the new commander, Mansfield.

The small, confined wooden pilot house was located on the upper deck. On this gray day, the polished brass fittings of the compass and barometer glimmered in the well-lit space. Looking through the door window, he saw three men with their backs turned, gazing toward the bow at the activity on deck. He recognized the back of one man—Ensign Albert Beecher—but not the other two.

The three men turned around as he entered. One stepped forward and extended his hand, saying,

16

"I'm Lieutenant Henry Mansfield, Commander of the *Patterson*."

The new commander was an 1867 graduate of the Naval Academy. He had worked his way from Ensign to Master, then promoted to Lieutenant in 1871. Later in life, he became the commander of the U.S.S. Iowa and served in the Spanish-American War, culminating his career as a Rear Admiral. His presence in the room was unmistakable, even without speaking in his deep baritone voice, the polished uniform and tall, erect posture attesting to his rank and authority.

"Sir, a pleasure to meet you. I'm Master at Arms Harry Ford."

"And this is Lieutenant Edward Dorn, Executive Officer."

"Oh, so Lieutenant Oliver isn't our XO this season?" asked Harry, shaking Dorn's hand. Dorn was about Harry's weight, a good three or four inches taller and five years older; in Harry's opinion, Dorn was too thin for an officer.

"No," replied Dorn, "Lt. Oliver was assigned to a revenue cutter due to the death of one of their officers, and I was selected as his replacement. I look forward to working with you." Harry picked up a hint of what seemed like a faint New England accent but couldn't find the state from which the new XO might be.

"And you know Ensign Beecher, I believe," said Mansfield as Harry and Beecher shook hands.

"Yes, sir. Good to see you again, Beech." Beech's real name was Albert, and his nickname was earned in boyhood from his thickset body, which somebody once likened to a Beech tree.

"You too, Harry. You look well."

"We will all get to know one another better over the next few weeks," said Mansfield, "but for now, did you have a restful break from service? How was your leave?"

"Busy," replied Harry." I spent most of it visiting my parents. They live a few blocks from me. My father is well—he sells life insurance—but my mother has tremors and a demanding time walking. The doctor thinks she might have shaking palsy."

To Harry's surprise, his new commander replied, "God bless her, son. May His healing power grant her health."

A knock at the door interrupted the conversation, and Seaman Ellingson entered the room. Ellingson was an old salt, a caricature of an ancient time, a bent-over sailor with a wrinkled face, long weathered hands, long thin hair on his head, and a bushy salt and pepper beard on his face.

"Beggin' pardon, sir, but Master at Arms Ford is needed down in the crew quarters. There are two guys arguing,' about to come to blows."

Before leaving, Harry asked Mansfield, "Are you aware that the *H.M.S. Swiftsure* is moored nearby? I saw her as we arrived."
"Yes, I am. We've already exchanged signals, and we will be paying a diplomatic visit. If you're interested, please join us."

"Yes, sir. I'd be honored."

Chapter Three - The *Patterson*

Harry and Ellingson left the pilot's house and headed to the crew quarters. By the time they arrived, the men that had been arguing had settled their dispute. Electing to go back to his quarters, he invited Ellingson to follow along.

"I was just thinking about last year," Harry said as he led the way. "We were anchored around Ketchikan. I was out in the *Vixen*, and you were out in the whaleboat, doing depth soundings. You fell overboard and started yelling. I can still picture you swimming to shore and then stripping. It was a funny sight! Was the water cold?" he asked with mock sarcasm.

"I tell you, it was cold, Mr. Ford. And I could have been fish food, no thanks to you."

"What happened?"

"You know, I've been in boats all my life. You'd think I'd know balance by now, wouldn't you? Well, I was hauling the sounding wire, my foot lodged under the seat so I could reach out farther, and wouldn't you know it—my boot slips out of that hold. Before I knew it, I was in the water. It happened so fast; I still can't believe it. The only time I've ever capsized myself," he chuckled. "The cold takes your breath away. Your body gets rigid, and your muscles are hard to move. The weight of your clothes pulls you down, and you struggle to stay up. Men die in minutes in that water."

"How did you do it, then? You must have been in for ten."

They arrived at Harry's quarters, and Ellingson immediately headed to Foust's empty bunk. Lying slouched, the tan wrinkles on his face arched downward; his maturity spoke to his world travels.

"I learned to swim as a child." Ellingson shifted to get more comfortable, reclining in the bunk.

"My mother taught me. I grew up back East, in Pennsylvania. My parents lived on a farm they bought from my grandparents—on my mom's side.

19

Mom had four sisters and three brothers, mostly younger than her. The place had a pond, really a small lake. When she was about fifteen, one of her sisters and one of her brothers drowned. The grief of losing her two siblings was intense, and she vowed not to let it happen to her children. She learned how to swim from a friend, and then she gave each of us swimming lessons when we turned five. I wanted to be a sailor, so she gave me extra training."

"Good for your mother. But the cold—how did you survive the icy water and the weight of your clothes?"

"I kicked my boots off first thing and pulled down my trousers. After you're in the water for a few minutes, you begin to feel numb, so the cold isn't as bad. Remember to keep your trousers with you. They can make a semi-floatation tube, and you'll need 'em once you're out of the water."

"That sounds like it wouldn't work."

"Yeah, well, I swam back to shore before I froze. It helped to have the current at my back."

Harry enjoyed the older man's company and his stories. Ellingson had been a sailor longer than the others and had visited far more ports. He wondered if Ellingson had ever married.

"Do you have any children, Ellingson?" Harry felt nostalgic in his quarters and in no hurry to work, so he figured he could engage Ellingson in conversation. He sat down on one of the two chairs in the cramped room.

"No, no children."

"You ever been married? Or in love?"

"Me, in love, heh. Oh yeah, ain't we all? Let me tell you a story. We bought Alaska from Russia in 1867, right? Well, I always wanted to go and visit this 'Seward's Folly,' as they called it. I heard wild stories of incredible riches. Gold, for one, but timber and fish too."

He waited while Harry resettled himself in one of the chairs in the room and continued.

"I hired on with a trading company in late summer of '82. I can spot a capable vessel and crew, but these—they sailed like greenhorns. I moved around on company-owned ships and worked at their trading posts in the southeast. I hitched a ride back to New York after the bad '83 winter. Once I warmed up, I missed Alaska and wanted to go back. I got wind of a new ship, the *Patterson*, built by the government just for Alaska—to sail the southeast on survey duty. Congress spent $100,000 to build it. I wanted to be on that ship."

Harry was skeptical that Ellingson knew how much the *Patterson* cost to build, and he wondered what this had to do with Ellingson being in love.

"How did you know that?" asked a skeptical Harry.

"I'll tell you how. Name the Coast and Geodetic Survey Superintendent who died in office in 1881."

"Well, that was before my time, but was it Patterson?" Harry instantly realized he was on the ship named in his honor.

"Yes, Carlile P. Patterson, Superintendent. I, Seaman Ellingson, was in love with his daughter, Katie."

Harry was stunned. *What are the odds?* He thought. There was no way this gentle but unskilled, uneducated man had somehow loved the daughter of one of the country's—if not the world's—foremost geodetic surveyors. It didn't fit.

Raising his eyebrows in doubt, he asked, "Go on. How did you meet and fall in love with this woman?"

"Only by grace, I say. Nothing happens by accident, chance, coincidence, or whatever you want to call it. All things happen by God's grace, mercy, or punishment. I had gone to Boston for a family matter—a death in the family. I got all fancied up with new funeral clothes, so at least I didn't smell like fish.

"For a reason I don't remember, one of the women helping with the funeral was Katie—a friend of a friend. She wanted to go to a fabric shop, and I agreed to assist her. We had the best time from the moment we left until we returned from the store. She was so happy, laughing at everything. She caught my attention; she captivated me with her beautiful smile. She had more sense than I did and asked if I could take her shopping the next day. I fell in love with her charm, strength, and humor. She was the person who christened this ship."

"She caught you, eh?"

"Aye, mate, that she did. She caught my heart. We spent three evenings together. I was in love with her when I left." Ellingson turned more somber. "I never saw her again."

"What happened?"

"Our worlds were too different. She was a socialite, and her mother wanted her to succeed or at least marry a man with money. I wasn't that man, and we both knew it. So, we said our goodbyes; I rated Fireman with the Navy, joined the *Patterson* on her maiden voyage in '84, and now here I am."

"Wait, you're telling me you sailed on this ship's maiden voyage?" Harry, by now, had enough of the hard chair and moved to his bunk to recline.

"Aye, Mr. Ford. Five years ago. We embarked in July of '84 from Hampton Roads. It may have been July, but it was cold and wet. All the hands were grumbling about the weather, and we hadn't even left port yet. Poor captain—he knew he had a long trip ahead of him and with a quarrelsome crew right from the start. Rather than face weeks and months of surly men, he decided to head for the Madeira Islands."

"This ship, the *Patterson*, sailed to the Madeira Islands? Off the coast of Africa?"

"Yes, sir, Mr. Ford. Those beautiful islands off the coast of Africa. I couldn't believe I was going to Africa, but we were soon steaming across the Atlantic Ocean."

"Why would the captain go there?" Perplexed by apparent insubordination or dereliction of duty, Harry didn't know which.

Ellingson grinned with a wise expression that confused the young seaman. "Mr. Ford, it goes back to your question about love. There are all kinds of love. I've seen men in all ways bent over it. They get messed up in their minds trying to understand what love is. They want real love, you know—

the love between a man and a woman, caring for each other the rest of their lives, no matter what."

Ellingson paused. "It's hard. So many men and women with so many different ideas of what love means, but to find two people who make it work—that's a beautiful thing."

Harry nodded.

"You love southeast Alaska, don't you?" Ellingson asked.

"Yes," Harry replied. "And I can't wait to return."

"But you ain't askin' about places, are ya? You're asking about a woman's love. Mr. Ford, love for and by a woman takes all forms. For some men, well, a few hours of a woman's touch is enough. There's a sayin' that goes, 'The sight of a woman's naked body is too great a part of the universe for a man's eye to behold,' and I'm of that belief. For those men, those few hours must last a lifetime. For others, only being married and sleeping next to a woman, night after night, will do.

With Katie, it wasn't an option; I couldn't have her. My other love—or lust if you will—was Carmen. Beautiful Carmen."

"She lived in the Madeiras?"

"Oh yes, she was a resident of Strangers' Rest. She was the most beautiful of all the women there."

"Strangers' Rest?"

"Yeah, a bordello, if I must say. Once word reached Washington about ships altering course for Africa with Strangers' Rest as the destination, the top brass objected, so we changed the name to the Seaman's Institute. We figured the Navy would assume we meant the Seaman's Church Institute. The irony was quite laughable. Wine and women. Everybody had a great time at the Seaman's Institute."

"So, what happened to Carmen?" Harry asked, trying to keep Ellingson focused.

"Well, two days with Carmen turned my head so backward I couldn't think straight. I loved her, wanted to marry her, and never left her. I imagined myself off the coast of Africa, living in love for the rest of my life. Mr. Ford, I thought I was lovestruck, but it was only lust. I got my senses back when the Master-at-Arms—Wallace, I think was his name; you two might know each other—came for me. He hauled my ass back to the ship. The Commander learned I almost went AWOL for a woman. He put me in chains and on light rations till I got my mind back. It took three days."

"Tell me, Ellingson, any other unauthorized ports of call on that trip? Off to Australia?"

Ellingson chuckled at the young officer's cynicism.

"No, Mr. Ford, just fueling and watering stops along the South American coast." He chastised him, saying, "Ya know, Mr. Ford, not all the world follows the rules like you do."

Harry knew what he meant. He took pride in his role and job as Master-at-Arms and did things to the best of his ability.

"It comes with the job description."

"We stopped at Rio de Janeiro, Montevideo, Chile, and Sandy Point before crossing the Magellan Straits. The *Patterson*, loaded with thirty tons of coal on deck when we went through those straits in a gale, rode the seas without takin' on so much as a cup of water. She's a fine ship.

After we passed through, I saw something I'll never forget. There was a village on the shore, and they sent out over a hundred canoes, maybe a hundred and fifty, to intercept us. They were Tierra del Fuegans, in full war paint, two or three to a canoe." Ellingson paused, remembering the details of their faces.

"What did you do? Did they attack?"

"It was a sight to behold—these small canoes bobbing in the waves while we stood looking down on them, hundreds of men staring back up at us. The captain cut the engines so we wouldn't run 'em over. We had no clue what they intended, so the Commander ordered up the Gatling guns to the ready and issued rifles and pistols."

24

"Definitely! I would have, too!"

"So, these canoes carried rope lines with hooks on the end, and before anyone had any idea what was happening, they were attached to the *Patterson*. Shouting, half-naked natives started to scramble aboard." At this, Ellingson flailed about and shouted gibberish, and they both laughed.

"Lucky for them, the Captain recognized they weren't there for any malicious intent but to barter—trading for tobacco and firewater. Some wanted food. I was able to trade for a goat and a beaver skin, and it only cost me three plugs of tobacco."

"Wow, so they wanted to trade. The world is getting smaller."

"Yes, sir, Mr. Ford, you can't go anywhere without running into somebody you know from someplace in your past."

"Mr. Wallace sure had his hands full on that trip, as did the captain. Turns out that pleasing the crew only lasted so long. When they voted to refuse duty, it got to their heads—the shore leaves did. Captain Clover read—or should I say shouted—the Articles of War to the crew, describing the consequences for refusal. Everyone went back to work but for one man. Turner, I believe his name was. Mr. Wallace kept him in the brig on bread and water for a week. He ate quite well, though, as we all went down after meals and brought him food."

Harry chuckled at the thought as he and Ellingson left for their duties. He, too—contrary to how Ellingson perceived him—would have offered extra food to a prisoner. The world didn't need to be that harsh.

Chapter Four - The *Swiftsure*

The *U.S.S. Carlise P. Patterson* crew exchanged diplomatic signals and messages with the crew of the *H.M.S. Swiftsure*, and after receiving permission, Mansfield and a contingent of his officers were to board. Visits between officers of foreign navy vessels anchored near each other were a naval and international courtesy; following Navy protocols of etiquette and precedence for such visits was required.

Lieutenant Mansfield trimmed his short blond beard, mustache, and sideburns with scissors, brushed back his hair, and then tweaked his bow tie. Taking his frock coat off a hanger, he put it on and attached his saber to his belt. He placed his cap—embroidered with a shield, a silver eagle, and two crossed foul anchors—on his head. His uniform was immaculate, as would be his British counterpart.

He set off to the main deck to meet the contingent boarding the *Swiftsure*. Assembled on deck were Lt. Edward Dorn, Ensigns Albert Wood, A.C. Almy, Albert Beecher, John McDonald, and Master-at-Arms Harry Ford. Ensign William Foust was staying behind on the *Patterson* in the absence of the commander.

The *Patterson* had three substantial-sized steam launches used in surveying support roles and for general sea-worthy transport. That afternoon, the *Cosmos* was tied to and waiting alongside the *Patterson*. The *Cosmos* and a sister launch, the *Pirate*, were fifty-two feet long and twelve feet across, built to float in less than five feet of water. These unassuming craft were too big to haul onboard for sailing, so they were towed behind or traveled independently under steam. They could carry a crew of seven and had sleeping quarters built on the deck for extended travel. The *Vixen* was the third and more modest of the three.

Towing a launch came with risks, and the *Cosmos* herself had once been stranded at sea with no power after her towline broke in a spring southeast Alaska storm. Waves large enough to smash the bunkhouse crashed over the deck, soaking the crew. One man trying to repair the damaged helm and steering wheel injured his hand when it became caught in the propeller gears.

The *Cosmos* was also famous among ships for being lost at sea. The crew had diverted to assist survivors of the *Ocean King*, a passenger liner that had floundered off Port Townsend, Washington. Taking extra time for the rescue, the *Cosmos* was late for a scheduled rendezvous with the *Patterson*. The *Patterson* sent out an official notice stating that the *Cosmos* was "lost at sea" before eventually seeing her arrival in Port Townsend with the rescued survivors.

For additional support when taking measurements in the launches, the *Patterson* also utilized unnamed smaller wooden steamboats built by the Herreshoff company, as well as four gigs, or sailboats, and two or three rowboats. These support vessels were hauled up and hanging by their davits. These smaller craft were more nimble and easier to maneuver in tight spaces and had the advantage of being hauled on deck for maintenance.

In preparation for the *Swiftsure* visit, Engineer Strickland stood at the *Cosmos'* helm, his trademark pipe hanging from between his yellow teeth, blue smoke rising between puffs. A rope and wooden gangway, rather than rope ladders, was in place. The bay was completely calm, so it took Strickland little effort to maintain the launch's position.

After the seven officers in full dress uniform boarded and the craft cast off, Strickland engaged the propeller, steering her toward the *Swiftsure*. As they neared, they saw the British flag hanging limp in the calm air on the flagstaff astern. Wood let out a soft whistle as they got closer, expressing his awe at the size and beauty of the ironclad battleship. The *Patterson* was a modest 163 feet long, while the *Swiftsure* stretched 475 feet. The former displaced 719 tons of water and sat 14 feet below the water line, while the latter displaced 7,020 tons and sat 24 feet below the water line.

"Those are 9-inch muzzle-loading cannons, and she has ten," Mansfield said. "In addition, there are four 6-inch muzzle-loading cannons, with ten 25-pound breech-loaders. The British command added those about ten years ago during a retrofit before sending her out as their flagship for the Pacific Ocean."

"You've seen her before somewhere?" asked Almy.

"No, but I've heard of her. She has a solid reputation. I studied her retrofit at the Academy. She was built around 1871, and I think she is the seventh or eighth in the British line of warships to be named the *Swiftsure*."

The *Patterson* officers motored into the battleship's shadow, and as they neared the gangway, they heard the British bosun's whistle piping the boarding call. The *Swiftsure* crew assumed positions along the rail to welcome their American counterparts onboard. Tying up to the gangway, Lt. Mansfield led the men up to the main deck. Officers in British uniforms stood at attention as the uniformed Americans presented themselves.

"Permission to come aboard? I am Lieutenant Henry Mansfield, Commanding Officer of the *U.S.S. Carlisle P. Patterson*, United States Navy, under contract to the United States Coast and Geodetic Survey."

"Permission granted! Captain James Hammet of *H.M.S. Swiftsure*, at your service." Dropping his salute, the British commander strode forward to shake Lt. Mansfield's hand. "It is a pleasure to meet you."

Commander Hemmet did not have the overwhelming presence or size of *Patterson*'s commander, but he carried himself with the same sense of dignity and seriousness as his American counterpart. The British Captain wore gold tasseled epaulets and embroidered sleeves smartly accenting his polished buttons and wide belt.

"The pleasure is mine," responded Lt. Mansfield. "Thank you for your hospitality. As I stand here looking at your deck, the *Patterson* seems so small, like a rowboat. What a fine ship!" he marveled.

Captain Hemmet straightened his stance even more. "Yes, we are very proud of her," he answered.

"Forgive me, I'd like you to meet Ensigns Albert Wood, Albert Beecher, A.C. Almy, John McDonald, Lieutenant Edward Dorn, and Master-at-Arms Harry Ford. Our engineer, Mr. Strickland, is staying with the launch.

"Very nice to meet you. Under my command are Lieutenants George Chase and Benjamin Crowley, along with Ensigns Darren Foster and Robert Giles and our Master-at-Arms Charles O'Brien." Harry immediately picked up the phonetic distinction between the American and British version of 'lieutenant,' the former sounding like *lootenant*, the latter sounding more like a *lefttenant*.

The officers spent several minutes shaking hands and greeting each other in turn. Captain Hammet then led a tour of the ship. He began at the bridge and worked their way past the gun deck and gunnery crew quarters to the

28

armor deck. The captain explained how the ship was designed to reduce the risk of damage from accidental explosions. They explored the decks below, and the Patterson crew compared the living and dining quarters provided for three hundred fifty British sailors to those provided on the *Patterson*.

When the tour concluded, it was time for an early dinner. Not prepared for a formal dinner typically associated with visiting dignitaries, the white-walled, well-lit wardroom where they were to eat remained undecorated, with only the officer's uniforms giving the room a formal appearance. The cook, however, prepared a special meal of steamed oysters, fillet of sole, sweetbread, and chocolate orange pudding cake for dessert, served with French Champagne.

Captain Hammet invited the American sailors to be seated and opened the discussion.

"Lieutenant Mansfield, as you know, living onboard a ship for six months with the same mates, you get to know each other pretty well. Habits, unpleasant habits..." The men in the room chuckled, knowing exactly what he meant by "unpleasant habits." He continued, "...preferences, opinions, and such."

"By the end of a season, we know each other pretty well, too," agreed Mansfield.

"And so today, we take the opportunity to engage in spirited discussion with your perspectives on various matters. I know what my officers would say about any given navy or maritime situation, but it's their views on public policy and the international stage that I like most to elicit. You see, those policy views are based on societal norms, likes, and dislikes; they're not as simple as operating procedures. Policy mystically transforms into politics, and that's where things get interesting."

"I had never thought of it that way, but go on," replied Mansfield.

"Our most recent discussions have centered on the Samoan Islands. Are you familiar with the ongoing issues in Samoa, Lieutenant?" asked Hemmet.

Lieutenant Mansfield sat back in his chair, pausing before answering. "Samoa, yes. The British, Americans, and Germans are ready for a fight—not to mention the internal power struggles between tribal leaders."

"Lieutenant Mansfield, beg my pardon," interrupted Ensign McDonald, "but Samoa is also where the cyclone hit last month. The Navy lost sixty-three men, and the *Trenton*, the *Vandalia*, and the *Nipsic* warships sank. The Germans lost close to one hundred men and three ships."

"And we almost lost the Calliope," added Lieutenant Chase as he and Captain Hemmet exchanged glances. "But I think the cyclone may have reordered priorities there. Diplomatic tensions between our three countries don't seem to be as high as a result."

"Germany is hosting a foreign policy conference in Berlin involving delegations from the United States, Britain, and Samoa. I hear progress is being made on deciding who should be the rightful king," added Captain Hammet. "Mata'afa won the islands' tribal war, but I don't trust him to govern fairly. Laupepa would be my choice for the king of Samoa. As for the Three Powers, what do you think, Lieutenant Mansfield? Is it proper for the United States, Great Britain, and Germany to rule Samoa?"

"A house divided against itself cannot stand," answered Lt. Mansfield, prompting laughter and conversation among the other officers. The tone shifted from serious to friendly as the men ate their dinners and engaged in more intimate technical and personal discussions. They shared stories about their wives, families, and life back home, passing around pictures and clapping each other on the back. They quickly became friends, bound together as brethren, mariners, and Navy officers.

Finishing a conversation with a British officer on his left, Harry turned to engage his Master-at-Arms counterpart, Charles O'Brien, as stewards served dessert.

"Where in England are you from?" Harry asked the heavy-set man.

"Born in Lancashire, '52. Grew up in the Royal Navy—my dad and uncles all served. My dad died a few years ago, and my mum is still at home. I stay with her when I'm there. Otherwise, my brother takes responsibility. She's getting frail," Charles said matter-of-factly. "I suspect I'll be in the Navy till they drop my limp body overboard. No wife, no children. The sea is my mistress, as they say. I've been doing this for so long that I wouldn't know what else to do. What about you, mate? Where are you from?"

"I grew up in Hudson, in the state of New Jersey," answered Harry. "My friends and I would go down and play in the mud and the eddies along the riverbanks—catching snakes and frogs, looking for kids' treasure. All the families owned boats, and I went fishing with my father all the time. It was a wonderful place. One year, most of the river froze over."

Harry paused, lost in thought. "Do you know what the Indians used to call the Hudson River?"

Charles shook his head.

"Muh-he-kun-ne-tuk. It's Mohican for 'River that flows two ways,'" Harry explained.

"My father was a captain in the Volunteer Army during the Civil War. I was born close to nine months after the war ended, so what does that tell you?" he joked.

"Your parents celebrated! I like it!" laughed Charles.

"They're still alive," Harry explained, "they live up the street from me in San Francisco. Sometimes, I think they didn't want a son as much as they wanted a farmhand. I worked day in and day out from the time I could walk—helping my mother at first, then my father with the harder chores. But my father didn't intend to stay a farmer. We moved from New Jersey to San Francisco when I was fourteen."

Charles nodded in affirmation but then said, "I have relatives in your hometown of Hudson. About five years ago, the *Swiftsure* docked in New York City, and I had the chance to visit; the two towns are right across the river from each other."

Harry paused, his eyebrows pulling together as he reflected on his boyhood. His demeanor turned somber. "My best friend..." He stopped, struggling with the words. Charles could see the anxiety rising in Harry's freckled face.

"My friend Thomas... he... he and I were playing one day down by the water, the river's edge. We were eight or nine years old. I went back to the

31

house for something to eat, leaving Thomas alone. When I returned, he was out in the Hudson in a small rowboat. The boat should have been tied to shore, but the knot must have slipped, and it drifted into the current with Thomas in it."

He pictured the tragic moment from years earlier. "It had rained for many days before that, so the river was at flood stage. On top of that, it was a full moon, and the incoming tide was colliding with the downstream flow. Remember, the Indians call it the River That Runs Backwards, so you can imagine—the water was nothing but chaos, swells and waves tossing the boat. I can still picture Thomas—the look of sheer terror on his face as he bounced around in the rapids. He couldn't do a thing about it, nor could anyone else. It seemed like forever. Then, suddenly, no rowboat. No, Tom."

He swallowed. "I feel guilty. I should have been with him. It never should have happened."

"It wasn't your fault," Charles said.

"I don't know. I was so young—I suppose that gives me some legal out. He was my friend; we were playing, and it wasn't like I was responsible for him. But did I ignore a voice in my head—my better judgment—when I left him alone to get myself something to eat? I sometimes wonder."

"It was a tragic accident. The sea, the river, our natural environment—it's more powerful than you or me, and it won't be challenged, much less conquered."

Harry nodded, and Charles changed the subject.

"How did you sign on with the *Patterson*?"

"After we moved west, my father secured a job selling life insurance. One of his clients, a man named Reeves, was a mid-level government accountant for a new federal agency surveying America and the coastline. At my father's invitation, our family met up with his family at a park. My father wanted to talk—well, sell—insurance, but instead, this Mr. Reeves did all the talking. He was excited about his job and wanted to talk about it. He explained—more to me than to my father—about working with math, earth science, astronomy, biology."

32

Harry considered mentioning how this man's son had ruined his life but thought better of it and held his tongue.

"So, it turns out this insurance client knows of an entry-level opening in the Coast and Geodetic Survey. Since I told him I liked science and did well in school, he followed up with a recommendation to the hiring manager. The next thing I knew, I was hired as an apprentice hydrographer. It was a clear case of 'it's not what you know, it's who you know.'"

After the stewards removed the dinner and dessert dishes, Captain Hemmet and Lieutenant Mansfield stood, followed by all the officers, as it was time to return. In a gesture of goodwill, Charles gave Harry a big bear hug.

"God calls us when He wants to call us. We don't play a part in that," he said, looking his new friend squarely in the eye.

Harry nodded, and the two shook hands before joining the others as they left the room to return to the *Patterson*.

"Captain Hemmet, you and your officers are welcome to visit the *Patterson*," Mansfield stated as he and Hemmet neared the gangway to the *Cosmos*.

"Thank you, Lieutenant Mansfield. It shall have to be an abbreviated visit. We are leaving in the afternoon, and I will need to prepare, so I won't be attending. However, I will send a delegation. Perhaps you could show them the equipment you Americans use for your coast survey? My crew would be very interested."

"Yes, we do pride ourselves on having the best scientific equipment available. We'd be happy to demonstrate."

The next day, members of the British delegation arrived for a tour of the *Patterson*. Mansfield welcomed them aboard. The sense of international diplomacy was no longer a concern; the group stood more at ease, as if on a fact-finding mission instead of a stage where they were watched.

"Good to meet you again, Lieutenant Crowley. I understand you depart in a few hours?"

"Yes, Lieutenant, we've been ordered to Hawaii."

Leading the small group of four along the main deck, Mansfield described the ship.

"Framed in white pine with cedar tops, with Georgia yellow pine used for the planks and beams. The upper and main decks are white and yellow, respectively." He stopped and turned. "Georgia is one of our southern states, and its forests are unending."

"I've heard of your wood. It's used in European shipbuilding as well," said Crowley.

"Propulsion is provided by two vertical compound engines that sit fore and aft. The *Patterson* can go seven knots under steam. The screw is four-bladed cast iron, eight feet in diameter." Nudging Crowley, the American commander quipped, "But who wants to use steam?"

"The *Patterson* is a joy to sail. Harbor maneuvers are easy by the wind. With square rigging in the foremast and gaff rigging in the rear masts, I can work the breeze and get her turned where I need her to go."

They entered the pilothouse, reviewed the navigational instruments, and climbed up the observation deck ladder to view the harbor. Mansfield then led them downstairs for the final part of the tour inside.

"Here is the wardroom, our primary meeting space," he explained. "There are twelve staterooms and a pantry. Forward is the deckhouse, an engine room, the Otis steel boiler room, a storeroom, a galley, and a forward pantry. And here is the drafting room, along with surveying equipment. These are the meridian telescopes. You'll see the Sigsbee-sounding machine on the aft deck when you leave."

Lt. Mansfield explained the organizational structure to Lt. Crowley while the British surveyors and their American counterparts took the opportunity to discuss surveying in detail.

"Mr. Ford is a good example of how our agencies work together," began Mansfield. "He is rated as a Master-at-Arms by and for the Navy, but for the Geodetic Survey, he is one of three hydrographic experts onboard. He provides security while also plotting shorelines, determining depth, taking tide measurements, and charting the location of obstructions. Another example is Ensign Wood—he's our primary navigational officer, but he is also an expert astronomer for the Survey."

"All of our salaries and wages are paid by the Survey from congressional appropriations. The Survey owns the *Patterson* and pays for its operation, but by law, it must operate under the command of Navy officers. The Navy and the Treasury Department have a love-hate relationship with our mission. Some years, we're organized under the Treasury Department; other years, we're in the Navy Department."

"I see," said Crowley with a grin. "Seems like American bureaucracy at its best."

The small tour group approached the main deck to examine the most advanced Sigsbee machine available. Mariners have taken soundings and depth readings using ropes and wires for centuries. As depths increased, it became more difficult to manipulate the wire used for distance measurements, with its total weight exceeding two hundred pounds pulled by the currents. Sigsbee modified the equipment, and his machine became the industry standard for depth soundings for the next fifty years.

Impressed with the American technology, the British delegation bade farewell to their American counterparts and departed for the *Swiftsure*. Mansfield retired to his quarters, satisfied that the United States Navy and the United States Coast and Geodetic Survey had passed a test of international diplomacy with excellence. He reclined in his favorite reading chair and picked up his book, turning the pages to where he had left off.

Chapter Five - Mare Island

The *Patterson* unmoored from the Washington Street dock and anchored off the Pacific Street wharf on April 6, 1889. Lieutenant Mansfield used the slight breeze to push the sails for relocation. Departure for Alaska was not for another four days, but with the amount of ship traffic around him, Mansfield felt that leaving from anchorage would be easier than departing from the dock, helping to minimize any delays caused by other ships crowding the harbor. The crew was busy onboarding supplies, loading water, plotting the course, cleaning the galley, repairing sails, calibrating survey equipment, and tuning engines, among other pre-departure tasks.

The ship's officers conducted navigational briefings, using lessons learned from five previous voyages to guide them on the early and most southern leg of the trip. However, much remained uncertain about the routes and anchorages in the northern part of southeast Alaska. They would be exploring areas for the first time.

By the night of April 8, the officers were burning the proverbial midnight oil in preparation for departure. Mansfield, Dorn, Almy, and Wood were in the wardroom, focused on Admiralty Island's Seymour Canal. Wood led the discussion with his slow, southern drawl.

"This area here, southeast of Mole Harbor, puts us close to the center of our survey sites, and it is well protected. The areas up here, to the north, start to shallow out about here," he said, pointing to a location on one of the maps spread out on the table, "and they catch the wind as it comes in from the west."

"I agree," said Mansfield. "And it's close to Mole Harbor for shore activities and our water source."

"And not too far from Juneau. I foresee going into town many times," said Dorn. "This may be my first trip on the *Patterson*, but it isn't my first with the Navy. Something always comes up."

"So, Seymour Canal, Cleveland Passage, and Holkham Bay will be our primary destinations, then?" asked Wood. "I'll begin plotting this part of our course first thing tomorrow."

"Thank you, Ensign. I think—"

Five sharp peals from the ship's bell and five short blasts from bosun's whistle indicated an emergency on deck. The men in the room dropped what they were doing and rushed topside. A loud commotion came from a group of sailors gathered near the main mast. Two of them rushed off as Mansfield, Dorn, and Wood approached.

"What's going on? What happened?" Mansfield shouted, working his way to the center of the group.

"It's Seaman Gronholm, sir," said one of the sailors. "He fell from the yard arm. It looks like he broke his leg, his collarbone's busted, and he knocked himself in the head pretty hard. We've sent for Dr. Percy. We don't want to move him till the doc gets here."

Mansfield slowly raised his head to look at the yard arm Gronholm had fallen from fifteen feet above. Seeing nothing obvious to indicate why he fell, Mansfield ordered Dorn to investigate and question witnesses for a report. He didn't want a similar incident once they were underway. And he wanted to know why Gronholm was climbing the mast and hanging on the yard arms at night when the *Patterson* wasn't under sail.

Dr. Percy arrived and examined the seaman, concurring with the crew's assessment that the compound fracture of his femur was his most acute injury, with the broken collarbone adding to his pain. He splinted the leg to immobilize it and then lashed a long cloth around his shoulders and armpits to keep his collarbone pulled back. The crew then carefully moved Seaman Gronholm onto a stretcher for transfer to the sick bay, where the doctor planned to set his broken leg more thoroughly. Lt. Mansfield and Ensigns Wood and Almy followed Dr. Percy to his quarters and waited for his prognosis.

After the examination, the doctor emerged from the curtained room and told Lt. Mansfield, "He'll survive, but I want to send him to the hospital at Mare Island so they can properly treat and set the fracture. They can put on a better cast than I can here. Can you get someone to take him at first light? At least we haven't left yet—that would have been worse."

Mansfield turned to Almy and directed, "A.C., tell Mr. Ford to organize a party to take Seaman Gronholm to the hospital on Mare Island first thing in the morning. A.C., I need you and Wood to stay here and continue our route plotting." Mansfield turned and left for his quarters to draft his report.

"Yes, sir. Right away," responded Almy.

Finding Harry still in the drafting room, Almy filled him in on the emergency and Mansfield's orders. Harry immediately returned to his quarters to gather clothes and rain gear and then lay down in his bunk for the night.

At first light, he found two crew from the crew quarters and then had them load Gronholm onto the *Cosmos*. After Harry learned their names were Jefferson and Tomkins, they set off into the harbor toward San Pablo Bay, skirting the south shore on their way to the Napa River and Mare Island. As they approached from the south, dozens of Navy ships anchored in the harbor created a maze of moving obstacles to navigate.

The hospital was three blocks west of where they had planned to dock, but due to heavy ship congestion, they decided to dock the *Cosmos* further south. They found a loading dock four blocks from the hospital. A small contingent of men on the dock were loading empty artillery shells onto carts and then hauling them away. They unloaded Gronholm and moved him in a makeshift wheelchair up bumpy Azuar Avenue, which ran through the industrial and warehouse district of the base. Along the way, Gronholm explained the only reason he was in the spars was to get away from the crew for a while.

At admissions, the hospital staff quickly took Gronholm for treatment, leaving Harry and his crew empty-handed and ready to return back to the *Cosmos*. After signing the necessary paperwork for Gronholm's admission, they began descending the front steps of the hospital.

A shock wave and heat from a tremendous explosion rocked the three-story hospital, shattering windows and sending glass shards flying. Everyone in the area felt the blast's heat on their skin but were otherwise unburned. All knew immediately that there had been an accident at the ammunition magazine. Acrid smoke began to billow their way.

Doctors and nurses ran out of the building toward the blast site. A massive cloud rose from the area while smaller explosions continued to ignite. The first firefighting crews arrived in a Jumbo 9-ton steam fire truck purchased a few months prior. The steam-powered engine provided both water pressure for the hoses and propulsion for the vehicle's lumbering rubber-tired wheels. Two teams of six horses hauling steam-powered water tanks arrived minutes later. The three units began pumping water to douse the flames, though most of what could burn had already exploded.

About an hour after the blast, mop-up operations were underway, with crews putting out fires and removing any remaining ordnance. When all was clear, Harry surveyed the damage. Charred embers and body parts lay scattered in the smoldering remains, blackened by the explosion. A firefighter sidled up beside him.

"What happened? Do you know?" asked Harry.

"We haven't had an accident in thirty years, but I knew one was bound to happen," the firefighter replied.

"How did you know one was going to happen?"

"See that man over there?" The fireman gestured toward a lifeless body lying off to the side. "He's not wearing any shoes. Most likely, he was a sailor ordered to fill shells—but without any proper training. The men who manage black powder need to be professionals. They wear the right clothing and use the correct tools. But when ships come in and want a quick turnaround, sometimes they use regular hands who aren't trained well and don't have—or don't use—the proper equipment."

Pointing to the dead man, he continued. "He should be wearing a pair of rubber boots to avoid static spark. They're hard to get on, so chances are he didn't lose them in the blast. Likely, he wasn't wearing them to begin with. That could be the cause of the explosion."

They watched, mortified, as the base emergency crews attended to the three survivors and the twelve men killed in the explosion. Deciding they had seen enough, they returned to the *Cosmos*, stunned to see it covered in ash, with its sunscreen fabric sung from the heat. Realizing that if they had been onboarding the *Cosmos* during the blast or had been walking by, they might have been burned or even killed. Their trip back to the ship went unnoticed as they talked non-stop about the explosion.

Mansfield spent the afternoon before departure overseeing his least favorite responsibility—last-minute personnel matters. Officers McDonald, Almy, Wood, Strickland, Beale, and Dorn were all in the wardroom with him.

"Commander, Landsman Ah Bo may have deserted—he hasn't been seen in four days," reported Dorn.

"Ensign Wood, please note in the ship's log that Landsman Ah Bo has deserted," replied an annoyed Mansfield. "I'll never figure out how zero money in the pocket is better than a decent day's wage."

Desertions always frustrated him, given the energy required to find and train replacements. It amazed him that someone would leave a job without warning, sometimes even abandoning their earned wages. He regularly held crew and officer meetings to reinforce why they were on the ship and to ensure everyone understood their mission. He often told the story of someone he knew who had been lost at sea because they didn't have accurate navigational charts. He wanted a crew that believed in their work, understood its importance, and saw it as more than just a job. The *U.S.S. Carlise P. Patterson* offered ideal opportunities for entry-level officers—not just the crew.

"He didn't work very hard if you ask me," said Wood as he wrote in the logbook. "Ah Bo, that is. I'm not sorry to see him gone as long as we don't get a similar replacement."

"If we all stayed home, nothing in this world would get done, and we'd all starve," added McDonald. "I'll personally interview Ah Bo's replacement while we're in Port Townsend, sir. I know a place where some decent sailors hang out."

"Thank you, Ensign McDonald. Alright, who's next?"

"Sir," said Dorn, "the men won't mind because they didn't like his food, but Cook Moriquet told me his father has taken a turn for the worse, and he's asked to be discharged so he can stay and help his family. I agree, pending your final approval. For his replacement, I recommend Landsman Yung to take over as the ship's cook. He makes excellent curry."

"Ensign Wood, please note the change of cooks in the ship's log."

A knock at the door interrupted the meeting as Harry arrived.

"Mr. Ford, welcome. I trust Seaman Gronholm is in the hospital?"

"Yes, sir, but you won't believe what happened while we were there. The base ammo depot blew up—a huge explosion. We were in the hospital when it happened. The blast was so strong it shattered windows. The *Cosmos* fabric was charred from the heat and covered in soot. If we had been at the launch when the depot exploded, we could have been burned or killed."

"Were there any casualties?"

"Yes, probably a dozen," reported Harry.

"Oh, that's horrible. Thank God you're okay—and the men who went with you," said a relieved Mansfield.

"Thank you, sir."

"We've been discussing crew matters. Lieutenant Dorn, continue, please."

"Commander, you need to make a decision regarding Landsman Lavelins. Should he be discharged?"

"Yes, discharge him. I don't want him on this sailing—he's trouble. He's been drunk on duty, smuggled alcohol onboard, and stirred up the men."

"With Lavelins discharged, Gronholm in the hospital, and Ah Bo, a deserter, we're down four crew members—we were already one short," Dorn noted.

"Like I said, I'll pick up some crew in Port Townsend. We can get by for the first three or four days without them. There should be plenty of men looking for work in Townsend," said McDonald.

"Paymaster Beale, any personnel issues? How is the new assistant working out?" asked the commander.

"Arthurs is performing well… for an apprentice."

"Engineer Strickland, any personnel matter to discuss?"

41

Strickland pulled out his pipe and replied, "No, sir, I have a full contingent of firemen and assistant engineers."

Lieutenant Mansfield continued his questioning. "Has the hull been inspected? The screw?"

"Yes, the underwater team completed their tasks yesterday. They inspected the entire hull. The propeller screw doesn't have any bends; we shouldn't have vibrations due to propulsion," assured Engineer Strickland.

"What about engine stockpiles? Oil, grease, seals?"

"I believe we have everything needed to maintain the ship. Of course, with the engines, boilers, and launches—one never knows what might go wrong," Strikland replied.

"Lieutenant Dorn, muster drill report."

"Yes, sir. I called the crew to their muster stations last evening. They lowered all life rafts into the water and found them to be fully provisioned and operable. The rafts were hoisted aboard and stored away. The crew performed well."

Mansfield finished with his questions and concluded, "Our departure tomorrow morning is scheduled for eight o'clock. I know you all still have much to do before we leave, so I'll let you get to your duties. Thank you."

As the group rose to leave the wardroom, Mansfield asked Harry to stay behind. Speaking quietly, he said,

"I've noticed a tendency for Paymaster Beale to delegate critical duties to Assistant Paymaster Davenport and, even though he's new, to Assistant Paymaster Arthurs as well. I spoke with Beale about it the other day, but he claims it's for training purposes. It seems to me he delegates too much. But what worries me most? I saw Davenport wearing a ring with an exceptionally large gold nugget—it must have cost a fortune. Where did a paymaster get the kind of money needed to buy that?"

"I saw Davenport showing it off to the crew. I wondered the same thing," Harry replied.

"Mr. Ford, I expect honesty, and right now, I'm not sure if I'm getting it."

"Sir, let me check into it. There could be any number of reasons why he may have a new ring, but I agree. He doesn't make enough money for the likes of what I saw."

The next morning, the skies were clear, with a moderate breeze from the northwest. The entire ship was active well before dawn. Firemen stoked the coal fires for the eight o'clock departure while riggers scurried up the masts, preparing the sails. There was an air of expectancy among the crew—the time for adventure had finally come again.

Mansfield stood in the pilot house, the center of activity for the officers. All the ensigns were on hand or busy with last-minute tasks. Harry was on watch for security. Lieutenant Dorn reviewed their course out of the harbor at the chart table. The bosun and one runner stood to the side.

As Ensign Foust adjusted the time on the ship's clock, now only minutes from high tide and departure, Mansfield eased into the captain's chair and said,

"Prepare to get underway. Bosun, pipe the order—general call."

Boatswains—derived from an English and Norse term meaning "servant" or "apprentice"—served as foremen for the deckhands. These men pulled the ropes, raised the sails, and hauled the anchor. After receiving an order from the captain, the boatswain needed a way to quickly get the attention of the crew to execute those commands. Sometimes, deckhands would race across the ship, repeating the order to ensure everyone heard it. But in unexpected situations, a faster method was needed.

That's why the boatswain's whistle was developed—a sharp, piercing sound that cut through the noise of the sea, signaling sailors to action. Varied in size and shape, the distinctive shrill of the boatswain's whistle defined it. The tone changed depending on one of the four hand positions. Additionally, the user could produce smooth, rattling, or undulating notes lasting five or more seconds by adjusting the position of their tongue.

Foust telegraphed the engine room to let Strickland know that departure was underway.

"Prepare to weigh anchor," ordered Mansfield. "Are the crew in position, Lieutenant?"

"Yes, sir, we can sail anytime."

"Hoist the anchor! Set the sails! Ahead slow!!"

The bosun's whistle sounded long and shrill; the telegraph repeated its tap-tap-tap, and verbal orders echoed across the ship's deck. The crew raised the anchor, secured the mooring lines, and set the sails for departure.

"Navigator, report," ordered Mansfield.

"Course is set west by northwest for Duxbury Reef and Drakes Bay, latitude 37.88, longitude -122.69," came Dorn's reply.

"Stations for leaving port. Lookouts to their posts."

"Sir, we have cleared the harbor."

"Engine room, ahead moderate."

At 8:15 a.m. on April 10, 1889, the *U.S.S. Carlise P. Patterson* embarked from San Francisco on a summer expedition to study the waters of southeast Alaska. It would take five days to reach Port Townsend, Washington, and more than a week after that to arrive at the southernmost Alaskan waters.

Chapter Six - Salt

The *Patterson* stopped briefly in Port Townsend to load coal and water and to allow McDonald to select replacement sailors. The daily sailing regimen since leaving San Francisco provided Harry with a much-needed routine. Now, when thinking of Clara, it wasn't with anger but more like the loss of a friend who had moved away. The amount of time spent thinking of her also diminished. He was open to new opportunities, new adventures, new friends, and even a new love.

Early every morning, Harry conducted a ship inspection. On training days, he mustered the appropriate crew for drills. His creative juices flowed as he engaged the crew in imaginary fires requiring them to use the firefighting equipment, pretending the ship was sinking and requiring them to lower the life rafts, or staging a scenario where a man had fallen from the masts and needed medical care. His energy level was high, and he was on a mission for safety. Lights out meant a final security check, where he would take time to talk with each watcher on duty that night.

The night was also his favorite time, as the quiet allowed him to reflect, collect his thoughts, and plan the next day's activities. Standing alone at the rail in the dark, all he could hear was the groan of the engine and waves as they lapped at the boat below him. He could see only a few feet into the pitch black on moonless nights, or he watched as the dark and foreboding wilderness passed by, silhouetted by the moon on clear nights, feeling the cool air on his cheeks and sniffing in the aroma of the sea. He was content with his position in the world, and each night, he looked at the Master-at-Arms insignia on his upper sleeve—three red chevrons connected by a red arch on which sat a white eagle—and recited the creed:

> *"I am a Master-at-Arms. I hold allegiance to my country, devotion to duty, and personal integrity above all. I wear my shield of authority with dignity and restraint and promote, by example, high standards of conduct, appearance, courtesy, and performance. I seek no favor because of my position. I perform my duties in a firm, courteous, and impartial manner. I strive to merit the respect of my shipmates and all with whom I come in contact."*

Harry enjoyed observing the world around him. He tended to ask questions rather than pontificate, trying to understand any situation's particulars. His approach and demeanor were not those of an enforcer or policeman. He didn't try to intimidate anyone but had the strength and skills to subdue an assailant. Usually, he stood back while his more eager shipmates fought the bad guys, telling them he'd oversee the paperwork. He chose restraint rather than conflict in both his professional and personal life.

He was fair and open when called to settle a dispute or investigate alleged misconduct. Everyone respected his balanced investigations, which tried to consider all sides of the story. His administration of justice was firm yet compassionate. He would ensure that all prisoners received blankets, pillows, and other items to make their stay more comfortable.

Not many days later, he ate breakfast with McDonald and Almy in the wardroom. The cook had prepared scrambled eggs and bacon, and the hungry men ate as much as they wanted. After a second helping of scrambled eggs, Almy intended to sprinkle salt, but the shaker was empty. Looking at the other empty shaker on the table, he condescendingly called the steward.

"What are you guys doing back there? Can we have more salt.? Both shakers are empty."

"The cook wants us to conserve. He doesn't think we have enough," came the steward's reply.

"Four barrels isn't enough?" asked Harry.

"We don't have four; that's the problem. We only have three."

"But I saw four being loaded onboard."

"We only have three," insisted the steward.

A couple of days later, Harry investigated the salt discrepancy. Unlocking the dark pantry and food storage room, he lit a lantern and looked around. It was hard to see, and the room was very cluttered, but he walked over to the barrels stacked against the far wall, counting three full of salt.

Dropping to his knees and holding the light, he peered at the open floor beside the last barrel. A mound of dust was pushed into a crescent shape, indicating a barrel had been there. Tiny dots of white salt crystals glinted from the pile.

"There were four barrels," he said to himself. "But where is the fourth, and how did it go missing?"

He left and hurried to the galley, where the cook was cleaning breakfast dishes.

"Cook, do you have a minute? I need to ask some questions." Harry hoped he could understand Yung's English.

Bent over the sink, Yung said, "OK," with a thick Chinese accent.

"Have you noticed anything unusual here in the galley?"

"What unusual, Mr. Ford?"

"Crew stealing food, getting into the rum, unauthorized people in the storeroom?"

"No, nobody here," replied the cook.

"What about salt? Do you have enough salt?"

Yung stopped washing dishes and said, "Salt. That's right. I only have three. Not enough. I should have four." He returned to washing dishes.

"Have you seen anyone in the storeroom? Was anyone hanging around, waiting for you to leave?"

Yung stopped his dishwashing and said, "Davenport. I saw him. Don't like."

"Davenport?" What was he doing?"

"Hanging around," he repeated. Harry needed to find out if Yung was repeating his words or if he meant it.

"Did he go in the storeroom? Did he have anything in his hands?"

"He shakes out his pants pocket. Salt came out of pocket."

"But a barrel of salt is missing. How could it be in his pants? He can't put a barrel's worth in his pants."

47

"Hide it. Move from barrel to somewhere."

By now, the cook had stopped dishwashing, his almond-shaped eyes squinting while his mouth scowled. He wanted to get back to his work.

"Yung, salt is as precious as gold to some people in these parts."

"Salt," said the cook, nodding his head in agreement or repetition; again, Harry wasn't sure which.

"But where is the barrel itself?"

"Don't know, on deck? Lots of barrels on deck" stammered Yung.

The cook returned to dishwashing, while Harry was convinced a barrel of salt was missing.

Asking Paymaster Beale a few questions was Harry's next objective, so he went back to his quarters to plan the next steps. Beale was a career Navy veteran who retired on the job, as it were. Beginning with exceptional reviews, he advanced from Assistant to Past Assistant and then Paymaster. Years later, his attitude changed in the position, and his attention to detail, concern for internal controls, and even desire to be in charge diminished considerably. His assistants assumed cash management, accounting, and inventory control. He claimed he spent his workday reviewing the accounts, but his penchant for napping cut a great deal into that time. Ultimately, he was accountable for the salt in the barrel, as he was the de facto quartermaster of the ship.

Foust was lying in his bunk when Harry returned.

"Harry, haven't seen much of you. What's going on?" William, or Fousty, as he liked to be called, was a newcomer this season on the *Patterson* but had put in five years on other Navy ships. A high forehead with protruding eyebrows and a crooked nose distinguished him from others, as did his limp. Harry hadn't yet spent much time getting to know him, but now was not the time to start.

"I know you haven't been around much, but what do you know about Beale?" Harry asked, ignoring Foust's question as he lay down.

"Beale? Why him? What's going on?"

48

"I believe we are missing a barrel of salt. It's Beale's responsibility to account for it, and I have a suspicion he may be behind its disappearance. I want to talk to him, ask some questions, but not let him know why."

Foust thought for a moment before saying, "I don't know much about him. I don't spend any time with him. I do know he likes food. Join him at dinner. He doesn't pay attention to table talk; he focuses on the food, the smell, taste, the spices. Get him focused on eating, and he'll be unaware of what you're talking about. And he always eats at six-thirty."

Harry followed Foust's advice and arrived at six-thirty-three that evening, just after Beale's arrival but before the stewards had served the meal.

As he entered the room, he caught Beale's attention by pointing at the seat beside him and asking if it was available. Nodding yes, Beale waited as Harry sat down. Beale was a large man, about forty-five, with a pot belly and big hands.

"Mr. Ford, how are you this evening?"

"I'm well, Mr. Beale, thank you. I trust you are well, too?" Harry didn't believe Beale was well, his bloated red nose and yellowing skin betraying a long-time, overweight drinker.

"I am Mr. Ford, I am. Last night, we had stew, and I found it delicious. It had the right proportion of meat to potatoes and perfect seasoning. Tonight, the cook prepared salmon on rice with a side of peas and almonds and a cookie for dessert; I look forward to a hearty meal."

"I hope this cook stays with us longer than the last."

"Cook Yung is one of the best we've had if you ask me. He doesn't use too much hot spice like some of the others."

The stewards served the meal, and Beale enthusiastically enjoyed it, trying to smell or taste each spice or flavoring. He worked with Foust's insight about food.

"So, how is the salmon?" Harry asked.

"Delightful. This sauce is perfect—lemon, garlic, and mustard. Mmm, it's delicious."

"Oh yes, it is, I agree," said Harry as he tasted the fish. "We should encourage Lt. Dorn to mobilize a fishing party today to replace what we are eating. I could eat salmon, halibut, or crab every day of the week."

"A fine idea, sir. You have my approval to proceed." Beale signaled the steward over and asked for more salmon.

"Can you bring a saltshaker, too, please?" Harry asked.

Once the stewards brought an additional plate, he leaned over to Beale and said, "I learned as a child to salt my peas in order to eat them."

Beale was treasuring each bite taken from his plate; eyes closed as he sensed every taste and smell.

"Yes, salt—one of the most desired of all the tastes. One of the treasures of the ancient world. Currency for the Romans."

"Really?" Harry asked in surprise. "Currency?"

Taking another bite of the salmon and sipping his water glass, Beale continued, "Yes, it has been valued over the centuries, even today."

To Harry's disappointment, the discussion generated no noticeable "I'm guilty" reaction from Beale. He knew more about salt than most people, but it wasn't enough to suggest he was stealing it. Harry changed the subject.

"Hey, I just remembered, tomorrow is payday," said Harry.

"Yes, first thing in the morning," was Beale's reply.

"Can I help you with anything other than security, of course?"

"No, Mr. Ford, we have it covered. Davenport and Arthurs will be in charge. Under my supervision, of course."

"Of course."

Up until now, Harry's only concern was salt, but the mention of the two underlings being responsible for the pay reminded him that Davenport was inventorying the salt loaded onboard. Maybe it wasn't Beale, but one of his assistants.

"Say, when did Davenport and Arthurs ship on? Were they with us last season?"

"Mr. Ford. Davenport's been with me for two years now. Arthurs joined us this past winter. Any reason for asking?"

Harry emphatically denied any reason other than to say he couldn't remember if they sailed last year. Finishing dinner and wishing Beale goodnight, he returned to his quarters. Foust was not there, so he sat down in his chair at the table.

He decided to write a letter to Clara. She hadn't been on his mind too much lately, but he was moving beyond the breakup and wanted a final say. He felt that he could close out the relationship on his terms by writing.

Dear Clara,

I am well as I write this. We are sailing daily in fair weather for the most part. The food is satisfactory, and everyone is getting along. We have a new commander, Lieutenant Mansfield. I doubt he will be with us after this season. He is an outstanding officer, and I'm sure he will be promoted and assigned to a new ship.

I wanted to say I'm sorry for what has happened. I didn't realize what you were going through; I wasn't aware of your feelings. That alone discredits me for not putting you first.

I understand how difficult it would have been to say something, and I don't fault you for not telling me until now.

I do put my life at risk; it's what I do, it's my job. Every man I work with takes the same risks daily, but we are there for each other, and I know they have my back.

But I understand your point about not knowing from day to day. It must be agonizing. I trust that you will be safe while I'm gone, but I know you need more than reliance on God.

Please forgive me for what you hold against me; I have nothing against you. I hope we can someday agree on what's white and what's black. Good luck to you and John.
Respectfully,
Harry.

Putting down the pen, he sighed. A burden lifted; he could move on without the anger that would otherwise gnaw at him. Forgiveness released him from his hurt. He put the letter in an envelope and addressed it to Clara, but he wanted to personally take it to the post office in Juneau.

Foust arrived, and the two settled in their bunks for a brief rest before something else required their presence.

"He knows a lot about salt, does he?" asked Foust after describing the dinner encounter. "That may not seem like much to you, but to me, it does. I'll bet he knows something about the missing salt."

"Fousty, you may be right, but given the loose reins he has on the other paymasters, I'll bet they may be involved as well."

Silence overtook the room as neither had more to say. Snoring soon replaced the silence.

Chapter Seven - The Stikine

The Stikine River flows 380 miles in a wide arc from the high country of Canada through the Coast Mountains, west and then south, to its outlet in Southeast Alaska. North America's fastest-flowing navigable river is fueled by snowmelt, glacial melt, and rainfall and provides dramatic access from the Pacific Ocean through the Grand Canyon of the Stikine to the interior of Canada and the entire continent.

For centuries, the Tlingits used this route and its largest tributary, the Iskut River, gaining access to the resources it provided, fish and furs foremost. The river also offered easy access to the Sacred Headwaters—the drainage basin surrounding Klappan Mountain, which is the source of the Stikine, as well as the Nass and Skeena Rivers. The clans settled on an island just at the mouth of the river and, until the late 1700s and early 1800s, lived alone in their village, notwithstanding trading with other tribes.

During the mid-1800s, four nations claimed ownership and control of the Stikine River, the island, and the native settlement: Tlingit, Russian, British, and American. As with countless Indigenous peoples throughout history, the original owners—the Native Tlingits—were forced to give up what they had. They resented watching white men use their ancient sacred trade and travel routes, but they were powerless to stop them.

Through the Anglo-Russian Convention of 1825, Russia granted the British the right to cross their territory along a line through the Portland Canal, the main body of water providing access. Britain could use navigable waters beyond that quasi-boundary if no Russian settlements existed. In the early 1830s, both the British and Russians took an interest in the Stikine at the same time. The Hudson's Bay Company dispatched the sailing frigate *Dryad* from Vancouver, intending to sail the Stikine and establish a post upriver. In response, the Russians quickly built a stockade on Wrangel Island near the village—named after Ferdinand von Wrangell, the Russian governor there at the time—to prevent the British from proceeding.

As the British ship approached the river's mouth, the Russians fired cannons from the fort and the sailing ship *Chichagof* to protest their incursion. The two countries reconciled in 1839 by executing an agreement that leased the fort to Britain for ten years at an annual sum of two thousand otter skins. Britain renamed the site Fort Stikine in 1840 but lost sovereignty when the United States purchased Alaska in 1867, renaming it Fort Wrangell.

Twenty-two years after the purchase, on the night of April 26, the *Patterson* lay anchored two hundred yards offshore. The officers gathered in the conference room to present the summer work plan to Lieutenant Mansfield. Gas lighting fixtures cast shadows across the room, and maps and charts lay strewn across the wardroom table. Mansfield arrived and claimed an unoccupied chair, cleared his throat, and began.

"Good morning, gentlemen. I trust everyone slept well?"

"Harry went out like a light, and I think I followed right behind him," injected Foust. "I woke up very refreshed, sir."

"I must have passed out," confessed Harry.

"I felt the same way—went right to sleep," said McDonald. "But Almy here stayed up looking at charts."

"And now I wish I was back in bed," quipped Almy.

"You'll get another chance tonight, Ensign," chuckled Mansfield. Bringing his grin to a more serious look, he continued,

"Since neither I nor Lieutenant Dorn were on last year's survey, I've asked Ensign McDonald to brief us on last year's efforts. I know Lieutenant Commander Thomas does excellent work, but with limited time, one can only accomplish so much. I understand that relocating the *Patterson* from Juneau to Ketchikan cut the survey season short, and we hope that doesn't happen to us again this year. Given that we plan to have more time, I aim to complete twice the amount of work. Ensign McDonald, if you will."

"Thank you, Lieutenant." Standing up and using a pointing stick, McDonald jabbed at an easel holding a map of the Southeast as he mentioned geographic locations.

"The mission last year, as given to Lieutenant Commander Thomas in his general instructions from the Superintendent, was to continue from the

54

northern limits of the 1887 effort—moving north into Stephens Passage and Frederick Sound. Survey work last year took place out of Snettisham Bay before they repositioned to Canada to conduct boundary surveys for the State Department. As you know, there was a dispute regarding the boundary line between Alaska and British Columbia," he concluded.

"Mac, that dispute," interrupted Woods, "began with an 1825 treaty between Russia and Great Britain and carried over when the United States bought Alaska. It won't be resolved for years. Sorry, Mac, I didn't mean to interrupt."

"I don't mind," shrugged McDonald. "The statistics I'm sharing include last summer's entire field season, with results from both the Alaskan and Canadian efforts. I didn't have time to separate the Alaska totals from their report.

Of course, triangulation is one of our primary objectives. In this regard, last year went very well, building and occupying 625 monument stations and observing 16,990 angles of declination, each using the theodolite."

"Those are impressive numbers," Mansfield injected.

"I'm assuming the majority were at the boundary location; the stations there would have been easier to build than the ones in Alaska," added Almy.

"Good point—that's probably true," agreed McDonald. "Moving on to their topography work, last year the crew surveyed 1,000 square miles, plus 661 linear miles of shoreline."

"That should help keep ships off the rocks. That's a lot of shorelines," said Harry.

"And to the crew's credit, their hydrographic work was outstanding last year," said McDonald. "They ran over 1,400 miles in soundings, taken from 6,224 individual soundings."

Ensign Woods took the pointer from McDonald and described the astronomical work.

"I was the assigned astronomer, so I can fill you in on last year. As you may know, astronomical north varies by latitude and longitude, so we built three stations specifically for latitude and longitude observations. We completed nineteen-night latitude studies, which is reasonable considering how poor the weather was. We also recorded over 174-star pairs. It took most of the night just to get sixteen or so pairs."

"Sounds like a tedious process," said Mansfield.

"Yes, Lieutenant, it is. We use a method called the Horrebow-Talcott technique for observations. It's very time-consuming."

Woods handed the pointer back to McDonald, who resumed the presentation.

"Thank you, Albert. Regarding last year's magnetic work, we built two stations resulting in sixteen magnetic declinations, seven gravity dips, six deflections, and six oscillation records."

"What does all that mean?" asked Strickland. "I'm an engineer, not a surveyor."

"Well, declination measurements help determine the distance in degrees between geographic north and magnetic north, ensuring that geodetic surveys align with geographic coordinates rather than local magnetic directions. Dips help us understand the Earth's geoid—the sea-level surface of the Earth—and the deflections caused by uneven mass distribution. As for deflection, imagine a plumb line. Deflection causes it to deviate from an ideal vertical position. And oscillations allow us to track wobbles in the Earth's axis. Does that help without being too technical?"

"Not really," Strickland moaned.

"They also collected 51 new marine specimens off the ocean floor," added McDonald.

"How many have we collected so far this year?" asked Beecher.

"I've counted fifteen so far," said Lt. Dorn. "They are being stored before we send them to Headquarters."

"What kind of specimens, these sea creatures?" Almy asked.

"Well, one that I saw had a mouth the size of your fist but was only about six inches long. It had short fins and spines sticking out of its body. Huge bug eyes. They want to give it a scientific name, but I think the best name would be 'Double-Ugly,'" laughed Dorn.

"Mac, do you have anything more to report?" asked Mansfield.

"Yes, sir. Mr. Ford and his staff completed three hydrographic sheets for Frederick Sound, from Dry Strait to Cape Fanshaw, scale 1:80,000." Using his pointer to indicate locations on the map, McDonald continued. "They also completed sheets for Duncan Canal, scale 1:20,000, and Brown Cove, Thomas Bay, Farragut Bay, and Portage Bay, all in the Frederick Sound area. That is all I have."

"Does anyone have anything to add?" asked Mansfield.

McDonald raised his hand. "With all due respect, and through no fault of Lieutenant Commander Thomas or the crew, the *Patterson* did run lightly aground in Oakland Creek at the end of the trip."

"Yes, I know," said Mansfield. Mac, can you provide a brief explanation for those who aren't aware?"

"There were calm airs that morning, so weather was not the issue. About an hour after entering San Francisco Bay, she got stuck as she headed up the creek. The Commander tried backing the engine while the crew heaved on the chain attached to the stream anchor on the port quarter. Twice, the anchor came home. We tried lowering the boats and shifting weight to the starboard side, but she didn't budge. The frigate *Alameda* took lines but couldn't hold them. It wasn't until well after noon that we attempted to set her free on high tide. We backed the engine again and heaved in on the hawser. The anchor came up once more. Finally, about twenty-four hours after getting stuck, a steam tug named the *Wizard* pulled her off the mud bank. We steamed up to the foot of Broadway Avenue in Oakland and moored as if nothing had happened. Commander Thomas immediately ordered a full inspection of the ship, but there was no damage. I don't know if he reported it or not, but it's in the log."

"I can't believe Commander Thomas found himself in a jam like that," added Mansfield. Do you know if the investigation ever determined what caused the grounding?"

"No, sir. The watch did not call out, nor did the helmsman stray off course. They concluded one of the river bars shifted due to recent rains."

"Thank you, Mr. McDonald." Turning to his engineer, Mansfield asked,

"Mr. Strickland, would you be so kind as to brief everyone on last season's maintenance issues?"

"Aye, Lieutenant. Right from the beginning, the *Pirate* was a headache. She broke down on May 1st and was laid up for several days after a crankshaft busted. Later that summer, she hit a rock and sprung the shaft—the same day, her skiff swamped and sank in Frederick Sound. Two months later, she lost a propeller. She was a real pain last season. I've gone over her thoroughly, and I think she's going to be okay. I've stocked just about every part we might need."

"Thank you, Mr. Strickland. Dr. Percy, do you have anything to report from last season?"

"No, sir. It was uneventful. Several landsmen were sent ashore to medical facilities, but nobody died during the trip. For me, that is a huge success."

"Yes, and for me as well," added Mansfield." Let's strive to stay safe and keep out of mortal danger, shall we? Thank you, Dr. Percy. Master-at-Arms Ford, do you have a report from last season?"

Harry's face flushed as his stomach tightened. Though thorough and confident in his work, he sometimes struggled with speaking in front of groups. His social anxiety often manifested physically, making his face turn red and his skin sweat.

"I placed Seaman Silven in double irons for disobeying and abusing Petty Officer Stewart and for leaving the ship without permission. I put two seamen in double irons for four days for being under the influence of alcohol while onboard."

Mansfield noticed his rigid expression and downward gaze, sensing his discomfort.

"Mr. Ford, are you ill?"

"No, sir. I'm fine. Just a hot flash, that's all."

The officers burst into laughter, and Harry tried to laugh along, wiping the sweat from his brow.

"Alright, let's move on to what we're doing this season." Mansfield stood up and took the pointer from the table. "Here is where last year's work left off." He pointed at the map, tracing an arc on the northernmost part of Stephens Passage, south of Juneau near Taku Harbor. "The *Patterson* anchored out of Taku Harbor and Snettisham Bay before heading south. This year, we will drop anchor below Snettisham, working around Holkham Bay, Seymour Canal, and Windham Bay." He indicated each location on the map.

"Let's make sure we know who is doing what this year. Mr. Ford, we'll start with you."

Still tense, Harry focused on steadying his breathing.

"We know you will be doing excellent hydrographic drafting and serving as our Master-at-Arms," said Mansfield.

"Lieutenant Dorn, of course, is Executive Officer. Ensign Woods, since you were the astronomer last season, you are again in charge of astronomical observations."

"Absolutely."

"Ensign Beecher, I understand Ensign Oliver was responsible for tidal observations last year, and since he is not with us, would you take that responsibility?"

"Yes, sir. My privilege."

"Mr. Ford, you will be responsible for all watch duty. I don't want anybody getting onboard who shouldn't, and I don't want anybody leaving without us knowing about it."

"Yes, sir. Thank you."

"Ensigns Slocum and Almy, I want you to focus on navigation and share the duties. We are going into uncharted waters. Ensign Foust, I'm putting you in charge of magnetic observations. Ensign McDonald, you will oversee field duty. Any questions?"

59

Silence followed.

"Let me remind you: what we are about to do is very dangerous," Mansfield continued. "Surveying the Southeast Alaska coastline will be one of the most challenging things you ever do." He shook his head in wonder at the thought. "You must always be alert. Rely on your training, your shipmates, and your instincts. We will fix what needs fixing, and if we don't have what we need, we will acquire it. I intend to stay the full season.

These tides make those in San Francisco Bay seem weak. Ice floating in the water can puncture a hole in your launch. Whales can breach beneath you. You name it—it could kill you. I don't want any dead men on my watch. Godspeed to each of you."

"Godspeed," came the replies.

Chapter Eight - The 4th of July

Admiralty Island is *Kootznoowoo* to the Tlingit, meaning *Fortress of the Bears*. It is the second-largest island in Southeast Alaska, measuring ninety miles long and thirty miles wide, and home to the world's highest concentration of brown bears. There is one bear for every one of the island's 1,600 square miles, or approximately eight bears per Tlingit inhabitant. Named by George Vancouver in 1792 for the Admiralty, his Royal Navy employer, the island is a stunning display of wilderness and wildlife.

The *Patterson* worked in a Cleveland Passage anchorage through May before moving on to Admiralty Island's Eliza Harbor for most of June. By the 24th, they anchored at Snug Cove, outside Gambier Bay, at the island's southeast corner, where Frederick Sound meets Stephens Passage. To the east, the coastal mountains rose four to six thousand feet above sea level, lifting the Juneau Icefield, with glaciers and rivers spilling out below.

Mansfield called his officers to the wardroom for a briefing on the upcoming activities out of Snug Cove.

McDonald pointed to two locations on a map spread across the table. "Sir, our first objective is to build two triangulation stations we're calling Blunt and Rocks, here and here. We estimate it will take seven to eight days per signal, starting with Rocks. I'll take the *Vixen* out with my field crew for construction."

"I can help. I'll go too," interrupted Harry. He wanted to get out and experience the dense woods firsthand.

"Thank you, Harry," responded McDonald. "I've been using the same four landsmen—Carpenter, Marshall, Yang, and Lee—as my crew. They have expertise in constructing monuments and signals and are currently gathering supplies. Once we build Rocks, we'll move on to Blunt." He finished and asked if there were any questions.

"Alright, sounds good," said Mansfield. "Ensign Foust, I'm placing you in charge of general field duty. The first thing I'd like you to do is organize a wood-gathering party. We need four cords of wood." Foust nodded in agreement. "Ensign Beecher set up a course for depth soundings and put the Sigsbee to use. Mr. Strickland will support you in the *Pirate*."

After the meeting, McDonald caught Harry outside the room and asked, "What do you know about taking observations, Harry? Did you take any last year?"

"No, I didn't go out last season and don't understand how theodolites work. I'm hoping you'll shed some light for me."

The next morning, Harry, McDonald, and his crew of four left in the *Vixen* to locate the two sites along Admiralty Island's shoreline suitable for survey monuments.

"We are looking for a flat area above high tide; it needs to be prominent." McDonald pointed across a small inlet to where they would build Signal Blunt. Finding the exact location, he beached the *Vixen*, and they began hauling supplies ashore.

"Put the wood and all the tower-building materials and tools beside the site for the monument," he instructed after jumping into the surf and pulling a mooring line to tie the launch to a tree. "Marshall, take all the camping gear and begin setting up camp somewhere over here." He gestured toward the upper beach. "I'm putting you in charge—you pick the spot. Yang, Lee, and Carpenter listen to him and do what he says. He's in charge."

All hands helped set up tents and tarps to keep the rain off the tables and chairs hauled in from the *Vixen*. One tent housed books, charts, instruments, and other items that needed to be kept dry. Seventeen-year-old Marshall chose a flat location in a clearing under a grove of four-hundred-year-old Sitka spruce trees towering two hundred feet into the air. It was free from tree falls and upturned roots, which prevailed in the woods, and a thick carpet of moss blanketed the site, surrounded by abundant blueberry bushes. The landsmen placed rocks in a ring, cleared out a firepit, and scrounged the woods for dry pulp found in downed trees. The ability to start and maintain a fire in the wet rainforest conditions was critical to their success and comfort.

By early afternoon, they had finished setting up camp, and with plenty of summer daylight remaining, they began the physical build of Signal Rocks, a rocky outcrop above high tide. Their first task was to set a permanent monument from which surveyors would take measurements, linking that point to other known set points on Earth.

Using iron rods, the crew pounded out a three-foot-deep hole in the rock, one-foot square. McDonald placed a small earthen cone with a one-inch-square tapered end in the bottom center of the hole, with the small end facing downward. This one-inch location provided a subsurface monument, serving as a redundancy should the monument at ground level be disturbed.

McDonald prepared a sulfur compound by heating it in a fire, then poured the liquid sulfur into the hole around the cone, sealing the rock and preventing moisture from entering and cracking it. Once the sulfur cooled, he placed a metal bolt with a rounded top into the firming liquid, two crossed lines etched into the middle of the bolt head. Near the newly installed monument, they placed a flat, two-square-foot quartz stone and used chisels to inscribe it with U.S.C.&G.S., June 1889, B.M.

They then assembled a ten-foot wooden tripod and placed it directly over the monument's center. Anchored to the ground and reinforced with six-inch cross-boards, the tower had to support the weight of men, heavy instruments, and exposure to the elements. A small platform was secured at the tripod's top to hold the theodolite and bolt the instrument to it. Wooden rungs were attached to enable access to the platform.

About one hundred yards away, on another rock outcrop above the tideline, McDonald instructed the men to build a reference monument so future surveyors could locate the benchmark they had just installed. Positioned at a location easily visible from the channel, they used the same methods as the benchmark, but with one key difference: instead of B.M. for Benchmark, the metal bolt head was inscribed with R.M. for Reference Mark, and instead of two crossed lines, it bore a pointing arrow directed toward the benchmark site.

With the reference mark set, they built another ten-foot signal tower. Securing a ten-foot post atop the tripod, they topped it with a large metal cap to reflect light to aid in locating it from long distances.

The men completed Signal Rock and returned late for dinner before settling into their cots for the night. After breakfast the next day, they crossed to the other side of the inlet and repeated the process to build Signal Blunt, named after one of McDonald's cousins.

With the stations and towers complete, the crew lifted the heavy theodolite onto Blunt's platform and secured it to the tribrach. When they climbed up to inspect, McDonald was satisfied that it was centered over the surface monument they had set earlier.

"Harry, come up and have a look." He wanted to mentor his colleague in the use of the theodolite.

"Bring up my dark blue logbook. Yes, that one."

Harry grabbed the tome, carried it up the rungs, and handed it to McDonald. A small walkway surrounded the top of the tower, providing access to the eyepiece.

"Here, stand here," McDonald said, pointing to a spot behind the instrument.

"Peer through there and locate the survey rod we placed last week at Signal Oar. Do you see the numbers on the rod?"

"I'm not sure."

"Align your crosshairs with the zero-line painted on the rod. Loosen the upper clamp and turn the upper plate."

Harry moved the plate, trying to align the lines precisely, but gave up.

"It's quite precise, isn't it? I can't set it properly." He stepped back from the instrument, allowing McDonald to look.

"Well, mate, you came close," McDonald said, clapping him on the back. Looking up at the darkening sky, he was no longer interested in continuing the lesson.

"We'd best get back to the *Patterson* and not spend the night at camp." With his record book still under his arm and no new observations to add, he descended the rungs, preparing to return to the ship.

They still needed to set additional monuments for the gravity station mark, the magnetic station mark, and the tidal benchmarks, but the weather turned sour as an intense low-pressure system settled over Southeast

Alaska. A steady, heavy rain fell for four straight days, and the temperature barely varied more than a degree or two above or below 52 degrees.

Lieutenant Mansfield suspended all activity as the rain created too much risk for the survey teams. With no work and the dreary monotony of rain, clouds, and darkness, morale plummeted. Conversations were brief, if spoken at all, and the men slept to escape the oppressive gloom. Watch duty became especially demoralizing.

As always, the weather eventually improved. The drizzle stopped, and a glorious blue sky appeared, dotted with white cumulus clouds drifting east. In an instant, the men's spirits soared, and the sun erased the memory of the miserable, rainy days. From Mansfield down to the newest landsman, everyone gladly resumed their duties, offering to help wherever they could.

Mansfield wasted no time putting them back to work.

"Mr. Foust, organize a wood-cutting party. I realize it only just stopped raining, but there's never any dry wood up here, so why wait? Let's get wood onboard to dry out.

"Mr. Beecher, resume the soundings in Gambier Bay.

"Mr. Wood, fetch fresh water.

"If I haven't called your name, help out wherever you can. Let's keep the crew busy again, gentlemen!"

A chorus of hoorays erupted from the grinning men.

Harry joined Foust on the *Vixen* for the wood party, along with landsmen Carter, Simon, Fredricks, and Ming. They landed at a location on the island within sight of the *Patterson*, anchoring the launch and rowing to shore.

"Harry, you, Carter, and Simon go up through there. Fredricks, Ming, and I will go over in this direction," Foust instructed. A big man with broad shoulders and massive forearms, he was an asset when it came to cutting firewood.

Each three-man crew carried an axe per man, a two-person, six-foot crosscut saw, and two smaller bucking saws. They felled trees, removed limbs, and hauled what they could to the beach by hand. Though exhausting, the work was welcome after the cold, damp days, and the warmth of the sun made it even more enjoyable.

Harry's crew remained within shouting distance of Foust's group, and the two teams soon turned their task into a friendly competition, challenging each other to collect the most wood.

By late afternoon, the two groups had wandered far apart in search of the best trees. Harry's crew drifted off while he stayed behind to trim smaller limbs. Sitting on a log to catch his breath, he stopped for a second and noticed an eerie stillness. There were no sounds—no men talking, no axes striking wood, no trees falling. The once-loud voices of the landsmen had fallen silent.

He realized he was alone. He closed his eyes and took in a deep breath, relishing the moment.

Suddenly, a horrific scream pierced the air from his left, sending him to his feet. He could hear loud grunting and growling about seventy-five yards away.

"Carter!" Harry called. "Simon! Where are you? Where are you?"

He sprinted toward the screams and growls by following an animal trail. As he crested a small rise, he saw the massive brown bear strike Carter, its claws ripping a deep gash across his chest. Blood gushed from the wound as Carter collapsed, curling into a ball with his hands behind his neck.

The bear stood over him, growling, swiping at his head, sniffing, and swatting again.

"Help! Oh God!" Carter screamed. "Help! Help!"

The bear showed no sign of stopping.

Harry pulled out his .38 revolver and fired four shots, striking the beast in the neck just below the jaw and in the chest near the heart. The grizzly groaned but remained on its feet, still incredibly dangerous. It reared up, shaking its massive head from side to side, growling.

Harry fired twice more, hitting its chest again.

With a final groan, the bear turned and staggered fifty yards before collapsing in the underbrush.

Carter lay on the ground, battered and bleeding but alive. He had deep gashes covering his chest, face, and arms. Kneeling beside him, Harry ripped open Carter's jacket to treat the wounds, brushing against a hard wad of something in the coat pocket.

Pulling it out, he realized—this was why the bear had attacked.

It was a large piece of beef jerky.

Foust and the others arrived moments later, breathless.

"Get bandages on those wounds—stop the bleeding as best you can!" Harry ordered.

Foust tore into his first aid kit and worked quickly to stem the blood flow. They carefully lifted Carter and carried him to the *Vixen*. Laying him at the bottom of the launch, they wrapped a blanket around his blood-soaked clothes, hoping they could get him to Dr. Percy in time. Simon hurried to stoke the launch's fire. Foust semaphored ahead to alert the ship to Carter's injuries. Dr. Percy met the *Vixen* upon its arrival. Carter was lifted aboard and sent to the sickbay, where the doctor attended to his wounds.

As they stood at the rail, Lieutenants Mansfield, Dorn, Harry, and Foust held an impromptu briefing.

"What happened out there?" asked an astonished Mansfield.

Harry was relieved that Carter was still alive. More importantly, however, he had the answer Mansfield wanted.

"This," he said, holding up the jerky. "It was in Carter's pocket. It's why the bear attacked, I have no doubt. Bears don't behave like that without something provoking them or if they smell something to eat. Like jerky."

"Lieutenant Dorn, see to it that all the men are instructed not to take food on their persons during shore parties. Anyone caught violating the policy will either end up like Landsman Carter or in chains for three days, whichever comes first," ordered Mansfield.

Dorn concurred, and the men went about their duties.

Three days later, just after midnight on Thursday, July 4, 1889, the night was clear and pleasant with a slight breeze. At this time of year and at their latitude, well above the rest of America, the midnight hour wasn't pitch black; you could see what you were doing if you were outside.

Nautical twilight occurs when the sun is below the horizon but still lights up the sky. It is one of three twilight stages. Stars are visible but not entirely dark. For the *Patterson* crew that night, nautical twilight occurred between 11 o'clock p.m. and 2:45 the following morning.

Civilian twilight is the brightest and provides enough light to conduct most human activities. Beginning at the end of nautical twilight at 2:45 a.m., civilian twilight went until 4 a.m., when it was daylight. Civilian twilight would return at 10 o'clock that evening, followed by nautical twilight at eleven. In other words, it is light enough for the crew to see throughout the entire twenty-four-hour day.

The third stage, astronomical twilight, is the time of day when the sky is dark enough for astronomers to see objects in the heavens without interference from the sun.

Due to the abundance of daylight, the crew had difficulty sleeping. Coverings were placed over the windows to block light from entering the sleeping quarters. The crew covered their eyes with heavy cloth. Most had difficulty regulating their internal clocks, staying awake late, and not realizing how late it was until the following day. Sleep came whenever one could find it.

"Lieutenant Dorn, order the men to raise the ensign," Mansfield said as they gathered for the call to order on that July 4th morning. "Today is our national Independence Day, and it shall be a day of celebration. No shore duties, no station building. I want the cook to cater a picnic, and we'll set up tents, chairs, and activities over on that sandy beach," he said, pointing to a location on shore. "See that large boulder next to the beach? With high tide this afternoon, I challenge each man to jump off that boulder into the ocean, boulder diving! And at nine o'clock tonight, Lt. Dorn, two rounds of rum shots for the crew, and fire the cannon! We're going to celebrate our independence! We're going to celebrate the United States of America! We're going to celebrate Alaska!"

Beside the beach Mansfield chose for the picnic, an unnamed stream flowed from the mountains into Gambier Bay. The salmon were plentiful—King, Sockeye, Coho, and Humpbacks swimming upstream or staying offshore on their way to their ancestral spawning grounds. One could drag a hook across and catch any number by yanking the hook. Harry organized a fishing competition where participants had to catch salmon by the mouth, with the heaviest King winning. Most of the fish were Cohos or Humpbacks, while the fewer Kings waited in deeper water before beginning their upstream journey. A few of the crew used launches to troll where it was deeper water. Others didn't care about the fish and set traps for King crabs.

The number of salmon caught was far beyond the needs of the picnic, the winning King weighing in at forty-four pounds. The icebox was full of fillets along with two dozen crabs. The smell of freshly cooked salmon wafted from the beach fires the entire evening. At nine o'clock, the cannons fired from the ship, culminating the celebration. The crew returned under a pale Aurora Borealis.

Chapter Nine - Sitka

Two days after the holiday, Dorn, Strickland, Harry, and Ellingson prepped for departure to Sitka in the *Cosmos* to transfer the recuperating Carter to the *U.S.S. Pinto* hospital for continuing treatment. The *Pinto* was an iron-sided, double-masted steamship of the Navy, commissioned in 1865 but recently renovated for Alaskan service. She carried two 30-pound Parrott rifles—cannons weighing sixty-five hundred pounds. The cannons could fire twenty-seven-pound shells filled with three pounds of black powder every minute, effectively reaching two and a half miles, with a maximum range of five. A twelve-pound howitzer was also on board for smaller, closer targets.

Anchored in Snug Cove on the south end of Admiralty Island, Sitka lay due east of the *Patterson*, about sixty miles as the crow flies. To reach it by launch, however, they had to round the southern end of Admiralty, head north in Chatham Strait, and then follow Peril Strait to the eastern side of Baranof Island to Sitka Sound, one hundred and fifty miles. The trip would take about sixteen hours one way, and they would need to spend the night anchored somewhere along the way.

It was a fair morning when they departed, with light winds and clear skies, about 55 degrees at 4 a.m. The *Cosmos* bobbed alongside the *Patterson* as the men clamored over the railing and down to her deck, the fires stoked. Before Strickland engaged the propeller, Mansfield appeared above, shouting,

"Ahoy, Dorn!" He waved, and Dorn went back onboard for a quick conversation.

"Once you deliver Carter to the *Pinto*, stop by the governor's office. He has a message for you to relay on your trip back."

"Yes, sir. Did he say what the message was or where we were to take it?"

"Yes, you are to take it to Angoon. The message is from the Navy Department, Washington, D.C."

70

"I'm guessing it's about the bombing a few years ago?"

"Correct. The village requested an investigation. You are delivering the results of that investigation. It's not the answer the natives want to hear. The Navy isn't backing down from its position. Angoon won't be a happy place once you deliver the news," concluded Mansfield.

"Yes, sir, good to know."

Dorn climbed back down into the *Cosmos*, and Strickland steered out of the harbor and into Frederick Sound. Getting up to speed at eight knots, he turned southeast and then due east across Chatham Strait. A slight breeze came from the northwest. The waters were calm, so the craft didn't rise and fall on the swells but made easy progress. Their wake was the only disruption to the ocean water.

They went about five miles across the strait to the western side of Baranof Island and veered north. The men talked about fishing to pass the time. Strickland and Dorn took turns at the helm while Harry and Ellingson maintained the fire. Finding a protected location in Rodman Bay, they anchored for the night. They had gone about one hundred miles, and it was nearing four in the afternoon. Plenty of sunlight remained, but they didn't want to travel Peril Strait this late in the day.

The fifty-mile-long Peril Strait produces extreme currents, tides, and whirlpools, making navigation challenging. Named by Alexander Baranof in 1799, nearly one hundred fifty crew members died there, inspiring the name. Remarkably, they didn't die from poor navigation or dangerous currents but from eating poisonous shellfish. In that vicinity, Poison Cove and Deadman's Reach were also named for the calamity.

It would take six or seven more hours to arrive in Sitka. Not wanting to arrive too late in the day, the group decided to depart their anchorage at 6 a.m. The sun was shining as they took their time through the narrow Peril Strait, then passing north of Kruzof Island into Salisbury Sound. Turning south, they passed through Neva Strait to the east of Partofshikof Island, working their way through Kristof Sound. As they passed the Magoun Islands, Mt. Edgecumbe came into view.

"A volcano!" cried Carter. Wrapped in a blanket the whole trip while sitting to the side, he gripped the rail and peered at the white-topped cylindrical cone, awed by the snow-covered formation.

At only 3,201 feet tall, it was one of the lower peaks in the area. Its most prominent feature was the volcanic cone top, which opened like the mouth of a grouper chasing bait. Tlingit natives called it L'ux Shaa—a mountain blinking, spouting fire and smoke—but its last eruption was four thousand years ago.

"We are about fifteen miles out from Sitka," Dorn stated. "We'll anchor in the harbor, aside the *Pinto*. Carter, how are you doing?"

"Doing well, sir, thank you. I'm looking forward to leaving. Thank you, Dr. Percy and everybody, for helping me."

"We are glad you are getting better. Here, let's get you up."

After pulling aside, the men assisted Carter up the gangway to the *Pinto*. With the injured man transferred, they returned to the *Cosmos*, where they paused to consider what to do next. It was now one o'clock in the afternoon. They were hungry and still needed to visit the governor's office. They decided to visit the marine base to find a meal.

Dorn had been to Sitka several times and considered himself a Russian historian. He was fascinated by Russia's occupation of North America and filled the others in on its history as they headed the launch to shore.

"In 1799, Alexander Baranof established a trading post here and named it Fort St. Michael. Unfortunately for the local natives, the Russians treated them the same way they treated the Aleuts, who, as you know, are nearly extinct. Here at Fort St. Michael, the natives were aware of the slaughter and tried to avoid the Russian cruelty. They rebelled, attacked the fort, and burned it to the ground."

"Baranof hated this insubordination. In 1804, he sought revenge, defeating the Tlingit and forcing them to flee. From the ruins, he rebuilt the trading post, renaming it New Archangel. It was the Russian colonial capital of North America and one of the earliest known settlements on the continent's west coast. It had eight hundred residents at a time when San Francisco only had ten. After the town was sold—I mean, when Alaska was sold to the United States—the town died as all of the Russian businesses pulled out."

Landing on the rocky beach, they saw, to their left, above the high tide line, the area called the Native Village. It sat in a bleak existence, with bleak

72

houses constructed in the same square fashion and a similar bleak house beside it. Its closeness to the town and the fact that Tlingits worked, shopped, and conducted business in Sitka meant that, at least, whites in Sitka accepted them more than in most other Alaskan towns.

They walked up to a dirt road used as a boat launch. Above them stood what was once Alexander Baranof's castle, now a plain structure replacing the original elaborate mansion symbolizing Russia's influence and power. Dorn couldn't contain his enthusiasm for the history.

"This location was an obvious choice," he said, pointing at the current building on a rocky outcrop over fifty feet above the high tide line. "Fire destroyed the original castles, but Baranof rebuilt them again because he knew the importance of this location. The Tlingits of the Kiksadi Clan used this spot as a Native stronghold before that. The first castle had three floors, with an upper fourth floor. A small cupola sat atop the roof, a porch at the front entrance, and a long flight of steep steps leading up from the beach. It was surrounded by sunrooms and decks, constructed as part of the rock outcrop."

The structure before them did not resemble that grand design, and fire would again destroy it nine years later. In 1889, it was a plain, square, wooden-sided two-story office building, nothing close to a castle or mansion. The Navy had painted the building a reddish color, trimming the windows and doors in white. On October 18, 1867, it was the site of the ceremony commemorating the transfer of Alaska to the United States.

They moved past the site and into the town of about 1,500 people, mostly Native Tlingit and many Russians. Only a few Americans, besides the contingent of Navy personnel, resided there.

Their boots clamped loudly on wooden sidewalks as they walked downtown, looking into the shops and saloons. A group of Natives stood outside the entrance to Three Crows Market while two white men entered the low door. Customers bartered and bantered in English.

"Too bad we don't spend the night. I'd be up for a beer or two." It was Harry as they passed a brewery, and for a moment, he allowed himself to feel the loss of his relationship. "A couple of beers," he said, "or maybe even a couple of shots of rum."

"Oh, that does sound tasty. I'll join you," said Ellingson.

73

"No, we can't. We're on duty, and we still must go to Angoon," said Dorn, ending the discussion.

Once beyond downtown, they walked uphill on Lincoln Street, past a coal shed, and then turned left on Marine Street. To their right, they noticed a prominently situated grave. The men stopped so Ellingson could run over and read the monument. He came back and reported,

"Princess Maksotov, wife of Prince Dmitry Petrovich Maksutov, Chief Manager of the Russian American colonies," he recited. "What's best is it's a Lutheran cemetery, not Russian. She must have converted."

The barracks and Custom House stood ahead. Grassy, open parade grounds faced the buildings, with a small contingent of marines practicing a drill off to the side.

Passing the parade grounds, they entered the barracks, hoping lunch would be available. By chance, it was, and they enjoyed a meal with men stationed there. The *Patterson* crew listened during dinner as the marines told stories of living and working in North America's most remote outpost.

After eating, they thanked their brothers and went to Governor Lyman Knapp's office to collect the message. One of the marines from lunch walked with them and then escorted them into the governor's office for introductions.

Governor Knapp was fifty-two but looked much younger, maybe because he had only just arrived in Sitka in April following his nomination to the post by the recently sworn-in President Harrison. Knapp was originally from Vermont, and after graduating from college, he joined the Vermont Infantry Regiment, where he would be wounded in the battles of Gettysburg, Spotsylvania, and Petersburg, rising to the rank of colonel. Though seen as an outsider and mocked for his military uniform, he was determined to improve mail delivery to remote southeast Alaskan communities.

His office was minimally furnished, modest by Washington, D.C. standards, but one of the more elegantly appointed rooms by Sitka standards. Knapp adorned the walls with photographs of President Harrison and George Washington. Heavy red velvet curtains hung open by the windows. An American flag stood near the desk. Soft armchairs in a semicircle faced his desk, and he gestured for the men to sit there. With not enough chairs for everyone, Ellingson stood off to the side.

Sitting behind his desk, the Governor opened the discussion: "Gentlemen, again, thank you for coming. I wasn't sure how I was going to deliver this to Angoon until I heard you were coming into town, and then I thought, there's the answer. The *Patterson* crew will be going right by there, and they can take it. So, I appreciate you accepting the task."

"You're welcome, sir. And you are correct; we don't have to go out of our way," Dorn responded.

"I trust your trip was uneventful?" the governor asked.

"Yes, sir. It was quite an easy journey. We spent the night near the entrance to Peril Strait. We are hoping for pleasant weather on the way back," Dorn replied.

"The weather is to remain calm the next few days. But give it an hour, and who knows? Well, let me get to the point. The Angoon Elders requested a federal investigation into the bombing. This envelope contains a letter signed by the Secretary of the Navy confirming the determination that the destruction of Angoon was justifiable, regardless of the shaman's accidental death, given the kidnapping of two white men and the theft of trading post property. They requested a review about nine months ago, and this is their answer. Please deliver it to the Elders." He handed the manila envelope to Dorn, who stowed it inside his jacket.

"Yes, sir. We will make sure they receive it."

"Gentlemen, may I remind you that these Natives cannot be trusted and that when you go to their village, you must stand at the ready. Mr. Ford, is it Master at Arms? Be prepared. You are delivering unwelcome news. Do not let them kill the messengers. You are on a diplomatic mission with savages, so you must act with total authority and show no fear. Protect the interests of the United States of America at all costs." Then, with a clear hint of condescension, he added, "At least the Natives in Sitka are domesticated."

"Yes, sir, we will be ready for any contingency," replied Dorn. "Mr. Ford is able to anticipate any danger that may be at hand." Harry scoffed at the compliment.

Following another round of handshakes and goodbyes, they returned to the *Cosmos*, where they stoked the boilers and prepared to leave. It was 3:30 in the afternoon. Even though they were gaining ten minutes of daylight daily, the six hours back to their overnight anchorage would have them arriving close to ten o'clock, with just enough twilight to see what they were doing. The village of Angoon was several hours more travel, which would have to wait until the next day.

The three officers—and, to a lesser degree, Ellingson—disagreed with the governor's attitude regarding Natives, that they were savages and needed to be taught hard lessons, lessons that might mean the destruction of their village. Harry, Dorn, and Strickland found it abhorrent that their government would consider such a policy, let alone enforce it. Ellingson perceived the Indians as impoverished but did not believe that killing them was justified. He appreciated their ability to live in this environment, use the resources here, and thrive as a culture.

Chapter Ten - Hot Springs

Arriving near Chatham Strait around eleven o'clock, they crawled into their bunks without dinner—hungry but too tired to cook. Strickland woke everyone early the next morning by clanging a cast-iron skillet after preparing scrambled eggs and coffee. He chatted as the others ate, though nobody but him was energetic. He even cleaned their dishes.

As they stowed away their gear in preparation for departure to Angoon, their conversation and activity levels picked up, spurred by caffeine and daylight. Seizing the moment, Strickland turned to Dorn and asked,

"Lieutenant, are you feeling adventurous today?"

"I hadn't thought about it, but now that you ask—no."

"Ha! No, that's funny, Lieutenant. You probably want to follow orders, don't you? My mistake, of course."

"Why do you ask Strickland?"

"Well, sir, I'd like to take us on an adventure."

"What kind of adventure? Where?"

"Permission to change course and head north in Chatham Strait. I want to show you something."

"What is it?"

"It's a place I know. I found it a few years ago."

"Where? How far? We have our letter to deliver. Wherever it is, we can't be so late getting back to the *Patterson* that they think we're lost—or worse."

"I don't want the commander worrying about us either, but if we hurry, he may not notice we're late. It's not that far north of here, and it's on this side of Chatham Strait. We can stop at Angoon on the way back. This should only add three or four hours to our schedule."

"I think you should tell us where we're going," Harry interjected. He wasn't too keen on impromptu changes to the itinerary.

"Harry, I know you want to follow orders, but no—it's a surprise. I'm not going to tell. Let me just say I wouldn't insist on going there if it wasn't worth it. I don't want to get in trouble any more than you do. But I do think it would be worth it, even if we did catch hell."

After more questioning—but no further answers—Strickland convinced Dorn to change course. They traveled north along Baranof Island for about two and a half hours before veering left into an inlet. Five miles in, they passed a cannery on their right, slowing their speed another five miles after that.

As they drifted along the shoreline, a hidden river outlet emerged from the dense, thousand-year-old forest. Salmon leaped from the water, splashing upstream to spawn.

"Up ahead," Strickland said, peering intently at the beach. "Lieutenant Dorn, steer her by the outcrop—over by that huge treefall, the one with the giant spruce behind it." He was animated, giddy even. "I can't believe I'm here again! Oh, you're gonna be happy—something to cleanse the soul and soothe the spirit."

"This isn't a still, is it, Strickland?"

"No, Mr. Ford—much better than a still. This is healthy."

The *Cosmos* eased toward the beach and anchored. Dorn lowered a rowboat for transport ashore. The tide was slack, about to turn from low to high. Ellingson remained at the launch to keep it from beaching and to tend the fire.

The steep beach posed little difficulty for the men as they clambered up a large outcrop of solid rock. The moment they reached the top; one thing was evident. Steam.

A sizeable crevice, about five feet wide, ten feet long, and six feet deep, exhaled a warm mist. Freshwater filled the opening, its walls sloping inward so that six feet down, the pool was only three feet across, bubbles rising from its depths. A natural rock ledge surrounded the springs, with stones piled up for sitting, legs dangling in the steaming water. The high tide would not reach it, keeping the springs free of saltwater contamination.

"Hoonah Hot Springs!" Strickland shouted, stripping off his clothes and easing into the water.

Dorn and Harry laughed at the sight of the short, skinny sailor, now naked, slipping into the steaming pool.

"Strickland, how did you find this place?" Harry asked.

"These springs have been known around here for a long time. Oh, Mr. Ford, let me soak a minute."

Strickland closed his eyes and sank below the water before resurfacing to catch his breath. Steam curled around him, hot water lapping at the rock. Wiping his face, he continued,

"Before I was in the Navy, I ran around here with some guys out of Seattle. They weren't the best characters. I'll admit they cheated, robbed, got liquored up, cussed, spit, and fought. I did, too. I wasn't of quality character back then, either. We did a lot of trading that certainly favored us."

"Strickland, that doesn't sound like you. You're one of the most honest people I know," Harry said.

"Yeah, I had no idea you were a rogue," Dorn added.

"I haven't always been. I decided to go straight after what happened here."

"What happened here?" Harry asked.

Strickland took a deep breath and submerged for a moment before resurfacing, exhaling through his nose, eyes still closed.

"My crew and I were trading in Hoonah when this new kid on our crew said he knew about some hot springs nearby. We finished our business in Hoonah, and the kid led us here, where we camped for about a week, loving every minute. These springs do get busy, though—fur traders, fishermen, and loggers came here to relax, some to winter over.

On the evening before we intended to leave, a group of lumberjacks showed up, already liquored up and acting crazy—hollering, getting rowdy, shooting into the air. We camped off to the side, watching, and I knew something bad was going to happen.

Sure enough, one of them fired his pistol and hit the new kid in the arm. He didn't die, but my crew pulled their guns and started shooting back - a gunfight.

When it was over, only three of us were left alive, including me and the kid. We killed all of them. There was no law out here, so no one investigated.

That was when I knew I was on the wrong path. I figured I'd end up dead someday if I didn't change. So, when we got back to Seattle, I signed up with the Navy. It was my best shot at becoming a better man."

"Wise choice, I'd say," Harry responded. "I hope we don't have that kind of fun."

Turning to Dorn, he asked, "Have you determined the justification for our visit here in case Mansfield wonders where we've been?"

"I'm not sure yet," Dorn said as he undressed.

"What? You too?"

"Why not? I might as well enjoy it—we're here. And I want to know what I'm going to be in trouble for."

Stepping into the pool across from Strickland, he let out a long, satisfied sigh as he sank into the water beside his shipmate.

"Come on in—the water's fine," said Dorn.

Harry considered it but decided it would be best to scout the area first. No one had checked the surroundings when they arrived. Dense undergrowth of berry bushes, willows, and Devil's Club blocked his sight at ground level.

Finding a small stream trickling from the forest, he followed it, using the rocks to keep his feet dry. Once past the initial vegetation, the forest opened. The terrain was level where he stood, but thirty yards inland, the slope rose steeply. A narrow path paralleled the beach, an animal trail, though people may have walked it as well, given the springs' proximity.

He heard birds and small animals calling as he moved cautiously along the trail. Five minutes later, the sound of rushing water grew louder—the river they had passed on the way in. Deciding to push forward, he continued toward it before turning back.

The rushing sound grew louder as he drew near. Eighty feet from bank to bank, the river carried mountain snowmelt to the ocean. As he gazed down, he could see salmon making their way inland. Then he heard a sound that made his skin crawl.

To his right, about twenty yards away, a grizzly bear sat on its haunches on a sandbar in the river, paws out in front of its massive chest, its big black nose sniffing the air. Interrupted from its fishing, the bear was looking at him.

His first thought was Carter—how severely injured Carter had been from that attack. He replayed how he had shot the bear multiple times, how it had continued battering the poor man, bloody gashes across his face and chest.

Harry considered all his options before moving. If he ran, the bear might chase him. If he shot it, he might only wound it, making it furious and even more dangerous. His best option was to ease away, rifle at the ready, until he was out of sight.

He chose the latter and slowly moved backward, keeping the rifle shouldered. He continued this way for about twenty yards before feeling safe—at least for then. As far as he could tell, the bear remained where it was.

Turning, he ran full speed back along the trail. Reaching the hot springs without being followed, he burst through the narrow opening in the brush and onto the beach, where Dorn and Strickland were still soaking.

"Lieutenant! Strickland! Bear! Grizzly bear! Run! Ellingson, prepare the launch!"

81

He experienced another close encounter with a grizzly bear and successfully lived to recount the event. He kept yelling at the naked men to hurry as he made his way to the *Cosmos*, wanting to be on the water as soon as possible. He had no idea that a grizzly was an excellent swimmer and could follow them back to the ship if it wanted to.

Dorn and Strickland struggled to pull their limp, pink bodies out of the crevice.

"Where are my clothes?" Strickland shouted, confused about where he had left them. He scurried about, the tender soles of his feet hurting on the rocks.

"Over here," Dorn said, pulling up his trousers. Neither of them had paid attention to where they had tossed their clothes, and now they regretted their carelessness. The two naked men grabbed their garments, dressing as quickly as they could on their way to the launch.

Still aiming his rifle at the tree line, Harry kept watch as Dorn and Strickland climbed into the launch. He followed, scanning for any sign of the bear.

As they looked down the beach, it became clear that no bear was coming—there was no immediate danger. They shoved off, with Ellingson at the helm, pulling away from shore. Heading east toward the mouth of the inlet and on to Angoon, they laughed as they recounted their not-so-harrowing escape.

"Watching you two trying to haul your butts out of that crack is the funniest thing I've seen in years," quipped Ellingson. "And poor Mr. Ford here—he looked like he'd seen a ghost! You were as pale as a sheet, Mr. Ford."

Harry laughed nervously at his own bear anxiety.

"He was the biggest animal I've ever seen. Sitting on his haunches, he must have been ten feet tall. His paws stuck out six feet from his chest. His teeth…." He trailed off as the men smirked at him. "He was at least twenty yards away, just enjoying the day. I panicked," Harry finally admitted.

They all nodded in agreement.

"Don't worry about it," Dorn said. "We probably would have done the same thing."

"I've been close to big grizzlies, and they're something else. God created a monster of a creature if you ask me. At least if a beast like that eats you, someone may find your bones. If you go down in the deep, no one ever finds you," Ellingson mused.
"But did you like the hot springs?" Strickland asked. "Isn't that the best place? We need to come back here."

"If we come back, I want to get in," said Harry. "But for now, we still need to deal with Angoon."

Lieutenant Dorn nodded. "Yes, we still need to deal with Angoon."

Heading east out into the open waters of Chatham Strait, the small launch carried Harry, Dorn, and Ellingson effortlessly over the calm sea. The warm afternoon July sky stretched before them.

Chapter Eleven - Angoon

To the Tlingits, Aangoon means "Isthmus Town." Changed to Angoon by the Americans, it is the only inhabited village on Admiralty Island. Situated on the western side, the outline of the physical isthmus where the village is located juts to the northwest, its silhouette resembling a quill pen. The village of about two hundred people sits a mile south of the tip on a thin sliver of land—about a thousand feet wide—separating the waters of the Pacific Ocean from Kootznoowoo Inlet. Ocean currents pass in and out of the inlet twice daily, filling and draining Mitchell and Kanalku Bays, immense bodies of water inland on the island.

The Tlingit follows matrilineal lines to determine groups and clans. The Raven, Wolf, and Eagle moieties are the dominant kinships in Angoon, with several clans within each group, including Raven, Needlefish, Dog Salmon, and Killer Whale. Clan houses decoratively painted with orcas, eagles, bears, ravens, and fish define the village.

When the *Patterson* crew arrived that day in July, it looked as though Angoon was barely surviving. Despite the abundant resources that surrounded them, the villagers struggled due to considerable damage caused by the Navy seven years earlier. On a personal level, Angoon's scars ran deep, and wounds had yet to heal. Hatred of the Navy remained intense, as federal policy still deemed them savages—an inferior people. The bombing of their village as a punitive measure for what the government called an "insurrection" was a festering wound. Other military reprisals against the Tlingit only deepened their distrust, such as when the U.S.S. *Saginaw* destroyed all but one cabin in Kake, another southeast Alaska village, following a dispute over the deaths of two villagers.

Dorn contemplated how to approach the village without causing alarm or disruption. He feared that at the sight of their Navy uniforms, the villagers might assume they were there for another punitive action.

"Do any of you know any Tlingit words or phrases? I don't want to scare the villagers when we arrive. They might think we are hostile."

"Yes, sir," Strickland replied. "I know a few native words. Can't say 'em too great, but I can conduct business if I must. I picked up greetings in my other life before the Navy. Who I'm talking to can usually work out what I'm sayin'".

Native Tlingit conversations are complex and sound unlike discussions in English or other languages. Vowels and consonants are pronounced distinctly different, with consonants in particular spoken with an intense burst of air. Although used less frequently, vowels require lowering the soft palate to allow airflow through both the nose and mouth simultaneously. Word articulation follows a staccato-like rhythm as Tlingits glottalize—partially closing the glottis, the middle region of the larynx. Syllables are short and precise, while pitch variations change the meaning of words.

Struggling to articulate the deep, resonating sounds, Strickland sputtered, "Sh y-a awudanEixil."

"What does that mean?" asked Harry.

"I hope that means 'noble people.' "

"GunalchEesh haa x-ntxi lyaggodi," he continued. "That means 'thank you for coming.' Y-a yeed-t xat tsu, Ax tuw-a sigUo xiAx w dataani. At this time, I'd like to talk to you."

"Okay, decent enough to show some respect," said Dorn. "Stick to the 'noble people' part. One of them must be able to speak English; I can't see how they could get along otherwise."

Dorn decided a cautious approach was best. He ordered his men to leave their revolvers aboard the *Cosmos* and remove their hats, sashes, and medals to downplay their uniforms. Regardless of what Governor Knapp had said, he didn't want to upset the villagers at the sight of armed Navy personnel. If he returned in the future, he resolved to come as a civilian.

"I'll stay with the *Cosmos*," said Ellingson. "I'll turn her around and be ready to leave, keeping the fires burning and the steam on the boil." He had been particularly quiet before their arrival, but now he seemed agitated, tying knots in a rope as he spoke.

"Good idea, Ellingson. We want to be ready to leave at a moment's notice. We won't be here long," replied Dorn.

The launch anchored in the bay as villagers emerged to see who was arriving. Everyone except Ellingson climbed into the rowboat for the trip to shore. The slope made for an easy landing as they jumped out and hauled the rowboat above the high-tide line.

The Navy, in its compassion, had not shelled or burned all the villagers' homes that winter; a few remained. These surviving houses stood starkly among the burned-out ruins and the handful of newly built structures made of fresh-hewn lumber. As the crew walked up the beach, the scene was eerie. The sky was overcast, and the threat of rain added to the sense of gloom.

More than twenty-five village men, wrapped in brightly colored blankets, approached. The oldest among them—the clan elders—formed a small group in front of Dorn and his crew. Women and children remained behind while the shaman stood apart. The crowd was silent, watching closely for any sign of hostility from the Americans.

Strickland addressed the group with his extremely poor Tlingit.

"GunalchEesh haat yee. aadi. Thank you for being here."

The villagers murmured their vibrant blankets and hats, which were a stark contrast to the bleakness of the town.

One man with dark eyes and a scar on his chin wore a wide-brimmed hat with tassels and a pointed top painted with a red and black bear. A blanket with a similar red and black bear rested over his shoulders. Dorn whispered to the others that he was an elder. Beside the man with dark eyes stood a younger man—Dorn hoped he was an interpreter. The two men spoke quietly before the younger one turned and said,

"Speak in English, I will interpret. My name is Yáx góos.'"

"My name is Lieutenant Edward Dorn. This is Mr. Ford, and this is Mr. Strickland—officers of the United States Navy. We are delivering a message, but before we do, we would like to express our appreciation for your hospitality."

Yáx góos' turned and spoke to the older man while the other villagers listened. After a brief exchange, he turned back to Dorn.

"This is Ka'jaḵ'tii, our leader," he said, nodding toward the Elder. "He said a gesture of appreciation would be acknowledging the United States government's illegal use of force on a defenseless Tlingit village."

Ka'jaḵ'tii's wrinkled face remained expressionless, his black eyes unblinking.

"Honorable Elder, I cannot speak for the government. We are messengers and have brought a letter from the Secretary of the Navy."

Yáx góos' translated, and the villagers began murmuring excitedly. Dorn handed him the envelope.

"I will read this later. Tell us what it says now."

"It says the United States government did nothing wrong when they destroyed your village and killed your people. They maintain it was an accident that killed your shaman, thus absolving them of responsibility. You won't be financially compensated for your losses."

Yáx góos' repeated Dorn's summary of the letter for the others, and it was clear the villagers didn't like what they heard.

"I want you to know, not all of us agree with the Navy," Dorn added. "The three of us—Mr. Ford, Mr. Strickland, and I—don't think the Navy should have bombed you. You have our regrets and apologies."

Ka'jaḵ'tii stared back at him while Yáx góos' translated his words. Then, the younger man said, "Ka'jaḵ'tii wants you to leave."

Without further discussion, the villagers turned and went about their day as if nothing had happened, while the elders headed to the Raven house to discuss the letter with Yáx góos.' In the shadows, the village Shaman watched Dorn and his men.

The three sailors noticed the shaman's intense gaze but felt relieved as the rest of the villagers dispersed.

"What's he doing over there?" Strickland asked, the shaman chanting loudly.

The village's spiritual leader, wearing a wolf hat and robe, began performing a rhythmic, synchronized dance to the beat of two rattles he held. He turned in slow, deliberate circles, raising his hands to the sky before lowering them to the ground, all in time with the beat. His moccasin-covered feet pounded the earth as he pranced about, eyes closed, seeking wisdom from the ancestors regarding these white men.

"You're the one who knows Tlingit—you tell me," Dorn said. "I don't like it regardless. He might be casting a curse on us. Let's move out of here. We're already behind schedule, thanks to you. The wind will be at our back going down Chatham, so let's try to make up some time."

"Lieutenant, can we do something first?" Ford asked.

Knowing Dorn was in a hurry, he didn't wait for an answer but walked across the main street to the edge of the isthmus on the inlet side. Dorn and Strickland followed, watching him squat down, peering at the current. They wondered what had so captivated him.

The Kootznoowoo Inlet tide was coming in, filling the two vast inland bodies of water. Seawater surged through the shallow, narrow opening, creating a torrential rapid.

"This current is amazing. See that?" He pointed to a nearly submerged buoy. The Navy had installed it in the channel after the bombing. It was solidly anchored to the seabed, defying the current's strength to pull it from the ground—but the force of the water was powerful enough to drag it under.

"I've read about tides like this. The Hudson, where I grew up, wasn't this strong—it's farther south in latitude. When the tide comes in, it backs up and creates waves, but it's not this forceful when it reverses. Angoon has greater tidal pulls. And instead of a wide river like the Hudson, this has a very, very narrow channel." He pointed up the inlet toward the mountain peaks. "I've seen the topography of Admiralty, and the two bays feeding this are enormous."

Harry's inner hydrographer was alive, his mind racing to calculate the interplay of depth, velocity, volume, and tidal forces. He marveled at the rare and unique geological and hydrographic features before him.

"Mr. Ford, I appreciate your enthusiasm, but let's go," Dorn said. "We have to get back. The villagers may decide to take us prisoners. And it's getting to the point where Mansfield might question our whereabouts. I'd rather not explain our hot spring adventure."

Dorn and Strickland turned toward the rowboat, leaving Harry to his observations. As promised, Ellingson had repositioned the launch and was ready to depart. As the two officers neared the boat, three Native men in colorful blankets emerged from the clan house and began walking toward them.

Ellingson, unable to contain his concern, shouted, "Hurry! Natives are coming. We need to leave now! Get down here, Mr. Ford!"

Turning at Ellingson's warning, Ford saw the men approaching and realized he needed to move fast. As he walked toward the rowboat, the Native men altered their course, heading directly toward him.

It was Yáx góos,' Ka'jak̲'tii, and another man—massive, built like a sumo wrestler.

"We have a question," Yáx góos' said. "Where is your warship? What is its name?"

"We don't have a warship," Ford replied. "We are surveyors. Our ship is named the *U.S.S. Carlise P. Patterson*. It belongs to the United States Coast and Geodetic Survey. The Navy operates it, but not for war purposes— we make maps and charts for mariners."

A discussion in Tlingit followed as Yáx góos' tried to explain these foreign concepts to the elders. Ford could tell they weren't convinced.

Interrupting, he asked the younger man, "How do you know English? Do you understand what I mean by surveying? Do you know what geodetic means?"

"I was sent to Chemawa, an Indian school in Forest Grove, then Salem, Oregon. I studied science and blacksmithing. I understand the concept of surveying, but my Elders do not. They are concerned that you are here to plan a military attack. I have tried to explain what you do, but they still assume you're lying."

"Oh no, tell them we only want to draw the coastline on paper. They have my word."

Yáx góos' did his best to explain to Ka'jak̲'tii and the other man that these visitors were not enemies seeking to attack. Ka'jak̲'tii looked at Harry, then turned away, the other two following him. Harry and Yáx góos' exchanged a nod of mutual respect.

Ellingson, growing impatient, yelled for Harry to get into the rowboat and return to the *Cosmos*. As soon as they were aboard, he gunned the engine. The boat shuddered as it picked up speed, heading south along the island's west coast. Ellingson turned one last time to look at Angoon.

Noting the tension in Ellingson's face and his barely contained impatience, Harry sensed something was wrong.

"Ellingson, what's bothering you? You look concerned about something."

"I have something I need to tell you. You and the Lieutenant. Strickland, you should hear it too—you've been scurrying around these parts for years, so you'll know what I'm talking about. But I don't want to talk now. Let's wait until we're back on the ship—eat, sleep—and I'll tell you in the morning. It's a story that needs coffee," he said.

Chapter Twelve - Ellingson

The four men met in the galley the following morning, chatting over pancakes. McDonald and Almy were also there, but Ellingson didn't want them listening in, so small talk continued until the room was empty except for the stewards, who paid no attention.

"Alright, Ellingson, what do you have? What's got you so nervous?" Dorn asked.

Ellingson took a sip of coffee before beginning.

"Back in '82, the Northwest Trading Company hired me. I was a greenhorn, only two months on the job before trouble started. I was still learning the ropes as their whaling ship apprentice—engineer, pilot, or whatever you want to call it. I cleaned the hull, maintained the engines, repaired the spars, stoked the fires, and took control of the helm when needed. The company required that whaling boat to be ready to go at the first sight of a whale, so I worked constantly.

"But it paid well. They traded everything and anything—legal and illegal. We had furs, food, fuel, and household goods, but our most profitable item was a whale. Whale enabled the company to produce hundreds of candles, hundreds of pounds of soap, dozens of barrels of oil, and enough food to feed a town. The income from one of those giant mammals was enormous. A gallon of whale oil alone at that time brought in $1.50. Each carcass provided about three thousand barrels of oil. Each barrel was thirty-one and a half gallons. You do the math."

"That's almost $150,000," Dorn said, jotting the numbers on a piece of paper.

"Exactly, vast amounts of money. Sure, they had to pay for gear that went overboard, and they lost a few boats, but they were still making a solid profit. The money allowed the company to replace their lost equipment and buy the best boats. They built outposts around the Southeast, including one in Angoon. Business was good, and I was making a good living."

"I know traders. They're unscrupulous. One made over $25,000 in a year," said Strickland.

"It wouldn't surprise me," Ellingson replied. "But what was surprising was how few white men wanted to work whaling vessels, even for decent wages. They figured it was too dangerous. So, we had to go around to the Indian villages looking for crews. The Natives were willing, but the language barrier and other differences made it a challenge. And if there was alcohol around, none of them could go to sea for days.

"One day, my company put together this Indian crew to go whaling. There were three or four of them under the supervision of two of the company's men. Have you ever hunted whales, or do you know how they're hunted?"

Harry shook his head. "Ah, no. I guess a harpoon?" Strickland and Dorn both shrugged.

"Sometimes, but the world has changed. At present, a whaling harpoon gun is used. It looks like a regular rifle, but it shoots a six-to-eight-inch lance out of the barrel. Filled with black powder, the lance explodes when it hits the whale.

"So, I worked with these two white guys. They had been with Northwest Trading Company for a couple of years but had been in southeast Alaska even longer. They managed the whaling crews. Their names were Frank Stevens and Thomas Cantwell. They were dangerous and ugly. Stevens had only one eye—his right—so he wore a patch over his left. They ran roughshod over the Natives, hated 'em."

"Seems to be the prevalent attitude around here," Dorn quipped.

"It has been and will continue to be for a while," Ellingson replied. "Anyway, one day, I was outside behind the trading post in the privy. Nature had called, and while I was there, it was quiet, and I heard something..."

"You're not quiet! I've heard you!" Strickland interrupted, making the others laugh. Getting up to leave, he added, "Sorry Ellingson, I need to leave, I have a crew repairing a leak in the main boiler that I need to check on."

92

"I was quiet because I was finished," Ellingson shouted at Strickland as the other man left the room. Refocusing on Harry and Dorn, Ellingson continued. "I stepped out and saw Stevens and Cantwell in the back storeroom of the trading post. They sounded like they were arguing, so I worked my way closer, where I could see them more clearly. I presumed they were unable to see me as I was concealed, and the sun was positioned behind me. I could hear them talking about Teel' Tlien.

"He was one of the Indian crew that day, but he was also Angoon's shaman—very important to the village. They were talking about him and his wife. I knew who she was—beautiful. I'd seen Stevens around her, and I could clearly see the lust in his eyes. He wanted her."

"Oh, I see where this is going," Dorn muttered.

"I was watching through the window when I saw Stevens shove something down the barrel of a whaling gun. He crammed a rod in to ensure it was set. Just then, clouds covered the sun, and they must've seen me—I'd tripped over a root, and when I looked up, they were looking right at me. They dropped what they were doing and ran for the door. I knew they were coming after me.

"I bolted through the brush as fast as I could. I dove into a dense stand of Devil's Club, hoping they wouldn't follow. They did come out to look, but I was well hidden. This happened right before they needed to go whaling, so they left without me. It didn't matter that I wasn't on board—they could manage it without me. Not long after, I heard a loud boom out on the water. It was the gun going off—it killed Teel' Tlien.

"The village came out when they returned to shore, shouting and shrieking. It sounded like all hell had broken loose. I stayed put in the Devil's Club.

"After an hour or so, it was darker, so I ventured out to see what had happened. I looked in the trading post and saw Stevens and Cantwell tied up and gagged. The Natives, as they do, were demanding payment for Teel' Tlien. The whaling company wasn't gonna pay, so the Indians took Stevens and Cantwell prisoner. They also confiscated the company's property."

"So, how did you escape?" Dorn asked.

"I stole the launch from the Indians. I waited until the entire village was wild with anger, yelling and jumping around. I snuck south through the woods, dropping down to the low tide line—well below their line of sight. I untied the launch, pushed off, and started moving. I paddled out before starting a fire, let the steam build, and then took off for Juneau.

"Several hours later, the Navy bombed the village. I found out later that Stevens and Cantwell were released, and I figured they'd try to kill me if they ever saw me again."

"Wow, Ellingson. Quite the story. Have you ever told anyone this?" Dorn asked.

"No, Lieutenant. It's never come up. I went to Juneau and didn't say a word to anyone. I ditched the company's launch, collected my things, and took off for the East Coast. The last thing I wanted was to be anywhere near them."

"And that's when you met Katie and ended up on the *Patterson's* maiden voyage," Harry said.

"That's right, Mr. Ford. You listen well."

"That's a story I'd like to hear someday," Dorn said. "But for now, what happened to them—Stevens and Cantwell?"

"The Navy held a trial, but nothing happened to them. The court concluded that the shaman's death was accidental—a faulty whaling gun. Last I heard, they went up to the Yukon and were headed out to Bethel. They know I saw them sabotage the rifle. They know the Navy would reopen the investigation if added information became known, even holding the trading company liable. They'd kill me to prevent that."

"So, the Navy's conclusion—that it was an accident—is incorrect. It was sabotage," Dorn interrupted. "If this was sabotage..."

He paused, trying to grasp the implications. "It means the Navy was set up, in a way. They bombed Angoon for an uprising that was instigated by a white man, killing the shaman to have his wife. It's a story as old as King David."

"Did they examine the whaling gun?" asked Dorn.

94

"The gun wasn't on the launch when it returned. Stevens must have thrown it overboard after it exploded."

Dorn opened his file and pulled out a letter from the Collector at the Custom House in Sitka, dated October 28, 1882.

"It's a letter to the Secretary of the Treasury from the head customs agent, Mr. Morris. He's reporting on the incident. 'Severe lesson taught...'" he read. "'...the men were still prisoners...'"

"That would be Stevens and Cantwell," said Ellingson.

Dorn continued reading. "'... So, temporizing has been the policy pursued within the past two years by the Navy towards the Swashes, and they evidently thought this a game of bluff. They were surly and impertinent... The Houchens's are a rich and warlike tribe, very insolent and saucy towards the whites. As long as the native tribes throughout the archipelago do not feel the force of the government and are not punished for flagrant outrages, so much more dangerous do they become and are to be feared... The punishment has been most severe, but eminently salutary, and in my judgment, the very thing that was needed...'"

Dorn trailed off. "I guess Mr. Morris didn't think much of the Natives, did he? What did I say earlier? That seems to be the prevalent attitude around here."

He put the letter back into the file and flipped through other pages, pulling out a document with the Navy's insignia. It was from the Commanding Officer of the *U.S.S. Corwin*, the Navy vessel that fired on Angoon.

"It's Commander Merriman's official report from the *Corwin*." Dorn read aloud. "'...Fishermen in the act of discharging a bomb at a whale—the bomb accidentally exploded, killing a medicine man instantly. Indians at once seize the small steamer and two fishing boats.'"

"Everybody thinks it was an accident, and I would too if I hadn't seen it with my own eyes," Ellingson said. "That's not the first whale gun to explode in someone's hands. I know of two other whalers killed by a whale gun. It happens. But this was no accident."

Dorn picked up where he left off. "'...With the weather proving boisterous, I did not think it advisable to cross Chatham Strait with the steam-powered vessel. I held a powwow with the Indians... I explained to them the fallacy of any claim when the death is purely accidental.'"

"What if it was sabotage?" Dorn asked rhetorically.

He read on. "'I ascertained that they attempted to destroy the boats and that they were only waiting for another white man to be put to death. One of the men captured had but one eye, and they wanted a whole one—one with two eyes.'"

Dorn laid the report down and looked at Ellingson. "Old man, what have you done?" He slapped him on the shoulder. "You're an eyewitness with testimony that could rewrite history. Employees of the Northwest Trading Company outright murdered an Indian—a shaman, at that—making it seem like an accident. Angoon should be compensated by the trading company, not the Navy. This was no accident. Stevens and Cantwell should be charged with murder."

"I agree, sir, but I'd prefer if they weren't around to be arrested. They cause trouble wherever they go, so if they're in the area, we may hear about it. In any event, I don't want to see them again unless they're behind bars."

"Let's hope they're in the Yukon, like you say," Harry concluded. "Maybe we should report this to Lieutenant Mansfield. Do you concur, Lieutenant?"

"Yes, I think I'll brief him," Dorn answered. "He can decide what to do with the information. Ellingson, be prepared to tell your story a few more times."

"Aye, Lieutenant."

The three men sat in silence for a few moments before adjourning to their duties.

Harry took a little time to search for the salt barrel. Climbing to the deck, he checked every barrel he could find but saw none filled with salt. Disappointed, he headed to the drafting room to catch up on his work.

Chapter Thirteen – August

Summer was passing quickly. It was now August, and evenings were darkening earlier; the light that lingered through the night at solstice shined no more. The nighttime air temperature dipped lower, carrying the first hints of autumn. Rain remained a constant factor in everything they did, but at least it wasn't snow.

The survey crews worked diligently to establish their network of triangulated one-inch monuments, aligning them with the rest of the country's geodetic markers. The measurements had to be first-level and as accurate as humanly possible. They took astronomical, magnetic, tidal, and other readings multiple times to ensure the data met the highest standards.

Drafters created detailed field sheets that were sent to the Coast and Geodetic Survey headquarters in Washington, D.C., where technicians etched corresponding copper plates. These were coated with wax and graphite and placed in a solution containing salt and copper. An electric current was used to deposit metal in the etched areas, creating a replica plate ready for mass-producing charts used by mariners.

The *Patterson* anchored in Seymour Canal's Mole Harbor for the last ten days of August before moving north to Windfall Harbor and then a few days later to Holkham Bay.

Lt. Mansfield addressed the officers at their regular Monday staff meeting.

"Lieutenant Dorn, the weather forecast in Sitka calls for wind and high swells. Because of that, the steamer *Ancon* has changed course and will not be coming alongside to deliver our mail as scheduled. She's heading directly to Seattle instead. She'll be back with mail on her return trip next week. I have correspondence that needs to go out, and I'm sure others do as well. Please organize a mail party to Juneau."

"Yes, sir. Right away. I'll let the crew know."

"Lieutenant, I have a request," Beale interjected. "It's a financial matter. The cash I used to purchase coal from the freighter the *George Elder* has caused our reserves to fall below my projections for the rest of the trip. We still have additional significant purchases to make—more coal, for example—before we return to San Francisco."

"Why are we short? Didn't you budget the expenses?" asked a frowning Mansfield.

"Yes, sir, I accounted for everything, but now I'm projecting a shortfall. The price we paid the *Elder* for coal was fifty percent more than I estimated. I propose we cash one of our two gold certificates. That would provide $5,000 in currency, leaving us another $5,000 certificate for emergencies."

The officers murmured among themselves, with Harry reacting first.

"I'll go with Beale. I'll get a couple of the crew for security." While he wanted to provide security for the cash, he also wanted to mail his letter to Clara.

"Oh no, no, I'm not going," Beale said quickly. "Davenport will oversee the transaction."

"Are you sure? Why not you?" Mansfield asked.

Beale hesitated before answering. "I'm retiring after this season. The *Patterson* will need a new Paymaster, so I'm training Davenport."

"Don't you need to supervise him?"

"He watched me manage the last transaction before we left on this trip. He also has several small packages to mail."

"Ensign McDonald, I want you to go with Harry," Mansfield ordered. "Pick one or two more crew. You'll need the support."

"I'll take Seaman Ellingson," Harry said.

Mansfield nodded. "Carry arms, but don't wear uniforms. Blend into the town—don't draw attention to yourselves. Don't travel as a group; position yourselves strategically to ensure the safe transport of that certificate to the bank and the cash back to the ship. Mr. Ford, I want you shoulder to shoulder with Davenport at all times."

The next day, the rain had stopped, but the overcast sky threatened a downpour at any moment. At the helm of the *Pirate*, Dorn had a fire burning in the firebox, ensuring steam was available. The water was choppy, and he wanted power at the ready. Ellingson managed the lines while Harry, McDonald, and Davenport stepped onto the launch.

"Lieutenant, are you going too?" Harry asked, surprised to see him.

"Lt. Mansfield spoke to me this morning. He thought it best to have one more officer come along, so here I am."

He glanced up to see Arthurs standing at the railing, passing small packages down to Davenport.

"Arthurs, what are you doing here?" Dorn asked.

"I asked him to come," Davenport said. "You said you wanted more security. I figured you'd be focused on the bank, and I need someone to help carry these." He gestured to the packages.

"What's in them?" asked Harry.

"Marine samples. We're sending them to headquarters for identification."

Keeping the launch at ten knots, they bounced hard over the water for the three-hour journey, finally reaching the calmer waters of Gastineau Channel, Douglas Island to their left.

Tying up at the dock serving Juneau's harbor, Ellingson agreed to stay behind with the *Pirate*, keeping the fire burning and the vessel ready for departure once they secured the cash. McDonald walked ahead while Harry and Davenport stayed together. Dorn took the rear, watching from behind. Arthurs, carrying the packages, made his way separately to the post office.

Juneau was founded after the discovery of gold in 1880. It clung to the base of Mt. Juneau, trying not to slide into the Gastineau Channel near the terminus of Gold Creek. Unlike Sitka and Wrangell, neither the Tlingits, Russians, nor British had ever claimed Juneau. Built on a steep mountainside, the townsite was covered by a densely wooded old-growth forest. Once loggers cleared the land, little thrived beyond mud, fed by the area's 120 inches of annual rainfall.

A row of wooden cabins stood above the high tide line, further up the hillside. Main, Seward, Front, Franklin, and 1st through 6th Streets provided the town's primary access routes. Horse-drawn wagons hauled rocks and tailings from the gold mines, dumping them into the harbor to expand the waterfront.

The Alaska State Bank stood on Main Street, a river rock building just ten feet wide and ten feet deep. A single window with steel bars embedded in cement allowed minimal light into the interior. The heavy wooden door, reinforced with wrought iron hardware, locked the building at night. Inside, two clerks sat behind a counter with ledgers, scales, weights, and a small cash box. A cold potbelly stove stood in the center of the room. Behind a curtain in the back, a six-foot safe loomed in the corner, partially lit by two oil lamps on the wall.

Given the small space inside, Davenport went in alone while the others positioned themselves outside, keeping watch. Davenport returned, and the clerks locked the heavy bank door behind him. Once the building was secure, they opened the safe, withdrew $5,000 in various denominations, deposited the certificate, and locked the safe once more. When they were ready, Dorn went in, where he counted and confirmed the $5,000 in cash. Satisfied, he placed the money in a bag, secured it around his waist, and tied it in place.

The four men assumed their positions for the return trip to the launch. By the time they stepped onto the street, it was nearing three o'clock in the afternoon. They encountered no threats—only the usual town activity. Their journey back was uneventful, and they reached the *Pirate*, where Ellingson was waiting with the launch. Arthurs, however, had not yet returned.

With the money now safely aboard and guarded by Dorn, Harry decided he had time to mail his letter. Pulling it from his pocket, he caught McDonald glancing at the addressee.

"Clara, eh?" McDonald remarked. "What are you saying to her? Trying to change her mind—asking her to reconsider?"

"No, nothing like that. Don't worry—it's nothing dramatic," Harry replied. "I told her I understand her point of view, and I'm not angry at her."

"Good. Let it be over."

Turning onto Main Street, Harry took a right on Front Street and was about to turn onto Franklin when a familiar figure caught his eye. Up the street to his left, Arthurs stood outside the entrance of a blacksmith shop, engaged in an animated conversation with three or four Native men. The group huddled in a circle, focused on something in their hands. The rhythmic clanking of the blacksmith hammering iron on the anvil echoed from within the shop.

From below, Harry saw Arthurs hand a box—identical to those meant for mailing—to the men. They continued speaking, and as Harry watched, they handed Arthurs cash. Then, without hesitation, he disappeared into the narrow passage beside the blacksmith's building. The men turned and started down Franklin Street toward Harry.

Thinking quickly, he staggered forward, pretending to be drunk, and limped toward them, mumbling and slurring his words.

"That man… up there… I'm looking for him. He said to meet me, but now he's gone. Do you know where he went?"

The men regarded him silently, offering no response. As if losing his balance, Harry lurched forward, reaching out to steady himself. In doing so, he caught hold of one man's arm, knocking the box loose from his grasp. It tumbled to the ground, white granules spilling out.

The Native men scowled and shoved him to the ground as they hurried to gather the spilled contents. Still playing the drunk, Harry picked up the box and squinted at its label.

"Rare fish?" he slurred. "Where can I get rare fish?"

"Hoonah," one of the men answered as they scooped up the salt.

Hoonah? Why Hoonah? The question lingered in his mind as he watched them disappear down the street.

Pushing the incident aside, he remembered his letter and made his way to the post office. Perhaps sending the note would soften the lingering tension with Clara.

Returning to the *Pirate*, he felt a growing curiosity about Arthurs' whereabouts. As he reached the launch, he saw Davenport standing on the dock, tending the mooring lines. Deciding against telling Dorn and McDonald about the rare fish with Davenport there, he stepped aboard quietly.

Something beneath the bench seat caught his eye—something that hadn't been there before. Bending closer, he wet his finger, rubbed it into the material, then brought it to his lips. Salt.

Arthurs soon arrived, acting as if he had simply been to the post office.

"Where have you been?" Harry asked. "You said you were going to mail the packages. What took you so long?"

"I went for a walk. It's not raining, and it feels great to be on land again."

"Oh? Where'd you walk to?"

"Sheep Creek."

"Sheep Creek? What's there to see? The mining camp?"

"No, I just wanted to go on a walk."

Arthurs offered nothing more, and Harry let it drop—for now. As they returned to the *Patterson* through choppy waters, he observed Arthurs fidgeting with something around his neck. A gold chain with a nugget.

Harry hadn't noticed it before. He doubted it was new, but Arthurs kept tugging at it as if he weren't used to wearing it.

Shifting his gaze, he studied Davenport, who sat deep in thought, a frown creasing his face. Harry was glad Dorn controlled the money. Watching the two paymasters, he came to an unsettling conclusion—he didn't trust either of them.

Chapter Fourteen - Beale

Anchored in Holkham Bay during relentless rain, Mansfield joined officers in the pilot house one morning. Ensigns Beecher and Slocum were with Lieutenant Dorn and Harry, sipping coffee. The dreary weather cast a somber mood over the ship, though the gray-white morning mist drifting along the mountainside provided an eerie beauty. The flickering lights in the pilot house offered a small reprieve from the darkness.

"Gentlemen, it is August 22. We have a four-week window of opportunity before us. After that, the storms will pick up, and snow will reach sea level. I, for one, don't want to be marooned by an early-season winter storm."

The men around the table nodded, murmuring in agreement.

"I suggest we focus on three areas: first, completing the monument stations currently underway. Second, shoreline and depth measurements in the two fjords to our east. Third, there are tidal measurements in those fjords as well. Finishing the season by charting these two bodies would be a trophy for us all. I realize this is still a great deal to accomplish, but we must do as much as possible. Lieutenant Dorn, can you brief us on the details?"

"Yes, sir. Two days ago, we cleared the area for the baseline monuments on Tiedeman Island—signals Sick and Snap. Cab and Coach start next week. Yesterday, we returned to signals Brew and Trap to re-whitewash the wood for better visibility. Monument towers are built at Fizz and Clear. Tomorrow, we'll set up the theodolite for Ensign Wood to start astronomical observations this week. That leaves the construction of Clot and Dust, which should be completed toward the end of our four-week window."

"I'm heading out today for tidal observations," Beecher interjected. "Mr. Ford, would you like to join me? We can continue with your training."

Harry, eager to get off the ship and do physical labor, accepted the invitation. With the meeting concluded, the men dispersed to their respective duties.

He met Beecher while loading the gig, one of the smaller launches, usually rowed but equipped with a short mast for favorable wind conditions.

"Need a hand?" Harry asked, stepping in.

"I've got it. Oh, can you tie down that gauge?"

They set off to take tidal measurements south of the *Patterson's* position. The gig, slower than the other launches, took an hour to reach the designated location.

"We'll start here," Beecher said, pointing to a tide staff offshore—a white post with red lines and numbers standing five feet out of the water. Dropping anchor, he added, "What time is it?"

Harry pulled out his pocket chronometer.

"I assume you calibrated your chronometer with the ship's before we left?" Beecher asked.

"Yes, this morning."

"Good. What's the time?"

"Three minutes to ten o'clock, precisely."

"Tell me when it's exactly ten."

There was a pause, and then Harry said, "Now. Ten o'clock."

Beecher jotted down the time and the water height in a small notebook. "We'll take measurements every fifteen minutes for the next two hours. Then, I want to install that gauge farther north, up around that point," he said, motioning toward a rocky beach.

They sat bobbing in the water, passing the time between readings. Beecher, well-practiced in waiting for the quarter-hour increments, pulled a fishing line with a lead weight from his pocket. Then, from a small tin, he retrieved a herring, threaded it onto the hook, and dropped the bait to the bottom. Pulling it up two feet, he leaned back and waited.

Within ten minutes, he was hauling in a twenty-five-pound halibut. Reaching for a mallet kept for such occasions, he struck the flat fish on the head between its wide-set eyes, killing it before it could thrash about.

"Alright! Halibut!" Beecher cheered. Then, remembering their task, he asked, "What time is it?"

"Ten twelve. Three more minutes."

Beecher ran a rope through the fish's mouth and dropped it back into the water to keep it fresh. "The cook will like that," he remarked.

"Ten fifteen," Harry called out. Beecher logged the reading.

With the next check still fifteen minutes away, they opened the crate containing the gauge for installation. Metal tubes lay on the boat's floor.

"This is our new system," Beecher said, lifting one of the tubes. "With these, we won't need to come out and manually record readings; they'll do it for us. The tube houses the gauge, protecting it from the tide's movement, and the gauge is connected to this rod to record the heights."

Harry was examining the equipment when a sudden boom interrupted them—the ship's cannon.

All boats were being recalled to the *Patterson*.

They couldn't see the *Patterson*, obscured behind a spit of land, but as they stowed their gear, they spotted the other launches hurrying back. What struck Harry as odd was the *Pirate* speeding north—away from the *Patterson*.

They rowed back as fast as they could, though they still arrived second to last, with only the whaleboat trailing behind.

Once aboard, they quickly learned why they had been summoned.

In the wardroom, Paymaster Beale sat pale and shaken, gripping a glass of water. A blood-soaked bandage wrapped his head, and dried blood streaked his ashen face. Mansfield, Dorn, Dr. Percy, and the ensigns gathered around him.

"What happened?"

"Davenport assaulted Beale," Dorn replied grimly.

"Davenport? Why?"

"Theft. He's been stealing from the Survey."

Mansfield turned to Harry. "Form a search party and leave for Juneau. You are to locate and arrest Davenport and Arthurs for battery and theft of the launch."

"Arthurs, too?"

"Yes," Dorn confirmed. "He was there during the assault, and they left together."

Harry frowned. "What were they stealing?"

"I was looking into the books," Beale said, his voice unsteady. "I had a suspicion that Davenport was up to something. I thought he was skimming from the pay account. It turns out an extra twenty dollars went missing from each pay. So, I asked them to come to the office so I could show them the books, and the next thing I know, Davenport sucker-punches me, knocking me to the ground. He started kicking my head." He reached up, touching his bandages gingerly.

"The cuts aren't deep, and they should heal soon," Dr. Percy assured him. "I'll make sure he doesn't have a concussion or any internal bleeding, but otherwise, he'll be fine."

"Lieutenant Dorn," Mansfield said, "take a full inventory of the ship's stores and double-check the accounting ledger. Let's find out exactly what's missing."

"They're stealing salt," Harry interjected. "While I was in Juneau, I saw Arthurs handing something to the locals. It was salt. There is also a barrel of salt missing. And there was salt on the floor of the launch as well. Rather than call it salt, they refer to it as 'rare fish.'"

Beale was sent to the sick bay for observation, which concluded the briefing. As the officers dispersed, Harry stopped Foust in the passageway.

"Could Beale be involved in this as well? The injury could be a cover."

"I don't know. Maybe," Foust admitted. "He and Davenport have been working together for a couple of years now."

As they discussed their concerns, a commotion erupted from the deck above. They rushed to investigate.

Reaching the rail, they saw the whaleboat tied up alongside the ship. A soaked figure, wrapped in a blanket, stood shivering as crew members helped him aboard. At first, Harry assumed it was a sounder who had fallen overboard while retrieving the weights. Then, he got a better look.

"Arthurs?"

Almy stepped forward. "We found him floundering in the water as we turned back toward the ship after the cannon signal. We saw the *Pirate* speeding toward Juneau, and then—just by chance—we saw a figure fall overboard. If we hadn't been looking at that exact moment, we would have missed him completely. We went over and pulled him out. He claims Davenport pushed him."

Mansfield stepped in. "Lad, I must warn you—you are in serious trouble. It would be in your best interest to cooperate. Otherwise, very unpleasant things will come your way. Do you understand?"

"Yes, sir."

"You need to get out of those wet clothes. Dr. Percy, take him to sick bay."

"Thank you, sir."

Dr. Percy led the shivering assistant paymaster below deck. Mansfield, Dorn, Harry, and Almy followed, arriving at sick bay as Arthurs, now in dry clothes, cradled a steaming cup of coffee in both hands.

"We have some questions for you," Mansfield said. "Start by explaining what happened."

"I didn't think he would hurt anyone. I didn't know he was going to hit Beale. But when Beale confronted him with the missing money,

107

Davenport lost it—he flew into a rage. He might have killed him if I hadn't pulled him back."

"Is he stealing money from the pay account?" Mansfield asked.

"He is. Davenport is. I found out right after we shipped out, but he convinced me to keep quiet."

"How did he do that? How much was he giving you?"

"Five dollars."

"And how much was he keeping for himself?"

"Fifteen."

Harry leaned forward. "What do you know about the salt barrels? I saw you selling a box of it in Juneau."

Arthurs groaned, shaking his head. "I should have walked away when I found out about the salt. Davenport assured me we wouldn't get caught because Beale never double-checked the numbers. I went along with it; the extra five dollars was helpful. Then it was the salt. He produced this elaborate scheme to sell it at discounted prices to the natives. I thought he had stolen a pound or two, but then he showed me where he'd hidden an entire barrel. And yesterday, he said he had another plan. I didn't say anything. I should have—before it got to this point."

"What plan?" Mansfield pressed.

"He got greedy. He figured if he could steal salt without getting caught, he could steal other things."

"Like what?"

"Rum. He hid the rum and salt barrels in the hold by stacking them among the garbage, so they'd blend in. He made me help move them last night to the deck, rolling them along their edges."

"That's where they were, with the garbage!" Harry exclaimed. "I couldn't find them."

"He planned to sell rum and salt to the natives," Arthurs admitted.

Mansfield's face darkened. "This is outrageous."

"But sir, you haven't heard the worst of it," Arthurs continued. "As we were loading the barrels into the launch, we got word that Beale wanted to see us. We went to his office, and he confronted Davenport with the missing pay funds. Davenport snapped—knocked him down and started kicking him in the head, knocking him unconscious. Then, while Beale was out cold, he opened the safe and took $5,000 in cash. He pulled a revolver from his waist and aimed it at me, threatening to shoot if I didn't help him. He forced me to help him load those heavy salt and rum barrels onto the *Pirate*.

Mansfield's expression hardened. "$5,000 in cash. He took the cash from the gold certificate."

The room fell silent as they absorbed the weight of the theft. Harry felt a tight knot in his stomach.

Mansfield turned back to Arthurs. "How did you end up in the water?"

"Davenport pushed me."

"Why?"

"I told him I wanted out when we reached Juneau—I was done with his stealing," Arthurs said. "He tricked me. Said a launch was coming up from behind us and told me to turn around. The second I did, he shoved me overboard. If you hadn't picked me up, I would have drowned."

Harry clenched his jaw. "I should have stopped him."

Mansfield turned to him. "Could you have?"

"I suspected he had stolen the salt, but I couldn't prove it. I was watching to see his next move, but I never imagined this."

Dorn placed a hand on Harry's shoulder. "None of us did, mate. We all bear responsibility for what happens—no one man is to blame."

Mansfield took a deep breath. "Lieutenant Dorn, I appreciate your willingness to share in this, but I assume full responsibility for anything lost on this ship. Harry, as I said—take some men and find this man. He must face military justice."

Harry nodded. "Commander, Arthurs said Davenport threatened to kill him if he didn't comply. This man has battered a superior officer, stolen a ship's boat, and taken $5,000 in cash. We know he's armed. As mild-mannered as he was on the ship, from this point forward, we must consider him dangerous. We should each carry arms and be authorized to shoot if necessary."

Mansfield didn't hesitate. "Agreed, Mr. Ford. Try to take him alive, but given the money and rum he has, that may not be possible. Good luck, gentlemen. Find Davenport—and retrieve our launch." He turned to Arthurs. "Take him to the brig. Full rations. We'll deal with him later."

The disgraced paymaster lowered his head as the guards led him away.

Chapter Fifteen - Juneau

Preparations to capture Davenport began that evening. Dorn, McDonald, Almy, and Ellingson joined Harry in the search party. Each gathered a three-day supply of clothes and food in a duffle bag. They holstered revolvers, outfitted five rifles in the *Vixen*, and stowed extra wood for possible extended travel.

They departed north into Stephens Passage early the following morning. The rain and a strengthening northwest wind had come down hard since midnight. Once in the passage, three- to four-foot waves and a strong headwind slowed them to five knots. The Taku Inlet crossing proved a formidable challenge. High waves, combined with the tide flowing from the inlet and the Taku River, churned the water, tossing the *Vixen* about and scrambling the men to hold on tighter. Once past the inlet, they entered the calm Gastineau Channel, named for an English surveyor. The channel continued north past Juneau until it reconnected with Stephens Passage at the island's northern end.

Their first stop was Sheep Creek, a mining camp eight miles south of Juneau. The mine was on the mountainside, but the townsite sat near the shoreline. Tree stumps dotted the hillside around the cluster of a dozen wooden cabins.

As the *Vixen* approached, the men scanned the camp for Davenport. The *Pirate* was not among the boats moored there. Harry took the rowboat ashore with Dorn and McDonald while Almy and Ellingson stayed behind with the *Vixen*. The town had one store, so they headed in that direction, scanning the townspeople as they walked. Most were miners and paid no attention to the men. After speaking with the men in the camp, it became clear that no one had seen Davenport. They concluded there was no need to climb the hill to the mine site to double-check. That could be an option later if their search continued to turn up empty.

Back on the launch, they headed north for the short trip to Juneau. The rain continued unabated, storm clouds obscuring the summer meadows of Mt. Roberts. Mt. Juneau's peak was obscured, but the cascading streams showed heavy rainfall. Mists floated below the cloud layer.

Dorn maneuvered the craft through the harbor to search for the stolen launch. Seeing no sign of it, they turned around and docked. They walked up the floating platform to the loading areas and surveyed the town of Juneau rising from the shore. Now nineteen years old, Harry felt a strange sense of destiny tied to this place, as if important things were to happen here beyond the wealth of gold.

They split up, with Ellingson staying behind to tend the *Vixen*. The town had grown to about twelve hundred people. Another four hundred or so lived across the channel in Douglas, and a significant Tlingit population of about three hundred and fifty resided ten miles north in Auke Bay. The men walked up and down the steep streets, from Second to Sixth Street at the top of town to Gold and Harris Streets bordering the city on Starr Hill. No one they spoke with had seen Davenport.

Two hours later, they reunited with no new leads. Deciding that a trip up Gold Creek might be worthwhile, they hiked into the narrow canyon separating Mt. Juneau from Mt. Roberts. They often crisscrossed the creek bed, which also served as the path. Thistle-laden Devil's Club scratched their hands when they brushed against it. As they neared the mining operations at the head of the canyon, a gaping hole in the earth began to emerge on their right. The pit was over a hundred feet deep, formed by earth being washed away through sluicing. Locals called it the Glory Hole, given the amount of gold extracted from it.

Five dirty men were operating the sluice guns, but none had seen Davenport. Reluctantly, they followed the flowing trail back to town. The rain and lack of information on Davenport soured the men's morale. Pulling Ellingson from *Vixen* watch duty, they checked into the Alaska Hotel. After changing into dry clothes, they gathered at a restaurant a few buildings up Franklin Street to eat and reassess their situation.

"I hate the rain. I hate this much rain every day," said Almy, slinging his wet outer gear onto a wall peg while the others did the same. "Juneau is the worst. Or Haines. I don't know—the whole area. I'd rather be in Sitka right now. Or Gustavus. Anywhere but here."

"I find it refreshing," said McDonald. "My parents settled along the Oregon Trail in eastern Oregon. Have any of you ever been to eastern Oregon?" None of the others had. "It's very dry, desert-like. Months can go by without any rain."

Almy wasn't impressed. "Like birds that want to be in the air or fish that want to be in the sea, we each have a place that suits us. Mine isn't a northern rainforest. Maybe a rainforest in Mexico, where it's warm and doesn't snow."

"I love it," Harry echoed. "Didn't you notice the waterfalls cascading down Mt. Juneau? Beautiful. That's a four-thousand-foot drop! And the smell—ancient forest scents, that rich, earthy aroma."

"That's grease from the kitchen," joked Ellingson.

Harry ignored him. "And what about the streams, the creeks? The clearest, freshest water ever, with so many salmon swimming upstream you could walk across on their backs. Gold. Timber. Fish. Berries. This place is like a Garden of Eden."

"You wouldn't last two years up here," countered Almy. "You'd be begging to go back to civilization, rain, or no rain. Eden? You'd find this place hell."

"I could live here the rest of my life, leave the rest of the country behind. I love my work with the agency, but it's not just what you do—it's where you do it. Juneau is going to grow into a big town someday. I could live here."

Dorn agreed with Almy. "Harry, it can be overwhelming. I feel it. The constant pounding on the roof, the dripping. Everything is always wet. You can never start a fire when you need one."

"Some people can manage it, some can't," Harry countered. "If you hate the rain, you won't be happy. It'll drive you crazy. You must love the rain—to challenge it, to appreciate it. People come up here with the wrong clothes, cotton instead of wool, and then wonder why they're cold. You must have the right gear to thrive here, as well as the right mindset. Let the rain wash over you. Be like a duck."

"I'll bet if you asked the people living here whether they like it, most would say they don't," said Dorn. "They're only putting up with it for gold, salmon, or Sitka spruce—whatever brought them here in the first place. Once the gold or timber runs out, this town is dead. No one will be here to be born or buried."

113

"I disagree. What's to stop this town from growing? Okay, it can't go up the mountainside, but there's open space north in Gastineau Channel, up Lemon Creek. Even Mendenhall Valley could be a townsite someday. Rain won't stop this area from growing. And it won't stop the babies that will be born here."

Table service interrupted the conversation, and they gave the server their orders. Dorn changed the subject, much to Harry's relief.

"Gentlemen, we need to find Davenport. Ideas?"

"Could be anywhere," Almy started.

"Yes, but he must go somewhere. Did he know anyone here?"

"I have an idea where he might be." Ellingson leaned forward as the server brought the food. "A few years back, I was here in Juneau. You think it's wild now—you should have seen it then."

He paused, reflecting on the time. "It was uncivilized." Murder, theft, assault—no law. It's not as bad today, but it's still bad. But murderers and thieves have one thing in common: they are predictable. And I have a hunch where our Davenport is. In fact, one could look back on it as a tradition. Commit a major crime, go upriver to The Hideout."

"The Hideout? Is that a joke? Who would escape to a place called The Hideout?" snickered Dorn.

Ellingson smiled. "Too obvious, isn't it? But have you ever tried to go up the Mendenhall River?"

"No," Dorn admitted.

"Well, I'll show you why it's called The Hideout tomorrow."

They gathered in the lobby the following morning and walked to the restaurant for a late brunch. The rain had soured everyone's demeanor, and no one was in a hurry to go out hunting Davenport. After noon, they had no choice but to board the *Vixen* and proceed north through the Gastineau Channel into Lynn Canal. Rain fell constantly, but the tide was creating a problem.

114

As they neared the mouth of the Mendenhall, the tide was ebbing, but the river flowed strongly from the summer melting of the glacier upstream. The wind blew from the west, creating waves that pushed against the left side of the launch, forcing it near the flat, sandy river outlet to their right. Icy water soaked their clothes and boots. By the time they arrived late in the afternoon, they realized it was best to pull back from shore and anchor farther away from the mouth of the river. They had little desire to go upstream until the tide turned and their clothes dried.

First thing in the morning, Harry and Dorn set out in the rowboat for more wood. Pulling the rowboat onto the beach, they immediately saw the tall beach grass bent down and flattened in a twenty-square-foot area.

"Grizzly bear. They've been sleeping on the matted grass. Mr. Ford let's get our wood and begone. You hold the rifle, and I'll buck up this log. We don't need a lot." The woodcut was anxious but uneventful, and they returned to the *Vixen* with a small load of tree rounds.

The crew stowed their gear and brought the *Vixen's* firebox to life. They wanted an early morning departure, as the glacier's melt flowing downstream would be at its lowest due to the chilly night. Fortunately, the flood tide was near high tide, providing enough draft so they didn't bottom out as they started up the glacial-silted river. The launch struggled in the current. Only fifty yards upstream from the mouth, it was evident the *Vixen* wouldn't make it far upriver.

The men did their best to gain traction in the current, even throwing empty crates and old ropes overboard to lighten the boat. Lieutenant Dorn was at the helm, struggling with the rudder. Minutes passed with truly little distance gained.

"Lieutenant, we need to turn around. We can't make it against this current," yelled Almy, trying to be heard above the engine and the river noise pounding against the launch's bow.

Dorn hesitated, realizing what it would take to turn the *Vixen* around.

"Let's go a little longer. She is gaining a little now—let's see what it takes to make it to the bend up ahead."

The steam engine billowed smoke as they stoked the fire to keep it at peak performance. Tree falls dotted the river, their massive roots blocking the water, creating whirlpools, and shifting the sand.

"Lieutenant, we need to go back." Ellingson, Almy, and McDonald had joined Harry in trying to convince Dorn it was time to turn around.

Dorn hesitated again, knowing they could capsize while turning in the middle of the river. To their left was a log jam, and to their right was the deepest, fastest part of the channel. There was no safe place to turn.

He pushed the engine for all the power possible. After what seemed like an eternity, they made it far enough upstream to pass the jam, finally reaching a spot where a turn was possible. A downed tree lay ahead in their path, forcing Dorn's hand. He turned as sharply as possible to port.

Immediately, the current caught the keel and pushed the launch perpendicular to the flow. They were out of control, drifting sideways toward the jam they had just passed.

"Power! I need power!" Dorn shouted as he tried to nudge the bow farther downstream. He pounded on the helm as the Mendenhall carried the small boat downriver sideways.

Terrified, Harry saw the mass of trees out of the corner of his eye and realized the danger they were in. He screamed as loud as he could. "Move to the bow! Move to the bow!"

The three men instantly shifted forward, redistributing nearly seven hundred pounds. Before they were pinned against the jam, the extra weight forward changed the dynamics, and the Vixen motored past it, only bumping a small tree limb sticking out as they went by.

Drifting out of the river's mouth, the men sat in stunned silence, realizing how close they had come to drowning—how easily their bodies could have been swept out to sea, never found.

Chapter Sixteen - Man Overboard

They arrived back at the *Patterson* hours later to clean up and regroup. Mansfield called for a briefing in the wardroom, and soon, the room filled to standing-room-only capacity.

"Davenport was nowhere to be found," Dorn reported. "We didn't find the launch, either. We talked to a lot of people, but nobody acknowledged him, or they don't want to be involved."

Up until now, Mansfield had assumed they would find and apprehend Davenport. Now, he wasn't so sure, and everyone sensed his frustration.

"What are we missing?" Mansfield pondered aloud.

"Sir, we should talk to Arthurs and Beale. There wasn't time to interrogate them before we left. Arthurs was still in wet clothes," Harry said.

"Ellingson, bring them down here, but one at a time—starting with Beale." Mansfield looked solemnly at the men in the room as Ellingson exited.

"I haven't filed my report yet. I don't want to report that $5,000 was stolen during my shift. That would require involvement in reviews that I don't want to go through. We need to find that money, the rum, the salt, and the launch, too. They can be missing for a short while—borrowed, if you will—if we find it all and get it back."

Ellingson knocked and entered, followed by Beale.

"Beale, do you know where Davenport might have gone? Did he ever tell you about any places he'd go to?" Harry asked.

"No."

Since the attack, Beale had become noticeably quiet, almost sullen. Dr. Percy had concluded he didn't suffer a concussion and had no internal bleeding. Regardless, he seemed out of sorts to everyone—bordering on uncooperative.

"Nothing? He said nothing to you. You worked with him every day, in close quarters. What did you talk about all day?" asked an exasperated Harry.

"Nothing."

The absent look on Beale's face told Harry they were wasting their time.

"Ellingson, bring in Arthurs."

Released from his irons, Arthurs, hands tied together, and his face drawn into a sad, despairing look, entered the room.

"Not your best day, is it?" asked McDonald.

Arthurs looked glumly—even remorsefully—at the floor.

"I want to help you," said Harry. His sincerity seemed evident, and Arthurs perked up a little. "Your situation may not be as gloomy as you think. If you can provide us with information on where Davenport is, and we find him, I'm sure the lieutenant will consider your cooperation when reporting what happened."

"But I don't know where he went. He didn't tell me."

"Think back. In your cabin, while working, did he mention going anywhere? Any friends or family he might go to?"

"No, none that I can think of," Arthurs said.

"Did he mention any places he would go? Any towns?" asked Mansfield.

"No, no one I can remember."

Mansfield's question triggered Harry's memory.

"When we went to Juneau, I saw Arthurs selling the salt in packages labeled rare fish."

"Rare fish?" Mansfield and Slocum said in unison. "Why would he be selling rare fish?"

"He's not. He's selling our salt. That's how they cover it up. The topic of salt is rarely discussed; instead, rare fish is used as a form of code.

"As an agency, we pull strange sea creatures from the water and send them back to Washington for cataloging. It's something we do—nobody would think twice about it," confirmed Almy.

"That's not the point. I asked the man where to get rare fish, and he said Hoonah. I'll bet Davenport is hiding there. Let's leave first thing tomorrow."

"Damn it!" Mansfield shouted. "How are we supposed to get anything done? It's late August, and we're wasting time trying to catch a criminal. Yes, search Hoonah. But before you go, ensure things are going okay in the drafting room. Check on your team and ensure progress is being made.

Mansfield seemed angry, and Harry felt uncomfortable, as if the lieutenant were blaming him for Davenport's criminality and the lack of survey progress.

He went to the drafting room to review what his fellow technicians had accomplished. As expected, he found them working. J.D. Smith and Liam Sandford were first-year apprentices, and he appreciated their enthusiasm for studying hydrological work as much as—if not more than—the technical skills they assisted him with.

The room was well-lit for the tedious drawing, and the gas lamps gave off enough heat to warm it. McDonald's blue logbook for Signal Blunt lay on the table while Sandford studied the data inside.

"Gentlemen," Harry announced, entering the room, "I'm glad to see you two again. I apologize for my absence."

Smith and Sandford appreciated Harry's guidance and mentoring and respected his role as a Master at Arms on the ship. They also liked the freedom they had to manage the drafting program while he was off doing officer duties.

"Mr. Ford, it's okay. We know you have other responsibilities. Have you found Davenport yet?" asked Smith.

"No, but I think he may be in Hoonah. Unfortunately, I'll be leaving tomorrow to go there again. Can you two continue…?"

"We've got it, sir," Smith said. "You do what you need to do."

"Lieutenant Mansfield is feeling stress and ensuring him that our chart activity continues as planned may help relieve his anxiety. Now, tell me what you are doing. Where are you?"

The three men huddled around the table while Sandford began explaining their work.

"Here is the base data. Soundings are on this page. And here is the chart I'm drafting. Known obstacles are shown here and here." Sandford pointed to both numbers in the blue logbook and locations on the chart, and Harry tracked the numbers as well. "The shoreline needs more detail here and here. The depth contours in this area require revision. We went off scale somehow when we did our calculations," he said.

"Easy to do. I've made that mistake." He picked up the calipers and measured lines on Sandford's base map. "Have you been calibrating the instruments daily?" he asked.

"Yes, first thing each morning," Smith claimed.

He put the calipers down and chose one of the pens on the table. Moving his finger along the chart, he carefully wrote "Slocum's Inlet" on an area south of the Taku River, placing an X on the spot.

"For Ensign Slocum, is it, Mr. Ford? asked Smith.

"It was named after George last year. It's a small inlet, partially protected. He was out on one of the launches and fell overboard. Commander Thomas named it for him," Harry explained.

"How does that work? How does the Commander name geographical features? By what authority does he have?" asked Sandford.

"By virtue of his rank and the fact that no one else has named the place yet. Our job is to be the first to chart the coastline of Alaska. How do you do that if you can't name locations?"

120

Sanford didn't seem convinced. "But it seems so arbitrary. Someone falls into the water, and they have the place named after them. Big deal."

"Rumor has it that President Harrison is going to change things," said Harry. "I've heard he is establishing a board—a geographical naming board. They will have the right to accept or reject names, so if Mansfield were to name those shoals 'Killer Reef,' for example, the board could overturn it."

"What a great way to be immortalized," said Sandford. "Have it put on a map. It will be there forever."

The three men continued discussing the charts they needed and the required data for those charts. They agreed that with Harry gone much of the time, the remaining few weeks were critical in keeping up with the planned work program. They discussed this for over an hour when Dorn burst into the room carrying the accounting ledger.

"Harry, excuse me. I want you to look at this," Dorn said, plopping the book down. "Mansfield asked me to check supplies against the ledger." He pointed to a line-item titled *Payment for Services*. "Do you have any idea what that means?"

"I don't know. I don't do the books," said a bewildered Master at Arms.

"Neither does anybody else, only the paymasters. But look, all the other contracts and vendors are listed by name. This has 'Payment for Services' but no name. Now look at this." His finger pointed to $15. Beside that were initials: *GB*. "What do you think GB means?" asked Dorn.

"I don't know. Glass and bottles. They are an expense," shrugged Harry.

"Okay, yes, it could be glass and bottles. Or George Beale. I went back to check this date each of the preceding six months, and the entry was the same: same amount and same initials at the end."

"Maybe he was paying for some things out of pocket and reimbursed himself?" Harry asked.

"I thought of that, too," confessed Dorn. "So, a couple of days ago, I went to see him and asked about the entries and what they were for."

"What did he say?" Harry asked.

"Nothing at first. I could tell he was nervous. He assured me that the entry was for 'General Breakage,' a slush fund for accidents if you will. He paid for replacement items, and this was his reimbursement."

Stanford chuckled, "I didn't know we broke that much."

"Agreed," said Dorn. "I asked him why the same amount each month— how could it add up to the same amount every time? He promised to provide me with the receipts, assuring me everything was correct and legitimate. As he sat there, sweat formed on his forehead, and he was visibly shaking. I doubt he has any receipts to provide."

"So that's why Beale's been so quiet. He's been caught stealing. I'll bet he's involved with the missing salt, too," said Harry.

"How corrupt are these paymasters?" asked Smith.

Before anyone could respond, the ship's alarm bells sounded, and all four men hurried to the main deck.

A crowd had formed and was looking at a figure standing—or rather, stumbling—with his back against the aft rail. It was Beale, holding a revolver in his right hand and a rum bottle in his left. Splashing the brown liquid as he flailed his arm about, the gun cocked and ready to fire. The crew withdrew, realizing he could accidentally fire a shot at any moment. The paymaster was drunk—very drunk—and with a weapon in his hand after being caught stealing, he was also extremely dangerous.

Rather than watch where Beale was pointing the gun, Harry looked instead at a rope tied to Beale's right leg above the boot. Following the rope with his eyes, he saw it run from Beale's leg along the deck and up to the rail. He followed the rope to see it tied to a small barrel of nails sitting precariously balanced on the rail, held only by Beale's elbow resting on it. He watched as the heavyset paymaster shifted his body and lifted his left leg to straddle the rail. The barrel of nails wedged between his crotch, both man and barrel teetered over the choppy water.

Mansfield called out, "Paymaster Beale. Put the gun down and come off there. We aren't going to hurt you, but you need to get down from there.

We can help you." He turned to Almy and ordered him to prepare a launch.

Beale said nothing but took another slug of rum from the bottle and threw it toward the crew. Slurring his words, he yelled, "You caught me. I'm guilty. But you're not taking me off the sea and putting me in a cell. No way. This is where I belong."

He leaned to his left, bear-hugging the heavy nail barrel. With a blank look at the men on deck, he dropped into the dark water, clutching the gun and weight meant to take him to the bottom.

At once, everyone yelled, "Man overboard!" Those trained for such an occasion ran to their stations while other crew members threw life rings and ropes in the vicinity of Beale's splash.

Almy was still preparing the launch when Beale went in, and it would be several more minutes before he could move to Beale's approximate location, finally circling for any sign of the man. The *Patterson* stood in two hundred feet of icy water. Hypothermia only takes minutes to begin seizing the body in cramps, and that's without a barrel of nails tied to the leg. It had now been fifteen minutes.

"He's gone," Mansfield said to the men still on deck. "He's gone down to the deep."

Harry was stunned. He had witnessed his first suicide. The suddenness was almost surreal. One moment, Beale was alive; the next, he wasn't. He sat down to fathom how suddenly the paymaster's life had ended. He always assumed he would die slowly, giving him time to reflect on his life and say goodbyes. The thought of an immediate death scared him. The idea of suicide baffled him.

"Mr. Ford, are you okay?" Mansfield sat down beside him.

"I've never seen..."

"Don't think about it. It's a tragedy. We need to move on and do our jobs, work the survey. There was not enough time or anything we could have done to stop him. He surprised us."

Mansfield patted him on the shoulder and left him alone. Harry pondered what would make a man consider suicide. How significant must something be in a person's mind to convince them to end their life? Or is it a fear of something? Was his mind sick, like those who are mentally ill? The fear of watching other people die, loved ones passing on, perhaps? Or was it an escape, the ability to avoid accountability? Alcohol makes people do things they wouldn't do otherwise; it was that. He wasn't sure, nor could he make any sense of it. He wondered what God thought when men decided to take their own lives. He sat there for some time before going to bed that night.

Chapter Seventeen - Hoonah

Almy and McDonald had other duties, so Strickland and Slocum made the trip to Hoonah to search for Davenport along with Harry, Dorn and Ellingson. From where they anchored in Holkham Bay, the best route would be north up Stephens Passage, making a sharp turn to the south after passing the northern tip of the peninsula that would later bear Lt. Henry Mansfield's name. They veered west into Icy Strait and headed toward Hoonah on the northeast side of Chichagof Island.

The *Pirate* was still missing with Davenport, and Ensign Wood was near Ketchikan on the *Vixen*, trying to find a large piece of copper to fix one of the *Patterson's* boilers. Hence, the civilian-clothed Davenport hunters loaded the *Cosmos* for the trip to Hoonah. Fitting themselves with three days of rations, clothing, rifles, and revolvers, the men clamored into the launch. The sky was overcast, but it had stopped raining. A light southwest breeze would catch their backs as they traveled.

They sped along the east side of Stephens Passage until they reached the divide separating the Strait and Gastineau Channel. Opting not to go by way of Juneau, they steered through Admiralty and Douglas Islands. Inside this narrow passageway, both the water and the wind were calm. A parting of the clouds allowed a brief view of blue. Dorn throttled back the engine and reduced speed a little, providing a smoother and quieter ride.

Dorn took the opportunity to ask, "So, Hoonah. What are we getting into?"

All heads turned to Strickland.

"It's interesting when you think about it, why this place is here," Strickland began, pipe hanging from between his yellow teeth. "From what I understand, they are known as Xona Kwaan, From the *Direction of the Northwind*. Generations ago, Tlingit clans used to live further north of here, in the huge bay with all the glaciers. The cold and ice became too much to endure, even for them. The glaciers advanced and drove them out; the refugees came to this location to settle down. Because of this loose affiliation, they don't take the clan structure as rigidly here as in a place like

Angoon. They see themselves as related but don't emphasize common descent. Last I heard about five hundred people live here year-round, while more come and go seasonally."

"What's their attitude toward white people, the Navy?" asked Dorn.

"Skeptical at best, not likely hostile. I'd be more afraid of whites myself. The Northwest Trading Company has a post in town. Lots of illegal activity. If any white man is around, it's a safe bet he's up to no good."

"Okay, here's our search strategy to find him," said Dorn. "We cruise the harbor and look for the launch, then we search the town. Strickland, explain the layout of this place and where we'd want to look for him."

"We will be mooring off Front Street; it has all the bars. Start there. If he's not there, I'd go to the Presbyterian Mission. They provide free food, clothing, and shelter, a place for drunks to sleep it off. And if he's not there, you'll need to check the trading post. He might be conducting business."

"Ellingson, stay with the *Cosmos*. Remember everybody, be humble and show respect, but be prepared to defend," said Dorn.

Arriving mid-afternoon, they checked the harbor but did not find the *Pirate*. Several steam launches anchored offshore, but not the *Patterson's*.

"Well, he may be elsewhere or even sunk it to hide the evidence. We need to check the town. I'll take Front Street and the bars. Harry, you scout the mission. Slocum, the trading post. Strickland, check around the docks. Don't let them know you are with the Patterson."

The men blended in as best as they could, acting like longtime locals. Once on Front Street, they set off in their respective directions, Dorn continuing past three native men lying drunk on the sidewalk. Dorn thought of the directive to interdict alcohol and could see why. Alcohol devastated native communities, and even though he disagreed with the way the government treated natives, they were right to try to stop alcohol. Stopping in each bar, he asked the bartenders if they had seen Davenport or had heard of a barrel of rum for sale. Not one had, so he returned to the launch to wait with Ellingson and Strickland.

Harry proceeded to the Presbyterian Mission. Both men and women were about, wrapped in colorful blankets adorned with clan symbols. They were waiting for the evening meal. Three white men loitered about the mission, but not Davenport. He entered the shelter and scanned the cots to see if Davenport might be napping. Not finding him, he too returned to the *Cosmos* as Strickland was returning too.

Slocum went to the Northwest Trading Post off 2nd Street and stood across the way, monitoring the steady flow of white and native people entering and leaving the store. Other men, natives, hung by the door entrance, one man staring back at Slocum.

After fifteen minutes, he walked across the street and followed three women inside. It was dark, smoky, and smelly. He watched two clerks banter, barter, and cajole their patrons as they exchanged goods. He saw salt sold but couldn't tell if it was from the *Patterson*. Easing his way out the door and into the sunlight, the native man watching him earlier confronted him as he exited.

"What do you want?" Slocum asked as the large man blocked his exit.

"Are you looking for rare fish?"

Dorn was confused by the question, but then he remembered hearing the phrase at Harry's briefing.

"Yes, I'm looking for rare fish."

The native man stared at him before turning to his companions. After a brief conversation, where they each pointed to Slocum, the man who first confronted Slocum said,

"We have no rare fish to sell you."

"But you said..."

"What are you here for?"

"Well, a barrel of rum? A steam launch? One of our sailors."

Again, the man turned to his companions and conversed in Tlingit. His gaze softened, and he said,

127

"The white man is a liar. He steals and murders. He has cheated us for years. Then he brings white man's rum to our villages. You can see what happens; look—our people lie drunk in the street, thanks to white men like you."

Slocum didn't know how to respond but was glad he carried his revolver.

"I'm not here to sell rum; I'm here to find rum and take it from here. One of our men stole it, and we want it back."

Weighing Slocum's answer, the native man said,

"You are searching for a white man who stole salt, rum, and a boat from you?"

"Yes, yes, I am."

"The man you seek sells rum to my people at high prices. We don't want him around. I will help you find him because he brings much trouble."

Slocum felt relieved. "We, I, would be very grateful."

The native remained silent, gazing into Slocum's face as if reading his mind.

"He left here for the springs. Do you know where they are?"

"Yes. South of here?"

"Yes. Look in the forest west of the springs. There is an animal trail. It leads up the hillside. Two miles up the trail is a camp. The man you seek is there."

"How do you know this?"

"Alcohol makes a man talk, does it not?"

Thanking him, Dorn returned to the *Cosmos*.

"The springs!" he shouted as he approached. "I know where he is!"

As the men discussed their approach before departure, the late August afternoon sky morphed into the evening. The weather was balmy, the skies

128

clear, and the water in Chatham Strait was still. They recognized an opportunity to strike. Heading out of Hoonah into Icy Strait and then south into Chatham Strait, the waning gibbous moon provided enough light with the twilight to enable their navigation. In no time, they rounded the spit separating Freshwater Bay and entered the unnamed inlet.

Passing the opening, they killed the engines and put up the sails. Finding the springs in the moonlight would be difficult at best, but at least Harry, Strickland, and Ellingson had been there not long before. Passing where they thought it should be, Slocum finally spotted steam rising above the tide.

"Anchor here," Dorn said, and they lowered the anchors without a splash. The rowboat carried them to shore, and they stopped to decide on their next steps.

"The native said west of the springs was an animal trail. Follow it two miles."

"Do you smell that?" asked Harry, sniffing the air. "Smoke. He has a campfire burning."

They spread out to find the pathway. Slocum found it, and they walked through the forest, silhouetted in the moonlight. Twenty minutes later, they saw shadows bouncing off the trees around the fire that created them.

"That's him," whispered Dorn. They sat on their haunches and surveyed the site. "There's someone lying on the ground. Do you see him?"

They answered yes, grouping closer to discuss what to do. Before anyone could muster a proposal, Slocum tossed a twig near the prone man. No movement. He picked up a small rock, threw it, and bounced it off the blanket wrapped around the figure. Again, no movement.

Slocum stood up and walked briskly into the camp. Step by step, he closed in on the bundle, his weapon ready. Pausing just steps away; he motioned for the others to come over. The group quietly assembled near the fire.

The passed-out man was Davenport. Beside him lay two empty rum bottles. His snoring sounded like a bear in the woods, and he was oblivious to his surroundings.

"Davenport, get up. Wake up!" Harry shouted, poking the sleeping lump with his left foot. "You are under arrest for theft and attempted murder."

The snoring stopped, and a gurgle emerged from the blanket. He turned over and looked at the men standing above him through bloodshot eyes. After more prodding by Dorn, he sat up and tried to lift himself off his bed of hemlock branches, then fell back to the ground.

Recognizing that Davenport was in a total stupor, they holstered their revolvers and bound his hands and arms. His eyes barely open, the soon-to-be-former paymaster gagged and vomited. He was still gagging as he stumbled back to the *Cosmos*.

"Give strong drink to him who is perishing, and wine to him whose life is bitter. Let him drink, forget his poverty, and remember his trouble no more. Proverbs 31:6-7," said Slocum.

Davenport had beached the *Pirate* a hundred yards down from the *Vixen*, so Dorn and Harry stayed with him while Ellingson and Slocum retrieved the *Pirate* and returned it to the *Patterson*. The trip back in the *Cosmos* was notable only for the number of times Davenport threw up. It didn't help that Dorn purposely steered into the waves for enhanced bouncing.

"I saw our salt and rum barrels when I was hanging out at the trading post," said Slocum during the return with Ellingson. "They were being loaded onto a wagon out back. I could still see the letters USC, but the &GS was indistinguishable. They were all white men, too, all wearing dirty clothes. They didn't look like fishermen. My guess is they worked for the trading post. There were two mean-looking white guys working behind the counter. One of them had an eye patch."

Ellingson froze. "Eye patch? Did you say he wore a patch? Which eye?"

"Which one? Well, let me think," Slocum said. "It would have been on his left. He looked at me from his right," and he turned around to confirm which one it was. "Yes, it was the left eye with the patch. He watched me go over to the barrels when I confirmed the lettering was the USC&GS. I think he knew I was looking for the barrels. I turned around on my way back here, and he was following me. I saw him on the beach watching us when we left. Why?"

Chapter Eighteen - The *Ancon*

Harry placed Davenport in irons and on light rations, mainly until his stomach settled down. Evidence pointed to the theft of two hundred and seventy-five pounds of salt, less than a full barrel. Salt on the East Coast was sold for five cents a pound, while that sold in San Francisco was about ten cents a pound. The salt in Alaska, as with most other needed items, sold for far more, costing upwards of thirty cents per pound. Davenport sold the barrel for twenty-five cents per pound, which was discounted to move the product. He made $68.75.

The thirty gallons of rum cost the Geodetic Survey $1,500. Davenport sold it for $4,500. Found in Davenport's coat pocket was nearly $9,000 in cash, more than enough to cover the stolen $5,000, rum and salt. He sold the rum in Hoonah for more than three times its value, then skipped town after buying camping supplies, disappearing at the hot springs with five bottles of the stolen spirits, captured before he had a chance to spend his ill-gotten gains. With the extra cash, Mansfield ordered funds to replace the salt and rum and a $500 donation to the Presbyterian mission in Hoonah. To the crew's delight, he also ordered $100 bonuses paid to each, Davenport notwithstanding.

After receiving reports on the incident, Mansfield prepared his own report and sent it off to Headquarters. From there, he received his orders to transfer Davenport to the Navy tug *Pinto*, which would arrive in Juneau in three days. Davenport would continue to sit in irons with partial rations until then.

Harry's reaction to the three-day wait was one of relief. He wished to stop pursuing criminals and go back to hydrography. It was getting late in August, and he knew the survey season was nearly over, with the first dusting of snow already on the highest coastal mountain peaks.

He joined Smith and Sandford at the drafting table the first morning after capturing Davenport. For the next three days, they worked uninterrupted, pouring over numbers and data and drawing lines on charts, shorelines, and underwater hazards appearing on paper. They were there to chart the untamed southeast Alaskan wilderness. Working ten-hour days, they completed charts that had stalled during Harry's pursuit of Davenport.

It was the morning of this third day of dedicated drafting that Harry awoke, unaware of its coming significance. It was not a remarkable day; it was rainy and overcast as usual, and he remained warm under his blanket, giving himself time to gather his thoughts from his sleep. Foust was still sleeping in the other bunk, and he didn't want to wake him. He rolled onto his back and closed his eyes.

"Dear Lord, thank you for this day. Please protect this ship and the men onboard. In Jesus' name, Amen."

Foust awakened, and they both rose to dress for the day, engaging in cordial conversation until proceeding to the galley for breakfast. After a plate of eggs and potatoes, Harry's first order of business was to check on the well-being of Davenport in the brig.

"Wake up," he said. The prisoner was lying prone with a shackle on his left ankle and a chain attached securely to the wall. "Here's some food and coffee."

Davenport struggled to shift his body to a sitting position, allowing him to stretch his legs. Harry sat down in a chair across the room.

The prisoner said nothing, and Harry didn't expect him to. He had spent time with him the day before, taking his testimony of the events. He wasn't remorseful; he had no conscious guilt for trying to kill his co-worker, nor did he care that his boss committed suicide. He fully understood where his actions placed him with the Navy, and he accepted that. Attempted murder would trump the theft charges and put him squarely under the death penalty.

"You have a few more hours, and then we'll take a walk," he said as Davenport finished his plate.

"I don't want to go to hell." He tossed his tray on the table and leaned back to sip his coffee.

"What are you talking about?"

"Yesterday, you asked me if I was ready to go to hell."

132

Harry remembered the question that had just popped out of his mouth.

"How do you know there's a hell?" he asked. "You ain't dead, you've never been there."

Harry pulled up a chair, sat down, and crossed his legs. He yelled for the guard to bring two cups of coffee. Of what he was about to say, he was certain.

"When I was fourteen, we, my family, moved from New Jersey to San Francisco by ship. At that age, everything fascinated me: the ships, the natives, the sailors, the ocean, you name it. It was all so intriguing and new. But do you know what sticks in my mind the most from that journey? The scene that I most vividly remember?"

He waited until Davenport shook his head no.

"On the ship was this old man—well, to me, an old man, but probably in his late fifties, early sixties. He had somehow enamored himself to my mother, to my father's chagrin, and spent the entire journey as part of our family, without the quarters.

I found out later that the old man had died, although I didn't see his dead body. I've been to funerals, and the ship was like a funeral home. Mom, Dad, other passengers, and his family discussed his passing."

"How did he die?" asked Davenport.

"He had fallen to the floor in a faint and didn't revive."

"I go to bed, and the next morning at breakfast, everyone is talking about this old man. It turns out he wasn't dead; he was alive. Sure enough, he came to dinner that night, as real as you and me." He pulled his chair even closer to Davenport.

"Now for the best part. We were eating dinner. The old man was quiet, eyes closed. There were little conversations going around the table, but he wasn't involved. Suddenly, he opens his eyes and blurts out, 'I saw Heaven, and I almost went to Hell.' The room went quiet. Then, he starts describing his physical body on the floor with people attending to him. His spirit, as he called it, had risen above, and he was looking down on everyone, including himself."

"The next part is what gave me actual shivers. He described that black, ghostly shapes took him from the room and began poking, scratching, hitting, and burning him, while darkness started to black out all the light. He said he felt alone, falling helplessly, tormented at the same time. He said he was so scared and afraid that he called Jesus' name out of sheer panic. Immediately, the dark shapes disappeared, and the tormenting stopped. He said a white light began to build, then bright lights of many colors, and an intense feeling of love and acceptance."

"And just when I thought I heard it all, he said he saw his grandmother. He said his grandmother came to him as a young woman and told him it wasn't his time and that he needed to go back. The light faded, and the dead man said he woke up in bed covered by a sheet. To my dying day, I'll never forget what that old man told us. It comes down to this, Davenport: You can accept Jesus and go to Heaven, or don't accept Him and go to Hell. It's as simple as that."

Davenport didn't say anything. Harry headed down to the drafting room, asking the sentry to escort Davenport to the water closet for his morning rituals.

A recent sounding near the south arm entrance indicated previously uncharted rocks. Harry intended to convert the depth measurements to lines on a chart for the day. Smith and Sanford were already at work around the table when he arrived.

"Gentlemen, good morning. I see the depth numbers from Ensign Beecher here. My goal is to spend the entire day working on this." He gathered his pencils, pens, compasses, and scales as he prepared for drafting.

"Good morning, Mr. Ford. I've reviewed Beecher's numbers and confirmed their consistency with previous records." Smith was a seventeen-year-old from Columbus, Ohio. Harry liked his enthusiasm and, more importantly, his attention to detail. Sanford, a Seattle native, ten years older than his co-worker, was fully accurate, too, but he didn't have the enthusiasm the younger man had.

"J.D., what scale are you using for the coastline?" Harry asked.

"I'm using 1:100,000 for the coast, but 1:50,000 for the port area, to give it some detail. I've clearly marked the scale bars so there isn't any confusion."

"Liam, what about you? What are you working on?"

"I'm showing the rocks for the south entrance to Cleveland Passage, the ones Almy found at mean high tide."

Hours later, lost in their drafting, they barely heard the call for officers to report to the wardroom. Excusing himself, Harry dropped his pencils and headed out. The wardroom was at capacity when he arrived at the same time as Mansfield and Dorn. Two chairs remained, so he chose to stand along the wall beside Strickland.

"I need your attention for a moment, and I apologize for the interruption of your duties. I have just received word that the *Ancon* has wrecked and is stranded on the rocks in Loring Cove, north of Ketchikan," said Mansfield.

"That's horrible," interrupted McDonald. "If that ship goes down, so does a lot of mail."

"Quite true, but it's the people we're concerned about," he admonished. "The good news is the passengers and crew are safe."

"What happened?" asked Harry.

Mansfield looked down and chuckled. "Stupid mistake by the captain. Accidents like these are why I insist we relay all orders to the entire crew. Captain Wallace intended to keep the shorelines tied to swing the ship out from the dock, but someone released the lines, allowing the *Ancon* to drift. She hit a reef a few yards offshore and immediately took on water, listing twenty degrees. She sank within walking distance to shore at low tide. As I said, the 130 passengers and seventy crew are safe. They have taken provisions ashore and found shelter as best they can. Unfortunately, Loring Cove has nothing to provide; it's a canary with a dozen cabins."

"They might as well be on a desolate stretch of beach," Wood injected.

"Agreed," said Mansfield. "The *George Elder* is enroute to pick them up and should be there in a few days. Once rescued, they will return south. The *Ancon* was hauling tons of canned salmon."

"What does this have to do with us?" asked Harry.

"The *Ancon* had more than mail and salmon, gentlemen. You may recall when we transferred mail the last time, the number of well-dressed men and women lining the rails?" Mansfield asked.

Harry didn't know about the mail exchange, as he didn't participate with the crew. For passengers and crew of both vessels, transferring the mail sacks between ships was a festive event that everyone liked to watch.

"As you know, Ensign Wood is in Ketchikan with the *Vixen* for boiler parts. Several of the shipwrecked passengers have requested permission to travel with the *Patterson* for the next few days rather than return to Seattle on the freighter the *Elder*. Wood will be returning with six of them. I understand one is a famous painter and wants to continue his artistic journey."

"Do you know who the others are?" asked Beecher.

"A politician from Colorado and his family, and a lawyer from the East."

Mansfield then got down to the order of business he didn't want to bring up. "Gentlemen, I need several of you to volunteer to empty your quarters, so our guests don't have to sleep with the crew."

"Harry and I can bunk in the crew quarters for a couple of days," exclaimed Foust. "You don't mind, do you, Harry?"

"Very generous of you to volunteer, Mr. Foust," said Mansfield. "Almy and McDonald, you can join them as well. Please see that both your quarters are available by this evening. Oh, and the transfer of Davenport is on hold pending the arrival and transport needs of our guests. They, too, will likely end up on the *Pinto*."

"I don't mind bunking with the crew," Harry lamented to Foust. "But you could have waited for someone else to volunteer, though."

"It's only a few days. Once we get them to Juneau, they'll be out of our way."

"Wood should be arriving in the next hour or two with our guests," concluded Mansfield.

Harry turned to leave and said sarcastically, "I'll be in the hold if you need me. Move the rice sack, and you'll find me underneath."

"No such thing as a coincidence, my friend," laughed Foust. "This might be the best downgrade that ever happened to you. Rice might be what you need."

A dejected Master at Arms went to gather things from his quarters. He thought about two times last year when guests created weird situations for the crew. Most were dignitaries, and many felt entitled to ask for privileges, like private dining or to use the launches for sightseeing. He didn't mind losing his bed for those who appreciated the work the *Patterson* did, but for the upper class, he did mind. He was hoping they wouldn't be too annoying.

In the crew quarters, he found an empty hammock beside a resting Ellingson, waiting for his shift at the bell.

"Ha, looks like the cat has come down to live with the rats; oh my!" he cackled. "I'm guessing' your lot was chosen to provide lodging for our castaways, eh?"

"Sure enough," he said as he dropped his duffle and climbed into his hammock. "Another politician trying to figure out how to spend our money, if you ask me."

"Derision and scorn don't become you, Mr. Ford. Not all politicians are bad."

"I know. It's the last bunch we had on board that soured me about having guests. These folks may be better, and they'll have something to offer us; you never know."

"You'll know soon, Mr. Ford. They're due any time."

Chapter Nineteen - Guests

The bell sounded, rousing them out of their hammocks. As they pulled on their boots, they could tell from the noise that the *Vixen* had arrived. Harry decided to go to work rather than greet the guests with the other officers, still not convinced that having strangers on board was a promising idea. Once in the drafting room, he and his companions immersed themselves, rarely speaking while engrossed in detail, limiting their talk to technical issues.

Less than thirty minutes later, a knock at the door diverted their attention. Harry opened the door to find Mansfield talking to a contingent of people in the hallway. He entered, followed by two middle-aged men, a boy, a younger woman, and an older woman.

"Mr. Ford, I'd like you to meet Benjamin Fairchild, Esquire." Harry stepped forward and shook the slender man's hand, noticing the deep cleft in his chin. "Mr. Fairchild is from New York."

"Actually, I was born in New York, but I've lived most of my life in Washington, D.C. Mr. Ford, you are the ship's draftsman?" he asked.

"We..." He pointed to Smith and Sanford, "...we are the draftsmen."

"Yes, of course, the three of you; my apologies. I'll have you know not too long ago, I was a draftsman. I was an engraver in the Patent Office. I have great respect for the work you do."

"Thank you."

Mansfield continued with the introductions. "This is William Adams from Alamosa, Colorado, and Mrs. Adams, his wife. Mr. Adams is a State Senator. His older brother is Colorado's Governor."

"A pleasure to meet you, sir," said Harry, shaking his hand.

"Call me Billy," replied the cowboy politician. "This country of yours isn't the wild west of Colorado, but it is frontier. Tame it for us, son."

Harry didn't know what to say, so he said nothing.

Mrs. Adams spoke up. "Mr. Ford, this is our daughter Hannah and her son Mark."

Paying little attention to the boy, he stared at the beautiful woman standing before him, dressed in Western cowgirl clothing, her hair braided in long ponytails. With a coy smile on her face, she greeted Harry.

"Mr. Ford, I've always admired men in uniforms. What rank did you say you were?"

Blushing, he felt all eyes on him, and his anxiety grew. Breathing deep, he mustered, "I'm Master at Arms, ma'am. I, I try to keep order on the ship."

"Oh, I like order."

"Hannah," chided her embarrassed father. "Girl, mind your manners." Billy was known for being short on words, but his stern look at his daughter made up for what he didn't say.

As the introductions went around the room, Harry kept his eyes on Hannah. Something about her ignited him, and her radiant smile captured him. Her face was beautiful, and her dark eyes seemed to dance with happiness. He pictured himself kissing her neck.

"Mr. Ford!" It was Mansfield. "We are going to continue our tour. Would you like to come with us?"

"Uh, no, I have too much work to do. I'll catch up later."

"Can I stay?" It was Hannah.

Before Billy could protest, his wife Emma touched his arm, intending to quiet him, saying, "Hannah, can't you see these men have important drafting to do? You'd be interrupting them. You could come back another time."

"Mother, please. Mr. Ford, would I be interrupting your work if I promised not to interrupt?"

He tried following the logic before simply saying, "No, you'd be no interruption at all."

"Are you sure, Mr. Ford? She can come with us if you like," concluded Mr. Adams.

"No, it's fine. Hannah, let me show you what I'm working on."

The tour resumed without her. Smith and Sanford, recognizing the situation, excused themselves to lunch, leaving him alone with her. He began to move a chart to show her the contours when she asked, "Wanna hear a joke?"

"A joke?" He hadn't heard one in a long time and didn't know what to think. Men told all the jokes he had ever heard, and they usually weren't very polite. Was she going to tell him a dirty joke?

"Yes. My mother told it to me."

"Oh, well, if your mama told it to you, go ahead, tell me this joke of yours."

"Okay. A man said to a preacher, 'That was an excellent sermon, preacher, but it wasn't original.' The preacher was taken aback; he had written that sermon himself. The man told him he had a book at home with every word he said. The preacher couldn't believe it. 'Prove it!' the preacher demanded. So, the man leaves and returns a few minutes later. With a dictionary."

Harry listened as if more were to come.

"That's it. That's the joke. Don't you get it?" she said, laughing.

With a limp smile on his face, he said, "Yeah, I get it. I don't think it was that funny."

"Oh, don't be such a prude. Show me what you do."

He felt a tingle as she touched his arm to review the chart. She was a few inches shorter than he, and as he showed her the charts, he looked down at her dark hair and back.

"These are our field book notes showing the rocks we discovered. I'm adding them to the charts over here. And then I need to start another base map of another area, here at Station Blunt," pulling another large sheet of paper in front of them.

"Do you like what you do?" Hannah slipped away from him and wandered the room, looking at the myriad items strewn about.

Putting his compass down, he replied, "I love what I do. I live in an ocean hotel for six months a year, exploring Alaska. What's not to like?"

"The rain, the awful, never-ending rain." She said, picking up a pencil and twirling it in her fingers.

"Those who live in the rain yearn for the desert, while those in the desert yearn for the rain. Why is that?" Harry replied, enjoying the banter. She had a confidence that he liked, a demeanor to which he was drawn.

"I don't like the rain. Father insisted I come on this ill-fated trip. I wanted to stay in Colorado. The weather is beautiful this time of year. If it rains, it's usually from a thunderstorm. I love the sound of thunder." Turning to him, she asked, "Where do you live?"

"San Francisco." He stopped abruptly, remembering his last time with Clara at his apartment. He didn't know what to say next.

"Do you live alone?"

"Yes, I do."

Hannah didn't wait for any more information; she had enough. He was eligible, and she would learn more about him, but now her instincts told her to leave.

"I'm sorry, I must go. Let's talk again soon." She gave Harry that captivating smile and darted out of the room.

Standing at the table, he felt giddy. There was something about her that attracted him.

He returned to the crew quarters to lie in his hammock. He wanted to think about what the evening was to bring. He wanted to prepare mentally for a big social event and have his anxieties under control in advance. He looked to see Ellingson lying in his bunk, sleeping fitfully under his blanket. The man never goes to bed early, he thought.

Dinner began at 6 o'clock. Harry visualized the wardroom where dinner was served. It seated twelve comfortably, although at times they jammed in sixteen, but he didn't think the lieutenant would do that with dignitaries. He started by counting the six guests, two lieutenants, and himself to make nine, leaving three more seats at the table. Five would be on either side, and the lieutenants would sit at the ends. Hannah would sit with her parents and son, leaving one officer beside them. If all went his way, he could sit beside her for dinner or at least be across the table to talk with her.

With a plan in mind, he dressed in his uniform. It was seven minutes after six when he arrived in the hallway outside, as dressing in the crew's quarters had taken longer than expected. Dinner guests filled the hallway. Hannah, her mother, and her father were there, but neither her son nor the artist had arrived. Fairchild, the attorney, was there. Mansfield, Dorn, Dr. Percy, Wood, McDonald, Slocum, Foust, and Beecher were present for the officers.

The last to enter and sit at the only seat available, he found himself at the opposite end of the same side of the table as she was, completely out of sight and conversation range. He was in the least desirable position at the table, and as he looked around, he noticed the looks the other ensigns were giving Hannah.

"Mr. Ford, I'm surprised," said Mansfield. The commander sat at the end, as he predicted. The serving crew came and went from the kitchen, delivering water and a salad. Harry was pleased to have fresh vegetables this far into the summer.

"Surprised by what, sir?" he asked.

"That you were the last one seated tonight. You are so punctual. I can hear you saying, 'If you're not early, you're late.'" The diners chuckled, and he felt obligated to explain.

"Dressing in the crew's quarters, sir. The ship's painters came in to clean up while I was getting ready. I had very little room."

Leaning over and looking down the table at Harry, Hannah asked, "Ford. That's the name on the door. Are we in your room?"

Mansfield moved on before he could answer.
"So, I understand your son Mark has found a new friend, the artist?" he asked Hannah.

"Yes, he has. He seems captivated by painting, and now he wants to be a painter too."

Senator Adams interjected. "Mark's a bit of a dreamer. Art and music have always appealed to him. Hannah is the practical one; she isn't a dreamer. He wouldn't inherit any artistic talents from me anyway," he said, holding Mrs. Adams's hand. "You are where he gets his talent from. You play the piano so beautifully."

"But Mark wants to watch him paint, and Mr. Bierstadt was gracious enough to let him stay, so neither Mark nor Mr. Bierstadt, the artist, will be joining us tonight," clarified Mr. Adams.

"I have yet to meet this artist. Why didn't he want to join us?" Dorn asked. Other than Lt. Mansfield, none of the other officers had yet to meet him.

"He wanted to start right to work, painting in his cabin. I think the *Ancon* wreck has given him inspiration for a new painting. He couldn't stop talking about it while we were coming here on the *Vixen*. He held his supplies in a sack closely under his arm, not wanting water to damage them," said Mrs. Adams.

"What is his name, Bierstadt? Is he Dutch? It sounds Dutch," said Dr. Percy. "Van Gogh was Dutch, Rembrandt and Vermeer too."

"You studied art, Doctor Percy?" she asked.

"No. I only know what I like. Are you an artist as well as a musician, Mrs. Adams?"

"She is a great painter," interjected her husband. "Her painting of the Rocky Mountains at sunrise has been shown at the Denver Art Gallery."

"Mr. Bierstadt is Prussian," she said as the galley crew replaced the salad plates with bowls of venison stew from a Sitka blacktail deer Beecher killed

143

while on a wood-cutting party. After stewards had served, Dr. Percy brought the painter's nationality back to the table.

"Prussian," you said, Mrs. Adams. Mr. Bierstadt is Prussian?"

Between bites of food and without looking at anyone, the senator's wife explained, "By birth, but he has lived in the United States most of his life. He and I talked a great deal before the sinking. I admire his talents. He is a far better painter than I will ever be."

"Oh honey, don't sell yourself short. You're a fantastic painter." Everyone at the table could tell he expressed his compliment with love and sincerity, and Mrs. Adams smiled for the first time Harry could remember.

Returning to Bierstadt, she continued, "He did return to Germany to study at Düsseldorf, but he lives in New York, part of the Hudson River School."

"Mr. Bierstadt promised to come out of his quarters tomorrow," said Mansfield. "He will be joining us for dinner tomorrow."

"How long will our guests be with us?" asked Almy, his eyes on Hannah.

"The Navy will be sending the tug *Pinto* to Juneau. Our guests will be escorted there, where they will continue their journey south with them." Sensing the motivation behind Almy's question, he continued addressing him directly.

"The day after tomorrow, I want you and Mr. Ford to take Davenport to Juneau. I've decided not to wait."

"Why not take Davenport while we escort the guests?" asked A.C., hoping to get to stay and know Hannah better. Harry saw Almy's look and then confirmed he had a ring on his finger.

"It doesn't look proper, does it? Taking a prisoner in irons along with senators and famous painters? Would you want a prisoner transported with you?" answered Dr. Percy.

"Exactly," said Mansfield.

The room's volume increased as they talked amongst themselves during dinner. Harry realized Hannah was having four conversations with the officers beside and across from her.

He hated being at the end of the table; he wanted to be by her side. Instead, he was engaged in a discussion with Mansfield and Fairchild regarding drafting. It was work-related and meticulous, and he couldn't listen to what she was saying.

"No, really, the submittals that we dealt with were awful. So many of the initial drawings and specs received from the patentee were inaccurate. How is the Patent Office to engrave inaccurate data?" Fairchild shrugged his shoulders. "Mr. Ford, are the numbers you receive from the field accurate, or do you have to adjust them somehow?"

"No, sir. Baseline, tide height, locations—everything we do has to be first-level accuracy. Ours is the foundation; all subsequent tie-ins start from our work. We double and triple-check. We have to." He was proud of their accuracy.

"Yes, I can imagine it must be," replied Fairchild.

Dessert service interrupted the work discussion, for which Harry was grateful.

"By the way, did everyone enjoy the venison stew? I thought that was excellent!" said Mansfield as they ate dessert.

He ate his cake quietly while Mansfield and Fairchild chatted. The lawyer mentioned he was considering running for Congress.

"Oh no," Harry thought.

He stayed at the table, toying with his cake as the rest of the group slowly departed from the room. Hannah was also one of the last to leave, continuing a conversation with Almy that A.C. didn't want to end. Without a firm goodnight, she excused herself and sat across from Harry. Harry tried not to smile at Almy.

"We didn't get a chance to talk tonight," she said. "Let me ask you a question: Where were you born?"

"I was born in New Jersey."

"You're from the East Coast? Wow! Do you miss it? After all, Boston, New York, and Philadelphia are great cities! So refined. It is so, so different from here or even San Francisco."

"I lived in Hudson, Massachusetts, until I was fourteen when my family moved to California. I don't remember the East Coast at all. Give San Francisco and Alaska time; they'll refine themselves someday."

"I think cities and towns west of the Mississippi are brutal, dangerous, ugly, and dry. Even Colorado is too dry for me. And here, it rains all day, every day, and if it doesn't rain, it's probably snowing."

"Locations east of the Mississippi are old, run-down, dirty, crowded, and tiring. Out west, the air is clean, you can drink the water, and you can live as you want."

"Do you always disagree? I know I'm right." She stopped and looked at him. "I like that about you. You're an Alaskan man. Strong, honest, independent, resourceful. I like that." Smiling the look that melted Harry's heart the first time, he thought the smile seemed more sincere and personal this time.

"You could show me Station Blunt tomorrow."

Harry sensed his hypocrisy as he jumped at the chance to take her out on a sightseeing tour. "I'd be honored," he said. "First thing after breakfast, the tide will be right."

They smiled at each other before she turned and walked out the door. He stood as the kitchen crew removed the dishes and silverware. These guests were different from what he expected. He exited and went up on deck. The evening sky had darkened, and the stars shone faintly. The fall equinox was approaching. He gazed up, always in wonder at the brightness of such little points of light. Sighing, he thanked Jesus for such a day full of grace— a day with Hannah. Who was this woman? He gazed at the heavens one last time before heading to the noisy and cramped crew quarters.

Chapter Twenty - Art

The following day, he had the galley prepare a lunch of fried chicken, mashed potatoes, gravy, and Cole slaw. After some back-and-forth, he and Beale negotiated a small bottle of rum in advance of his daily allotment. Dropping the whaleboat into the water from its davit, he tied a small rowboat to the stern and placed the picnic basket with the rum inside.

While preparing the launch for his date with Hannah, he saw Ellingson standing by the main mast, shivering. Walking over, he could see his face was pale and sweaty. Motioning for the old sailor to sit down, he asked if Ellingson was okay.

"Nah, I don't feel very well."

Even though the weather was a balmy 62 degrees, he had a blanket wrapped around him.

"Let's take you down to see Dr. Percy. Have you been to see him yet?"

"No, I haven't. I started feeling bad yesterday, but I thought I'd get better. I took a nap, thinking that would help, and I only got worse."

"Here we go," he said, putting his arm around Ellingson's waist for support. Then, he slowly walked him to the sick bay.

Dr. Percy had Ellingson lie down for an examination. With the old sailor under his care, Harry returned to the deck, looking for Hannah. Huddled around her and her family were Dorn and several other officers, including Almy. He walked up to greet them.

"Mr. Ford, good morning," said Dorn. "It seems the Adams were expressing their desire to go sightseeing, and they were hoping you would go along with them."

Summoning all his inner courage, he asked, "If I may, Mr. and Mrs. Adams, your daughter, Hannah, asked if I could show her one of our survey stations. I would like to take her out to Signal Blunt if you have no objections. We will be very careful."

Mrs. Adams spoke first. "I think that is a good idea. Enjoy yourselves."
"Wait, are you sure?" protested the girl's father.

"He's a navy man. I trust him."

Hannah entrusted Mark to his grandparents, and with a pouty face, Mark let everyone know he wasn't happy at being left behind.

"Remember, he likes to hide. Always keep your eyes on him," she told her parents.

They held hands as he led her to the rail above the whaleboat, and she lifted her leg over the rail and descended the rope ladder.

"Have you done that before?" he asked, impressed with how she managed to climb down.

"No, that's a first. I slid down a firehouse pole once if that counts."

Harry chuckled. "Where did you do that?"

"Boston."

The ocean surface was calm, and the sky was blue, but clouds drifted in from the west. It was a phenomenal fall day for southeast Alaska, and he was glad he had this opportunity with Hannah. He directed the boat northeast with three destinations in mind. He could tell she seemed fascinated with the coastal range as she stared at the rounded mountain tops four and five thousand feet above them, rising from the lush rainforest. He hoped she'd get to appreciate their whitened peaks after a snowfall.

Station Blunt was the first stop. They beached the whaleboat and walked over to the monument while he explained the basics of surveying. They climbed the station ladder to the platform, but without a theodolite, he could only point to the tide staff across the way and explain how it operated. It didn't matter; they enjoyed looking out over the water from the tower, talking and laughing.

Returning to the whaleboat, he surprised her by explaining that their visit to Blunt was only the first of three destinations. Steering the *Cosmos* back into Stephens Passage, they traveled as far as Taku Harbor before heading up the Taku River. About an hour later, pushing against the river's current, she gasped in astonishment at seeing not one but two tidewater glaciers in front of her.

"This place is amazing," she exclaimed.

"Truly," he said as he cut power to the propeller, letting them drift in the water flow. "The icefield above this is even more amazing."

"What's an icefield?" she asked.

"A glacier about the size of Rhode Island that makes baby glaciers like these."

Hannah laughed at the use of the word. "Babies are small; these aren't small. But they are stunning."

"God's creation at His finest."

He engaged the propeller, turning the craft around to head out of the inlet. His third destination was on the far side of Stephens Passage on Admiralty Island. Again, it was a trip of about an hour, and the two didn't talk much as they took in the stunning scenery while scooting across the water.

As they neared Admiralty, he scanned the shoreline, looking for one location. He directed the whaleboat into a small, crescent-shaped cove with a beach of smooth rocks. Ramming the whaleboat onto the beach, he jumped out and hauled it above the high tide, tying it to one of the spruce trees that lined the cove.

Lifting Hannah out of the boat to avoid getting water in her boots, he carried her to shore and put her down gently, holding on while she steadied herself on the rocks. She didn't pull away but instead looked into Harry's eyes. They held each other for a moment, not moving, not saying anything. Their worlds had collided in the Alaskan wilderness, and they knew they were on the verge of something. He broke the tension.

"I need to get something."

Returning to the launch, he maneuvered the rowboat from its stern tie and pulled it to the beach so he could pull it ashore.

"What are you going to do with that?" she asked. She had found a downed tree and was sitting on the trunk.

"This." He went to the whaleboat, lifted an axle set with two steel wheels, and attached it as a dolly under the little boat.

"And this." He reached in and pulled out the picnic basket. "Lunch?"

"Oh, my. You clever fellow. You've thought of everything, haven't you?"

"I try to," he said, smiling. Lifting it on the dolly, he said, "It's not that heavy, but why work harder than necessary? Follow me."

"Where are we going?"

"Through there."

"I need to tell you; I don't like surprises. Where are we going?"

"To a beautiful spot for a picnic lunch."

"In the forest?"

He towed the rowboat up a well-used animal trail, and Hannah followed close behind. Massive spruce and hemlocks rose above, covered in moss, and the earthy smell permeated everywhere.

"I love this aroma," Hannah said, breathing deeply.

"Me too. It's so rich."

"How did you find this place?"

Pausing to catch his breath and survey where he was going, he replied,

"Pure luck. I was doing tidal observations and landed in that cove to relieve myself. I spooked a buck, and he took off this way. I followed him here, and lucky for me, I did."

"How much further?"

"Don't worry, our destination is over that next moraine."

He struggled to pull the little rowboat over tree roots, and Hannah wondered if they were lost when finally crossing over a third moraine. Climbing to the top, she caught her breath, gazing at the pristine mountain lake before them. She put her arm around his and pulled him close.

"Beautiful. Does it have a name?"

"No, not yet. I didn't tell anybody about it, so no one at the Survey knows, and they're the ones that name things. What would you call it?"

"Lake Harry," she quipped, pulling on his elbow.

"Ooh, I like that. Lake Harry. Sounds impressive."

"Well, you need something named for you."

The two worked their way down the slope to the shoreline, where he put the rowboat in the water. Helping Hannah inside, he shoved off, gently paddling in its stillness.

"Lunch?" he asked. "Grab that basket, yep, that one. Open it. There should be a cloth to cover the seat."

"You thought of a tablecloth? What kind of a man are you?" She placed the packaged chicken, potatoes, and slaw on the cloth and pulled out plates and silverware.

"See that bottle? Pull that out." He hauled easily on the oars, guiding them to the lake's center.

"What's this? Did you bring liquor?"

Embarrassed, he replied, "Yes, I hope you don't mind."

"Mind? For what have you been waiting?" She set the glasses on the bench and poured two shots.

"To Harry Lake," she toasted.

"Wait, I thought it was Lake Harry."

"No, we agreed it would be Harry Lake. I'm always right."

He held up his glass, saying, "To Hannah, may she always be right, even when she's wrong." Laughing, the two downed their shot of rum.

After the third shot and stories about their childhoods, the two sat in the rowboat, drifting, enjoying each other's company and the serene quiet as the alcohol worked its influence. The clouds covered the sky above, and rain was likely.

"I need to come here," he said, occasionally watching fish break the glassy surface. "It's calming. On the ocean, there's always movement: waves, tides, currents, wind. Nothing is still; the ship is always moving. The sails catch the breeze even when hauled in. But here, complete stillness. The lake doesn't move. There's no noise from the waves, nothing other than birds and the animals."

"It is so quiet," said Hannah. She was leaning over, her hand in the water, staring into the lake's depths.

"Hannah, can I ask you a personal question?"

"Sure."

"Mark's father, what's his story? Where is he?"

"He's dead, killed when Mark was four. It will be two years next month, now that I think about it."

"I'm so sorry. I didn't mean to bring up bad memories."

"You're not, I mean, it's okay. Frank had gone into town, and on the way home, he... well, the best we can figure is his horse reared, likely from a rattlesnake, throwing him off. They found his body on the side of the road, bleeding from his head. A large rock beside him had blood on it. He must have hit the rock when he fell off the horse."

"I'm so sorry for you. That would be awful, dying alone on the side of the road like that."

"When he didn't return by dusk, I grabbed Mark and went left for town to find him. A family in a wagon heading to town was there when we arrived, having tended to Frank as best they could. He didn't make it. It had a devastating effect on Mark. His demeanor changed. He's so aloof now, rebellious, even for his age. Everybody in the house is on edge, trying not to set him off into some childish tantrum."

"I haven't seen that in him. He seemed well-behaved, but then I only saw him for a few minutes."

"He's quite outgoing. He tries to impress adults with how smart he is or how strong he is." Hannah paused before asking, "Harry, have you ever thought about being a father?"

"No, not really. Other than to assume I'd be one someday. Clara and I didn't talk about children; we hadn't gotten that far in our relationship."

"I have to be careful not to let a man into my life, my son's life, only to have him leave and devastate two hearts."

She nudged his leg with her boot, and the boat rocked softly.

"Whoa."

Just as the first raindrops began to fall, he said, "We should be getting back. We have a ways to go, and we don't want to miss dinner with our artist guest tonight."

"It's raining again," a drunk Hannah exclaimed. "It rains all the time here. I can't stand the rain." He took off his wool sweater and gave it to her.

"It itches."

They arrived back at the *Patterson* after sunset, much to the chagrin of her father. After a parental admonishment not to keep his daughter out so late next time, Harry departed from the family to his temporary quarters to prepare dinner. Seeing Ellingson's empty hammock, he remembered he was in sick bay and headed that way instead.

When he entered the room, the doctor was the first person he saw. He stood over Ellingson, who was lying on the bed with a cloth covering his forehead and eyes.

153

Dr. Percy turned to him, saying, "He's not well, Mr. Ford. He's burning up. He has an infected cut on his leg, and I'm afraid sepsis may have started. He needs better care than what I can give him. You need to get him to Juneau first thing tomorrow. Take him straight away to Dr. Bartlett. I'm out of carbolic acid, but he should have some to clean out the wound. Then he'll probably need to be transferred to the *Pinto* for hospital care."

Harry returned to the crew quarters, conflicted between wanting to have a meal with Hannah and getting ready to transport Ellingson. He decided he would go to dinner but leave before dessert. He also needed to develop a plan for the Davenport transfer.

Once again, he was the last to enter the room. Bierstadt had replaced Fairchild across the table; otherwise, the guests had remained in yesterday's positions. A.C. was talking to Hannah, but he couldn't tell what they were discussing.

Mansfield again oversaw introductions. "Mr. Bierstadt, this is our ship's senior draftsman and Master at Arms, Harry Ford."

"Mr. Bierstadt, a pleasure to meet you."

"The pleasure is mine, sir."

He smiled at Hannah as he passed her to his seat. Turning to Mansfield, he told him about Ellingson.

"Lieutenant Mansfield, I need to go to Juneau tomorrow to take Ellingson to the doctor in town. Dr. Percy doesn't have all the medicine he needs to treat him, and Ellingson is really bad. His infection has spread."

"Yes, go and take Davenport with you. You can leave him in the town jail until the *Pinto* picks him up from there. Take extra crew with you for support."

This night's dinner was quieter, and the conversations were less lively as the group listened as the painter talked nonstop. Harry recognized Bierstadt's narcissism when McDonald mentioned he once trained to be a painter, but Bierstadt ignored the comment and continued to discuss himself.

154

"Ah, my apologies," he said through his thick European accent. "I have sequestered myself in my room and haven't been very social. I get a vision, and I can't get it out of my head. I can't wait to sketch it. That's what I've been doing. I don't have all my supplies, but I can draw with a pencil and work with the image in my head."

"What are you painting or drawing, should I say?" asked Almy. He didn't care; he only tried to impress Hannah but said it loudly enough that Bierstadt had to respond.

"Our shipwreck. The *Ancon* is lying on her side in Loring Cove. The poignancy struck me, lying on her side like that, the snow falling gently. She needs to be commemorated."

"But the wreck almost cost you your life. Why would you want to paint that?" asked Hannah.

"Almost is the critical part, dear child. I almost died, but I didn't. Why not use that experience in my work? I want the painting to express the beauty of the moment, the sensation of something as unique as a ship floundering on the rocks in a snowstorm. I take that moment and memorialize it in painting."

"I can see that," said McDonald. "I tried to capture the essence of a mountain in a painting. It's not easy expressing your thoughts and emotions about a stationary object when putting them on canvas."

"Think of the western expansion," said Bierstadt, "and the tragedy of the buffalo, the Indian. They are both hunted to extinction. I painted *The Last of the Buffalo* to memorialize the passing of a part of our history, of our culture."

"Is hunting Indians to extinction a tragedy? The savages rape and murder women."

As often occurs in a group conversation when just one comment is overheard, the room fell silent after Hannah's outburst. Harry felt embarrassed for her, but no one in the room knew that her grandmother and aunt had suffered that very fate when her family first settled in Colorado.

Bierstadt broke the tense silence.

"My dear Hannah, I believe that the killing of the Indians for the sake of killing them is immoral. They are people like you and me; we just live in different worlds."

"Maybe I was too harsh, but I don't like Indians. They can move to a reservation and continue their culture there."

The meal service interrupted the flow of conversation, and small discussions began. Not being part of one, Harry remembered he needed to go to the galley to ask for a travel lunch for tomorrow. He listened as Bierstadt explained to Mansfield about his losses in a studio fire a few years back, but he didn't engage in the talk, leaving that to Mansfield. Although meeting this famous person was an honor, he was more concerned with Ellingson.

"I miss the painting of my wife Rosalie the most," Bierstadt said as Harry regained focus on the conversation around him. "Once I leave Alaska, I'll head to Nassau, where she is while I'm traveling. She struggles with tuberculosis, so the Caribbean is the place for her to be."

Turning to Hannah, Bierstadt said abruptly, "You are as beautiful as my wife was at your age. Now, she and I are both old, and our bodies show it. It's like we are ships wrecked on the rocks, just waiting for the ocean to claim us. Yet, we exist, living and breathing. I would want someone, were they to paint us, to be able to capture the vibrancy that is still in our lives, even though our bodies have been wasted. There's a spirit to everything."

As the stewards cleared the venison roast from the table, Harry excused himself, explaining that he had an early departure tomorrow and wanted to prepare. Stepping out the door, he looked at Hannah. She gave him an expression of dismay that she couldn't say goodbye. He cocked his thumb and gestured for her to come out. Excusing herself, she went to the hall and shut the door.

"I won't see you in the morning, and I'm not sure what time I'll return. You leave the day after next." He didn't know how to express his feelings. "I had a wonderful time with you today. I had a lot of fun."

"Me too; I loved the tour. And the stillness of the lake. I'm missing that right now as we rock in this wind." She smiled and held his hands in hers.

"Thank you. And goodbye until we see each other again." She leaned up and kissed him on the cheek. "You are wonderful," she whispered in his ear.

He looked back at her, wondering if he would spend more time with her before she left. And what about after that? He stayed in the moment and said, "I'll see you tomorrow." He bent over and kissed her on the cheek, turned, and walked down the hall.

Chapter Twenty-One – Dr. Bartlett

September 1st dawned cloudy and pleasant, a cool 45 degrees. The *Patterson* bobbed at anchor in Holkham Bay, with the crew beginning preparations for relocation to Taku Inlet later in the day. Harry rose early, preparing for a challenging day with two key goals. He dressed in civilian clothes and holstered his navy-issued Colt .38 revolver on his hip. Looking at Ellingson's empty hammock, he paused to pray for his friend. Walking to the brig, he gave Davenport a change of clothes in preparation for transport.

Davenport was sitting on the bunk. Seaman Jones was standing at the door, assigned as an escort to Juneau. Harry entered, and Jones left the room to check the launch preparations.

He unlocked the shackle on Davenport's ankle and waited as he changed. Shackling him again before transport, Harry explained that he'd be back. As he opened the door to leave, Davenport asked, "Want to know what I decided?"

He paused, trying to figure out what he meant. "Decided? About what?"

"Heaven and hell."

"Oh, right, that discussion." He hadn't given their conversation any more thought.

"You don't sound as if you care."

"I do. I have a lot on my mind. What's your decision?" He sat down in a chair, but Davenport didn't continue.

"Look, I'm not a salesman; I wouldn't be able to convince my mom to birth me."

Davenport didn't respond, so he continued, "You know what? It's up to you. Just remember that old man's story, okay?"

The tension between them indicated nothing further was to be said. He left the room, failing in his evangelism skills but glad he had said something. The unfortunate timing had him more focused on a man's life than another man's soul.

He headed to where Ellingson lay in a bunk, Dr. Percy tending to him. "His fever held through the night; it didn't worsen," the doctor told him as he entered the room. "But you need to go. I've sent a message to Dr. Bartlett; he knows you are coming. Hurry."

Before escorting his sick friend, he went to check on the launch. He found McDonald and two sailors—Jones and Walker—preparing the *Pirate* for their departure. They had already stoked the fire and loaded wood and other supplies.

"Mr. Ford, Lt. Dorn asked me to go with you. Let's organize for your trip today," McDonald put down the chart he was looking at and said. "Our two objectives are to transport Seaman Ellingson to Dr. Bartlett and take Davenport to the town's brig. Nothing else, we get in, and we get out."

"I'll take Ellingson. I want to make sure he gets treatment as soon as possible." Harry's empathy was evident, so McDonald asked, "What endears you to him? It shows on your face."

"I think I've accomplished so much and know so much. But when I listen to Ellingson's stories of the places he's been and what he's done, like being on *Patterson's* first voyage, I realize how limited my life has been. Mac, he's more than a sailor. He's what this agency and this mission are about. He is the ultimate adventurer and explorer. He shouldn't have to die from sepsis. That's not right."

McDonald concurred and agreed to escort the prisoner with Walker, allowing Harry and Jones to take Ellingson to the doctor.

Walker retrieved Davenport while Harry escorted Ellingson to the *Pirate*. The weather worsened, with rain falling in a steady drizzle and the wind beginning to whip around. The patient was not doing well, and Dr. Percy wanted to hold until the last minute, afraid the trip in the rain might kill him before getting treatment. Harry and McDonald wanted to get going, as the swells would push the launch to its limits.

With four- to six-foot swells, waves crashing onto the *Pirate's* deck, winds drifting them off-course, and rain steadily coming down, the trip to town was miserable. Davenport chummed over the side often. They arrived with a steady downpour and had already soaked their clothes. The weather and lateness of the afternoon cast a dark pall over the town.

McDonald set the plan to escort Davenport to the territorial jail up Main Street and wait for the Navy to pick him up. No one was sure when that would happen. If they were still waiting for the Navy at 7 p.m., it would be too late to return to the ship that night, owing to the unfavorable weather and tides. If that were the case, they would meet at the Alaskan Hotel for the night, keeping the prisoner captive in jail.

In the meantime, Harry and Seaman Jones would take Ellingson up Seward Street to the doctor's office. The sick man could barely walk. He was very weak, shivering from the pain, rain, and cold. The doctor was available to treat the wound and infection but wouldn't be staying the night to attend to him; that would be up to Harry and Jones until the Navy medics showed up. If they had not arrived by seven, Harry would stay with Ellingson while Jones checked into the hotel, switching places in six hours.

The *Pirate* landed at low tide, and they helped the ailing sailor walk up the gangway to the dock. The wood was wet and slippery due to the rain, and the steepness of the walkway made it difficult. They bumped into dock workers and sailors as they struggled toward Franklin Street.

The bars along Franklin and Front Streets were busy this rainy Friday evening. Fishermen, loggers, miners, prospectors, and businessmen were celebrating the end of the workweek. The bell rang often, signaling a well-paid patron was sponsoring drinks for all. It was a festive atmosphere inside with the dark deluge outside.

Dr. Bartlett's office was on Seward, three blocks up from Front. The crowded wooden sidewalks made maneuvering difficult. People walking toward them would step aside, either into the muddy street or against a building. Others forced the three men to turn sideways. Together, the people, rain, and steepness of the street made the task of carrying Ellingson extremely hard.

The trio passed multiple businesses and buildings built with narrow passageways between them, allowing people to access the next street up the hill rather than walking around the block. They could see the doctor's building as they approached, a darkened walkway to their right.

Before Harry or Jones could react, three men jumped from the dark alley and attacked them. Two of the attackers were large, burly men, while the third was smaller in comparison. The smaller man stood and laughed, kicking Ellingson as he lay on the ground, where he had slumped. The two larger men struggled to subdue Harry and Jones. Jones was getting a severe beating as Harry and his attacker rolled and wrestled in the muddy street. Escaping from Harry, the man pulled out a knife and went over to Ellingson, plunging it into his stomach without hesitation. From the mud, Harry could see the man's eye. It was Stevens.

"Mr. Ford!" yelled Jones, but before he could say more, the other attacker landed a punch to the seaman's jaw, knocking him unconscious. Guttural sounds were coming from Ellingson's mouth while blood pumped from his gut as he lay in a heap in the rain. Stevens turned and thrust the knife at Harry, but he stepped back into the street and fumbled for his revolver.

The second man, Cantwell, knocked Harry over, beating him about the face with his fists and then choking him by the throat. Harry could see the dark figures of Stevens and the small man standing nearby. What seemed like the ghoulish laugh of an evil man watching another man die emanated from the small man's mouth.

As bystanders began to gather and shout, Harry's attacker got off, and the three ran back into the pitch-black alley they had appeared from.

"Ellingson!" he yelled, crawling to his friend. Townspeople were beginning to help Jones to his feet after he regained consciousness. Blood was oozing from Harry's eye socket.

"Help me move him to the doctor!" he commanded, and several men raised and carried Ellingson the rest of the way to the doctor. Dr. Bartlett was expecting a patient with sepsis but instead found one with a lethal knife wound.

Ellingson was alive, but not for long. The knife had cut into his liver, and the doctor had neither the skill nor the materials necessary for the extensive surgery required. If Dr. Bartlett could keep him alive for a few more hours, the Navy might be able to save him. But they had not arrived, and Harry knew Ellingson was about to die. He knelt beside him and held his hand.

"I'm so sorry I let this happen to you," he moaned, tears forming. "May God have mercy on your soul."

Ellingson never regained consciousness, passing away minutes later. Harry stood in the corner of the doctor's room, stunned, his mind paralyzed by the murder of his friend he had witnessed. The doctor tended to the cuts on Harry's face and eye, putting bandages over the wounds.

Seaman Jones entered the office, finding Ellingson dead and Harry in a daze. Jones had a massive welt around his eye, but otherwise, he was unharmed. Seeing his superior immobilized, he took charge.

"Doctor, thanks for your service. The Navy will reimburse you for your efforts. However, I need to take Mr. Ford here to meet the other members of our party at the hotel while we wait for the *Pinto*. We will return in the morning for the death certificate."

"No, I can get that for you now," Dr. Bartlett replied, walking over to his desk. He pulled out a sheet of paper and began writing. "What's his first name?"

"I don't know. I've only known him as Ellingson," Harry murmured.

The doctor finished the death certificate and handed it to Harry. He then said softly, "Mr. Ford, your friend would have died anyway; his infection was beyond treatment, and the sepsis had spread throughout his body. The knife quickly ended what otherwise might have been prolonged pain. Don't blame yourself, son. There was nothing anyone could have done to help him."

The information comforted Harry, as he knew Ellingson had been quite ill before the attack. Regaining balance in his emotions, he and Jones left the doctor's office, leaving Ellingson's body behind for the officers of the *Pinto* to pick up.

It wasn't 7 o'clock yet, but there was no reason to wait now that Ellingson was gone, so they went to the hotel to change into dry clothes for dinner. An hour later, McDonald and Carter met up with them to discuss the day's events.

162

"You two took a beating," McDonald said, looking at the bruises on their faces. "I don't remember that was part of our plan." Harry's left eye had filled with blood, but it wasn't seeping out anymore.

Harry smiled a contorted smile and seconded the teasing. "I know we talked about having fun, but we never defined it. Did you guys have fun today?"

"Harry, I almost forgot," said McDonald. "Davenport wants us to give you a message. He said to tell you that he believes. Does that make sense to you?"

He smiled. "Yes, that makes sense. Thanks."

"Can we focus on what we're doing?" interrupted Jones. "Ellingson's dead."

The mood turned as the table reflected on the gravity of the day's events.

"It was Stevens, the man with the eye patch—the man Ellingson predicted would try to kill him. The other guy must have been Cantwell, but I don't know who the third man was; he was much smaller. They must have watched us carrying Ellingson up the street, knowing we were going to the doctor."

"Why did he want to kill Ellingson?" Carter asked. Harry explained Ellingson's role in the Angoon bombing.

"Damn it, I'm angry," said McDonald, pounding his fist on the table. "Mr. Ford and Jones here have been beaten up, and one of our crew was murdered."

"He would have died even without the knife. That's what Dr. Bartlett told me."

"It doesn't matter. It's still attempted murder. The Navy won't care that Ellingson was sick. They care that someone tried to kill him," McDonald concluded.

Harry listened, then spoke up. "I reckon they are still in town, and I bet they now want to kill both witnesses to the stabbing. I propose we find them before they find us."

"This place is out of control tonight," said Almy. "Everybody has money. Somehow, payday landed on the same day for everybody—the fishermen, lumbermen, and miners. The bars won't close till morning if they do then. I wouldn't be surprised if Ellingson isn't the only murderer this weekend. If we go out looking for them, they have the element of surprise, watching who comes and goes right now."

"What if they have already left town? Other people can identify them. Maybe they felt it was safer not to be here." Harry imagined various scenarios of where they could have gone. "I'm guessing they're using a company boat. A launch with a name on it, perhaps?"

McDonald spoke up. "Alright, I have a plan. My first thought was we should stick together, but now I think if we split up, we can more easily blend in. They might be looking for us to be staying together. We're all armed, right?"

"I am, but that didn't help," Harry said. "They can knife you in a second."

"I think we all agree that under the authority of the Navy, we can pursue and apprehend by whatever means necessary a man who killed one of our shipmates and his companion who battered our two friends here." McDonald's demeanor left no doubt about what he meant, and he continued,

"Harry, you mentioned the launch. Why don't you go down to the harbor and look for it? If you see it, come back, and let us know. Jones, check out the diners and businesses. Carter wanders the neighborhoods. Be careful of houses or sheds that are broken into. I'll go barhopping, starting at the Imperial."

"What time should we be back? What if we find them? How do we let the others know?" Jones seemed apprehensive at the thought of a nighttime search, his swollen face reminding them of the kind of men they were dealing with.

"Let's give it till one o'clock," replied McDonald. "If we don't locate them by one, we probably won't. Meet back here by that time; we'll sleep and then head back at first light."

"And if we do see them?" Jones asked again.

No one had a response, so the group pondered what to do.

Harry devised a plan: "If someone finds them, stay put. Don't go anywhere unless you need to follow them. Then, when that person doesn't arrive at one o'clock, say it's you, Jones. Then the rest of us start looking for you in the bars and the stores. Or if you know Stevens is stationary and not going anywhere, be here at one and lead everyone back."

The group concurred and left for their respective destinations. Harry headed down to the harbor, bundled against the rain. It had only let up a little, and the darkness seemed to penetrate everywhere. He could hardly see twenty feet in front of him. Anyone hiding in the shadows could quickly jump out and attack him. He thought of the two men jumping him on Seward Street.

He had taken his revolver from the holster and placed it in his jacket pocket, held firmly by his right hand, with his finger off the trigger. Fishermen were coming and going with lanterns for their night work, so he used their light to wander the docks looking for their company's vessel. The smell of the ocean and the fish catch filled the night air.

At the end of the main dock, away from activity, he found a boat with "Northwest Trading Post" painted on the side. No one was in it, so he went aboard. Seeing a small barrel under a blanket, he popped the top with a nearby mallet. A quick smell and taste, and it was clear it contained rum. It had to be Stevens's boat. The barrel, however, was not from the *Patterson*.

Pulling the blanket back over the barrel, he got out, hid behind a stack of fish crates on the dock, and waited for the two men or one o'clock, whichever came first. He wasn't sure how to subdue two men, so he began imagining scenarios using his revolver. Realizing this was risky, he decided to sabotage the launch engine to strand them. Climbing back into their boat, he took a mallet and beat one of the rods, bending it enough to inhibit its movement.

He climbed back out and returned to his hiding and his revolver. Hours passed slowly, and he ached from sitting in an uncomfortable position. As one o'clock approached, he wondered what he should do. Deciding he should stay past one and have the others come to him could help them develop the next strategy at that point. He was afraid that if he went to the hotel, the two men would arrive while he was gone, and he would miss them.

About thirty minutes after one, McDonald approached.

"Mac, is that you?" Harry asked apprehensively. "Where are the others?"

"Carter is out looking for Jones. He didn't show up at one o'clock, either. I came here to find you."

"I found their launch and disabled it, but they haven't been around. I figured you all would show up, and we could decide what to do," said Harry, anxious to go.

Dorn had other plans. "If that's the case, I say we go back to find Carter and Jones. Then we can come back here together."

They left the docks for the town, walking the streets and peering in windows and down alleys. By now, fewer people roamed the streets, but many remained, each bundled up against the rain.

As they were about to turn down Franklin Street, they heard Carter.

"Hey, Harry, over here." Carter was motioning for them to come over. As they approached, he was half-hidden in one of the narrow ways between buildings, bending over something. They walked over and peered into the shadows. As their eyes adjusted, Jones's body became visible.

"Is that...?"

"I'm afraid so. Knife to the throat. These guys are serious. They are on home turf, and we are not. None of us are safe now, especially Harry. We need to get back to the hotel and leave town as soon as we can. Before they kill again."

McDonald hoisted Jones's limp body onto his back, and the four men went down to the launch to place the dead seaman onboard. Watching everyone around them as they walked, McDonald and Carter returned to the hotel to gather their things, leaving Harry behind to guard Jones's body and the *Pirate*.

Waiting in the dark, cold, rainy night, afraid that at any moment the man with one eye would jump out and kill him, fear gripped him as he pushed against Jones's dead body. He shivered, both from fear and from the cold. He thought of Hannah, the neck he desperately wanted to kiss. That thought, and his revolver stirred his resolve. The death of two men, one a close friend, bore heavily on his shoulders, and he pondered if it was his fault. Was he somehow responsible? The arrival of Carter and McDonald interrupted his introspection, and the three huddled in the pilot house for the next two hours until there was enough light to leave for the *Patterson*.

Chapter Twenty-Two: Burial at Sea

When the *Pirate* came alongside the *Patterson* that morning, the crew was busy repairing sails as the rain had lessened considerably. McDonald and Carter hauled Jones' body on deck, generating gasps from those nearby and creating a crowd. Others, seeing the commotion, came out and stood around. Word of the activity on deck reached the commander, and he and other officers soon began to arrive, but by then, the *Pirate* had been unloaded. McDonald, Harry, and Carter remained with Jones; his body covered by a blanket. The crew was throwing questions at the men, but they waited to answer Lieutenant Mansfield.

"Sailors," Mansfield shouted at several seamen watching, "secure that launch better—it's banging against the *Patterson*." Several sailors responded immediately as he bent over to look at the body, finally concluding in a quiet voice,

"Someone bring Dr. Percy to examine the body. Lieutenant Dorn, I want everyone involved in the officer's room immediately. You, sailors, wait for Dr. Percy and then follow his orders on where he wants the body taken. And treat Jones with respect."

Mansfield stormed off, angry at the men who cut Jone's throat.

By now, the guests had arrived to observe the commotion, and Hannah was standing by her parents, holding Mark's hand. Harry, McDonald, and Carter had blankets brought and wrapped around their shoulders, preferring not to change their wet clothes before they debriefed the lieutenant. Walking to the door leading to the wardroom, Harry looked over at Hannah, her hands clutched to her chest and her eyes wide with apprehension as she took in Harry's beaten face.

Dr. Percy popped out the door onto the deck just as Harry was about to enter the hallway. The doctor went over and peeked at Jone's face, placing a large white cloth over his throat to hide the hideous cut. He ordered the men chosen by Mansfield to haul Jones onto a blanket and take him to the sick bay. The doctor intended to complete an autopsy as per regulation and prepare him for burial at sea.

The Adams family went back to their quarters after the body was removed. Hannah waited nervously, which her father noticed.

"Hannah, are you alright? You look pale. You shouldn't have looked at that dead man. There are things in this world we shouldn't have to see."

"Harry—his face, his eye—it was all bloody and bruised."

Her parents turned to each other and realized it wasn't the dead man that affected her; it was the severely beaten officer she was so taken with.

"Mr. Ford, he looked hurt, didn't he? But the doctor is tending to him. He will be alright." Mrs. Adams moved to embrace her daughter. "How brave he must be, helping that poor sailor. He must put his life in danger often."

"He looks very hurt; I hope his vision will be alright."

"I didn't realize you were in…."

"In what? In love with Harry? I don't know, am I? Maybe. I know it's only been a few days, but he has a special quality; he has good character, he treats me so nicely, and he makes me laugh. When I'm with him, I don't feel lonely; I don't feel like I'm on my own. Can I go and see him?"

"But dear, think about what you might be getting into. This is how he lives: dangerously. Do you know how many ships have sunk in these waters or how many men die here each winter?"

"He lives in San Francisco during the winter."

"You see my point, though. Are you prepared to love a man who is gone half the year facing deadly risks each day he's away?"

"I think so."

"And what about Mark? Is that the kind of father you want for him—only home half the time and maybe not coming home at all?"

"Mother, enough! I will have plenty of time to think about it. It's way too early for that. Regardless, he's hurt, and I'd like to go see him now."

169

Mrs. Adams looked at her daughter with sympathy and nodded with a smile. She had prayed for a good man for her daughter, and from what she had seen, Harry seemed like a fine man—although his work in Alaska was concerning.

Hannah kissed her mother and then her father.

"What about you, Father? What do you think?"

"My daughter, you are on a grand adventure. Everything and everyone around you are new and wonderful. People seem to be more special for some reason. Keep your focus—we have a lot of work to do in Colorado. We're not going to win my next election with you in San Francisco."

Walking through the hallway, she needed to hold her arms out to catch the sides—not because the *Patterson* was moving, but because she weakened at the thought of Harry's significant injuries and how to reconcile her strong feelings for him with her parent's strong opposition.

Arriving at Dr. Percy's office, expecting Harry to be in bed and attended to by the doctor, she was instead greeted by a group of officers talking excitedly over each other. Due to Harry's injuries, the doctor determined it was best if he remained in sick bay, and they wanted his input while they held the debriefing there.

Positioned at the wardroom door, A.C. turned to her as she approached and said, "Hannah, you shouldn't be here. This is an official inquiry. You should probably leave. I'll fill you in later."

"Oh, I'm sorry, I didn't know. Thank you." She turned around and went back down the hallway.

"Hannah, wait!" Mansfield shouted over the room, waving her to come back.

"Everyone, quiet," he commanded, and the officers fell silent.

"Hannah, please come back. Harry wants you here. Almy, we can have our meeting with her present—we're not violating any code of conduct. Please, come over here."

Mansfield shifted over, allowing her to stand by Harry as he lay in bed. She rubbed his hand in hers but remained quiet during the discussion. He looked at her through his one good eye, caressing her hand with his thumb. Once she was settled, Mansfield continued. "Carter, so again—you had gone looking for Jones when you found him in the alley, murdered. You said you didn't see anyone. But what about before that? Did you see anyone while you were on the lookout?"

"Commander, the streets and bars were packed, people everywhere except where Jones was found. Given the amount of blood on the ground, he must have lain there for some time."

"Witnesses?"

"I didn't have time to investigate, sir. Once the others showed up, we hauled the body back to the *Pirate*, got our stuff from the hotel, and then waited out the rain. With all those people in town, the dark night, and not knowing Juneau well, we agreed it wasn't safe for us. The one-eyed guy could have hidden anywhere and jumped us at any time."

Mansfield turned to Harry. "Tell me about Ellingson's murder."

Harry drew a deep breath and closed his eyes. He squeezed Hannah's hand and began, "I saw the one man, Cantwell, I'm sure, sucker punch Jones and knock him out. He and Stevens then jumped me in the street in the mud. I was fending off Cantwell when Stevens got up, went over to Ellingson, and stuck the knife in. Cantwell was getting the better of me...."

He paused and squeezed Hannah's hand again. "If the townspeople hadn't come right then, I'd be dead too. Doc Bartlett says Ellingson was nearly dead from infection anyway. The knife just finished him off sooner. Here's the death certificate," he said, pulling it from his inside coat pocket and handing it to Dr. Percy.

"And Ellingson's body?" the commander asked.

"Dr. Bartlett was holding it for the Navy. He expected the *Pinto* to pick it up by today or tomorrow," injected Carter.

"Harry, can you identify those two men?"

171

"Stevens, the one-eyed man, for sure. Cantwell—I didn't get a good look other than he was as big as Stevens. There was a third guy, smaller. I don't know. It all happened so fast."

Mansfield stopped asking questions for a moment before concluding, "I will need a report from each of you—Carter, McDonald, and Ford—by noon tomorrow. I'll let my command know what's going on; they may have orders for us. I'll keep you informed. In the meantime, we have work to do."

"Are we going out to find Stevens and Cantwell, Lieutenant?" Harry asked.

"You're not. You're out of commission. Right now, I think the *Pinto* is better staffed and prepared to deal with locating murderers. We will support them in any way we can, but unless directed otherwise, I am not sending out my officers to find these men. We don't even know where they might be, and I can't risk more men. The *Pinto* can handle it for now. Dr. Percy, you have your charge. Hannah, can you help him?"

Lieutenant Dorn, please organize a burial at sea and a wake for Seaman Jones and Seaman Ellingson. Place something in the shroud to represent Ellingson's body. Collect their belongings and sell what you can. The proceeds will go to any family they named on their enlistment paperwork. If Ellingson didn't have a family, we can donate it to one of the missions on the way home."

"Ensign McDonald, clean up, eat, and write that report. Ensign Wood, you'll assume Watch Command. Double security and provide firearms. I don't want anybody we don't know near this ship. There's no telling what Stevens and Cantwell may try."

Mansfield paused as the men nodded in agreement. Ending the meeting and releasing the men, he stopped at Harry's bedside.

"Harry, I'm glad you are safe. I hope you heal quickly. I know you are in good hands," he said, winking at Hannah before leaving the room.
Dr. Percy departed as well, ostensibly to get more supplies from the storeroom.

Hannah leaned over and kissed Harry, this time on his lips, careful to avoid the cut on his lower lip. Tears fell from her eyes as she looked at his bruised face and bandaged eye. She squeezed his hand tighter.

"I had no idea your life was like this—so dangerous," she sputtered. "You could have been killed."

Harry's heart sank. "Oh no," he thought, "here it comes, like Clara."

"But you are a draftsman, right? Draftsmen aren't always Masters-at-Arms. You don't have to be in the Navy, do you? You can do drafting from an office, can't you?"

"I suppose so."

"Harry, I know it's only been a few days, but I like you. I like you a lot. I'd like to get to know you much better. I don't know if I could cope with things like this, though—you getting beaten and killed."

He listened, understanding better now what Hannah—and Clara before her—must feel.

"But I'm willing to try."

It was enough to make him sit forward. "Hannah, you have taken my heart. I'd like to get to know you, too. I won't be going out to sea for the rest of my career, I can assure you. But I will be going out for the next few years. If you can make it through a couple more years…?"

She smiled and held both of Harry's hands.

"Yes, a couple more years. I look forward to it."

They leaned into each other and kissed passionately before pulling back.

"You are an angel," he murmured, moaning slightly as he lay back in bed.

She kissed him again and laid her head lightly on his chest, feeling the rise and fall of his breathing as he stroked her long brown hair undone from her pigtails.

A sharp knock at the door startled them, and Hannah stood up. Dr. Percy entered, his arms filled with bandages and other supplies. He set them on a table and walked over to the couple.

173

"How is the patient?" he asked, removing the eye patch to check Harry's wound.

"He is doing very well, Doctor. Thank you for your care."

"Oh, it's no trouble."

Dr. Percy paused, then looked at them. "I was asked to inform you that Lieutenant Mansfield has received orders that all guests from the *Ancon* are to be escorted to Juneau at the earliest favorable tide tomorrow. The Navy is concerned about further violence, and until these two men are caught or killed, they believe your safety is at risk. The *Pirate* is scheduled to launch at 7 a.m. Miss Hannah, you'll need to be onboard. I'm sorry."

That evening, Dorn organized a funeral for Ellingson and Jones. Dr. Percy embalmed Jones' body as best he could, then wrapped it in a white shroud and placed him on a flat, eight-foot board. His arms and legs were bound and attached to lead weights. A similar board was prepared for Ellingson, with cordwood used for the body, wrapped in a shroud, and placed on the board nonetheless.

After a few words from McDonald, Bible verses, and a moment of silence followed by the firing of the cannon, the pallbearers first lifted Jones' body and dropped it overboard, then repeated the process for Ellingson. The crew remained silent as the shrouds disappeared beneath the water.

The ship's organ, normally stowed away, was moved to the deck. Mrs. Adams began to play hymns. The crew of the *Patterson* had purchased the organ several years ago after raising funds from duck and geese hunting on Mare Island while in port for the winter. At that time, the ship's wardroom steward, an avid musician, had a keen eye for pipe organs. This one had seven pipes, with a wooden casing featuring an intricately carved façade. The worn carpeting on the push pedals indicated extensive use.

Mansfield ordered rum brought to the deck, and as Mr. Adams played *Amazing Grace*, Mansfield poured drinks for each man. One after another, both officers and crew shared words about Ellingson and Jones, recalling stories of their time serving together. It was a sad, solemn evening filled with occasional laughter, punctuated by the haunting sound of the organ and rum-fueled singing echoing across the water and into the dark, starless night.

Chapter Twenty-Three: Redfield

Upon learning from Dr. Percy that she was leaving in the morning, Hannah returned to Harry's cabin, where her parents were already preparing to depart for Juneau. Dr. Percy required Harry to stay in the sick bay as he was extremely worried about Harry's eye and wanted to monitor him for a concussion. Harry objected to no avail and then settled into a melancholy state, demoralized by events beyond his control. He could lose an eye, Hannah was leaving in the morning, and his friend Ellingson was dead, murdered.

The doctor released him early enough the following morning to say goodbye to Hannah. Standing on deck with her parents, Hannah paced back and forth, hoping she would see Harry one last time. Ensign McDonald readied the *Pirate* for their trip to Juneau. When Harry emerged on deck, she ran to hug him. Wanting some privacy, they noticed the stern was devoid of people and walked that way. Looking over the rail, neither knew what to say, but they seemed to understand what the other was thinking.

"Here is my address," she said, handing him a slip of paper. "Don't lose that."

"I won't. And here's mine. Don't lose that." Neither knew what to say next, so they just looked at each other, smiling, until Hannah's father called for her. She said,

"I'm sorry, I don't know what to say. There are too many moving parts to sort through right now. Let's take time and reflect on it."

Still baffled by his feelings, Harry simply agreed. "You're right."

"See, I'm always right." She leaned in and kissed him on the lips, wrapping her arms around his neck. They lingered in their embrace, locking eyes and looking deep.

"I love you."

"I love you too."

The bell rang, and they walked back together. Hannah was the last to board, and as they pulled away, she continued to wave. Harry continued to wave back, an aching feeling settling into the pit of his stomach that he might never see her again.

Returning to the sick bay, he entered the room and faltered, leaning against the wall for support. Dr. Percy escorted him to the bed and had him lie down. Using his stethoscope, the doctor checked Harry's heart and lungs.

"What was that all about?" the doctor asked. "Are you feeling weak? Are you sick or nauseous? Your heart rate is elevated."

"All of a sudden, I felt faint. I was fine until now."

"Let's take a look at that eye."

Harry lay down as the doctor removed the bandage and inspected the eye socket.

"Now that the swelling has gone down, you don't appear to have any broken bones, so your hyphema isn't from that. And there's not much blood anyway. I'm not too worried. Your vision will be blurry, and you'll be sensitive to light, but if you rest and keep your eye covered for the next three to five days, it will improve enough that you won't even know you were almost blinded. There may be some pain—here's some willow bark to chew on. Wash your eyes carefully four times a day, followed by twenty minutes with a warm cloth resting gently on your closed eyelid while lying down. Do you have any questions?" he asked, looking sympathetically at his bruised, battered, and broken-hearted patient.

"Mr. Ford, I've seen a lot of things in my day, but you, young man, have lived a lifetime already. You'll be fine, but I want you to stay and sleep. I'll lock the door so nobody can come in and disturb you."

Sleep never came as his mind raced with thoughts of Hannah. He couldn't stop saying her name. He imagined her moving into his apartment and marrying somewhere along the coast. He pictured her sitting at the table, eating dinner. He even tried to picture the two of them with Mark and other children at the table but shrugged off the idea as an intrusion into the time spent with her.
Then his imagination took off, and he speculated about living in Colorado. Not familiar with the state or its cities and towns, he knew it was east of

176

California but west of the Mississippi River. He decided it didn't matter where she was from; it would be a new environment, a change from what he knew.

She had told him they lived in Alamosa, on a ranch outside town. He imagined it overlooking a red-rock valley with blue skies and very little rain. He pondered life in an arid climate devoid of the daily precipitation in the Southeast. He felt he could live and thrive there or anywhere.

But to leave Alaska and never come back? That was a lot to ask. Still, he rationalized at least two ways it would work. One was that he was only a *Cheechako*, a greenhorn. He had yet to spend the winter in the Alaskan bush; therefore, he wasn't truly an Alaskan. Second, he figured Alaska would always be there and wouldn't change. He could always come back in the future. His imagination soared as he considered the drafting opportunities in Colorado. A new state would need surveys in every town.

His vision was interrupted by a knock at the door and the handle rattling. Barely alert, he listened as whoever was outside muttered a low profanity and walked away. A few minutes later, another knock came, followed by jingling keys unlocking the door and the sound of several men entering. He opened his one eye to see Mansfield and others standing before him.

"Mr. Ford, at my request, Ensign McDonald has written your report. Mac, can you please read it?"

After listening to McDonald's iteration of the events, Harry concurred, sat up to sign and date the document, and handed the paper to Mansfield.

"Lt. Mansfield, have you been able to find them yet?" he asked.

"We haven't. I have orders to let the *Pinto* take charge of the case."

"But sir, they have other obligations, like getting the Adams family back to Colorado. They won't focus on this—it's no big deal to them. We need to find Stevens and Cantwell before they leave the area."

"Mr. Ford, orders are orders. And you have yours. You are to recover, relax, and regain your strength. Nothing else."

"But sir, with all due respect, I'm fine. We need to find Stevens."

177

Mansfield appreciated Harry's resolve, but with one eye, he knew the young man wasn't capable.

"Tell you what—I'll send out a party to scan the usual hiding places south of Juneau, you know, Sheep Creek, the logging camps in the area. No engagement, but at least we can look."

With the report signed, the officers left Harry alone again. He fell asleep within ten minutes, physically and emotionally drained, only to be woken up five hours later by Dr. Percy.

"You are free to go, Mr. Ford. In my opinion, you don't have a concussion, and your eye is healing very well. You'll have that bandage off in three or four days. You must, however, continue with compressing and cleansing as I instructed. Stopping your treatment too early will only lengthen the healing time."

Still groggy from his nap, Harry remembered that he had been bunking with the crew and that his belongings were still there. The memory of Ellingson and his murder flooded his mind again, and he had to sit down as he thought of his friend.

After collecting his belongings from the crew quarters, Harry struggled down the hallway to his cabin. Still not fully aware of his surroundings, he opened the door. Hannah's scent immediately caught his nose. He dropped everything to the floor and breathed in the aroma, picturing her there at that very moment.

He walked in, and on the table, he noticed a small box with a note attached. It read:

> *Dear Harry,*
> *Remember, I'm always right.*
> *Love, Hannah*

Inside the box, she had left a white cloth the size of a handkerchief. She had embroidered an irregular blue circle filled with wavy blue lines, surrounded by green stitching resembling trees. In the center of the blue circle was a brown square, which Harry assumed represented the rowboat. Beneath the circle, she had stitched *Lake Harry*, dating it and placing her initials in the corner.

No sooner had he found the cloth than the ship's bell sounded the fire alarm. Rather than leave the present behind, he jammed the fabric deep into his pants pocket.

When he arrived in the kitchen a few minutes later, the crew had already extinguished a small fire, and the cleanup had begun. A pan of oil left unattended over a lit burner had ignited, setting several nearby cleaning rags aflame. A quick-thinking steward had grabbed handfuls of salt from a nearby barrel and doused the flames before they could spread further.

"I want a full report by tomorrow morning," Harry told the steward bluntly. "What, why, who, when, and how?" His sense of responsibility had returned with the emergency, and his old self was ready to go back to work.

"I will schedule a fire drill. We need to be better prepared," he thought to himself.

With that business behind him, he walked back to his cabin. Hannah's faint scent still lingered, and he tried to visualize her arriving in Juneau with her family. He dozed off as he dreamed of kissing her neck.

After that, life on the *Patterson* reverted to relative normalcy. Harry's eye healed, and with the guests gone and Ellingson and Jones now only memories, the crew responded with enthusiasm for the final part of the season. They had less than a month before returning to San Francisco.

Several days later, in the early hours of September 9, the *Patterson* finished receiving 20 tons of coal from the freighter *Elder*. At 5 a.m., firemen lit a fire under the main boiler, and by nine, they had left Taku Inlet, moving to anchor at latitude 57.7, longitude -133.5—their home in Holkham Bay for the next several weeks. The weather was clear and pleasant, and the crew's spirits were high, though Mt. Sumdum had received a light dusting of fresh snow overnight. Mansfield called his officers together for a final briefing on their last month of activities.

"Gentlemen," he began, "we are nearing the end of the season. I want to congratulate each of you on a job well done." The officers gave themselves a round of applause. "But our most challenging landscape may still lie ahead this week—these two fjords that we've been dancing around. I've decided it's time to name them. The north arm will be named for President Harrison's Secretary of the Navy, Secretary Tracy. And to be fair to the

179

two administrations, I am naming the south arm for Secretary of War Endicott from the Cleveland administration."

"Tracy and Endicott Arms. Very good choices, sir," chimed in Woods.

"These fjords are extremely dangerous, and I can't emphasize enough the risk we take each time we launch a boat. Ice chunks the size of the *Pirate* are everywhere. The currents are strong, the tides are extreme, and the winds are unpredictable. You and the crew, especially those in the smaller whaleboat and skiffs, must always take every precaution and exercise extreme care. This is by far our most high-risk location, and we don't need to increase that risk through our own stupid actions."

The gathering broke into a chorus of comments when a youthful-looking seaman knocked on the wardroom door. By his trim uniform, sharp facial expressions, and hand gestures, he appeared to be a bright young man eager to work his way up.

"Sir, with your permission and apologies for the interruption, Seamen Walker and Halvorsen appear to be intoxicated."

The room settled down as everyone turned to hear what the seaman had to say.

"What's your name, sailor?" Mansfield asked.

"Redfield. Tobias Redfield."

"Go on."

"Yes, sir. I was in the crew quarters getting ready for duty when I smelled an odor—you know, stale alcohol. I traced it to Walker and Halvorsen."

"Oh? And then what did you do?"

"They were unresponsive. I shook them and yelled at them, but they didn't wake up. Drunk as skunks under a blanket. I pulled off the blanket, but they didn't even notice. I let the watch know, and he said I should report it to you."

"Very good, Redfield. Thank you. Mr. Ford, will you please handle this? We can brief you later regarding the fieldwork."

180

Harry followed the seaman down the hallway to where Walker and Halvorsen lay passed out, two empty rum bottles nearby.

"Tell the watch to send two men down here with leg irons," he ordered. Redfield left and soon returned with two other seamen, bringing the irons they locked around the drunks' ankles. The intoxicated men were not small, and at this moment, they were dead weight. Before anyone could say anything, Redfield grabbed one of the two crewmen and sped off. Moments later, they returned, buckets of water in hand. With a nod of approval from Harry, they threw the water into the faces of the inebriated duo.

"Great idea. Thank you."

"You're welcome, sir… Mr. Ford."

The drunks were no longer completely unresponsive, though they were still sluggish. Chained and placed in security after staggering through the ship, they were given wash buckets for the inevitable vomiting.

"Redfield, I was thinking that you and I could go out and run a shoreline. Do you have any interest in drafting or hydrography?"

"I can picture what drafting is, but I don't know anything about that hydro... stuff. I like learning all kinds of things; it doesn't matter to me what it is. I do like having a mission, though—a reason to do something. Otherwise, some things ain't worth doing."

It was late, and Harry was exhausted. He bade Redfield good night and returned to his quarters, where Foust was sound asleep in his bunk. Trying not to wake him, Harry crawled into bed as quietly as possible.

His introduction to Redfield helped him feel a little better about Ellingson. The old sailor had been with him a lot that summer, and though Ellingson wasn't replaceable, Redfield seemed like a likeable fellow.

Chapter Twenty-Four: Drills

Knocking at the door woke Harry up, and the continued knocking began to annoy him. It was an hour before he had planned to get up, and he hadn't slept well, waking up multiple times, his mind racing with recent events. Foust had left hours earlier for his watch, disturbing his sleep even further. Carefully wiping the sleep from his eyes to avoid re-irritating his injured eye, he pulled on his robe and opened the door to find Redfield.

"Good morning, Mr. Ford. I brought you some coffee."

"Seaman Redfield, what are you doing here? You're not my steward."

"I know, sir. But last night, we talked about going out to measure the shoreline. Don't you remember?"

"We talked about it, but we didn't agree to do it right now."
Harry's mind was occupied with preparing for the fire drill he had scheduled for that morning.

"I have a fire drill I need to conduct. I can't go." Somewhat annoyed by the eager seaman, he was at least glad to have an excuse to turn him down. Harry's mood, he could tell, was sour.

Redfield looked disappointed but replied, "Oh, that's okay, Mr. Ford. We can do it another time. Here, enjoy the coffee anyway." Handing over the cup, he turned and walked away down the hallway.

The coffee tasted weak and lukewarm, adding to his lack of enthusiasm for the day. He needed to draft the drill outline and plan the topics he wanted to cover with the crew, but he couldn't focus. Instead, his thoughts kept drifting to Hannah, Ellingson, and Jones. He wondered if five months at sea was wearing on him. Was this job what he should be doing? Being away from home for so long had already cost him Clara; would the same happen if Hannah wanted to be part of his life?

It was raining, which, Harry thought sarcastically, was perfect weather to match his mood. The deck was slick with water as he met the assembled men after a breakfast of scrambled eggs. About a third of the drill crew was missing, and he considered calling it off, but then several more arrived. No one spoke—likely just as miserable as he was, standing in the rain.

Within a few more minutes, the entire contingent had arrived, except for Walker, who was still in chains. With hats pulled low against the rain, he could hardly tell who was who. He hated the moment, but duty called, so he began the drill.

"Firemen, you have a very important responsibility, and I expect you to take it seriously. This week, we had a kitchen fire that could have easily spread and sunk the ship. Several of you responded immediately and helped extinguish the flames. To those who acted quickly—job well done."

The group clapped half-heartedly.

"Today, given the rainy conditions, we will have an abbreviated drill…"

The crew cheered, drowning him out.

"…an abbreviated drill focusing on alternatives to water for fire suppression. We witnessed how well salt worked, so today, I want to place five pounds of salt in various locations around the ship that are susceptible to fire."

He had intended to sketch out the locations on paper, but he hadn't completed it yet. Besides, the rain would have ruined it anyway, he thought.

"You three men, I want you to examine the entire ship for flammable materials. Ensure they are properly stored or discarded. Also, make sure all aisles are clear for safe passage. Check every nook and cranny in every part of the ship."

"The rest of you will inspect and test the fire hoses, properly stowing them when finished. Any questions?"

"How will we know if a hose leaks? It's raining!"
The crew laughed, and Harry dismissed them, giving them one hour to complete their tasks.

The men quickly scattered, and for a moment, he hated what he was doing and wished he were anywhere else.

Shuffling off the deck, he reluctantly made his way to the brig to check on the two prisoners. The steward was cleaning up their dishes, and the guard had already taken them for their bathroom break. He stepped inside and sat in a chair between them as they lay in their bunks.

"Lieutenant Mansfield has ordered five days of restraint with full rations. You should be grateful he didn't toss you overboard like I would have."

"My head hurts," complained Halvorsen.

"Drink some water."

"I can't stay here for five days. I'll go crazy," added Walker.

"Then go to sleep."

"What if the ship catches fire again? Who's gonna save us?"

"Nobody. Why would anyone risk their lives to save the likes of you two?"

Harry's angry words echoed around the room, and he realized he had gone too far. There was no need to take his bad mood out on others. There was no need to tear his prisoners down.

Unconsciously, he lifted his hand to his eye, sensing a dull throbbing pain. Thinking of his injury and the aches from being assaulted, he realized that his bruised body and ego were likely fueling his anger.

Humbled, he added, "Don't worry. If the ship catches fire, I'll come and get you. You have my word."

Leaving them under guard, he should have gone to review the drill crew's performance. Instead, he headed to the hold, found a barrel to sit on, and, with no one around, hid for some much-needed downtime. He questioned why he felt the way he did. Closing his eyes, he let the ship's motion calm his nerves. The quiet break worked, and after fifteen minutes or so, he felt more like his old self again.

He went about the ship, checking the salt deposits, ensuring clear passageways, and confirming that the fire hoses had been properly tested and stowed. Satisfied with the drill, he dismissed the fire crew and climbed into the pilothouse, where Mansfield, Dorn, and McDonald were scanning charts.

Without looking up from the table, Mansfield asked, "Mr. Ford, what can I do for you?"

"Sir, I wanted to report that the fire drill was successful this morning. We now have salt for fire suppression located at strategic points throughout the ship."

"Very well, Mr. Ford. Thank you. Your drills are critical to our efficiency. Keep up the good work."

"Next week, when it isn't raining, we will conduct a lifeboat drill as well."

"And how are our friends Walker and Halvorsen? Are they showing any signs of repentance?"

Feeling a little guilty about his treatment of them, he said, "Yes, I think so."

"If that's the case, they have my permission to go on our end-of-season shore leave in Juneau—on the condition that they do not get drunk or bring alcohol back on board. If they can meet that test, the rest of their time in irons will be waived. If they violate those terms, they will be dismissed from Navy service and left behind."

"Yes, sir. I will make sure they behave while in Juneau."

"Will you let me know how they do?"

"Yes, sir, I will. Again, I'll go with them to make sure they stay sober."

"Thank you. Now, we only have a week or so before hauling anchor for the season. What are your plans until then?"

"My next stop is to check in with Smith and Sanford. I haven't worked on any charts in a while. I need to catch up—to know what they are working on, what data is missing, and what we absolutely must finish."

"All the launches are in demand and will be in use daily, so check early with Lieutenant Dorn—he's in charge of their schedules."

"Yes, sir. I will be needing one, I'm sure. I know some depth measurements for the south arm of Endicott Arm need to be remeasured, and there are probably others."

Mansfield paused to reflect on other tasks, then asked, "How is the eye?"

"It's better. I still have some cloudiness, but it's less than before. Dr. Percy says it should be gone in another few days. It did ache a little today, though."

Changing the subject, he asked, "Any word on Stevens and Cantwell? Have we found them?"

"No, nothing. The *Pinto* investigated and they think the two jumped town, but there's no confirmation. Nobody in Juneau knows anything. I suspect they're all afraid of getting killed."

Harry thought of the upcoming shore leave. "Will it be safe for us to go ashore in Juneau?"

He wasn't afraid to know they were still at large, but he was well aware of how deadly they could be.

"Yes, Mr. Ford, I doubt those two would be so brazen as to attack any of our crew members while we are all in town. Nevertheless, we will need to remain vigilant."

Leaving the pilothouse, Harry headed to the drafting room. Both of his colleagues were there when he entered.

"Well, if it isn't Mr. Ford. You haven't been around in what—a week?"

It was Sanford, reaching out to shake his hand.

"It seems like it, doesn't it? I don't remember when I was here last."

"Good to see you, sir. How is the eye?" asked Smith.

"Better. I'll admit I've been reluctant to stop by. I'm afraid I won't be able to see the details. Doc Percy said I should wait another day or two, but I want to know now."

"Of course," Sanford smiled. "Take a look at this one. I just worked on it and then noticed something wrong when I compared it to this one. It's a rendering at 1:25,000 of the south arm—Endicott Arm—south shore, west of this choke point. My contour isn't correct. Can you see what I did wrong?"

Bending over the chart, he grabbed a ruler and studied it. He examined it for a few more seconds, moving the ruler slightly. After a moment, he said,

"No, I can't. It's too blurry and cloudy. I'm trying to focus with just one eye. I'm not ready yet. I'd be putting the shoreline on the mountainside."

"Mr. Ford, we've got this. Smith and I can do the drafting, and we can keep up. But remember, we need data, too—accurate numbers. You get the measurements, and we'll build the charts. We need at least two, if not three, shoreline remeasurements, plus more depth measurements.

"Mr. Ford, I know how much drafting means to you, and I'm sorry your vision isn't better, but you can still help us," implored Sanford.

"And your eye will continue to heal. You'll be able to draft again one of these days," added Smith.

Harry smiled and nodded. "You guys are right. I can still help. There's no sense in feeling sorry for myself. So, show me what areas you're talking about."

They proceeded to brief him on their needs.

Half a dozen deckhands were busy hauling the *Pirate* out of the water for repairs, but there was a leak at the propeller exit. Dorn supervised, giving orders as the men used a boom with pulleys and ropes to lift the craft from the water, hoisting it above the deck. They then pulled another set of ropes to center her and finally tied her corners and ends down to keep her from swinging. Ladders were swung into position to allow access to the raised launch. Taking advantage of the situation, Dorn had the crew scrape barnacles and other crustaceans from the hull.

The *Cosmos* was also alongside. Almy directed his crew as they hauled cordwood from the *Cosmos* to the ship, moving it down to the wood storage compartment near the boiler. The time and effort required to cut and transport dozens of cords of wood were significant, but the savings over coal made it worthwhile.

Harry meandered up to the deck and watched the activity for a moment before approaching Dorn. The engineer was explaining the repairs needed to fix the leak. After convincing the engineer to do only what was necessary, Dorn turned to Harry and said,

"The old gal ain't what she used to be. How many times have we had to haul her up this season? Three? Not to mention the times we've fixed her in the water."

"She does seem to be breaking down more, I agree."

"What can I do for you, Mr. Ford?"

"Tomorrow morning, I need to use one of the launches for shoreline measurements."

"I think you're in luck. Beecher is due back from tidal observations at about nine. Is that too late?"

"No, that's perfect. I'll use his launch, and I guess he can get some sleep. Thanks, Lieutenant."

Harry turned to leave and saw Redfield approaching. He remembered the coffee incident from earlier and realized how much better he felt—he had come out of his mood slump. Smith and Sanford's support had lifted his spirits.

"Redfield, I want to thank you for the cup of coffee this morning. I wasn't quite awake when you knocked. It surprised me."

"You're welcome, Mr. Ford. I won't do it again."

"I think that would be best," he agreed. "I do need a crew for tomorrow. I'll be measuring the shoreline. Are you available?"

"Yes, sir, I'd like that. I'll be there. Thank you."

He looked at the young man, probably no more than seventeen, and remembered his own enthusiasm at that age.

"Thank you, Redfield. I could use your help. Now, I'm off to visit my two prisoners."

He bade him good night and headed down to the brig. As he walked, he replayed his morning interaction with Walker and Halvorsen and was relieved he no longer felt the same anger. He wondered what had triggered his bad mood, then recalled Redfield knocking at the door, the ache in his eye, and his bruises.

The two prisoners sat on their bunks while the watch stood outside. He pulled the chair between them and sat just as he had earlier.

"Are you in a better mood, Mr. Ford? You seemed a little out of sorts this morning. Granted, you have every right to be," Halvorsen admitted. "Walker and I have been talking—we shouldn't have done what we did. It's the alcohol. Once you start, you can't stop. Anyway, we want to apologize to you and Lieutenant Mansfield. We won't do it again. We promise."

"Yes, yes, we won't do it again, we promise," Walker echoed.

Harry looked at them both, wondering if they truly meant what they said. Their *mea culpa* had come before they knew about the upcoming shore leave. Maybe they had come to repentance on their own.

"I want to believe that it won't happen again."

"No, sir, not ever again," they both pleaded.

"Alright. I believe you. In a couple of days, Lieutenant Mansfield will be allowing shore leave for all crew members, including you. You have two options: one is to not get drunk, and two is to not get drunk. Do you understand?"

Walker raised his hand. "Are we getting paid anytime soon?"

Harry wondered if he would regret letting them go to Juneau.

Chapter Twenty-Five: Chung

Eleven hundred islands covered in old-growth forests make up the two-hundred-mile-long Alexander Archipelago. If one were to fly over them from south to north, subtle differences would emerge between the groupings of these islands.

The southern group includes Revillagigedo, Prince of Wales, Dall, and Wrangell Islands. Dixon Entrance, north of Graham Island in Canada, serves as the gateway to these southern islands. The peaks in this group are generally shorter and more rounded than their northern counterparts. Nine of the ten highest peaks in the whole of the archipelago are in the northern group—only 4,592-foot Mt. Reid on Revillagigedo Island makes the list from the south.

The northern group includes Admiralty, Baranof, and Chichagof Islands—the ABCs—as well as, to a lesser extent, Kupreanof Island. These islands extend northward to the northwest flank and northern end of the Juneau Icefield, bordering Glacier Bay at the southern edge of the Wrangell-St. Elias Mountain range. The highest peak in the northern group is Kootznoowoo Peak on Admiralty Island, standing at 4,850 feet, while the high point on Baranof Island rises to nearly 5,400 feet. Adjacent to Baranof Island is the dormant Mt. Edgecumbe volcano on Kruzof Island, which rises to 3,200 feet.

With only two hundred miles separating the northern and southern tips, the climatic differences are striking. In general, the south receives more rain, while the north experiences heavier snowfall. Snowfalls in the north are earlier, deeper, and linger later in the spring, whereas in the south, snow is seen less often, both on the peaks and at sea level.

Similarly, if one were to fly over the archipelago from west to east, two other notable distinctions between the island groups would emerge, one of which lies underwater. To the west, the Pacific Ocean surrounds both island groups equally. However, a view of the ocean floor—if the water were removed—would reveal a stark difference.

In the north, the continental shelf drops off dramatically just twenty or so miles from the coast, while in the south, this shelf break occurs more than seventy-five miles offshore. The abrupt transition from deep ocean waters to shallow coastal waters in the north creates more navigational hazards than in the south, where the shift happens much farther out to sea.

To the east, the North American continent is rising, but here, too, there are notable differences. The Coastal Mountains form the edge of the mainland, with the Stikine River providing a natural line of separation between north and south. South of the Stikine, elevations are lower, meaning mountain peaks retain less snow and fewer glaciers remain. North of the Stikine, however, the massive Juneau Icefield spans hundreds of square miles, rising thousands of feet in the Coastal Mountains. The icefield feeds numerous glaciers, some of which reach the ocean, while others terminate in lakes, their meltwaters forming river outlets.

Roughly 1,800 miles separate Juneau from San Diego—a distance comparable to that between San Francisco and Kansas City, Missouri. Within that vast span, a mere five miles of an inlet opening provides access to two of the most dramatic fjords in the world, Tracy and Endicott Arms. These twenty-mile-long, glacially carved canals are flanked by towering mountainsides that rise four to six thousand feet above sea level. At the ends of these canyons, tidewater glaciers descend from the Juneau Icefield, frequently calving massive ice blocks into the frigid waters below. In winter, snowfall replenishes the icefield, while in summer, the melting ice imperceptibly slides downhill, inching ever closer to the ocean—and eventual extinction.

On September 21, the crew of the *U.S.S. Carlise P. Patterson* found themselves within this five-mile inlet opening south of Juneau, enjoying ideal conditions. They lay anchored in Endicott Arm, where a light breeze from the south and east kept them sheltered from stronger winds blowing north and west in Stephens Passage.

The *Patterson* wasn't the only vessel in the area. Fishermen and fur traders frequently ventured into these ice-choked waters, drawn by the region's abundant resources—otters, salmon, halibut, cod, and lobster. The native Tlingit also fished these waters. Between the survey launches gathering measurements and the fishing boats hauling in their nets, the area bustled with activity despite its remote location.

On this beautiful late fall day, the *Patterson's* launches were busy early in the morning. The conditions were excellent, and the crew appreciated their final days in the region being free of rain and snow. They enjoyed abundant sunshine, relative warmth, and an almost surreal, glassy calm on the ocean's surface.

The *Cosmos* was the first to launch, just after dawn. Piloted by McDonald and a crew of four, its mission was to conduct additional depth soundings using the Sigsbee. They headed out into Stephens Passage, turned south past Wood Spit, and were followed by a smaller skiff for support.

As a pale-yellow hue peeked over the mountains into a crystal-clear blue sky, the *Vixen* launched. Ensign Wood directed his four-man crew north to the entrance of Taku Harbor, followed by a second skiff. Their task was to take piano wire and measurement readings along the southern entrance there.

Almy set out in the *Pirate* and one of the smaller Herreshoff launches with his crews. Their assignment was to measure the shoreline from the northern tip of Rock Point, curving around the inside of Sanford Cove's southern base, down to the large creek that entered from the south. Given the bay's curved nature, Almy required numerous measurement points to minimize the straight-line effect.

Beecher arrived in the whaleboat as expected at about 8:30. As Harry watched him tie up alongside, he noticed Redfield approaching.

"Good morning, Redfield. Are you ready?"

"Yes, sir, Mr. Ford. Do you still want to go out and do shoreline measurements? I read about that last night before I went to sleep—I found a book on it in the ship's library."

"I'm impressed. Not many men on this ship have that kind of motivation."

"Thank you, sir. Someday, I'd like to be an officer."

"I think you'd make a decent officer. Now, about today—my drafters need some depth locations remeasured. So, instead of shoreline measurements, we'll be taking depth soundings. We're heading east."

Excited, the young seaman exclaimed, "Let's get to work!" Looking more enthusiastic than any man should be about such labor, Harry wondered what made the greenhorn tick—but he didn't ask.

Beecher, meanwhile, finished unloading his equipment and supplies from the whaleboat before climbing aboard the *Patterson* beside them. He dropped his duffle bag with an exhausted sigh.

"I made it. I wasn't sure I would."

Redfield asked, "What's the matter, sir? The water is calm, and there's no air this morning."

Laughing, Beecher replied, "Oh no, it's not the weather, seaman. I've been out three nights at Station Snap doing tidal measurements." Turning to Harry, he asked, "Did you notice the moon last night?"

Harry thought about it. "No, I guess I didn't. Why?"

"No, you didn't. It was a new moon. The moon affects tides. I've seen some big tides in my life, but in this vicinity, they're phenomenal—fifteen, sixteen feet. The first two nights I was out, I thought, yeah, these are pretty major tides. But last night—eighteen feet. I've never seen anything like that. So, I want to warn you, since I see you're taking out the launch, today's tide will be just as big, if not bigger. Be prepared."

Turning to Redfield, Beecher added, "I'm exhausted from battling tides for the past three days."

Harry glanced at his chronometer. "If I recall from the charts, today's low tide is at about one o'clock, and high tide this evening is around seven."

"Not around one o'clock; it is at one. And tonight at seven twenty-five," Beecher corrected. "Minutes count with tides like these. An eighteen-foot tide changes at about three feet an hour—roughly an inch a minute. If you were off by twenty-five minutes, that's nearly two feet."

They loaded the whaleboat with wood, water, sounding equipment, and supplies. Harry had ordered two lunches and some snacks from the kitchen, knowing they'd be out for at least six hours. The steward brought the food at the requested time. Confident they had everything they needed, he instructed Redfield to handle the ropes. They were about to push away when Dorn approached.

"Mr. Ford, glad I caught you before you left. There's a Chinaman in a small skiff trying to sell something to our boats. His English is so bad that nobody's sure what he's selling, but he's been going around to each of the launches. He even went up to the *Pirate* twice. He gets animated, and we all think he's crazy in the head. One of the cooks was on the *Pirate* and was able to talk to him. Says his name is Chung and agrees he is crazy. Just wanted to give you a heads-up in case he approaches you."

"Okay, that's good to know. I don't like it when strangers show up."

Endicott Arm was calm when they untied from the *Patterson*, making for an easy time in the whaleboat. Harry watched the mountainsides drift by— gentle slopes covered in green forests, with water cascading down the flanks like braids of white hair. Small chunks of ice bobbed in their path, most too small to pose any threat. He let them bounce off the hull with a slight thud.

Their destination lay about nine miles to the east, toward the glaciers. The other launches were visible to their right but soon fell behind as they gained distance. As they progressed, he slowed the boat—the ice chunks ahead were growing larger.

According to Smith and Sanford, the site for their soundings was more of a line than a single location, stretching the entire length between the canyon walls. The line curved like an arc, its open end facing the glaciers. Depth measurements had shown inconsistencies in this area, and new readings would help confirm the underwater geography.

About twelve miles from the inlet opening at Wood Spit, they reached their first measurement point and began setting up for the soundings. The water remained calm, though a slight breeze had begun to stir. The air was warm, and both men took their time setting up, appreciating the stunning scenery around them.

They decided to take their first measurement near the north shore and work their way south across the channel. Sanford explained that the line they were measuring marked an underwater edge—a sharp drop-off, with a shallower area to the west and a steep drop-off of the ocean floor to the east. Their goal was to locate this edge and measure the depth on both sides along its entire mile-and-a-half curved length.

After about three hours, they had gathered enough data to confirm Smith and Sanford's suspicions. Endicott Arm featured a dramatic underwater cliff. Along the arc, in the very center of the canyon, there was a sudden drop from 950 feet to 1,150 feet—an abrupt 200-foot plunge. At another location to the north, near the entrance of an unnamed glacial canyon, they measured an astonishing 680-foot drop from the top of the edge to the canyon floor. For comparison, Horseshoe Falls at Niagara Falls is only half a mile wide and 180 feet from top to bottom.

Their concentration was interrupted when Redfield spotted a launch approaching.

"Harry, someone's coming. Is that one of ours?"

They stopped and watched as the craft continued toward them. Harry pulled out his binoculars to get a better look.

"No, it's not one of ours. I think it might be the Chinaman Dorn warned us about."

Sure enough, a man of Asian descent piloted the little steamer. They waited as the short, thin, wrinkled old man maneuvered alongside. Harry expected some desperate plea for supplies or assistance, but instead, the man simply stared at him.

For several seconds, their eyes locked. Then Chung broke into a wide grin and began speaking rapidly in his native language—excited gibberish neither Harry nor Redfield could understand.

Baffled, Harry glanced at Redfield as if to say, *What do I do?*

As they bobbed in the water, Chung abruptly stopped talking and began stuffing moss into his firebox. Almost immediately, a thick black cloud of smoke billowed into the still air. The old man laughed to himself as he alternated between blowing on the fire, looking at Harry, and glancing back toward the entrance of Endicott Arm.

"Mr. Ford, what's he doing?"

"I don't know. That moss is gonna put his fire out—that's what I don't understand."

Chung continued stoking the fire with more moss. By now, the smoke had drifted several hundred feet into the sky, dispersing as it met the breeze.

"Is he signaling?"

Harry tensed. Redfield was right—he *was* signaling someone. And he suddenly knew who.

"That laugh," Harry muttered, his body stiffening. "Now I recognize that laugh. He was laughing while Cantwell tried to beat me to death."

Chapter Twenty-Six: Marooned

Instinct warns us to stand, fight, or flee as fast as possible when confronted with danger. But how do you know which action to choose? The immediacy of a threat—or even distractions at the time—may cloud judgment, increasing the risk of making the wrong choice.

Deer hunting on Admiralty Island in bear territory is inherently dangerous. The hunter knows this going in, observing his surroundings and preparing for the dangers he may face. He's ready to defend himself if a bear attacks while he's hunting. But that same hunter, after killing a deer, will put down his weapon to gut it, leaving him defenseless against a grizzly charging after the carcass. At that moment, he has little to no time to react. Decisions that should take minutes must now be made in seconds—if there's time at all.

Imminent danger impacts our ability to reason. Depending on the physical or emotional threat level, a feeling of impending horror can strike with such intensity that it overwhelms the mind. Paralysis sets in, making fighting or fleeing impossible. Helpless and stripped of cognitive function, one is left to face terror, frozen in fear.

As Harry and Redfield watched, Chung continued stoking his moss-burning fire. He let out a long, loud hoot—a celebratory exclamation that echoed across the still ocean. Whether it was the call of a madman or someone expecting a great reward, Harry wasn't sure.

Realizing Chung was signaling to Stevens, Harry decided it was time to take action, and he turned to move toward the helm. Redfield, mindful of their well-being while out working, thrust a canteen of water to Harry and suggested he have a drink, which Harry did, but in doing so, swallowed too quickly. The water went down the wrong pipe. Choking and coughing, he stood abruptly, cutting off the oxygen to his brain.

His vision blurred.

He collapsed onto the floorboards.

Faintly, he heard Redfield calling his name, but the voice seemed distant, as if the seaman was far away. Slowly, Harry regained consciousness, finding himself face-down on the deck. Redfield pounded on his back and shouted,

"Mr. Ford! Mr. Ford!"

"Mr. Ford, you fainted. Oh Lord, are you alright? You hit your face on the ground. You're bleeding a little. Here, let me help you up. You fell like a rock. I didn't have time to reach out, and then—boom—you were down. Are you okay, Mr. Ford? You're lucky you didn't pass out and fall overboard. You'd have drowned."

Harry stood, testing his balance while gripping the helm.

"Wow," he muttered. "I could hear you calling me, but it didn't connect. That was strange. I'm fine, I think. It's over. My head just hurts."

Now fully conscious, he sat down on the launch's bench seat, looking around. The fjord's natural beauty and the clear sky suddenly sharpened his senses. No sound but the rush of a waterfall across the inlet. No wind except a whisper stirring the highest treetops. The ocean lay smooth and glassy, unbroken by ripples. At that moment, a calm settled over both the world of Endicott Arm and Harry's battered soul.

He flinched as Redfield pressed gauze against his bleeding face and taped it down. The bandage fell off, and Redfield tossed it overboard.

"I'm fine. It'll stop bleeding. Thank you."

Regaining his focus, Harry spotted Chung floating about a hundred yards away. The moss had indeed clogged his firebox, smothering the flames. Powerless in the water, Chung frantically tossed out smoldering moss to clear the firebox while shooting nervous glances at Harry.

Lifting the binoculars, Harry scanned west toward Stephens Passage.

"Boat coming this way. Redfield, I need to tell you what's going on."

He hesitated, looking at the boy in front of him. Despite Redfield's occasional annoyances, he was a good kid—thoughtful, well-meaning. He

198

brought him coffee. He tried to patch him up. Now was the time for honesty, not sugarcoating their situation.

"Redfield, I'm afraid I've put you in harm's way. I witnessed Ellingson's murder, and the killer wants to kill me, too. My assumption is—that's him coming this way. He doesn't like eyewitnesses. He's already killed two men that I know of.

"Ellingson saw him murder a tribal shaman in Angoon. Years later, they knifed Ellingson right in front of me. Seaman Jones saw it, and they cut his throat.

"This guy—Chung—I didn't get a good look at him that night they beat me in the street, but he was there. I remember his laugh. That high-pitched screech while Ellingson bled out. It was like he *enjoyed* watching a man die."

Harry pointed at the small craft still drifting nearby, tendrils of smoke rising from the firebox.

"Chung is an accomplice to murder. Are you armed?"

He knew Redfield *shouldn't* be armed, but he hoped the teenager had brought something along—maybe for shooting a halibut or some other reason. Harry now regretted not taking his rifle.

"No, Mr. Ford. I'm not authorized to carry a weapon."

"Well, if you don't have anything, we've got just six rounds in my .38.

Check under the tarps and inside the storage compartments. Maybe someone left ammunition or a weapon."

"I can shoot a pistol," Redfield said eagerly. "I'm a straight shot. My grandpaps taught me when I was a kid. We'd go out in our backwoods and shoot turkeys and raccoons."

Harry handed him the revolver.

"Here. Take this. I've got a plan."

Once again, they looked toward the approaching launch. It had closed the distance and was now clearly visible. Harry wanted to take another look through the binoculars, but it was too late. They had no more time to waste.

"Drop all our sounding lines, lead weights—any loose gear. Cut everything loose. Dump all that lead overboard. We'll deal with the quartermaster later."

Redfield moved quickly, throwing multiple fathoms of heavy line into the sea. Over a hundred pounds of lead splashed into the water. Then, he threw several pieces of wood into the firebox and filled the boiler with fresh water.

Their whaleboat was perfectly positioned behind Chung's disabled launch, obscuring them from view of the incoming boat.

"Redfield, stoke this fire as hot as you can. Use more wood if you need to. We need a full head of steam—*now*."

Designed to generate steam quickly, the *Herreshoff* was ready within minutes to engage the propeller and turn toward Chung. The Chinaman had not relit his fire and continued drifting with the current.

"Blow air into that firebox! Find the bellows if you have to—blow on it! We need steam!" Harry yelled at Redfield.

As they approached the Asian's launch, the small craft created ripples cascading across the mirrored water. Chung, his back to them, sat cackling. The whaleboat drifted in quietly after cutting power to the prop.

"I want to cripple his engine—flounder him. A crew from the *Patterson* can pick him up later. Take the helm and steer us to the stern. I'll board and take the engine out with this," Harry said, grabbing a hammer.

Redfield eased the bow to the rear of Chung's boat, close enough for Harry to jump over. He pounded on a steam valve, dislodging it from the boiler. Steam hissed through the opening as Harry rendered the small craft inoperable.

Chung flew into a rage, throwing a knife that missed Harry's arm by only a few inches. Screaming at the top of his lungs, he looked for something else to throw but found nothing. Harry slowly backed up, gripping the hammer as his weapon. Redfield maneuvered the launch alongside, allowing Harry to hop back in. With Chung's craft disabled, they turned their attention to the inbound launch, now closing in fast.

"Mr. Ford, what do we do?"

Mentally calculating the movement of the approaching launch, Harry estimated it was traveling at about eight knots. The whaleboat could also do eight knots—as long as they stayed at that speed, they could maintain their lead. But which direction should they go?

Glancing around at their surroundings, he weighed their options. The *Patterson* would be the best place to return to but given the angle and speed of the incoming boat, it would cut them off first. Stevens and Cantwell didn't need to get *to* them—only within rifle range.

Scanning the nearest shoreline to the south, he saw no possible shelter or landing spot. The mountainsides were stripped bare by the glacier's recent retreat, the granite walls plunging nearly perpendicular into the cold water. No footholds. No rocky beach.

He turned his gaze north, almost a mile away, but that shoreline was no better—just smooth, featureless bedrock at the waterline.

Then he looked east.

The tidewater glacier loomed in the distance.

"Mr. Ford, no! You *can't* be thinking of going up there. We'll never make it in this little whaleboat! Look at the size of these ice chunks—*we'll be crushed!*"

"Quiet."

He wasn't just looking east. He was looking at the water.

Pulling out his chronometer, he noted the time was twelve-thirty, then glanced up at the waning crescent moon still visible in the afternoon sky.

"Redfield, I've been at this location before—doing soundings. Remember where that large drop-off occurred, just in front of that canyon over there?" He pointed to the north shore.

201

He looked back at the approaching launch.

"That's where we are going. It's our only escape. We need to move—*now*."

He powered the *Herreshoff* to full speed and turned east. Looking back, he could see two bulky figures in the pursuing launch. The craft adjusted course, following them.

He handed Redfield the binoculars.

"Can you tell who they are?"

"Two men. White."

"Any features? Beards?"

"Yes, wait—one of them is wearing an eye patch."

Stevens and Cantwell.

"Stevens is piloting, and the other one's holding a rifle." Redfield turned to Harry, his voice filled with disbelief. "They're going to *shoot* us."

They maintained their distance, dodging ice chunks large enough to damage the launch. Both vessels slowed as the danger increased.

Harry spied an area at the canyon entrance that might serve their next move. The mouth was narrow, only a few hundred yards across. Like Endicott Arm's shoreline, the west canyon wall was sheer, smooth bedrock plunging straight into the water—no place to land.

"There. On the east side of the entrance." He pointed. "See how the bedrock drops less steeply? Unlike anywhere else around here, you can stand there without falling over. There are places to hide. Do you see it?"

Redfield followed his gaze and spotted several small outcroppings where trees clung to the rock. Unlike the sheer cliff on the opposite side, this formation jutted out like a finger, creating an appendage with footholds.

"I see it. But what do you mean *I* could stand there?"

"I'm dropping you off. I want you to hide."

"What? Wait—*no!* You *can't* do that!"

"I can. And I am. Stevens wants *me*, not you. They don't even know who you are. But if they see you, they'll kill you too. I *can't* let that happen."

He steered the *Herreshoff* into the small alcove the rock formation created, giving them a few precious seconds out of Stevens' line of sight—just long enough for Redfield to jump.

Redfield scanned the bare rock for hand and footholds, then leaped from the boat. His right boot slipped briefly into the water before he caught himself. Gasping, he scrambled up the rock, climbing nearly thirty feet until the ridge flattened out. There, he steadied himself, standing straight and still. From his vantage point, Redfield looked west into Endicott Arm, high enough to spot the *Patterson* in the distance. Scanning the water, he watched as Stevens slowed the launch near the canyon entrance, hesitating in unfamiliar waters.

"Stay out of their sight!" Harry yelled. "They know there were two of us in the boat. If they only see me, they might turn around and start looking for you. Go as high as you can into the trees, keep your eyes on 'em, and don't hesitate to shoot. Understood?"

Harry swung the whaleboat around, determined to evade Stevens by heading up the canyon, but his concern for Redfield gnawed at him. If Stevens decided to send Cantwell ashore where he had dropped the boy off, Redfield would have nowhere to run. He had to trust that the boy would know what to do.

Hidden behind a tree, Redfield watched as Stevens and Cantwell alternated their gaze between Harry's retreating boat and the canyon entrance near his own hiding spot. He knew they were unlikely to follow Harry into the treacherous water. More likely, they would turn back and come looking for *him*.

Shifting his gaze from Stevens' launch, he looked up at the impossibly narrow, steep canyon, his breath catching at the sight of the massive glacier towering at its head. Closing his eyes, he prayed that Mr. Ford would survive.

Chapter Twenty-Seven: The Herreshoff

The cold air dropping down through the canyon from the glacier, some six miles ahead, struck Harry in the face the minute he headed that way. The bright sunshine of Endicott Arm gave way to darkened canyon walls, all in shadow. Small spruces that had grown after the glacier's retreat clung to the upper hillside, but for the most part, the lower canyon walls were bare bedrock. In places, the grey-blue silty water flowed past the rocky shoreline, while in others, bedrock jutted into the water as a massive wall. A heavy flow of meltwater from the previous afternoon's sun poured out from under the glacier, either to flow with the outgoing tide or to confront it as it was coming in.

Stevens and Cantwell continued their pursuit, not stopping as Harry had hoped. He didn't want them to go after Redfield, but he assumed they wouldn't risk their lives in the current either.

During an anchorage in Holkham Bay earlier in the season, he and Beecher had made this trip just beyond the mouth. They had been out conducting soundings along the arc when they took time to check the imposing entrance. They went far enough to learn that the canyon bent almost 90 degrees to the left before doglegging back to the right. A ridgeline of bedrock, forty feet high and two hundred yards long, protruded from the mountainside, creating a natural choke point. Not only did this constriction narrow the passage, but the ocean floor also became very shallow at that point, with the bedrock submerged only at high tide. A glacier was their best guess as to what lay further upstream past the turn.

The pursuers had closed the distance and were now following within a quarter mile. He could see the two men in their boat as he approached the bend. Looking ahead at what he was about to navigate, it dawned on him that the combination of the constriction point, the canyon's geography, the incoming tide, and the extreme meltwater volume and velocity would place him in a torrent worse than that of Kootznoowoo Inlet. The walls were steeper and narrower, creating a faster flow, and, more menacingly, ice the size of small skiffs floated everywhere, swirled about by the currents, and in some places, grounded due to the low tide and exposed sandbars.

In a quick panic, he considered turning the whaleboat around and trying to speed past Stevens to the open waters of Endicott Arm, where he could likely beat them to the *Patterson* for help. Remembering they likely carried a rifle, he decided to stick with the plan to hide up the canyon. Turning around, he saw the two men behind him, slowed in their pursuit by the ice. Cantwell had moved to the bow, and as Harry watched, a puff of smoke came from the rifle he was holding. A bullet grazed by his jacket sleeve, terrifying him.

Timing his escape as best he could over the past fifteen minutes, the dynamics he had hoped for were now coming into play. It was 12:57, according to the whaleboat's chronometer, and the water flow out of the canyon was slowing. The tide level was 3 minutes from its lowest point. The ocean would be no longer draining but reversing, beginning to fill inland. The currents around him swirled as if uncertain which way to go. Recognizing that every second counted, he added more wood to the firebox. Ahead, he could see the mix of ocean and glacial river water in the shallow neck, which was now calm.

Harry had been out on the launches enough times during his tenure with the Survey to be well aware of their operating characteristics. He knew that this launch, in particular, was built for extreme conditions. Designed for the Greely Relief Expedition in 1884, it had features that separated it from the other Herreshoff launches. The propeller was not fixed in one position but could be unlocked and pulled up to protect it from shallow water. A $4\frac{3}{4}$-inch clasp enabled a center mast to be attached, allowing sails to be raised for wind-powered movement. Two iron runners, about two feet apart, ran along the keel on each side, acting like sled runners. Designed by the Navy to require minimal water, the engine's boiler could come up to steam in less than ten minutes. For the Greely launch, they added a grappling hook contraption designed to pull the launch over ice.

With only a slight bump on a gravel bar, he passed the narrow curve and continued up the canyon past the bend.

Within minutes, he sensed an increase in the current's strength, pushing him forward. Looking back, he saw the choke point beginning to churn, with water splashing into the air from the waves created by the constriction. The two men had not appeared—they apparently weren't willing to navigate through it.

Hesitating, he pondered his next move. He couldn't keep going—the glacier was further up. He only had a few minutes to decide, and he began to panic that maybe he should go back, risk the rising water, and face Stevens. He figured Stevens would leave rather than risk getting caught by the *Patterson's* search parties. He decided he wanted to get out, but turning and keeping the launch steady was challenging in the currents.

It was too late anyway.

The current had become so strong, fast, and voluminous that he could not pass the whaleboat through the choke point he had only minutes ago traversed. The churning rapids soon engulfed the entire canyon—and the whaleboat. One of the largest tides of the year, in one of the most remote glacial canyons on the continent, had caught Harry in its grasp.

He turned off the propeller and pulled it up to avoid snapping it off. A strong breeze funneled down the canyon. He considered raising the sails but then reconsidered. The water was controlling his position. The rudder provided no response, and the boat twisted and turned, remaining relatively stationary within the canyon. The ocean pushed one way, and the glacial river pushed the other. There was little he could do but sit and try not to be thrown overboard.

Splashes of ice water came over the gunwales, drenching his clothing. Scooting on his hands and knees, he moved closer to the firebox for something to hold on to. The air temperature was thirty-eight degrees in the shadows of the mid-afternoon September sun. Wet and cold, he pulled a dry jacket from his duffel bag and put it on.

"Beecher said high tide was at 7:25 tonight. I'm going to be here until 7:25. I'm not sure I'll survive," he said to himself. Crawling over to the helm, he carefully removed the lid covering the Herreshoff's chronometer.

"1:17. Six hours and eight minutes to go."

He didn't know how he would survive six hours in the tumultuous water. The waves and currents shook and pushed the launch violently, nearly careening him into the bedrock walls lining the channel. He could easily be tossed into the frigid water and drown.

He could not hold on to the engine compartment—his hands were too cold, his fingers too stiff. The boat bounced and rolled high into ten-foot waves, then dropped with a thud into the troughs. Struggling to pull a blanket from storage beneath the seats, he wrapped it around his shoulders and sat with his back against the engine enclosure, bracing his feet against the seat for stability.

As the minutes ticked by ever so slowly, an overwhelming sense of dread crept into his thoughts. His blood pressure rose, his pulse pounded, and his breathing became shallow and fast. Dizziness spun his head, and he fell over. Unhurt, he sat back up, unsure of what had happened. Desperate, he clutched the blanket tighter around him, covering his head, hiding from that which terrified him.

Fear gripped his senses. The pounding of the water against the boat resounded in his ears, drowning out all other sounds. He was going to be cold and wet for a long time. Closing his eyes, he remembered only a small part of a Psalm that he had been taught long ago. "Be still. Be still," he cried, imploring God to command the waters to stop. "Be still." As the minutes and hours passed, the vivid memories of his baptism in Christ one warm spring Sunday five years ago became his focus, a spiritual victory so needed at that moment that he was able to briefly accept the peril that swirled around him.

Meanwhile, Redfield had climbed to a flat spot in the trees overlooking the inlet and Endicott Arm. He watched as Harry passed through the narrow neck and disappeared from view. Then, he saw Stevens and Cantwell enter, stop, and witness the water transform from calm to chaos. Looking west into Endicott Arm, he spotted two *Patterson* launches off in the distance and the stern of the *Patterson* itself, partially obscured by Bushy Island.

Giving up on Harry, Stevens, and Cantwell drifted back down near the canyon entrance, just offshore on the eastern side. Cantwell, scanning the hillside with binoculars, caused Redfield to duck down, hoping he hadn't been seen.

"They're looking for me," he muttered. Carefully peeking out, he confirmed that they were indeed searching the hillside. Staying crouched, he moved behind the ridge to remain completely out of their line of sight. He descended along it for twenty yards before peering over again to relocate the two men.

They were closer now, only fifty yards from his hiding spot. Redfield watched as Stevens maneuvered their launch toward the rocky shoreline.

He assumed they were trying to get close enough for Cantwell to jump out. The boat rocked in the wake, and Cantwell, standing near the bow, looked unsteady as he assessed his landing area.

With a steady hand propped against a fallen tree, Redfield aimed his .38 revolver just to the side of Cantwell and fired three quick shots into the hull above the waterline. Cantwell startled, lost his balance, and flipped backward over the gunwale into the water. Stevens scrambled to keep the launch from smashing into the rocks before turning to search for his partner, but Cantwell had already disappeared below the surface. Quickly reversing course, Stevens steered the launch west toward Endicott Arm, pointing to where Redfield was standing.

The canyon walls echoed the gunshots for miles. Within ten minutes, launches from the *Patterson* arrived, responding to the sound, knowing Harry and Redfield were somewhere in the vicinity. Seeing the launches approaching, Redfield scrambled closer to the shore and fired two more shots. One of the launches fired a shot in return. Dorn and his launch crew were the first to arrive.

"Redfield, are you all right? What are you doing here? How did you get here?"

"Lieutenant, it's Mr. Ford. I think he's trapped. He went past a bend in the canyon, and then the tide came in, and the water went wild. It's impassable—impossible to get out. I don't know if he's still alive. And the two men chasing us—Mr. Ford told me to shoot if necessary, and I felt it was necessary. I shot at one of them, and he fell overboard. The other one, the guy with the eye patch, took off. You probably saw his launch heading out as you came in. You should have stopped him."

"Yes, but we had no reason to intercept it."

"Mr. Ford told me they killed his friend and would kill him too if they found him. The Chinaman in the boat signaled them—that's how they found Mr. Ford. After we figured out what he was doing, Mr. Ford disabled Chung's boat and took a hammer to it. He should still be floating out there unless Stevens picked him up on his way out."

"We saw him sitting there for a while, so I sent a crew to check on him. Chung started throwing things, so they left him alone. He's still there—we can pick him up."

208

"He was their partner," Redfield clarified.

At that moment, Almy arrived in a skiff, and Dorn turned to him. "Return to the *Patterson* and bring back a crew to take Chung prisoner," he ordered.

Dorn then turned back to Redfield. "You shot Cantwell?" he asked, taking the revolver.

"I'm not sure I shot him. I shot at him, and I think he fell in and drowned."

They departed from Redfield's landing and made their way partway up the canyon. Held back by the churning water, they knew any attempt to search for Harry would have to wait until the tide turned—still hours away. Reluctantly, they returned to the *Patterson* to wait.

Chapter Twenty-Eight: Rescue

Calling his officers and Redfield together in the wardroom, Lt. Mansfield demanded answers. Chung was a prisoner in the brig, Redfield may have shot and killed a civilian, and his hydrographer, Master at Arms, and fellow sailor was missing—possibly dead. The thought of Harry in danger, or worse, was deeply unsettling. His somber demeanor mirrored the mood of the men gathered around him. It was six-thirty, high tide was an hour away, well past sunset, and the new moon would provide no light. The room remained quiet as they reflected on the dire situation.

"From what Lt. Dorn has told me, we have an extraordinary problem involving Mr. Ford. I want search parties formed immediately. He and I believe Harry is still alive. We have an obligation to do everything in our power to help him. If the worst comes to pass, at the very least, we must find his body."

"What makes you think he's still alive?" asked McDonald. "I've seen water like that, and not many boats can take the kind of pounding he's going to get."

"Actually, the Herreshoff is the reason we believe he may survive. If the water is as treacherous as you say, that Herreshoff is his best chance. You can't swamp it—it's built to stay afloat."

"Or glide on the ice," added Strickland.

"But sir, the rock walls, the underwater hazards—he could hit something, puncture a hole, and sink. Herreshoffs aren't unsinkable."

Mansfield nodded in acknowledgement. "Yes, that's a possibility. However, I prefer not to dwell on what might go wrong. Until we find evidence to the contrary, he is alive and needs our help. Wouldn't you agree?"

"Absolutely," McDonald conceded. "I'm not trying to be negative, just realistic."

In the corner of the room, Redfield sneezed. Distracted, Mansfield turned to him. "So, what can you tell us about these men who were following you? Did you shoot one of them?"

"Yes—no—I mean, I think I missed him. I shot near him. From what I saw, he simply tripped and fell into the water when the bullets went by."

"Where did you get the revolver?"

"Mr. Ford gave it to me right before we dealt with Chung. He told me not to hesitate to shoot."

"Mr. Ford told you that?" Mansfield asked skeptically. "That doesn't sound like him."

"He did! He told me that—I'm not lying. Chung and those two men wanted to kill Mr. Ford. That's what he told me. He wanted me to protect myself."

"Okay, but he had gone up the canyon, and you were alone—watching, waiting. What made you decide to pull the trigger?"

"Honestly, I only meant to scare them away. They had been holding positions in the channel for a long time, waiting for Mr. Ford. When he didn't come out, they started looking for me—just like he predicted. They had seen two of us in the boat, then only one. They were searching the shore where he dropped me off, using binoculars."

"So, what made you shoot?"

"The one with two eyes—Cantwell—was about to come ashore right where I was hiding. I saw him in the bow, and I shot at him. I knew he'd come over and shoot me if I didn't. I didn't want to kill anybody, I swear."

"Lieutenant Mansfield, if I may, I'd like to get started on those search parties as soon as possible," said Beecher. "High tide is at seven twenty-five—less than an hour from now. He'll have about a five-minute window to pass through the neck once the tide turns. We need to be ready when he comes out—he's going to be wet, cold, and traumatized."

Mansfield agreed. "Yes. Get all the launches and skiffs in the water—full steam. Take as many lanterns, bells, and rifles as you can find for each boat. We need him to be able to hear us, find us. Move! Redfield, stay close."

The *Cosmos* and *Pirate* were the first to launch, veering east into the ice-choked water with two anxious search parties. The crews knew the danger but disregarded their own safety to help their shipmate in distress. By 7:10, they had positioned themselves inside the canyon entrance but below the choke point, where Harry would emerge if he was still alive. They had fifteen minutes to wait.

Meanwhile, Harry was doing his best to stay alive. For six hours, he had struggled to retain body heat and keep from being tossed overboard. The whaleboat lurched violently, caught between the incoming tide and the outgoing river. He wedged himself tightly between the engine compartment and a bench seat, huddling near the firebox for warmth. Although drenched, his wool jacket, cap, pants, socks, and gloves still offered some insulation. Wool retained heat even when wet, and its fibers generated warmth when moistened.

The relentless assault of the water battered his psyche. Over and over, he replayed a haunting memory in his mind—a boat capsizing, his childhood friend Tom vanishing into a watery grave.

He agonized over his parents, imagining their devastation when the Navy failed to find his body. He thought of Hannah, despairing at the idea of never seeing her again. He thought of Clara, knowing she had been right—he was going to get himself killed.

His mind conjured gruesome images—his body dragged underwater by the canyon's current, tumbling along the rocky bottom before being expelled over the arc's edge into the depths below, where ocean creatures would consume him.

At times, he sobbed so hard he could barely breathe. Yet, in his despair, he still found gratitude—thanking God for the two lunches he had eaten, the full load of wood on board, the sturdy launch keeping him afloat, and for keeping him alive. He pictured himself being pulled from the water, meeting Jesus in Heaven. He thought of Hell. He thought of the old man on the ship—the one who had died but didn't die. He thought of lost family members, wondering if he would see them again.

Other times, he was lucid, even exhilarated by the challenge. He analyzed the water's dynamics, trying to visualize the canyon's depths. He imagined soaring high above, looking down on his fragile launch as it battled the currents below. He calculated the impacts of mountains, glaciers, and the ocean on his position, filing the information away for the charts he would one day create.

By seven o'clock, as high tide approached, his mind had shifted. He was no longer praying or thinking of his family. The roaring water no longer deafened him. The gritty spray no longer tasted salty on his lips. He was in pure survival mode—his body shivering, his thoughts fading, his mind shutting down.

Physically, he was not doing well. The wool clothing helped, but the cold air and wet clothes had lowered his core temperature. Hypothermia could start at any moment, gradually impairing his critical thinking. He struggled to get more wood, crawling on his hands and knees to retrieve it from storage at the bow. He bumped his head hard on the bench seat when the boat lurched sideways, cutting a small gash across his cheek. The wet wood sizzled when placed in the fire. Closing the firebox door, he leaned against the covering. The faint heat was soothing, but he sat in a cold stupor.

The sound of a rifle shot echoing in the canyon didn't register in Harry's brain. A second shot rang in his head, too, but the third and fourth shots brought him to his senses. When the fifth shot rang out, he scrambled for the clock, checking the time. It was seven twenty-five.

"It's too late!" he screamed, struggling to pull himself up to the helm and hold the steering wheel. Looking at the water ahead, he saw none of the sandbars, only free-flowing water. Fortunately, he had put more wood in the firebox, and the steam he needed was almost ready. Not taking the time to add more water to the boiler, he hoped he had enough pressure for the ride out of the canyon.

With the quick steam buildup of the Herreshoff, it wasn't but a few minutes before he tried to engage the propeller, but nothing happened. Frantic for a moment, thinking the engine was somehow inoperable, he screamed at the top of his lungs. Panting, he looked and realized he had pulled up the propeller hours earlier. Lowering it as fast as he could, he glanced at the current in the bottleneck. The battle between incoming and outgoing currents had paused momentarily, and the deep-water traverse was now passable.

He put the propeller in gear and turned the launch around. After more than six hours of turmoil, the calm water was almost surreal to him. He could tell the incoming high tide was nearing its peak and about to turn, so he sped up to fully exit the bottleneck, passing into the calmer waters of the canyon entrance. At last, out of the watery prison he had been in for six hours, he shouted for joy and then collapsed in the boat from exhaustion. He was elated; he had survived, and the whaleboat had lived up to its name.

"I made it! I'm alive! Oh, thank God, I'm alive!" he shouted.

Not far ahead sat the *Pirate* and *Cosmos*, the men waving their lanterns and clanging bells when they saw the whaleboat. They fired three quick shots to signal *Patterson* that Harry was safe.

Once all the launches and skiffs had sided with Harry, several crew members, including Lt. Dorn, jumped into the whaleboat. Dorn was exuberant and quickly wrapped a dry blanket around Harry's shoulders, placed a dry cap on his head, and finally gave him a big bear hug.

"Harry, nice to see you, man. Here, let them help you up. I'll get your things. Are you alright?"

"I'm alive. That's all I can say. Thank God I'm alive."

"Lieutenant, we need to move Mr. Ford to the *Patterson* and get him warmed up. He could have hypothermia." Redfield grabbed one arm and helped Dorn transfer the stiff figure into the *Cosmos*.

Harry crumbled down in the heated cabin, with Redfield sitting beside him. One of the crew brought over a cup of coffee. About the time Harry quit shivering, they arrived at the *Patterson*.

Every man not involved with the rescue had lined the rails to welcome him back. Cheering erupted, and gunshots fired into the night. Looking up, he felt an overwhelming sense of relief and gratitude. The men he worked with had his back; they always had each other's backs.

He gingerly moved onto the *Patterson's* deck, and Lt. Mansfield was the first to greet him. Standing at attention, the Lieutenant saluted him as an honorary gesture before embracing him. Stepping back, he said nothing more as Dr. Percy led him to the medical quarters.

214

"Mr. Ford," Dr. Percy began after they reached the sick bay, "I take back what I said about you the other day, about having been through so much. Now—now that you've been through this—you've been through it all. I don't know how you're going to top this. We—I—wasn't sure I was going to see you again."

Harry removed his wet clothes while Percy found him dry ones. "When they told me you were behind a tidal wave and couldn't escape for six hours, I couldn't believe it. We all felt helpless."

Somewhat exhausted and still foggy, Harry replied, "Helpless sums it up."

The doctor made him lie down and started the examination. Percy covered him with a blanket to keep him warm and examined his extremities for frostbite. Hypothermia was not a concern as his body temperature had returned to normal. Aside from bruises and minor cuts, he was in relatively good shape. Dr. Percy placed a bandage on the gash on his cheek. It was Harry's mental health that most concerned the doctor.

"Harry, can you tell me what happened to you out there?"

In a soft voice that Dr. Percy strained to hear, he said, "I got caught in the canyon. I couldn't go anywhere. The launch was literally stuck. I just bounced around, hoping not to smash into the canyon wall."

"You said helplessly sums it up? Is that how you felt—helpless?"

"Yes. And hopeless. Well, then I'd pray, and the hopelessness would go away, not the helplessness, but I was never able to reconcile my death. I didn't want to die."

The horrible event was over; Harry was home, warm, dry, and tired. Percy left him to sleep, wanting to talk again in the morning. Anybody who spent six hours feeling helpless and hopeless in a horrific situation should discuss it.

Assigning a seaman for the patient watch, Percy moved down the hall to the wardroom, where Lt. Mansfield and the other officers debriefed. Mansfield asked about Harry's health.

"Sleeping right now, which is a good thing. Physically, he is okay—several minor cuts and scrapes, no frostbite or hypothermia. We will have to wait till he wakes up to assess how his mental health is. His mind probably took more of a beating than his body."

Mansfield looked around the room at the men sitting at the table and standing along the walls. The gravity of almost losing one of the officers weighed heavily on him. Beecher summed up the event.

"Endicott Arm has some of the largest tides I've ever seen. This is one of the most extreme environments on Earth if you ask me. How many glaciers are around here? There's Brown, Sawyer, Taku, and some we haven't named yet. And that canyon Mr. Ford was in? I'm surprised he's still alive."

"The whaleboat saved him," added Wood. "It would take a whale breaching underneath to tip that launch over. I'll bet he pulled up the prop and let it drift."

"He planned a lunch for us, so he had food. We didn't eat it all. That might have helped," said Redfield.

As in all meetings, the room descended into numerous conversations between the officers as they each submitted their assumptions about what he had gone through and how he had made it out alive. Mansfield wasn't listening; he was thinking of his next steps. He had fixed his gaze on Redfield.

"Mr. Redfield, do you fish?"

"Sir? Why, of course, I fish, who doesn't? I pulled in a ten-pound humpy just yesterday morning."

"And how do you catch a fish?"

"I use sardines when I can get 'em. Otherwise, I save the roe from when I catch females and use that."

"Okay, so you use sardines and roe. As bait?"

"Yes, sir, as bait."

Mansfield stood up, and the officers in the room did as well. Dismissing the men for the night, he concluded,

"Then you'll understand what I mean when I say I want to use you and Mr. Ford as bait. Goodnight. We'll talk more tomorrow."

Chapter Twenty-Nine: Frontier Justice

The following morning, Harry woke up in sick bay alone, the seaman assigned to watch him having left several hours ago. Lying there, warm under the blankets, he recalled the events from the day before. Reliving the horror of the boat tossing him around on the floorboards, he remembered how the cold had constricted his stomach to the point that it was too tight to breathe. He realized he had almost died. Turning his gaze to the room's window, he watched the red glow expand in the morning clouds. Thinking about how beautiful the sky was, he went over to the window and peered out, giving thanks to God.

Seeing the hospital clothes Dr. Percy had given him; he decided to go to his quarters and change. Walking down the hall, he encountered Ensign Wood.

"Harry, I'm so glad to see you, my friend. We were all so afraid for you."

"Thank you, Albert, I do appreciate it."

"How are you feeling? Are you okay?"

"Actually, I feel pretty good. I'm going to get a change of clothes, and I'm hungry. Have you eaten?"

"Just finished. I'm on my way to the wardroom. Hey, you may want to hurry. Lt. Mansfield was adamant last night that he was going after Stevens. He asked us to meet in the wardroom after breakfast. He said he had a plan involving you and Redfield."

"Redfield? Huh. Yeah, I'll get going. Let them know I'm on my way, would you?"

He reached his quarters and opened the door. As he stepped in, there was still a lingering semblance of Hannah's scent. Saying her name in his head, his thoughts and memories of her reassured him. He sat on his bunk, not out of exhaustion but out of personal change. Surviving the water had somehow reshaped his perspective. She was still the provocative woman to him, but when he thought of his life in Alaska, Hannah was less provocative, even problematic. He changed into his uniform and headed to the officers' wardroom, hoping for breakfast.

As soon as he knocked at the wardroom door and entered, the officers gave him a standing ovation followed by a round of handshakes. He worked his way around the table, exchanging greetings, finally coming to Lieutenant Mansfield.

"Harry Lord Ford, I think I speak for everyone here and every man on this ship when I say you had us pretty worried yesterday. Everyone cared what happened to you. It's hard to imagine what you went through, but we're very glad you're safe and well. You must tell us the story someday."

"Thank you, sir. Thank all of you. I appreciate your concerns. I kept praying 'Be still,' hoping God would calm the water."

McDonald interjected. "Harry, do you know that complete psalm, Psalm 46?"

"Not really. I just remember the 'be still' part."

Chuckling, McDonald began reciting the first few verses of Psalm 46:
"God is our refuge and strength, a very present help in trouble. Therefore, we will not fear though the earth gives way, though the mountains be moved into the heart of the sea, though its waters roar and foam, though the mountains tremble at its swelling."

"That's the beginning," McDonald continued. "The verses about Be Still are:

"Be still, and know that I am God; I will be exalted among the nations; I will be exalted in the earth."

'So Harry, it still applies to your soul, not the water," concluded McDonald.

"Harry, Hallelujah anyway," Mansfield exclaimed. With the formalities complete, he continued.

"Officers of the *U.S.S. Carlise P. Patterson* and Seaman Redfield, I believe that, unlike heaven, here on earth, there is no justice, only the laws of man. We have laws and processes that weigh the evidence and hope for a just outcome as judged by a jury of our peers. It's a good process, and for the most part, right and wrong are fairly determined. Unfortunately, in many places, like Southeast Alaska, that process is not in place, and justice isn't being served to the public. Mr. Stevens is one such case. We know he has murdered at least three people, including the shaman. We know he has attempted murder. And yet, he remains free."

"What are you suggesting, Lieutenant? That we take the law into our own hands?" asked Dorn.

"No, sir. I'm saying we use the law to stop him." Mansfield added, holding up a piece of paper. "Washington has issued a warrant for his arrest. It came in from Juneau last night. We're going after him."

Turning to Harry and Redfield, he added, "I want you two to be our bait. What do you say?"

Redfield didn't hesitate to say yes. Harry paused before answering, then said,

"Lieutenant, I'll do anything to catch that son of a bitch."

The men took notes as Mansfield laid out his plan.

"In two days, we haul anchor for the season, so we don't have much time. There are three parts to my plan: get the word out, pay the men, and then send the entire crew ashore for leave. Stevens will hear about the crew getting paid and getting drunk and will think it's time to act. Redfield, did Stevens get a look at you? Could he pick you out of a crowd?"

"I don't know, sir. He pointed at me."

"Let's assume he might go after you too, not just Mr. Ford. Now, to discuss the first part—getting the word out. Beecher, select a few of the crew and leave for Juneau as soon as you can. You might as well do a mail run while you're at it. Your real purpose is to let the town of Juneau know that the well-paid crew of the *Patterson* is coming for a good time. Talk to bartenders, barbacks, store clerks, fishermen, loggers—whoever will listen. Make it sound like a big deal—everyone on the ship is coming to town for

220

a good time. And I want the men to have an excellent time; they deserve it for a job well done this year."

Ensign Wood interrupted, "Excuse me, sir, about your idea. Stevens has already knifed two of our men. Once our men start drinking, they'll be easy targets. Isn't this plan putting them in harm's way? What if Stevens decides that killing a random crew member would suffice, just to send Harry and others a message?"

"Albert, this plan does come with risk, no doubt, and I wouldn't do it if I thought that risk was too high. But there's a risk in doing nothing as well— the danger that one of us, or anyone, could further suffer at this man's cruelties. However, I want everyone to be safe. So, each of you, the officers of this ship, will not be drinking. You'll blend in and pretend you're having a good time, even acting a little inebriated, but you are there for one purpose, and that is to guard the lives of your fellow shipmates. You will be acting as security the whole time, situated around the bars, watching the crowd. Especially Ford and Redfield—the bait. I'm hoping a loud and boisterous crew crowded together in a bar may trick Stevens into doing something stupid."

"How do we know he'll be there?" asked Beecher.

"I think he'll want revenge for Redfield killing Cantwell."

"I shot at him—he fell in," objected Redfield.

"Sir, they should drop my name if they can. Seaman Jones called out, 'Mr. Ford' that night—twice, if I recall."

"Excellent idea. Ensign Beecher, make sure to drop Mr. Ford's name. Drop it in a big way. And here's how. Harry, come over here."
Mansfield stood up and had him stand beside him.

"Harry L. Ford, Master at Arms in the United States Navy, as the commanding officer of the *U.S.S. Carlisle P. Patterson*, I hereby exercise the federal authority vested in me to name the area that held you captive 'Ford's Terror.' Congratulations."

Clapping filled the room, and the men cheered. Mansfield shook Harry's hand and said, "No one but you could have made it through."

Turning to Beecher, he continued, "Mr. Beecher, I want 'Ford's Terror' to be on the lips of everybody you talk to. Explain how this was a true wilderness survival story and that Mr. Ford himself will be in town to tell the tale—over and over."

A small groan came from Harry. "Really, over and over?"

"Stevens will hear Harry's coming to town, and I'll bet he won't be able to resist the glory being bestowed upon his archrival. Mr. Redfield will be at your side every minute—your personal bodyguard if you will. And Redfield, this is for you."

Mansfield gave him the revolver he had used to shoot at Cantwell.

"But sir, this is Mr. Ford's."

"It's yours now, Redfield. You keep it," Harry said with a smile.

Taking the unloaded revolver, Redfield grinned. "Yes, sir. Thank you."
Mansfield returned to his seat and continued. "Carry on with final measurements today—I want boats in the water. A.C., I need depth and shoreline measurements of Ford's Terror for the Geographic Names logbook."

"One last thing. Take Chung with you to the jail in Juneau. Stevens might want him back, and he could be another piece of bait."

"I doubt Stevens cares about Chung. No one understands him, and no one would believe anything he has to say," Beecher countered.

"Maybe not, but I bet if Chung sees Stevens in town, he'll let loose one of his shrieks. Back to the plan—who's paymaster now?"

"Sir, with Arthurs still in irons, we have no one," responded Dorn.

"Lieutenant, delegate the paymaster duties to one of the ensigns and have Arthurs released from irons long enough to supervise payroll tomorrow. I'll contact the *Pinto* to see if their paymaster can assist us. The men have to be paid for this plan to work.

"Finally, shore leave for everyone tomorrow. Dorn, schedule the use of all launches as tenders to get the crew to shore and back, but rotate the launch crews so everybody has a chance to go into town for a while if they want. Any questions?

"Alright. Now, let's get Stevens."

Beecher selected three talkative seamen who could keep a secret and spread a rumor. For transport, he chose the whaleboat—an unassuming craft to the unfamiliar fisherman or dockworker, yet perfect for subtly spreading the story.

It worked. None of the men at the docks paid the whaleboat any attention as they arrived, but by the time they headed to the bars, all the dockworkers knew the story and marveled at how the little craft had survived such a dangerous place as Ford's Terror. By four o'clock, dockworkers were finishing up their day and making their way to the bars, just as Beecher had planned.

Beecher and his men found their orders to go drinking one of the most enjoyable they had received all season. It was a Thursday evening, so the bars weren't too crowded, allowing bartenders and barbacks time to chat. He cautioned his men not to drink to intoxication—otherwise, they could drink freely. Mansfield had approved the use of the ship's funds for their efforts, so drinks were "on the house," so to speak.

They began at the Imperial on Front Street, the oldest and most popular bar among the locals. Sitting at the long wooden bar for about an hour, they ensured the bartender was well-versed in the tale of Ford's Terror. By the time they left, he was repeating the story to new patrons.
Eventually, dockworkers began arriving, describing the launch in detail.

Crossing the street to the Triangle Club, Beecher and his crew repeated their enjoyable routine—a draft beer for the Ensign while the crew sipped shots of rum. Later, they visited the Lucky Lady and the hotel bar, engaging all who would listen.

By midnight, the story of Ford's Terror was well-known in town—at least among those who frequented bars, which was nearly everyone. Along with Harry's survival tale, bartenders warned locals that the crew of the *Patterson* had been paid and were coming to town, ready to spend their money. The bell would be ringing through the night, much to the bartenders' delight. To the townsfolk, it was a sign to go home and lock up.

Beecher and the others returned to the ship, confident that word about Harry would reach Stevens if he was nearby.

Lt. Dorn was on duty in the pilothouse when Beecher arrived.

"The mission was a success. The name Ford is being tossed around as we speak," Beecher reported.

"Very well," Dorn replied. "Tomorrow, we play it out."

With binoculars to his eyes, Dorn focused on a launch in the water.

"Say, is that Almy? He's supposed to stay out sounding for another hour or so. Can you tell what he's got at the side of the launch?"

Beecher grabbed binoculars from the table as the launch approached.

"I'm not sure. It looks like... it could be a body."

The two immediately left the pilothouse, descending to meet Almy at the rail. By the time they arrived, three crewmen had already pulled the body from the water and lifted it over the rail onto the *Patterson's* deck.

"Don't tell me it's one of ours," Dorn said, staring at the corpse lying face down.

"No, sir," replied Almy. "I think it's the man Redfield shot—Cantwell. I was just outside Ford's Terror, sounding for Lieutenant Mansfield, when I found him at low tide, right about where Redfield said. He caught his boot between the rocks, and I had to twist his leg to haul him out."

"Let's take a look then, shall we?"

Dorn bent over the body and searched for signs of a bullet wound. Finding none, he concluded, "Redfield did miss. I can't find any bullet wounds— he drowned. And we can be fairly certain this is Cantwell because odds are nobody else has gone up there recently."

Dorn searched through the wet pockets for some form of identification. If Cantwell had any papers on him when he went into the water, they were gone now. Attached to his belt under his coat, Dorn pulled a knife from its sheath and held it up for the others.

"One less murderer roaming about," he said, ordering four seamen to take the body to Dr. Percy.

Dorn, Beecher, and Almy then left to find Lieutenant Mansfield. When they knocked on his door, he promptly opened it.

"Good evening, gentlemen. To what do I owe this visit?"

"Sir, good news. Ensign Almy found a body today, and we believe it's Cantwell. The dead man doesn't have any bullet wounds. He found him wedged in a rock, exposed at low tide."

"That is good news. With Chung in jail and Cantwell dead, Stevens is left alone, and I believe we will catch him. To that end, I will see all of you in the morning. Goodnight."

Dorn wanted to retire to his quarters, but he still needed to resolve the paymaster situation. He went to find Ensign Foust, instructing him to assume paymaster duties in the morning and to meet him in the paymaster's office within the next few minutes.

Next, Dorn went to see Arthurs, releasing him from irons until the following day but requiring him to join Foust at the office. Finally, he went down to the crew quarters, where he enlisted several men to set up tables and chairs on the deck for payroll distribution. He instructed them to avoid placing tables where they would have to be moved if it rained.

When Dorn arrived at the paymaster's office, Foust was seated beside Arthurs. Both were reviewing and recording names and figures in separate ledgers, with tall stacks of currency neatly arranged on a table behind them. Arthurs was verifying his records while Foust cross-checked and logged the information.

"Ensign Foust, be sure to pay Landsman Johnson at the higher Seaman rate. He has now completed his one year of service. His pay increases from $35 to $40."

Reaching into a box, Foust pulled out an envelope labeled *Johnson* and recounted the bills. "Yup, $40—that's what's here."

"And Fireman Stevens? Did you catch his promotion?"

Foust checked Stevens's envelope and recounted the cash. "$45."

"No, it should be even $50. He had a promotion."

Dorn eyed Foust skeptically. "Will you be ready?"

"Lieutenant, I assure you the pay will be correct. I've done this many times," Arthurs interjected.

With the late-night counting session concluded, Foust secured the currency in the safe. Arthurs, finally free of chains for the first time in days, went to the galley for a late snack before going to bed. Foust returned to his quarters, where he and Harry discussed the plan for the following day until they both fell asleep in their respective bunks.

Dorn, shuffling off to his own quarters, fretted over everything that he assumed would go wrong in the morning.

Chapter Thirty: Shore Leave

After six months of endless toil, the survey season had finally come to an end. The crew had done all they could. Eventually, the Southeast would be fully geodetically tied to the rest of the world, and all the hazards in the major waterways would be identified and charted, thanks to their efforts.

At five o'clock the next morning, the rain returned along with a cold breeze. Regardless of the weather, excitement among the men was evident. They took extra time with their morning rituals—trimming their beards, combing their hair, cleaning their fingernails, and changing into fresh clothes. Instead of the crew's usual subdued banter about work, they loudly swapped stories of far ports and past exploits. Drinking antics were common topics, but there were even more stories about women, while others wondered if there were any women in Juneau. All were glad to soon have money in their pockets.

Ensigns Foust and Beecher, along with a few seamen, would not be joining the festivities, as they needed to take the *Pirate* to conduct final tidal surveys at Point Hugh on the southern tip of the Glass Peninsula.

The crew Dorn had assigned the night before had set up two tables with chairs five feet apart on the deck along the port rail. At 6 a.m., Foust and Arthurs took their places at the tables, ledgers, and pay at hand. Harry stood behind Arthurs for security, while Slocum stood behind Foust. Ensigns Wood and McDonald stood to the side, observing.

The crew lined up in single file—those with last names beginning with A through M at Arthurs' table and those with N through Z at Foust's. The acting paymasters handed each crewman an envelope containing his pay and instructed him to count the money before signing the ledger to confirm the amount received.

A sailor named Cosgrove arrived after the rest of the crew had been paid. Cosgrove was the epitome of a weathered mariner—his face deeply wrinkled from years of sun and saltwater exposure, his hands calloused from hauling rope, his salt-and-pepper beard long and unkempt. He was in his mid-forties, and while his face looked old, his 220-pound frame was solid muscle. One of the strongest men on the ship, he was often called upon to help haul the heaviest loads. Unfortunately, every officer considered him to have the worst temper on board.

Approaching Arthurs's table, he opened his pay envelope and counted the money. Unsatisfied, he counted it again, shaking his head.

"Paymaster, my pay is incorrect. I'm missing $20."

Arthurs opened one ledger, then another, cross-referencing an entry. Turning to Cosgrove, he said, "On Tuesday of last week, during a sounding operation, you were observed deliberately cutting fifty feet of piano wire with a lead weight attached."

Harry and the ensigns stepped forward, ready to intervene as Cosgrove leaned over the table, placing his hands firmly on the surface.

"Who told you that?"

"I don't know," Arthurs replied. "It's in the ledger. There was a note to deduct your pay. You'd have to ask Lieutenant Dorn—he put it in."
Frustrated and angry, Cosgrove repeated, "Who said I did this? Who?"

"It's confidential," Harry interjected. "If a crew member reports inappropriate behavior by another shipmate, we keep the informant's name confidential. If sailors feared retaliation, they wouldn't report misconduct. Keeping reports confidential also gives us time to verify them."

"Confidential?" Cosgrove scoffed. "You mean you ain't gonna tell me?"

"That's what confidential means."

"This ain't right. You can't just take one man's word for it. He might be lying to set me up."

"We trust the person who reported it," Harry said. "And we double-checked with his supervisor at the time. The allegation was backed up with evidence—or lack thereof. The description of events was very accurate."

Cosgrove moved as if to shove the table, but Harry and the other ensigns stepped forward, silently warning him against it.

"Ah, never mind," he bellowed, turning away, clearly furious.

After Cosgrove left, Harry asked if anyone knew who had reported the incident to Dorn.

"Redfield reported it," confirmed McDonald. "I was with Dorn when he came in."

"We can't let Cosgrove find out," Harry said. "Not with Redfield as bait. If Cosgrove knew, there was no telling what he might do on a drunken shore leave. What exactly did he see him do?"

"Redfield told me he was out in *Cosmos* with a sounding party under Ensign Beecher," McDonald replied. "Beecher chastised Cosgrove for not hauling his lineup fast enough. Feeling slighted, Cosgrove cut the line when the ensign wasn't looking. Redfield, as you'd expect, didn't like his attitude and reported him."

"Redfield," Harry sighed, "can be a handful."

By 9 a.m., payday was over, and all the officers gathered in the wardroom for their departure briefing before heading to Juneau for shore leave. Mansfield addressed them.

"Gentlemen, well, we did it—a successful season, if I may say so. I want to congratulate each of you on a job well done. We'll wait for the final reports, but I think we outperformed last year in terms of overall effort. Here's to you."

Standing, they all gave themselves a round of applause.

"But we may have saved the best for last. Tonight, we intend to catch the man who has murdered and tormented our crew." Again, they applauded and cheered.

"Everyone knows what to do. Be aware at all times. Be ever vigilant. He might strike without warning from the shadows, just like he did with Ellingson. We can't let that happen again. Now, I think we all know our jobs, so rather than a lengthy departure briefing, we're finished here. It's time to bring the law to Stevens."

The *Patterson* arrived in Juneau around twelve-thirty that afternoon. It was raining, and strong southeast winds were building. Once the anchors were down, the sails stowed, and the fires left to burn out, the transfer to shore began. The disembarkation bell rang, sending the crew into a frenzy to be next in line.

A shuttle procession of the *Cosmos* and *Vixen* quickly transported all those eager to go ashore. Within half an hour, everyone who wanted to leave had gone. The larger launches were then anchored, and smaller skiffs handled the hourly transit of leave-takers back and forth.

In addition to the officers, Dorn had selected eight crewmen to act as security while in Juneau. They agreed to abstain from drinking in exchange for extra rum rations the next day. He instructed them to keep watch for a man wearing an eye patch. Two were stationed in each of the four bars. A small contingent of non-drinkers remained on watch aboard the *Patterson*.

Harry, Slocum, and Redfield waited until the rest of the crew had departed before transporting Chung off the ship. Since his capture, Chung had remained defiant, frequently throwing tantrums and hurling food at his jailers. Harry bound his hands for control and his mouth for silence.

By now, the Gastineau Channel had grown choppy as the wind intensified. They used the whaleboat for the hundred-yard transport to shore, Harry feeling the wind push the bow as he steered. Upon arrival, they tied the launch to a dock piling and climbed the ramp to the pier.

The gloom was pervasive, and none of them had thought to bring a lantern. With storm clouds overhead and the lateness of the year, it would be very dark in a few hours. The dock was littered with nets, ropes, and fishing gear, making for a rough, uneven path.

Climbing Main Street to Third, they arrived at the jail without incident. The presence of Marines from the *Pinto*, already on hand to take Chung into custody, may have been enough to keep Stevens away. After their prisoner was led off, the three men headed for the bars.

"Which bar are you going to?" Redfield asked. Having never been to Juneau, he was unfamiliar with them.

Harry and Slocum exchanged a knowing look.

"The *Imperial*," they said in unison. "It's the oldest, meanest, nastiest of the four. You'll know it by the blood on the floor."

Rain poured as they walked back down Main Street, whipped by the wind. Turning onto Front, they made their way through the crowded sidewalks and entered the packed *Imperial*. Harry was the last to step inside. As he pulled back his hood and removed his hat, a cheer erupted from the *Patterson's* crew.

"That's him!" they shouted. "That's the Ford of Ford's Terror!"

Someone rang the bar's bell, and another round of drinks began to flow. As planned, they made space at the bar for Harry and Slocum. Redfield stood behind them, leaning in for conversation. The two men Dorn had entrusted with security raised their shot glasses and winked, signaling that they were on duty. The bar, doors, privy, and hallways were all under observation.

"Well, we have a couple of hours to kill."

Harry frowned at Redfield's choice of words. "Yes. Try to enjoy yourself."

They shared a toast and then waited, their heightened sense of suspicion sharpening with each passing moment. One of Dorn's security men, Seaman Evers, squeezed between them.

"No one has seen Stevens. Everyone in town is talking about Mr. Ford's experience. There are a lot of people who want to meet you, Mr. Ford."

At that moment, the bartender appeared to refill their drinks.

"Harry, what will it be? This one's on me," said Slocum.

"No, no," the bartender interjected. "If this is the Mr. Ford, it's on me. And for you and your young friend."

Harry considered having a shot of rum in honor of Clara and Reeves but decided against it. "I'll have a beer," he said.

The bar was boisterous and loud. The crew of the *Patterson* drank heartily but maintained decorum and a level of sobriety. Other patrons, such as the drunken miners and loggers who got into a heated argument, were less restrained. Their fight escalated until the bartender finally forced them out the door and into the rain.

At about 8:30 p.m., the door swung open, and three men entered Cosgrove and two of his mates from the *Patterson*. Cosgrove immediately set his sights on Redfield. Striding over to where Redfield stood against the wall, he tapped him on the shoulder. Harry moved to intervene, but he was too late. Cosgrove swung his right arm and punched Redfield in the mouth, knocking him backward. Harry and Slocum grabbed Cosgrove's arms and pinned them down, preventing another strike.

"It was you who turned me in, wasn't it?" Cosgrove growled. "You ratted me out for dropping the line. That cost me a lot of money."

To Harry's surprise, Redfield confessed without hesitation. "Yeah, I said something. I saw what you did. It wasn't right."

He rubbed his chin, but otherwise, Redfield seemed unharmed. Struggling to free himself, Cosgrove shouted, "Who are you to say what's right?"

"We all can," Redfield replied calmly. "Any one of us can speak up and do what's right. The problem for you is that I saw you do it. You deliberately cut the line just to mess with Ensign Beecher for calling you out."

Cosgrove's anger dissipated as quickly as it had flared, and they released his arms.

"Let me buy you a drink," Redfield offered.

Looking sheepish for having punched the man now offering him a drink, Cosgrove accepted. Loud cheers erupted as the two shook hands.

With the distraction over, Harry quickly scanned the room to ensure Stevens hadn't slipped in unnoticed.

The three men sat and discussed their next move. Slocum suggested it was time to return to the *Patterson*. The crew had orders to be back on board by midnight, but many were heading back early due to the worsening weather.

"I hate to give up early," Harry admitted. "If we leave now, we'll never find him. We had too many men here, and he saw the setup."

"I agree. We pretty much stuck together all night. I don't know if any of our men actually checked the other bars," added Slocum.

"Why don't I go over to the hotel and the other two bars to check on our men? I hope they didn't linger there too long since everyone seemed to be here," Harry said.

"Take Redfield and make sure. We'll have to assume they went back to the ship. If not, we'll find out during the count."

There was still a dozen or more *Patterson* crewmen in the Imperial, but a small, drunken group decided it was time to catch the water taxi at the top of the hour. Slocum chose to accompany them to ensure they made it safely.

Harry and Redfield went over to the Alaskan in a drizzling rain. The hotel lobby was empty as they passed the reception desk. The bar to the rear of the hotel was much quieter than the much busier Imperial, and the two *Patterson* crew members assigned to watch there were nowhere in sight. A few local Tlingits sat drinking quietly at the bar and at one of the lounge tables in the middle of the room.

"I like this place," Harry remarked. "There's something about the character here. Let's have another beer. What do you say?"

"Are you sure, Mr. Ford? Stevens is still out there."

Ignoring Redfield, Harry sat at the bar and ordered two beers.

"I'd like to know who designed this place," Harry muttered under his breath, not wanting the bartender to overhear. "Look at that monster watching us from beneath the upstairs railing." He pointed to an intricately carved wooden gargoyle peering down from above.

They sipped their beers for a few minutes, nervously eyeing the door. After a long evening of drinking, though, Harry needed to relieve himself. He ascended the stairs to the privy, past stained-glass windows, and turned right into a dimly lit hallway. The bathroom was the first door on the right. Beyond it, the hall extended further, lined with several doors leading to hotel rooms.

233

When finished in the privy, he stepped into the semi-lit hall and noticed movement to his right. Startled, he tensed, ready to defend himself. The shadowy figure hesitated before stepping closer, revealing itself. It was an older man carrying a towel and soap.

"Oh, I'm sorry," Harry said. "You startled me."

"I'd say I did more than startle you," the old man chuckled. "You looked scared to death." He entered the bathroom, shaking his head in amusement.

Harry descended the stairs, taking a long swallow of beer at the bar.

"Mr. Ford, what's wrong? You look like you just saw a ghost."

"I did," Harry murmured. "I did see a ghost."

"Really? Did you see a ghost? I believe you, Mr. Ford. I believe in ghosts. I believe in beings from another dimension. This place must be full of ghosts. What did you see?"

"I saw the ghost of Stevens," Harry said, his voice hollow. "He's haunting me."

Chapter Thirty-One: Terrorized

Leaving the hotel bar, Harry and Redfield stopped as they stepped out into the dark street. Now nearly a gale, the wind whipped through town with a vengeance, forcing them to button up their coats and pull their hats around their ears. The rain pelted their faces as they trudged through the mud.

"Be alert. Stevens could be anywhere, and he might know where we are."

"Yes, sir, Mr. Ford. I'm looking out. This rain makes it hard to know what we're doing."

Stumbling in the dark, they visited the Lucky Lady and The Triangle Club to confirm the *Patterson* crew was no longer there. Most of the town had taken shelter from the weather, so anyone outside was deemed suspicious. The rain and wind dampened the entire town's morale; nobody they passed bothered to look at them as they walked the short distance down the pier. Fumbling along the rough-hewn wooden surfaces, they descended the ramp to where they had tied the whaleboat. It wasn't there. The whaleboat—their way back to the ship—was gone. They stood stunned on the floating dock, rising and falling with the large swells.

"Where's our boat, Mr. Ford?" Redfield almost yelled over the wind.

"Slocum must have taken it. Or Stevens. Either way, we're sitting ducks."

"What about the ship's boats? The water taxis run every hour. Can't we use one of those?"

"What time is it? The last taxi leaves at midnight from the other end of the wharf. We need to get down there."

The trip up the ramp and down to the other end of the pier in the gale forced them to lean forward and push through the night, shielding their faces from the rain as best they could. Both were beginning to feel the effects of the weather. Harry felt for his new revolver but doubted his cold fingers could squeeze the trigger accurately. He hoped it wasn't after midnight, but he knew *Patterson* would send a search party if they weren't on board after that.

When they reached the taxi location, no other crew members were waiting. Harry fretted that the time spent at the hotel was coming back to haunt him. He hadn't been paying attention to the time, and without his chronometer, he had no way of knowing how late it was.

As they waited in the dark, two figures emerged from the shadows and walked down the ramp toward them. Unholstering his revolver, Harry did his best to grip it tightly. The two men stopped twenty feet away.

"Who's there?" he asked, ready to pull the trigger at the slightest movement.

"Identify yourselves," he shouted.

"Cosgrove. And Anderson. We're with the *Patterson*. We're here to catch a ride back to the ship."

They exhaled in relief.

"Oh, thank God. Is anyone else coming?"

"No, I think we were the last of the crew—at least from the *Imperial*. I don't know about the other bars."

"We checked but didn't see anybody."

The last midnight launch arrived on schedule with Slocum at the helm. The wind had forced the *Patterson* to reposition in deeper waters in the Gastineau Channel as a precaution in case other ships broke free.

"I was hoping the four of you would be here," he said above the wind. "You are the last ones to board. Harry, Redfield, Cosgrove, Anderson— let's go."

"Slocum, our whaleboat. It's missing—gone."

"It's back at the *Patterson*," Slocum replied.

"Who took it back?"

"Almy was on watch. He told me he saw several crew members arrive and climb over the rail and head below deck, but they weren't on the scheduled taxi—they came on the whaleboat. By the time he got there to see what was going on and ensure all the lines were secure, only Seaman Johnson remained, too drunk to climb the rope ladder. He had no idea who brought him back. Almy didn't realize you and Redfield had taken the boat, so he didn't think much of it. I didn't put two and two together until I was heading to the pilot house and happened to see it tied down for the winds."

The gale continued to pound the *Cosmos* as it returned to the *Patterson*. Spray from the waves blew off their crests, and the rain came from all directions. It was hard to see at night, and Slocum had to pilot the unresponsive launch carefully. Nearing the *Patterson*, a wave lifted the smaller craft and slammed it against the larger ship. A life ring absorbed most of the blow, and neither vessel appeared damaged.

As the crew tied off the *Cosmos*, they noticed a crushed board where it struck the life ring, but fortunately, it was above the waterline. Slocum set off immediately to find an engineer while Redfield, Cosgrove, and Anderson hurried to the crew quarters. Harry decided to report to the pilot house before heading to his own quarters. With Foust still at Point Hugh with Beecher, he had the room to himself and wasn't worried about the time. He just wanted to get out of his wet clothes after checking in.

McDonald and Mansfield were in the pilot's house when he walked in, dripping from the rain.

"Harry, you made it. We were beginning to wonder about you again," Mansfield admonished.

"Sorry, sir. I lost track of time. I didn't find any crew when we checked the bars before leaving town."

"Thank you. Why don't you change your clothes and get something to eat? You look like you could use it."

Harry left the pilot's house and headed to his room. The officers' quarters were along the ship's long interior hallway below the main deck. The stairs led down to the crew quarters at the hall's end. Tired, he walked slowly down the dimly lit hall, careful not to slip on the water trailing from the crew returning from shore leave. Being so late, no one bothered to mop

237

up. He had slipped here last year, hitting his head so hard he couldn't turn his neck the next day.

Turning right toward the officers' quarters, the water on the floor was less noticeable, and he quit focusing on his steps. He reached his door, entered, and crossed the room to light a lantern before changing into dry clothes. He donned his bedclothes, wrapped himself in a robe, and headed to the galley, hoping to get something to eat. After convincing the night kitchen staff to give him milk and cookies, he returned to his room.

As he stepped inside, the lantern had faintly warmed the space. A slight squish under his foot caught his attention. He looked down and saw a puddle of water.

"That can't all be from me," he thought. "Did I drip that much water?"

A sharp, violent blow to the back of his head instantly blurred Harry's vision. Stars exploded behind his eyes. The impact sent a shockwave through his skull, producing a high-pitched ringing in his ears, like a windstorm howling inside his head. He collapsed onto the floor, struggling to rise to his hands and knees as the room spun around him. Dazed, he heard the door latch, the lock click, and then—the cocking of a revolver.

"Mr. Ford."

The voice was low and calm, devoid of anger, malice, excitement, or anticipation. It was spoken as if addressing an old friend.

Lying on the floor in his robe, unable to reach the gun in his duty belt hanging on the wall, Harry took in just enough light to see the movement before him. Enough light to verify that his assailant was wearing an eye patch. Stevens smelled like a wet campfire and looked as large as a bear. He exhaled a stale cigar odor through his open mouth.

"Mr. Ford," he repeated.

Still reeling from the blow, Harry was in no position to fight. He needed time to think, to get to a defensible position. He struggled onto all fours, then quickly sat on his bunk. Stevens didn't move—except to aim the gun.

"Here. Put these on." He picked up Harry's tall boots by the door and tossed them over. "I want you to wear them."

238

"While I'm wearing my robe? Where are we going?" He knew he had little time and struggled to pull his boots on.

"Not we. The question is, where are you going? You're going to the place you sent my partner. You're going to a watery grave." Stevens let out a little chuckle.

Harry tried to envision what Stevens had in mind. Most crew members were passed out in their quarters, so very few would be around. The watches were supposed to be out, but given the rain and the leaves, they were likely inside and not on the lookout.

"Get up. Let's go." Stevens moved away from the door into the room, continuing to point his revolver at Harry.

Brain racing, Harry imagined several escape scenarios before deciding on a basic plan. He felt emboldened and took a deep breath.

"That's right, Mr. Ford, take a deep breath. You don't have too many more, and you're gonna need all the air you can get." As Harry limped toward the still-closed door, Stevens stepped behind and poked him in the back with the barrel of the gun.

"Now, listen to me. When we walk out that door, you keep your mouth shut. Do you understand? I don't want to shoot you; I want you to die in the ocean. But I will shoot if you yell. I really don't care as long as you die one way or the other. I'm guessing you'll be quiet because you don't want me shooting your buddies when they come running."

A sense of déjà vu settled over Harry as he saw himself walking down the hall. It was as if he had been in this situation before—trapped, vulnerable. He needed to brace himself against the walls to keep from falling as the ship rolled gently. Momentarily unsure of what he was doing, he stopped.

"Keep going." The gun barrel pushed into his back, snapping him back to reality, and he remembered his escape plan.

While he was in his namesake rapids, the hours spent there were his enemy. The terror seemed to last forever, giving him plenty of time to replay his life and dreams. Now, he had only minutes.

"Ellingson was almost dead when you knifed him. You didn't need to butcher him."

The gun pushed a little harder into his back as they neared the end of the hall.

"You don't understand. I like to kill."

The admission struck Harry to the core, a terror so absolute yet so different from his ordeal in the water. The thought of being murdered chilled him to the bone.

"You're not going to make it off this ship. You'll be caught."

"Shut up. I told you to be quiet."

"The Navy will hunt you down. You'll never have a day of peace." Another smack of the gun across his head reignited the pain from the earlier blow.

They walked unnoticed through the hall and up the stairs to the main deck, quickly moving aft. It was dark except for a few lanterns that barely emitted any light. None of the crew, including the watches, were to be seen. The rain continued to pour, but the wind had died down to a strong breeze.

Harry pulled his robe collar around his neck to keep the water out. His body began to shiver as it tried to generate heat. His plan—if it could even be called that—wasn't working; he hadn't had a chance to get away. As they approached the aft railing, he wasn't sure what to do.

He stopped and turned, Stevens still behind him, holding the gun.

"Now what? I suppose you want me to jump?"

"That's right. I want those boots of yours to fill with water and take you down, just like they took down Cantwell. Now, take off that robe."

He had to quickly choose between two bad options—getting shot or going into the water. Given the close range, he decided the gun was more likely to kill him than jumping into the ocean. He thought of Ellingson and how he had swum to shore. Maybe he could reach one of the launches tied to the *Patterson*. On the other hand, a gunshot would alert the crew, but jumping overboard wouldn't.

The lantern was behind Stevens, so Harry could only see his silhouette. His breath hit the cold air, forming a mist under the black hood. His darkened figure appeared ghostlike, and Harry couldn't distinguish his features.

"If I don't jump, you'll have to shoot. Death by hanging."
Stevens lifted his jacket and holstered his revolver.

"No, I don't have to shoot." He charged forward, ready to throw Harry overboard.

Using self-defence techniques he had learned at Master-at-Arms training, Harry countered by sidestepping and throwing a right punch to Stevens' jaw. But Stevens quickly pinned him against the aft rail, where cargo crates hemmed him in. His only escape was through Stevens, but at six foot six and weighing two hundred and fifty pounds, Stevens was too big to overpower. Spinning again, they wrestled, throwing punches in a struggle for dominance. Harry's smaller frame allowed him to evade many of Stevens' wild swings. Neither man could subdue the other; neither could get a grip. They stopped in a momentary stalemate, and Stevens pulled out his gun.

"I'm done playing with you."

Just as the words came out of his mouth, an oar came from behind and struck Stevens squarely on the back of the head, blood spurting from the gash it created. Dazed, he touched his head and turned to see who had hit him. The oar was then thrust under his throat, pushing him backward against the rail with enough force and angle to send him tumbling overboard. There was barely a splash heard over the sound of the wind.

Harry stood frozen, watching the body drift from the ship before sinking into the channel. He turned back to see Redfield holding an oar.

"Oh Lord, am I glad to see you!" he shouted and rushed over to give Redfield a bear hug.

"Mr. Ford, are you okay? You have blood on your head."

"Oh, that? Yeah, he hit me pretty good. But otherwise, I'm fine. I'm alive, thanks to you. You saved my life."

They went to the rail and leaned over, ensuring Stevens wasn't climbing the ship's rope ladders.

"Redfield, what brought you out here? How did you know Stevens was on board?"

"Back from town, I went to my bunk for the night, but one of the crew members was drunk and very talkative with a couple of shipmates. I heard him slurring something about a one-eyed man. That got my curiosity up, so I went over to talk to him. He was hard to understand…"

"Was it Seaman Johnson?"

"Yes, as a matter of fact. He had sobered up somewhat by then, and he told me that he and his friends had left the Imperial and went to the taxi pickup at the south end of the wharf. They saw a figure in the dark and rain who said he was Mr. Ford and told them to take the whaleboat back, not the taxi. The man was hooded, and they couldn't see his face clearly. When they reached the whaleboat, the same man came running down the ramp and said he had changed his mind and was coming with them. Given the rain and darkness, they thought nothing of it."

"He was bigger than me. Didn't they notice?"

"They were all drunk or huddled under their hoods, trying to stay dry. They weren't paying attention."

"So, how did you find me here?"

"I left the crew quarters to find you and make sure you were alright. Your door was open, and the floor was wet. I followed the water trail up to the main deck, I turned to the aft and saw you two fighting. The oar was lying there, and the next thing I knew, I was hitting him in the head with it. It happened so fast."

They went over to the bell and rang the man-overboard signal several times. Watch officers arrived immediately, followed by various crew members.

McDonald was the first to arrive. "Harry, what happened? Who went overboard?"

242

"Stevens. He was trying to kill me. Redfield saved my life."

"Let's move out of the rain," he said. "Redfield, come with us."

The *Patterson* became a flurry of activity as many of the sleeping crew awakened at the sound of the bell. Lanterns illuminated the night as a search party looked for the body. The ship's officers gathered in the wardroom. Mansfield was the last to arrive, and the room quieted as he entered.

Turning to Dorn, Mansfield said, "Executive Officer, the emergency bell sounded. Please, what is going on?"

"Sir, according to both Mr. Ford and Seaman Redfield, an unauthorized individual by the name of Stevens was onboard the *Patterson* and threatened to kill Mr. Ford. Seaman Redfield found them fighting on the aft deck. Given Stevens' size advantage, Seaman Redfield intervened on Mr. Ford's behalf, striking Stevens with an oar and forcing him overboard."

"Harry, your version?"

"We got Stevens, sir!"

A crewmember interrupted by knocking on the door with a message for Lt. Mansfield.

"Sir, the crew has recovered a body."

The entire room emptied as they hurried to the deck. Going over to the group huddled in the still-pouring rain, the officers of the *Patterson* squeezed past and gazed at the man lying face down. As the one most needing to confirm their suspicions, Harry knelt and pulled the body over to reveal the face. Recoiling, it became evident why the one-eyed man wore an eye patch.

Chapter Thirty-Two: Potlatch

Both Stevens' and Cantwell's bodies were transferred ashore the following morning to Dr. Bartlett's place for retrieval by authorities. Internal Navy policy prohibited ships from investigating themselves in matters such as the death or murder of Navy personnel. Officers from the *Pinto* conducted a Navy inquiry into the Ellingson and Jones murders, requesting to meet with Lieutenant Mansfield and his officers who were involved with or had direct knowledge of the events.

Beginning with Lt. Dorn, the investigating officers sat in the wardroom and listened in amazement as he retold Ellingson's story of how Stevens maliciously sabotaged the harpoon gun to kill the Shaman for his wife, thus igniting the Angoon confrontation. Dorn explained how Ellingson had avoided Stevens for years until the night he was killed and how Stevens murdered Jones to eliminate any eyewitnesses.

The investigators then called Harry, who described Chung's smoke signals, which had led Stevens to chase him to Ford's Terror. For the first time since the day it happened, he retold the story of being trapped in the rapids.

Subsequently, they called Redfield, who animatedly recounted the tale of striking and pushing Stevens overboard. Eventually, the investigators questioned the other crew members who were material witnesses. By the time they departed back to the *Pinto*, they realized they had stumbled on a trove of background information that would be of interest to the lawyers at the Navy Department.

The *Patterson* spent three more days in Juneau, shifting from survey work to the necessary preparations for departure. They loaded food, canned goods, fuel, and water for the return trip. The crew worked tirelessly to complete final maintenance projects, including painting the ship's hull to protect it from rust. They raised the sails for inspection and repair, and the engines were brought to full readiness. Harry had the men conduct an emergency abandon-ship drill.

The harbor was bustling with activity. Fishing trawlers set out early each morning, returning later in the day with salmon, lobster, or cod. Cargo ships unloaded food, mail, and other necessities, then reloaded with wood, minerals, and exports. The passenger steamer *Corona* passed through, and Harry watched as its passengers used water shuttles to travel back and forth for access to services in Juneau. Nine years later, the *Corona* would wreck just north of Victoria, British Columbia, on a scheduled run to Juneau, losing all cargo and the vessel but rescuing all passengers and crew.

Harry was in his quarters when a seaman delivered a postcard from that day's mail. It featured a panoramic drawing of San Francisco on the front. It was from Hannah and read:

> *Dear Harry,*
> *I am with my parents in San Francisco. What a beautiful city!*
> *We leave for Colorado the day after tomorrow.*
> *I miss you. Stay safe.*
> *All My Love,*
> *Hannah.*

He was overwhelmed with affection for this woman he barely knew. He smiled at the irony of her being in San Francisco when he wasn't. He pictured her on Market Street, walking up the steps of his apartment as if she lived there. That triggered a thought of Clara, and after further introspection, concluding he would rather be with Hannah.

Lying back on his bunk, he envisioned a future with this cowgirl from Colorado. Now that she had seen San Francisco, she might have found it appealing enough that there would be no need to move to Colorado. His hesitation to relocate stemmed from his parents and his desire to stay close to them. His mother wasn't doing well with the palsy, and his father sometimes needed help caring for her. As his mother's decline continued, his father would also need support in his inevitable aging.

But Hannah, too, would likely want to stay near her parents. Harry's speculation about what to do only frustrated him. He wanted to discuss these things in person, which meant one of them needed to cross a large part of the West.

With the *Pinto* investigation into the murders complete, Lieutenant Mansfield decided it would be a meaningful gesture to send an unofficial delegation to Angoon. He felt the village deserved to know the truth— that Stevens had killed the Shaman out of an age-old motive-lust. Dorn convinced Mansfield not to have the men wear uniforms but to travel in civilian clothes, explaining how uncomfortable the uniforms had made the villagers feel during his last visit. They took a bundle of blankets to offer as gifts.

Departing in the *Pirate*, the morning weather was generally overcast and rainy. Ensigns Beecher and Foust were still with the *Cosmos* in Cleveland Passage, but the rest of the officers and a few crew were aboard. Slight swells rocked the launch throughout the trip. Heading south from Juneau, they went past the southern tip of Admiralty Island and then veered north, arriving in Angoon around noon. Anchoring offshore at low tide, they needed two trips in the rowboat to get all the men to shore. The crew member stayed behind for security and to tend the fire.

Dozens of villagers gathered near the clan houses, scouting the *Pirate*. Women and children scurried about, disappearing into and out of their small wooden huts. The village men also started assembling, pulling their colorful blankets around their shoulders. Twenty younger men stood aloof, ready to act if the Elders needed them.

Dorn turned and said,

"I'll lead. They'll recognize me. Strickland, I want you up here to offer a Tlingit greeting. Always be on alert and expect trouble but hope for the best."

By the time they climbed the sandy beach to the high tide line, the village Elders had formed a group, standing defiantly before them as the village's guardians. Dorn spotted Yáx góos', the young interpreter, among the Elders, and the two exchanged nods of acknowledgment. Turning his attention to Ka'jak̲'tii, the Elder, he sensed neither he nor the others were pleased with the intrusion. He quickly had Strickland issue the greeting.

"Sh y-a awudanEixil."

"Noble people," echoed Dorn. "We meet again. We have brought blankets as gifts."

Yáx góos' dutifully repeated the words. Dorn waited for a reply, but hearing none, he continued.

"We have good news. I'll let my Commanding Officer, Lieutenant Mansfield, give you the details."

Before Mansfield could speak, Ka'jak̲'tii raised his arms to stop him. Yáx góos' translated:

"No more. You said you had good news last time. The Navy letter told us nothing. Same excuses. There was no news."

"I—we," Dorn said, gesturing toward his shipmates, "have new evidence we want to share with you."

"Why should we believe you this time?" came the interpreted reply.

Mansfield broke into the conversation, his baritone voice booming,

"Because it comes at the cost of two innocent lives. Because two of my men were nearly murdered for it."

The Elder listened as Yáx góos' translated and then asked,

"What is the evidence?"

"We believe that the death of the Shaman was intentional, caused by a white man with one eye from the trading company. He coveted the Shaman's wife. He sabotaged the harpoon gun. It was not an accident. It was murder. We want you to know that this one-eyed man is has been killed, he is dead," Mansfield replied.

When Yáx góos' finished, everyone seemed to be either shouting or yelling at someone else as they spread the news. Eventually, Ka'jak̲'tii said to the *Patterson* delegation through translation,

"I remember that terrible day. It dawned, like so many others we have known for hundreds of years, peaceful, cool: the bear in the river, the eagle and raven in the sky. But by sunset, our village was destroyed, our Shaman and others dead. Our houses burned to the ground, with winter soon upon us. It was the saddest day of my life." Here, Ka'jak̲'tii paused, and his expression softened.

"Yáx góos' was not here, and the younger ones do not remember. Many of us who were here have passed on. Soon, it will be a forgotten story." Again, Ka'jak̲'tii paused, but this time he walked over and stood directly in front of Lieutenant Mansfield, Yáx góos' close to his side for interpreting.

247

"I saw how he looked at Nuwuteiyi in the trading post. I saw the look of lust in his one eye. I saw how he treated our shaman and people while they worked the whaleboats. I believe you tell the truth. We have waited a long time to hear this."

"I doubt the Navy will change their mind," Mansfield said.

"It doesn't matter anymore," Ka'jaḵ'tii confessed, "you have brought healing through truth. Come, we celebrate! Yáx góos', spread the word in honor of our new friends; let's have a celebratory potlatch tonight in honor of our Shaman."

"We'd be honored," Mansfield said proudly.

They followed the Elder to Angoon's Raven clan house, where they could take off their coats and sit by the fire as they waited. The impromptu and abbreviated potlatch, initiated with no planning when normally they would spend days or weeks, took over two hours to unfold. Elders listened intently as Yáx góos' translated Dorn's telling of the history and involvement of Seaman Ellingson with Angoon and the events that transpired up to and including Steven's death.

To start the ceremony, one of the elders wrapped in a blanket adorned with a bear stood in the middle of the house and addressed the crowd in halting English.

"This potlatch is for Teel' Tlein. May his spirit rest in peace now that the truth has been told. May his spirit soar like the raven."

The villagers of Angoon celebrated their beloved Shaman well into the evening. Relatives of the dead man went around the village, calling out to each house to invite them to the remembrance. Typically, potlatches would be planned well in advance, last many days, and include clan members from other villages, but for now, a hurried local version had to suffice.

Singing in partial harmony filled the air as the men dancers in their respective clan blankets moved about in motion relative to the animal they were representing, the halibut dancer moving with the least motion but with concentrated energy. Women engaged without moving their feet, swaying rather than dancing to the beat of the drums.

Salmon, bear, venison, and duck were soon cooking to perfection. It was as much a remembrance of Shaman Teel' Tlein as a thank you to the men of the *Patterson*, an unexpected celebration of redemption and forgiveness. Angoon, though wounded, would survive and flourish in the coming years.

The Elder addressed the men as they went outside the clan house for their departure.

"Return someday." Shaking their hands, he went back inside to join the laughter.

"They like to enjoy themselves," said Harry as they walked to the rowboat.

"Agreed, Mr. Ford. They deserve a party. Great job, Lieutenant Dorn, Strickland, and everyone. Let's go home, shall we?"

Harry stopped and looked over the inlet that had enthralled him earlier that summer.

"Lieutenant, I know it's late, but I'd like to see that current again." Convincing Mansfield and the rest of the small group, they went over to a point overlooking the water rushing through it. The tide practically submerged the navy buoy, and whitewater splashed high into the air.

Harry, conjuring memories of his time in the rapids, groaned. Mansfield noticed and asked,

"Trapped in the rapids again?"

"Yes, thoughts of being caught in that torrent."

"Terrorizing, wasn't it? Ford's Terror aptly sums it up, doesn't it, Mr. Ford?"

"This, while amazing, doesn't come close. The other is so much more chaotic and powerful."

"I can't imagine getting stuck here or there," said Strickland. "If this isn't as bad as what you were in, that must have been something."

They stood in the rain and watched the water rushing by before returning to the *Pirate*.

They arrived late that night at the *Patterson*, with departure for the three-day trip to Port Simpson only hours away. Most of the men didn't bother to get any sleep, figuring they could catch up once they were underway. Rain continued to fall, although the snow level was getting closer to sea level.

The *Patterson* steamed south out of Gastineau Channel around midnight. The rain had stopped, and the skies were overcast with occasional fog. They raised the square sail in Stephens Channel under a light to moderate northeast breeze. By early evening, they lay anchored at the entrance to the Wrangell Narrows. Foust and Beecher returned with the *Cosmos*.

The next day, under steam, they set off at noon to traverse the Narrows and Sumner Strait under cloudy but pleasant conditions. Juneau port pilot E.H. Francis was on board to direct the ship through the restricted passageways. His local knowledge from the near-daily passage of this route was critical to the many ship captains who didn't pass through very often or were traveling it for the first time.

Lieutenants Mansfield and Dorn and Ensigns Almy and Beecher were in the pilot house, Francis at the helm. As they neared the halfway point of the twenty-two-mile-long narrows, Francis moved to the forward window with binoculars and told the helmsman to slow down, keeping her to starboard. Intently, he peered as if looking for something. With a firm voice, he ordered the helmsman to a complete stop. The officers stopped their conversation when they heard the order.

"Something wrong, Mr. Francis?" asked Mansfield.

"Straight ahead, about one hundred yards. See for yourself."

Handing the binoculars to the lieutenant, he stared at the place Francis had indicated. Dropping his arms, he asked, "You were expecting this, weren't you?"

"Yeah, I thought conditions were right. I've seen it before: the moon and tide phases in early October. It happened last year about this time, too."

"What are you talking about?" asked Dorn.

Mansfield handed him the binoculars.

"A whirlpool. A big one."

Dorn watched the hole in the water through the binoculars, emitted a whistle, and said,

"Wow, that is huge."

Everyone crowded up to the pilot house window and peered at the spectacle. A gentle breeze came from the east, and the rain had stopped for the time being, so their viewing was unobscured.

"See how dark the center of the vortex is," Harry commented. "The opening is what, nine, ten feet in diameter?"

"More like twelve or fifteen," said Dorn, looking through the binoculars. "And it's deep."

"Has this been charted? Have we heard of this before?" Mansfield asked. None of the officers knew about it.

"First time I saw it," said Francis, "I was on a mail steamer. We were heading north when we came up to this spot, and the helmsman didn't see it until it was too late. We started into that current, and it was only by the grace of God that the engines gained enough power to push us past the hole, or we would have been sucked down."

"Why haven't we heard about it?" asked Dorn.

"No loss of life yet, I guess. A small boat goes into that, and there's no telling where it might—if it ever—come back up. No one would know. And it doesn't happen all the time; it's not consistent," explained the pilot.

"I heard about a revenue cutter that was caught in one south of here, but they managed to escape," Dorn added.

After half an hour, no semblance of the vortex remained, so Francis ordered the *Patterson* to proceed. Passing near where it had been just moments before, everyone apprehensively watched as they went by the vanished vortex location.

On October 8th, the Patterson anchored in Port Simpson, British Columbia, for several days.

251

Harry wanted to be home in San Francisco. He was tired. He stood along the railing and watched the stars. The shore was visible in the dark, with the water reflecting the light of the lanterns. It was cold, and the image of Stevens' silhouetted face flashed before his eyes. He shuddered from the cold and tried to push the memory away.

He ached to be warm and dry again. He wanted privacy—his home, not shared with forty other men. He wanted to be on land. He was tired of being at the whim of the ocean beneath him. He wanted to cook his food, have clean clothes, and, most of all, have a woman to share his life with.

He thought of Hannah and prayed for her health, trusting that she was safe in Alamosa.

The bell rang at the hour, startling him. He had been standing at the rail for several hours and now realized how late it had become. He needed to go to bed before the ship left Port Simpson for Departure Bay. Looking to heaven, he gave thanks for the day and headed to his quarters for some sleep.

Chapter Thirty-Three: Welcome Home

Harry couldn't shake the feeling that he was still far from home, even though they had left Departure Bay. They still needed to sail through the San Juan Islands to Port Townsend, and San Francisco was five days beyond that. Once they arrived in San Francisco, he would need to remain on duty as Master of Arms for three weeks before the *Patterson* would sail up the creek to spend the winter at the Mare Island Navy Yard, marking the completion of their mission. He was looking at another month—early November—before he could go home.

Arriving in Port Townsend was a relief; he was back in the United States after what felt like an extended stay in a foreign country. Port Townsend had originally been home to members of the Klallam Tribe, who called it Kah Tai. The first white settlers arrived in the early 1850s, but by the early 1870s, all the Natives of Kah Tai had been evicted and sent to the Skokomish Reservation.

This coastal town of forty-five hundred residents was a key entry point into Puget Sound, where all ships had to stop for inspection and pay duty at the Washington Territory Custom House. Having the Custom House in Port Townsend was a hard-fought victory for the town's citizens. It had moved from Olympia to Port Townsend in 1854, but in 1862, it was relocated again—to Port Angeles. The Collector of Customs at the time, Victor Smith, made the change, much to the dismay of Port Townsend locals. Townspeople were so incensed that they refused to turn over customs documents to Smith and successfully convinced President Lincoln to remove him from his position.

Still, Port Angeles retained the rights to the Custom House. In 1863, a dam burst, and the water that was let loose swept the Port Angeles customs building and all its records into the Strait of Juan de Fuca. Because of this, Congress reinstated the Port of Entry title to Port Townsend in 1865. Under this authority, officers from the Revenue Cutters *Rush* and *Walcott* pulled alongside the *Patterson* on the day of their arrival to board and collect the requisite duty owed to the Custom House.

That same evening, they hauled anchor and set sail for San Francisco. Like a horse turning for the barn after a long journey, everyone's morale lifted at the thought of heading home, and they went about their duties with a noticeably lighter step. The routine of raising and lowering sails became a thing of beauty, aided by the joyful cadence of the crew calling out orders in unison.

"Set the mainsail, jib, and staysail!"

"Set the mainsail, jib, and staysail!" came the reply.

Later, another command:

"All sails in! We're under steam."

"All sails in! We're under steam."

And then again, in only a few hours:

"Set the mainsail, topsail, jib, and flying jib!"

"Set the mainsail, topsail, jib, and flying jib!"

"Unbend all sails except the jib!"

"Unbend all sails except the jib!"

Harry took every chance to enjoy the rhythmic chanting as the men worked through this final leg of their journey. He watched them check lanyards and ropes, ensuring marline spikes and twine spools didn't slip from their hands and injure someone below. He studied the sail configurations, trying to predict when the navigator would adjust the sails for changing wind conditions.

A day out of San Francisco, clear and pleasant weather replaced the persistent cloudy, overcast, and rainy skies they had endured for the past week. They finally anchored in San Francisco Bay at about eleven-thirty p.m. on October 14—six months after departing.

Upon waking the next morning, Harry remained prone in his bunk. He was warm, the sheet and blanket pulled tight around his neck, and for once, he didn't need to use the water closet. His eyes roamed over the clutter of charts, clothes, books, uniforms, and grooming utensils in the room, but he felt no urgency to go anywhere—he could be ready in minutes. Foust had already taken his belongings and left the ship, as it was his job to transfer the *Cosmos* to Mare Island. The only task Harry had committed to was helping Smith and Sanford pack charts and ledgers in the drafting room after lunch.

Giving thanks to God for the new day, he was about to rise when a knock sounded at his door.

"Who is it?"

"Seaman Conrad. Lieutenant Mansfield would like to see you right away. He's in the pilot house."

Thanking the seaman, Harry readied himself and went to find the commander.

"Mr. Ford, good morning. Nice to be home again, isn't it?"

"Yes, sir. It feels exceptional this time."

"Given what you've been through this voyage, I'd say you're right. By the way, I want to thank you for a job well done this season. I'm glad to have you as an officer on my ship."

"Thank you. That means a great deal to me."

"You're welcome," Mansfield said, shaking Harry's hand.

"Seaman Conrad said you wanted to see me."

"Yes, I do. While we're anchored here, I want extra watches posted. Word has it our deserter, Landsman Ah Bo, is seeking revenge on Cook Yang for some perceived slight. Yang is staying aboard until we reach Mare Island, and I don't want any kind of retaliation while we're waiting to go upstream."

"Yes, sir. Right away."

"And Harry, I don't want you doing the work yourself. Assign enough men so you can go home for a couple of days, alright?"

"I'd love that, sir. Thank you."

Harry spent the next four days on the ship. Packing his personal and professional belongings wasn't the issue—he stayed aboard to personally oversee the day and night watches, ensuring the seamen assigned to protect Yang were doing their jobs. He would never ask anyone to do something he wouldn't do himself. The long night shifts allowed him to get to know more of the crew, but they also left him exhausted. Finally, after his fourth night on duty, satisfied that Yang's protective detail was well-trained, he slung his duffel bag over his shoulder and headed home in the early twilight.

As he stepped into his apartment, a slight breeze drifted through. Striking a match to light a lantern, he was startled as hundreds of moths erupted into frantic motion, reacting to the light. For a moment, he just stood in amazement, watching the multitude flutter about the room. Holding the lamp near the open windows, he hoped they would follow the light out, but they didn't. Grabbing a broom, he began swatting at them, trying to shoo them outside, but there were too many. Instead of seeing his parents or catching up on much-needed sleep, he spent the next several hours ridding his house of the pests.

By afternoon, with most of the moths gone, he walked over to his neighbor Carl's house to collect his mail from the past six months. Carl, a Civil War veteran who had lost an arm, lived under limited means, and Harry often found small ways to help him—such as paying him to hold his mail. Carl wasn't home, but he had left a bundle of letters in the door alcove with Harry's name on it. Harry shoved a wad of cash under the door in thanks.

Sorting through the envelopes, he found nothing of interest. Deciding to rest before visiting his parents, he stretched out for a short nap. Just after seven that evening, he knocked on his parents' door and stepped inside.

"Harry! Frank, look who's here. It's Harry. He's home. Francis!" his mother shouted.

She didn't rise from her chair, so he walked over, hugging and kissing her as she reached up to hold his face.

"You lost weight, my gracious. Are you hungry? Have you eaten? Sit down—I'll warm up our dinner leftovers. We ate earlier. You should have let us know you were coming."

256

"I am hungry, Ma, but let me get it. What did you have?"

"Seafood chowder. Do you like seafood chowder, dear?"

"I love it, Ma. Love it."

"Frank!" she called again.

"Yeah, I'm coming—I was busy in the privy," his father grumbled. "Harry, welcome home, son. It's good to see you and know you're safe."

"It's great to be home, Paps. It was a long survey season."

"So, how's the job? My client, Mr. Reeves, always asks about you."

Smiling at the irony, Harry replied, "The job is good, Paps. The job is good."

"Did you have any excitement while you were gone?" his mother asked.

"Oh, yeah, I sure did. You'll be proud to know the commanding officer named a place after me."

"Oh, Harry, you've talked about others getting their names on places. And now you have, too! Did he name an island after you or a lake?"

The mention of having a lake named after him flooded his thoughts with memories of that day with Hannah. He pulled the cloth from his pocket with the embroidered lake, but instead of showing them, he gently pressed it to his lips.

"Harry, your mother asked you—what feature did he name after you?"

"Oh, right. Ford's Terror."

Neither of his parents thought they had heard him correctly.

"Ford's Channel?" his mother asked skeptically. "Is that what you said—Ford's Channel?"

"No, Ford's Terror."

"As in horror? That kind of terror?" his father asked incredulously. "What happened? What is this place?"

"Yes, like horror."

Harry left for the kitchen to warm up the chowder before describing his harrowing ordeal in Endicott Arm and the events that followed. Not wanting to alarm them too much, he left out many details related to the murders and attempted murders. He explained that he had only been doing his job when some waves blocked him from returning to the ship.

Frank brought out the warmed-up chowder, and Harry ate heartily while his father sat across the room, reading insurance documents. He pondered how to tell the next part of his story.

"I met a woman this summer," he finally blurted out.

Mrs. Ford reacted immediately.

"I'm sorry, dear—do you mean Clara? We already know Clara. By the way, have you seen her yet? I'm sure she missed you. She hasn't visited in a long time. How is she?"

"Clara is gone, Ma. We're not a couple anymore. We ended the relationship the day I boarded the *Patterson* in April."
"Oh my! What happened?"

"She predicted something like Ford's Terror would happen, and I would get killed. She didn't want to live like that anymore. I can't blame her."

"So, who is this woman you met?" his father asked.

Hannah and the other guests became the topic of discussion as he described the brief few days they had spent onboard the ship. Frank thought he had heard of a painter named Bierstadt. Lizzie questioned him about the significance of this Hannah now that Clara was no longer in the picture.

"But dear," she began, "she lives in Colorado. Will she move here? You certainly aren't thinking of moving to Colorado, are you?"

"I don't know. I haven't thought about it much. I might go visit once we arrive at Mare Island, and I can go on leave. I'd like to see that part of the country."

The sadness in his mother's eyes was evident as she considered the possibility of him moving away. He stayed a while longer after dinner, and after beating his father in a couple of chess games, he returned home to sleep.

The following day, he returned to the ship and stayed aboard until they arrived at Mare Island. He then returned to his apartment on extended leave, intending to return to the *Patterson* for next spring's departure to southeast Alaska.

Once home for good, he walked over to Carl's for the mail, hoping to find a letter from Hannah. Instead of a letter from Hannah, he found a handwritten note from Clara, which she knew she could drop off at Carl's house.

"Dear Harry,
I'm sorry for how I behaved when you left in April. I want to
apologize to you in person.
Please meet me at the Palais Royale Saloon next Sunday, the 27th.
I will be there around noon.
Love, Clara. "

The Sunday morning he was to meet Clara, Harry woke up sure of his destiny. Arriving at the Palais around twelve-thirty, he found an unexpectedly large and loud crowd gathered. Struggling to push through the people at the front door, he had an even harder time spotting his former fiancée. After working his way through the main room, he saw her waving to him from a table in the corner in a white dress with a white bow, away from most of the commotion.

"Harry, over here!"

"Clara, it's lovely to see you." He leaned over and kissed her cheek lightly.

"Oh, you look great! You must have had a fantastic season!" she smiled.

"Yeah, it was. Challenging at times, but a fantastic season nonetheless."

"A toast! To a successful season doing whatever the Survey does!"

She had already poured two glasses of champagne, so he took one and clinked his glass against hers. She looked animated, and he wasn't sure why. He wondered what the crowd was there for.

"What's going on? Things seem celebratory."

"That is a perfect word to use—*celebratory*. Let's celebrate," she said, raising her champagne and sipping from the glass.

He looked at her and then the bottle to see how much Champaigne she already had been drinking. The barmaid passed by, and he ordered a beer.

"So, what is going on here? Why all the people today?"

"They're installing something called a jukebox. It's a small little box, and it plays music. They say it's the first of its kind. I don't know—I like the piano."

"*Jukebox*. Who came up with that name?"

"Good question, I don't know. Harry, like I said in the note, I wanted to apologize for my behavior the day you left. I should have been more honest with you a long time before that. I should have said something sooner. I should have considered your feelings, too. I'm sorry."

"Don't worry about it. It's okay. I understand—especially after this year. I have a dangerous job. And I put my job ahead of you."

"No, I was wrong, and I admit it. And I was wrong about something else, too."

"Oh? What's that?" asked Harry.

"John Reeves. I hate to say this, but I misjudged John. It turns out he can't control his competitive nature and has gambled away a lot of his family's money. It told me he needed to borrow some money for his rent, and he lost that, too. But what's worse, while he's gambling, he's also competing for the attention of any pretty girl around. I realized he's not capable of fidelity.

"I'm so sorry Clara. I had no idea he was like that."

Harry began to panic as he listened to her describe Reeves' failings in detail and how she had been reconsidering her issues with Harry's job. He could tell where this was leading.

"So, after a lot of thought, I've come to the conclusion that I'm okay with you being gone for six months a year; I do believe you'll be safe, no matter what. The Survey wouldn't send ships out if they never came back, right? So, I got my own place, it's very nice, over near Nob Hill, you need to come over and visit. After I moved in, I had plenty of time to think, and I began to think about us again, as a family. I realized…"

"Clara, I'm sorry—I need to tell you something. I'm leaving for Colorado in a few days. Alamosa, Colorado, for the next few months. There's someone I met, and I'm going there to visit her."

Clara gulped the champagne from both glasses.

"Who? Who is she?"

"Her name is Hannah. I met her in Alaska after her ship sank, and we helped rescue them. Her father is a state politician. She has a son named Mark. She and I talked about meeting up after my season was over. Two days ago, I received a letter from her asking me to visit her parents' ranch through the winter. I've decided to go and have begun to arrange my travel."

Clara glared, and he could tell her anger might boil over into outright hostility. The crowd noise muffled her angry response:

"How dare you? How can you choose her over me? You've only known her for a few days! This is insulting."

"Clara, please understand that our engagement was over, and you left me. How was I to know you'd change your mind?"

"I invited you here so we could get back together and have our own family. Sure, I ended our engagement, and with good reason, but I never expected you to pick up another woman while you were in Alaska. After I broke things off with John, I assumed you would come home, we could talk

261

about things, forgive, and forget, and get back together and finally get married."

"I'm just visiting. You can't blame me for that."

"Don't tell me that. Don't even think this isn't your fault. *Get out! Get out of here!*" she screamed, throwing his beer and soaking his shirt. "*Get out of my sight. I never want to see you again.*"

That night, he fell to his knees beside his bed, not so much out of worship but from emotional exhaustion.

Chapter Thirty-Four: Great Sand Dunes

The Sunday morning earthquake over, he left the rubble of the demolished relationship to return home to begin packing. Emotionally numb from the intense exchange with Clara, he hoped the journey and time with Hannah would help him forget this disastrous fight.

He had taken a leave of absence from the Survey, intending to return in March before the *Patterson* sailed again in spring. Arranging his transportation to Alamosa took time, so it was a week after receiving Hannah's letter before he left San Francisco. There were no direct stage routes or continuous rail lines connecting to Alamosa, so travel would take a week or two, so he was put at Hannah's house in late November.

Departing San Francisco, he headed east on a Southern Pacific train called the *Overland Flyer*. He passed through the coastal hills and into California's Central Valley, stopping at the state capital, Sacramento. By the time they arrived in Colfax, the weather had turned sour. They were beginning the eastward climb over the Sierra Nevada, and wet, rainy snowflakes were melting as they hit the ground. The train was held near the summit at Alta due to heavy, wet snow blocking the tracks. He sat in the quiet warmth of his berth, watching the snowstorm bury the Ponderosa and Sugar pine forest in white. It took crews several hours to clear the tracks, making them twelve hours behind schedule when they pulled into Reno for a twelve-hour layover.

With nothing better to do, he followed the advice of a local Reno resident and walked south on Virginia Street to the Lake House Riverside Hotel for a quick lunch. Seated by a window, he watched the Truckee River flow by, heading east into the desert. The headwaters of the Truckee begin high in the Sierra, in Lake Bigler—now known as Lake Tahoe. By either name, it is the largest and second-deepest alpine lake in North America. Its water is so clear the bottom can be seen at a depth of eighty feet. The entire two-state watershed is covered in pine forests with eight to ten-thousand-foot mountain peaks encircling the lake. The Truckee River drains the lake when water reaches and spills over its natural rim. A closed river system, lake-river-lake, the Truckee begins at Lake Tahoe and one hundred twenty miles later empties into the treeless Pyramid Lake basin.

Back on board the train, Harry found town and station stops in Nevada and Utah were few and far between. Finally, the train stopped in Ogden, Utah, where he transferred to the Denver and Rio Grande Western Railroad. The dramatic route from Salt Lake City over the Wasatch Mountains reminded him of the Sierra, and he again sat back to enjoy the views from his railcar. He passed into Colorado, switching to a train heading south in Grand Junction. He traveled as far as Montrose and changed trains again. Were he to continue to Ouray, he would be forced to take a stage over the Rockies, as the rail line ended there, and the rail segment to Wagon Wheel Gap was impossible to build due to the mountainous terrain. He faced the same situation if he took the train from Sapinero to Lake City, requiring an uncomfortable stage run over mountains to reconnect with the train service.

Instead, he traveled from Montrose to Mears, then switched trains to Villa Grove, where he picked up the stage line for a more comfortable ride through the flat terrain near the Sangre de Cristo Mountains, with the Great Sand Dunes to his left as he traveled south. He arrived in Alamosa tired and late in the day, so he rented a room for the night. The next morning, after a bath and a hearty breakfast, he rented a horse and buggy, paying an extra deposit for the three-month rental. Following Hannah's detailed route in her letter, he set out east for the family ranch at the western base of Blanca Peak.

The sun came out enough to provide warmth on what otherwise would have been a chilly day. After an hour or so of riding through desert sagebrush, he reached a turn in the road that Hannah's map indicated— the route to their ranch. Passing under a wooden arch with the Adams family brand built into the center, the road began an upward incline, and as he went further uphill, Ponderosa pines began to dot the landscape. Eventually, the sparse trees became a forest, and he marveled at the difference between this dry, desert forest and the rainforest of southeast Alaska.

Urging his horse forward along the winding road, he crossed a wooden bridge over a dry streambed. As he bounded up the embankment, he saw Hannah's house in a meadow surrounded by pines. Anxiously hoping to see Hannah approaching him, he remembered she didn't know when he was arriving.

Approaching the house, he could see Mrs. Adams in a second-floor window. She disappeared, and he wondered if she was surprised to see a visitor. Nobody else was about, so he got off his buggy and hitched the horse to the post. By then, she had reappeared at the front door and came onto the porch to greet him.

"Mr. Ford, is that you?"

"Yes, ma'am, Mrs. Adams. Good to see you again. Hannah sent me a letter asking me to visit. I trust you don't mind."

She descended the stairs and grasped Harry's hands with both of hers.

"Yes, Harry, I know she invited you, and I don't mind at all. It's nice to see you again. You look much better than the last time we saw you."

"Ah, that's right. I had just met Mr. Stevens before you left. I had forgotten about that."

"Did you ever find him—the man who beat you?"

"Yes, ma'am, we did. He shouldn't be causing any more trouble."

"Oh, that's good. Now, follow me."

Mrs. Adams held Harry's left arm as she turned and retraced her steps up to the house. Stopping at the top before entering, she turned and looked sternly at him, her eyes narrowing.

"Harry, I want you to know Hannah's been through a lot—the loss of Mark's father, raising a child on her own, supporting us on the ranch, her father's endless political meetings and rallies. Lord knows I want what's best for her and for a normal life, and I know she needs and wants a good husband and father for her son. She invited you here because she thinks you might be that man. So, I want to know what your intentions are. I will not have my daughter and grandson hurt by someone with less-than-honorable intentions. Why are you here? Is it for you, or is it for them?"

"Mrs. Adams, I can assure you my intentions are honorable. I understand that Hannah and Mark come as a package—there is not one without the other. I, too, seek a normal life, as much as my career will allow. I haven't known your daughter for long, but I do know that the time we spend together is special for both of us. I am very fond of her and would do nothing to harm her, including leading her to believe something that isn't true. I recently experienced that myself and I wouldn't wish it on anyone else."

"That suits me for now, Mr. Ford. I believe you. But be aware, I will intercede to protect the best interests of my children."

"Understood."

Mrs. Adams led him into the house. Looking to the second floor, she called for Mark, not Hannah.

"Mark, come here. We have a guest."

Footsteps sounded from upstairs, and the six-year-old quickly stood before his grandmother, jumping up and down for her to pick him up. Ignoring his request, she asked him,

"Do you remember after our ship, the *Ancon*, wrecked, we went on another ship run by the Navy? Mr. Ford was on that ship. Do you remember Mr. Ford from your trip to Alaska? He is here to visit for a while."

Watching him jump while standing before his grandmother, Harry remembered the challenges the boy had presented to his mother and grandparents while on the *Patterson*.

"Nice to meet you again, Mark," he said.

Ignoring Harry's introduction, the boy said to him, "Harry, I can climb trees upside down. Do you want to see?"

"I, ah, I..."

"It's okay, Harry. Hannah isn't here. Go ahead. I'll ring the dinner bell to let you know when she gets back. She and her father had some business at a ranch south of here. Go on, spend some time with him. It's best if you give him options."

Before he could ask what she meant, Mark reached out and grabbed Harry's hand.

As soon as Mark entered the pine stand, he let go of Harry's hand and ran ahead. Harry called for him to wait, but Mark only laughed and stayed well ahead.

After rounding a large boulder much further up the trail, Harry found Mark hanging upside down from a pine branch seven feet off the ground. Just as his tiny legs let go, Harry lunged forward, catching Mark before he fell.

Plopping him right side up on the ground and unexpectedly raising his voice, he said, "What are you doing? Why did you do that? Do not ever do that again."

Mark's facial expression changed from an exuberant smile to a hateful pout in seconds, and Harry could tell his whole demeanor had turned sullen. Mark crossed his arms and started walking away, only stopping when Harry intervened.

"Get back here. You can't wander off into the woods like that."

Still pouting, Mark turned in another direction and kept going, arms folded tightly. Exasperated, Harry ran ahead to block his exit before remembering Mrs. Adams's suggestion.

"Mark, you have a choice. You can go home to see if your mother is back yet, or you can stay out here alone with the coyotes while I go back and eat."

"No way! I'm not staying out here with coyotes!"

He took off running toward the house, and Harry followed to ensure he returned safely. Stopping short of the meadow, he watched Mark run inside. Breathing in the dry air, he looked around at the arid landscape, noting how different it was from southeast Alaska but not too different from the hills east of San Francisco. Could he live here? He asked himself.

Interrupting his thoughts was the arrival of two horses galloping in, with one of the riders climbing down and tying the horse to the post. He immediately recognized Hannah's trademark cowgirl western wear and pigtails and hurried to meet her while Mark ran into her arms. Watching her hug her son and seeing her beautiful smile in the sunshine with the mountains in the background, he decided that, yes, this was a life he could enjoy.

"Hannah!" he shouted, running to her as she put Mark down. Surprised and excited, Hannah ran to Harry. They smiled at each other, hugged, and kissed before Mark interrupted.

"Momma, I climbed a tree upside down! Didn't I, Harry?"

Harry wasn't sure how he felt about such a young child calling him by his first name. It felt inappropriate, but he couldn't quite understand why.

"Okay," Hannah interrupted, "I think it's time for you to go find Grandpa. I think he needs help putting Harriet and Bravo in their stalls and getting them fed and brushed down. Can you go help him with the horses?"

Mark took off to the barn with a six-year-old's speed, alternately running, jumping, skipping, and rolling his way there.

Alone and holding hands, Harry and Hannah looked into each other's eyes again, their faces beaming. It was a watershed moment—their lives colliding, intertwining even as they stood motionless. He didn't believe in chance or coincidence. Instead, he knew God had brought them together for a reason; only time would reveal what that reason was. They kissed again, this time long enough to stir their passion.

A spare room upstairs was Harry's quarters for the time being, and he put his belongings there before heading downstairs for an early dinner. Introductions were in order as he met Mr. Adams—Billy—again. Also joining them for dinner were Grandma Bessie, Hannah's grandmother on her mother's side, and Cousin Mary. They lived in one of the small cottages located a stone's throw from the main house. Behind it was the bunkhouse, where six or seven ranch hands stayed, though they did not join the family for dinner.

From Harry's first day there, time with Hannah seemed minuscule; there was always something to do or something going on. Everyone living on the ranch had assigned chores, and Harry was no exception, getting up each morning to collect eggs and help feed the hogs before joining whatever crew of men went out to complete the day's labor. Hannah had Mark to feed, bathe, and educate, along with her own chores and assisting her father with his political career. Billy relied on her campaign advice, and she always knew exactly what to say to constituents unhappy with public policy. She also had an uncanny ability—if that's what flirting was—to raise campaign funds from wealthy male donors.

It was only on weekends that he and Hannah could venture off for any significant amount of time—the time all young couples needed to truly discover one another. Their favorite destination was the sprawling dunes northeast of Alamosa. They would ride in Harry's rented buggy to the edge of the dunes and enjoy a picnic on the sand. On each trip, they explored a new part of the sprawling wonder, finding some alcove where the wind hadn't yet pushed the sand into a mound twelve feet high. Hannah loved hearing over again the story of Ford's Terror and the fate of Stevens.

Mark was always a factor in the day. Breakfast, lunch, and dinner required his reluctant attendance, and he disliked nearly everything put before him. Mark's time with Hannah was unremarkable—pleasant even—but when she wasn't around, he seemed to transform into an obstinate, unlikeable child. At times, his behavior made Harry outright furious, as Mark would gloat at having gotten under his skin. Invariably, whatever mood Mark was in would change at the slightest offense he perceived—and most things, to him, were offensive. Ultimately, Harry gave Mark options as best he could, but otherwise, he had no idea how to handle the child.

As winter passed, spending time alone with Hannah became more challenging, and their weekend trips to the dunes became less frequent. The weather was cold, and she spent more and more time supporting her father as he geared up for a November election—only a short nine months away in Billy's mind. Hannah began accompanying her father on legislative trips to Denver for a week at a time, and when she was home, she often joined him at fundraisers and rallies held at area ranches. In the brief moments they had alone, Harry and Hannah were more aloof. Instead of talking about their lives or future, they sat in silence, broken only by platonic chit-chat about the day's activities and what was happening the next day.

February was nearly over. Though still cold, the sun shone longer, bringing some warmth to the day. Harry felt restless, bordering on irritable. His horse and buggy rental ended on the last day of the month, and he had yet to decide what he was going to do—stay in Alamosa or return to San Francisco. His next cruise to Alaska would be departing soon, and after experiencing the long and arduous journey to get there, he knew how

269

difficult it would be to make his way back. He still needed to check timetables and schedules.

The following day, he saddled his rented horse and headed into town. Hannah and her father had gone to a barn-raising celebration and would be gone most of the day, and he was in no mood to watch Mark. Truthfully, he wasn't in the mood to watch Mark anymore at all. He spent the day at the train station and livery, extending the horse rental by one more day.

Hannah was sitting on the porch when he rode up late that evening.

"Where have you been? Mother says you've been gone all day. What have you been up to? Where's your buggy?"

Her smile was gone, as was the sweet way she used to sing her words—replaced instead by a cold frown and simple, direct sentences.

"Oh, I had to go to town. We needed some fencing wire."

He bent over and kissed her on the cheek, but there was no real feeling in either the giving or the receiving of it.

"Fencing? Don't we have enough fencing around here already?"

"Ah, no. I needed fencing wire, you know, to tie it off with."

Several minutes of silence passed. Out of the corner of his eye, he studied Hannah. She was looking down, her face downcast. He realized she already knew why he had gone to town earlier. Closing his eyes as if summoning the courage to say it, he confessed softly,

"I also bought my passage to San Francisco."

Unlike the last time he told a woman he was leaving, Hannah showed no reaction other than taking a deep breath.

"I'm leaving tomorrow, on the afternoon stage, to Villa Grove."

"You're not accepting my father's offer?"

"No. I'm not an accountant—I don't want to manage his political books."

270

"And my offer? You're not accepting my offer to stay?" Tears were beginning to form in her eyes.

"I want to, Hannah, I do. You are an incredible woman. But I can't—I can't stay. I promised you and your mother I would be honest and not pretend to feel or believe something that wasn't true. I don't feel I can be a loving father to Mark. I know that. He needs more than I can give him. My heart isn't there; I have no patience for him, and that's not right. I feel inadequate with him. You? Yes, I love you. But I know you two come as a package."

Hannah sniffed. "You'd be a great father. But that's why I asked you here—to see for yourself what you'd be getting into. I don't hold it against you. I understand. I'd rather you be honest with me now than later."

"I don't want to manage your father's books because I don't want to give up my career, either. I have something very important going on with the Survey, and I'd like to stay with them for the foreseeable future—if they'll keep me. I'm also having a hard time adjusting to the desert. I want to be near the ocean. I miss it."

Hannah blew her nose and wiped her eyes, calming her breathing.

"Come with me to San Francisco. Live with me there," Harry pleaded. Hannah chuckled and flung her pigtail behind her head. She turned and looked lovingly at the man she had once thought might become her husband, reaching out to hold his hand.

"I can't do that, and you know it. How would I handle Mark without my parents' help? Your parents can't replace mine in that regard. And my father needs me for his campaign. He would be devastated if I left. And honestly, the idea of you being gone six months a year doesn't appeal to me at all."

"I have a hard time justifying leaving my parents too. Dad's going to need more help with Mom as she progresses, and I'm their only child."

"Exactly. We have a child and parents to think about."

The two sat on the porch, gazing into a field colored red by the sunset. Harry's heart sank as he realized Hannah would no longer be part of his life. Tears dripped from his chin as emotion took hold.

271

"I'm sorry," he whispered. "I'm so sorry."

"I know. So am I."

They held each other's hands tight as they sat quietly on the porch that night, crying on each other's shoulders before they parted for their rooms. The truth hurt, and the breakup was hard to accept, but at least it wasn't the ugly end that had characterized Clara's response to similar news. They met in one last slow, poignant kiss, their lips trembling as they said their goodbye.

Harry's last morning at the Adams ranch was filled with hugs and fond goodbyes from the family and ranch hands. Billy hitched a horse to the family buggy, and he, Mrs. Adams, Hannah, and Mark followed behind as Harry set off to return his horse to the stable and catch the stage out of town.

Once settled with his horse, he met the Adams at the stagecoach station. Harry and Hannah hugged once more, neither speaking—their eyes exposing their sorrow while their tears confirmed it. He kissed Hannah again, burning the sensation into his mind, not wanting to forget the feel of her lips against his, to gaze in her eyes. He wanted to cherish forever the scent of her hair.

Tumultuous emotions inside him, he climbed aboard the stagecoach and took a window seat, gazing at Hannah as he departed. He waved goodbye until she was out of sight, then closed his eyes. He had just begun to express his gratitude to God for Hannah when the stage lurched sharply, breaking his concentration.

Gazing out the window, something in the air caught his eye. A shadow passed over, and turning to look up, a grin crossed his face when he saw what it was. Above him, in the blue Colorado sky, soared a bald eagle, rising in the warm updrafts and circling above—an instant reminder of his Alaskan dream.

About the Author

Richard Wiggins is a former resident of very rainy Juneau, Alaska, who now lives in extremely dry Washoe Valley, Nevada, but still calls Alaska home from Panguingue Creek near Denali National Park. After forty years of writing transportation planning documents, starting with local transit plans in small southeast Alaska towns, Mr. Wiggins has discovered an unknown desire to tell stories about special people behind special places. Relying on his experiences living in Juneau for inspiration, Mr. Wiggins rarely enjoys the rainy weather he writes so longingly about.

www.ingramcontent.com/pod-product-compliance
Lightning Source LLC
Chambersburg PA
CBHW071548110726
47908CB00007B/2040

* 9 7 9 8 9 9 3 0 3 4 9 1 1 *